A

FLORENTINE
DEATH

A FLORENTINE DEATH

MICHELE GIUTTARI

Translated by Howard Curtis

ABACUS

First published in Italy in 2005 by Biblioteca Universale Rizzoli as *Scarabeo*
First published in Great Britain in 2007 by Abacus
This paperback edition published by Abacus in 2008
Reprinted 2008 (six times), 2009 (three times), 2011

A CIP catalogue record for this book
is available from the British Library.

ISBN 978-0-349-12006-5

Typeset in Horley by M Rules
Printed and bound in Great Britain by
Clays Ltd, St Ives plc

Papers used by Abacus are natural, renewable and
recyclable products sourced from well-managed forests and certified
in accordance with the rules of the Forest Stewardship Council.

Mixed Sources
Product group from well-managed
forests and other controlled sources
www.fsc.org Cert no. SGS-COC-004081
© 1996 Forest Stewardship Council

Abacus
An imprint of
Little, Brown Book Group
100 Victoria Embankment
London EC4Y 0DY

An Hachette UK Company
www.hachette.co.uk

www.littlebrown.co.uk

To my wife Christa, who had the patience
to support me during the endless hours of
solitude which the work of a writer involves.

ACKNOWLEDGEMENTS

I have always liked the custom of certain novelists, especially in the English-speaking world, to thank those who have contributed, directly or indirectly, to the writing of their books. As with many of them, my list would be too long.

So thank you to all my past and present colleagues, the police officers, inspectors and superintendents. I cannot name them all individually, but I hope they all know how grateful I am to them.

I also owe a great deal to the passion and professionalism of my agents, Daniela and Luigi Bernabò, who encouraged me throughout the many drafts of this book. I can never thank them enough for all their advice and suggestions.

PART ONE

A LONG, STRANGE DAY IN FLORENCE

1 October 1999

7 a.m.: Michele Ferrara's apartment

That morning, Florence had woken up twice: from a night's sleep, and from the sluggishness of a summer that had been too hot and too long.

Chief Superintendent Ferrara looked out at the city from his terrace overlooking the Lungarno degli Acciaioli. He had just finished reading the newspapers. Even the news seemed to echo the morning's good mood: the Pope had declared that sexual intercourse encourages the growth of tumours. That was sure to delight his incorrigible friend Massimo Verga, who would see it as yet more evidence of how right he was to be an atheist. Meanwhile, in Granada, Spain, it had been established that Italian women, with a life expectancy of eighty-two or eighty-three, were second only to Japanese women for longevity. Petra, his wife – German by an accident of birth but Italian by her choice of husband, as she often said with a self-satisfied air – would smile about that when he read her the article in a little while over tea.

Right now, Michele was enjoying the breeze and watching the Ponte Vecchio slowly fill with people. Petra was still inside the apartment, because she'd had to answer a phone call, but the table was already beautifully laid.

Breakfast was almost a sacred ritual in the Ferrara household, perhaps because it was the only meal husband and wife always ate together. As a tribute to Petra's Teutonic origins, it was a big, hearty breakfast, a real German breakfast, but one that the Germans could only dream about. The cold meats were Tuscan, the olives Sicilian and even the strudel, which Petra ordered from the pastry shop in the Piazza Beccaria, was much better than anything you could find in her native city. A judgement confirmed by her parents, who often came to visit them, either because they missed their daughter or because they couldn't resist the charms of Florence.

Weather permitting, they always ate on the terrace, which Petra had transformed into a garden. This morning, it was full of the scents of jasmine, lavender and rosemary. Drifting from the stereo speakers was the muted sound of Tosca cursing Scarpia.

'Guess who that was?' Petra said cheerfully, appearing at last with a steaming teapot.

'Your *Mutti*?' Ferrara asked, with a touch of irony in his voice: his in-laws had only left a few days earlier, and had been on the phone for more than an hour the night before.

'The *tombeur*,' Petra replied. 'He wants to know if you can drop in and see him. He's got a surprise for us.'

The ladies' man – Petra also called him Peter Pan because of his stubborn determination, common to all Casanovas, to never grow up – was Michele Ferrara's best friend, Massimo Verga. A Sicilian like Ferrara, he owned a big bookshop in the Via Tornabuoni. They had been school friends, then Massimo had decided to study philosophy at university while Ferrara had opted for law. It had actually been Massimo who had introduced Michele and Petra. Massimo had been madly in love with her, but in the end she had chosen Ferrara. The two of them had then drifted apart, until they had met again by chance in Florence, where fate had somehow brought both of them. Once their old friendship had resumed, Massimo had made it a point of honour to rescue Michele from the pit of barren ignorance into which, in his opinion, the study of law and his career as a policeman had cast him.

It was Massimo, too, who had introduced them to the pleasures of opera. Neither Ferrara nor his wife was a real connoisseur like Massimo, and they never would be. To them, opera was something purely emotional, and they kept up with it whenever they could. They were as passionate about it as their grandparents and great-grandparents had been in the days when opera was a popular art, like melodrama, and seemed to touch people's lives directly; the days when film and TV had not yet entered the lives of Italians. In the Ferrara household, in any case, the TV set was little more than a piece of furniture to be dusted. Even the news they preferred to hear on the radio.

Where Ferrara invariably disappointed Massimo, however, was when it came to books. It wasn't that he disliked books – on the contrary. He just didn't have time to read, he'd always say.

Ferrara looked at his watch. 'I can't make it right now. Maybe I'll drop in on him around midday. Will you remember to get the mushrooms? I should be home for lunch today.'

'How could I forget?' she said, laughing. 'Chief Superintendent Ferrara coming home for lunch is quite an event!'

She sent him off after breakfast with a kiss on his forehead.

8.56 a.m.: Santa Maria Novella station

The Eurostar 9425, due to arrive at 8.46, pulled into the station ten minutes late.

Valentina Preti got off the train and headed straight for the Tourist Information office. She was in a hurry.

As she passed a group of three young idlers, one of them called out, 'Oh *schönes Fräulein*, if you want to wash your clothes in the Arno, I'll help you take them off, no problem!'

All three laughed.

'Go fuck yourselves!' she snapped back with a malicious smile, leaving them stunned.

She was used to hearing remarks like that – she'd heard a lot worse. And she was used to being taken for a foreigner. In Bologna, where she had been living for four years, it happened all the time.

Born in San Vigilio di Marebbe, in Alto Adige, where her parents owned a hotel, Valentina was tall, slim and athletic, distinctly Nordic in appearance. She wore her wavy blonde hair short, in a gamine cut: today, it peeped out slyly from under the bright orange and purple scarf she had tied into a bandana. She had clean, regular features, and although she wore a little make-up she did not really need it. Her clear skin was dotted with small freckles at the sides of the straight, thin nose, her green-grey eyes were slightly upturned, and her small, soft, slightly protuberant lips had that hint of a pout that men like so much. She was wearing tight-fitting jeans, a purple blouse and an Indian silk waistcoat.

There was a queue at the Information office, and she had to wait.

From time to time, she looked nervously at her watch.

'How do I get to Greve in Chianti?' she asked when she finally reached the front of the queue.

'There's a bus about once an hour,' the girl behind the desk replied. 'The bus station is on your right as you go out, in the Via Santa Caterina da Siena.'

'How about the university?'

'Here in Florence?'

'Yes, the faculty of letters and philosophy.'

'Just a moment, let me have a look.'

As Valentina left the station, she looked at her watch again. 9.25. Too late. Better take a taxi, she could still afford it.

10 a.m.: Police Headquarters

In the offices of the *Squadra Mobile* on the first floor of Police Headquarters in the Via Zara, Ferrara had summoned five of his men for a meeting.

They sat around the table opposite his desk: Gianni Ascalchi, a young superintendent with a pleasantly grumpy expression, recently transferred from Rome; Superintendent Francesco Rizzo, Ferrara's deputy to all intents and purposes; Violante, the oldest of the chief inspectors, deaf in one ear, nearing retirement age and not greatly respected by his colleagues; Inspector Antonio Sergi, known as Serpico because of his resemblance to the Al Pacino character; and finally, Inspector Riccardo Venturi, who had been in the Squad the longest and remembered everything.

Ferrara kicked off proceedings. 'Are we ready for Sunday? There's always trouble when Roma are visiting, and we'll be dealing with two lots of supporters who can't stand the sight of each other. The Commissioner's afraid there might be trouble at the stadium, especially if Fiorentina lose.'

'What do you mean, *if* they lose?' The ironic comment came from Ascalchi, already known as 'the Roman' because of his strong accent. 'They'll lose, chief, they'll lose. We're the better team!'

Rizzo, a Sicilian like Ferrara, shot him an amused glance,

but the others took offence and jumped in to counter Ascalchi's remark.

'We can take it!' Inspector Venturi said.

'We'll destroy you!' was Violante's contribution.

'Okay, cut it out!' Ferrara interrupted. 'I don't want any more predictions about the match, is that understood? We have to help out our colleagues in Special Operations. They're overstretched in a situation like this.'

'As if we didn't already have enough on our plates . . .' Rizzo complained. He had several operations on the go, and was hoping to bring them to a rapid conclusion. He didn't like to spare men from his own squad for jobs which, in his opinion, weren't even in their remit.

Ferrara ignored him. 'Let's see if we can get some decent tip-offs. We need to know if the Fiorentina hooligans are planning anything violent. Get some of our people into the bars where the supporters hang out. Gather as much information as you can.'

Rizzo objected again. 'But surely, chief, Special Operations are already doing that.'

'I know, but it's not enough. We know the territory better than they do – and anyway, these are the Commissioner's orders, okay?'

'I wasn't arguing with the orders. It just seems to me a waste of manpower.'

'Let's not underestimate the situation. As you probably read in *La Nazione*, Special Ops raided the homes of several known troublemakers yesterday . . .'

Inspector Sergi stopped playing with his long tousled beard. 'I read that,' he said. 'Apparently in one house they found explosives filled with marbles.'

'Three of them,' Ferrara said. 'Three lethal devices. Best case scenario, someone gets hit and is left with an indelible memory. Worst case scenario, these things get tossed into a crowd of Roma supporters, or at the police. If someone were to get killed . . .'

Rizzo surrendered. 'All right, chief. We'll see what we can do.'

'Good. So when we finish here, get yourselves organised. Search cars and houses, if necessary. We have the legal authority to do it if we have to. The important thing is that you tell me first, unless it's urgent and you don't have time to call me. If that's the case, I don't need to tell you, you just carry on.'

'All right, chief,' they all agreed.

'Any questions?' Ferrara asked. Then, as always when a meeting was coming to an end: 'Has anyone got anything to say about their current cases?'

Inspector Venturi gave a summary of that day's activities. Sure that everything was under control, Ferrara brought the meeting to a close.

12 noon: parish church of Santa Croce, Greve in Chianti

Father Rotondi – Don Sergio, as everyone called him – walked towards the sacristy across the central nave, annoyed as usual by the tourists disturbing the peace of his church. These were supposedly high-class tourists, but they were just as intrusive as the downmarket kind. And there were more of them every year. Germans, English, Americans, and Japanese – the latter the worst because they always went around in groups.

This morning, there were two groups. The smaller one

stood admiring the precious white varnished terracotta above the altar in the left nave, while the larger one crowded around Lorenzo di Bicci's triptych in the apsidal chapel of the right nave. In the middle of the group, incongruously, there was a tall, fair-haired young man who towered over the Japanese. It was impossible not to notice him, because even inside the church he had kept on his sunglasses.

'He's really going to enjoy the triptych,' Father Rotondi said to himself, even more irritated. What disturbed him most was the unpleasant impression that, behind those sunglasses, the young man's eyes weren't on Lorenzo's work at all, but on him.

When he got back to the sacristy, he set to work trying to prise open the door of the wooden cabinet, which was jammed. The cabinet contained the precious monstrance that was used only for the most important masses, and Father Francesco, parish priest of Santa Croce, wanted it at all costs for Sunday's ceremony.

He had brought a sharp knife in from the kitchen and was trying to force the door open with it when Father Francesco walked in.

'Careful you don't ruin the wood,' he said.

Taken by surprise, Don Sergio jumped in fright and the knife fell from his hand.

'You shouldn't be using tools like that, father,' the older priest said. 'And you seem more nervous than usual today. Anything wrong?'

'No, no. It's just that there's a lot to do.'

'There always is, Don Sergio. The care of souls doesn't leave time for idleness.'

But Don Sergio wasn't thinking about the care of souls. He was thinking about the normal, everyday administrative tasks which Father Francesco didn't bother about and which the elderly sacristan was increasingly neglecting. There were repairs that needed doing, bills to be paid. They'd almost run out of candles and if he didn't take care of it, Sunday mass would have to be celebrated without them. And there were other things that were worrying him, too; private things. He had made a lot of mistakes in his life, and he had to find a way to free himself from them once and for all, even if it meant doing something really drastic. That was in his thoughts more and more these days.

He applied more pressure with the knife, and the door suddenly sprang open.

'There!' he said triumphantly. 'Now the important thing is not to close it again, at least before Sunday. We'll call the locksmith next week.'

'All right. But take that knife back to the kitchen and try not to hurt yourself. If you want to see me about the accounts, I'll be in my study.'

12.30 p.m.: Verga bookshop, Via Tornabuoni

'Nice to see you, Superintendent!' Rita Senesi greeted him, as cheerfully as ever, in her enchanting Florentine sing-song. 'What can I do for you?'

Rita Senesi had been working here for as long as anyone could remember. Whether or not she was in love with her boss was a mystery, and nobody knew the answer – perhaps she didn't even know it herself. She was certainly resigned to Massimo Verga's inveterate womanising, which had caused more than a few problems over the years and had greatly reduced his considerable family fortune.

'I'm not here to buy anything, Rita. Massimo asked to see me.'

'He's up there, in a "meeting". One of those "summits", you know? . . . I'll go and call him. Wait here. Or would you prefer to go to his office?'

'Yes, I think I will. Tell him I'm there.'

It was a big bookshop, spread over three floors. The latest books were on the ground floor, along with a section for newspapers and magazines just inside the front door on the left, and a section for luxury stationery on the right. On the first floor were the art books, including the antiquarian volumes, as well as Massimo Verga's office. In the basement was the store room, the paperbacks, and the meeting room. Book launches were held in the meeting room, as well as impromptu gatherings of the city's best wits, who convened from time to time at a moment's notice to slaughter anything that took their fancy: the latest bestsellers or the policies of whichever government was in office, no matter the political complexion.

Ferrara was not at all sorry to have arrived right in the middle of one of these meetings. If Massimo was busy, he wouldn't have time to do something Ferrara had been dreading: grill him on how he was getting on with Henry James' *Turn of the Screw*. Massimo had been constantly lecturing him about that book ever since Ferrara had been unwise enough to confess that, when it came to horror, he preferred Stephen King.

The office was not large. It was dominated by a metal desk that was always cluttered with books, most of them open and annotated in the margins or with the pages marked with strips of coloured paper. There were also four chairs, various shelves full of files, and an outsize rack of carefully polished pipes.

That was another of the differences that united the two men: as far as smoking went, Ferrara maintained that cigars were superior to anything else, while Verga championed the nobility of the pipe. Both of them looked down on cigarettes, which they considered common and deadly.

'I did it!' Massimo exclaimed as he joined him, having finally managed to extricate himself from the passionate debate currently in progress.

'I could have waited. I'm in no hurry.'

'What?' He smiled. 'Oh, no, I wasn't referring to those four madmen.' He opened a drawer in the desk, took out a rather thick envelope and handed it over in triumph. 'Look at this, and spare me the gratitude. When the time's right, I'll remind you that you owe me one.'

The surprise wasn't entirely unexpected. The envelope contained return tickets to Vienna, for two people, for a period of two weeks over the New Year, as well as tickets for the first night of *Cavalleria Rusticana* with Placido Domingo, which were now quite impossible to find.

1 p.m.: Michele Ferrara's apartment

Ferrara returned home, humming *Bada, Santuzza, schiavo non sono* under his breath, making sure no one could hear him because he was very out of tune and was well aware of the fact, even without Petra there to remind him. He was in a good mood. He had quite forgotten that the world never stops breathing down our necks, doesn't give a damn how we amuse ourselves, and is always there, ready to deal us a new blow in order to remind us that we are human and are born only to suffer.

Petra was in the greenhouse on the terrace, which was one of her two kingdoms, the other being the kitchen.

They lived in a top floor apartment, which Ferrara had been lucky enough to find seven years earlier. The apartment was small, though perfectly adequate for the two of them, but its great advantage was that it had a beautiful terrace, very large by Florentine standards. Petra had fallen in love with it immediately, and with a little time, patience and determination had transformed it into a garden that was the envy of their friends.

This was the time of year when she spent a lot of time in the greenhouse, sowing, transplanting, fertilising. The greenhouse was a small mobile construction of wood and glass, complete with air-conditioning, placed against the wall of the apartment on the south side of the terrace.

As he embraced his wife, Ferrara felt a strange sensation. When two people know each other so well, it takes the slightest thing, a pressure that lingers a moment longer than necessary, a glint in the eyes, an unexpected pause.

'What a wonderful day, Michele!' Petra said, freeing herself from his embrace with a forced smile that did not deceive him.

If she didn't want to come out with it straight away, he was happy to humour her. She was not the kind of woman to hide things. When the time was right she would tell him what the problem was. That was what he thought, anyway.

'You have no idea how wonderful,' he replied, taking her by the arm and walking her to the arbour, where the table was already laid.

'What do you mean?'

'Massimo's surprise.'

'A nice one?'

'To say the least.'

They sat down, but he found it hard to concentrate on the tempting salad with porcini mushrooms and slivers of Parmesan. 'So,' he said, 'don't you want to know? What's the matter? You seem distracted.'

'No, no, tell me. What is this great news?'

He told her as he handed her the envelope, and for a moment at least the joy of the surprise seemed to dispel whatever anxiety was nagging away at her. But immediately her expression grew pensive.

'So,' Michele Ferrara said gently, unable to restrain himself any longer, 'do you want to tell me now or do you prefer to keep it bottled up until tonight?'

'What, Michele?' she said, making a small attempt to defend herself but knowing it was pointless.

Petra's greatest gift was that she was a practical, down-to-earth woman. She always overcame her fears and anxieties, always tried to find ways of dealing with even the most difficult situations, and never let herself become discouraged. The important thing was to do something: that was her credo in life. That was another reason he didn't like to think that something had unsettled her.

They looked at each other intensely for a few moments. Then she took a letter out of the big pocket of her gardening smock, and handed it to him. As he held out his arm to take it, he uncovered his watch, and he instinctively noted the time: 1.46.

It was an ordinary commercial envelope. It bore the letterhead of a mail order firm and a gummed label with Michele Ferrara's name and address printed on it. Inside, an ordinary sheet of A4 paper, folded twice.

He unfolded it.

What he saw was like a collage made by a mad artist with a taste for the macabre.

MEMENTO MORI

'Remember that you will die.' Or else, That you *must* die. A pleasant little gift, Ferrara thought. The warning was pointless: death is the one thing we can be sure of in our lives, we don't need anybody to take the trouble to remind us. But if someone deliberately, and anonymously, sends a warning like that to the head of the Florence *Squadra Mobile*, it's hard to take it as a joke.

Petra certainly hadn't.

The letters had been cut out of a newspaper, and the sender had put the finishing touch to his work by spattering the words and the paper with red stains, and then holding it up to allow the liquid to trickle a little. A realistic touch that achieved the desired effect, whether the bloodstains were real or fake.

Ferrara put a cigar in his mouth but did not light it.

Petra stood up and started clearing the table. Neither of them had done justice to the porcini mushrooms.

He would have liked to put his arms around her and hold her tight. Perhaps she would have liked it, too. He would never know because at that very moment his mobile rang.

It was his deputy, Francesco Rizzo.

A man had just been murdered.

2.40 p.m.: in the squad car

'There was a call to 113,' Officer Sebastiano Franchi, the driver, said as they crossed the city with sirens blaring.

'Who's on the switchboard?'

'Grassi.'

'What time was it?'

'2.23, chief.'

'Do we know who called?'

'A woman, the cashier in a bar on the main square of Greve.'

'What did she say?'

'Just that they'd found a dead body. It was a murder. She sounded very agitated, according to Grassi.'

'What else?'

'That's it, chief. She hung up immediately.'

From the way he said it, it was clear that he was quite indignant at the woman's lack of civic responsibility. He couldn't have been more than twenty, was new to the job and unaware that, in a situation like this, such behaviour was, unfortunately, only to be expected. By way of compensation, he drove as if he were at the wheel of a Ferrari at Monza. Like all drivers, he insisted on showing off his skills.

They had left the city and were starting to climb towards Greve. Ferrara asked Franchi to turn off the siren and slow down a little. As he never tired of repeating: when a murder has been committed, five minutes more or less won't make any difference to the victim.

Especially as Rizzo had already gone on ahead, setting off immediately while the driver was still on his way to pick Ferrara up from home.

He was pleased with Rizzo, who'd turned out an excellent detective. Ever since, as a novice barely out of the Police Academy, he had been involved in the investigation of a series of prostitute murders, he had made great strides. His instincts were good, and he combined the old fashioned virtue of dogged commitment – an increasingly rare gift in policemen these days – with an ability to use the most up-to-date tools. In some ways he reminded Ferrara of Marshal Monaco, now retired, but whereas Monaco had hated even typewriters, Rizzo was perfectly at home with computers.

He had preferred to send him on ahead because he trusted him, but mainly because he needed an oasis of peace and quiet during the brief journey out of the city. He needed to think.

So someone wanted to eliminate him.

Who? And why?

Like everyone, he had his ghosts, personal and professional. After more than twenty years on the force, holding key posts, it was natural that a lot of people had grudges against him. Not only among those who lived on the margins of society and threatened it, but also within the establishment. Theoretically, he had a surfeit of choice. And yet he couldn't think of a single person among his possible enemies who might take things as far as this.

Cases of released prisoners seeking revenge were rarer than might be imagined. And he also tended to exclude political motives: things had been quiet on that front in the last few years, the Red Brigades had long since left the scene, and nothing had happened recently to suggest that anyone was looking to rack up the tension again. Besides, politically motivated murders tended to be claimed after the event, not announced in advance. And certainly not this way.

Of course, there was also the case of the Monster of Florence. The perpetrator of eight double murders, sixteen horrible crimes in which the victims had been dismembered, the Monster had been arrested before Ferrara had become head of the *Squadra Mobile*. Many people would have preferred to think of the case as closed, but Ferrara had insisted on reopening it, had demolished the theory of a lone serial killer, and had tracked down the killer's accomplices, all of whom were now in prison. That might have been enough for a lot of people, but not for him. Stubbornly, pigheadedly, he had continued searching for the people behind the crimes, and his search had taken him ever higher, as well as into the darkest corners of the city, uncovering a world of satanic rites and black masses – a lot of nonsense, according to those who still clung to the theory of a single killer.

It can be risky to stir things up like that, and he had certainly made enemies, but he found it hard to believe that they could really be planning his physical elimination. They could ruin his career, trap him in a compromising situation, or scheme to have him 'promoted', which usually means 'removed'.

They had already tried.

But killing him was too great a risk: his men would move heaven and earth, not to mention the prosecutors who had followed his investigation, the journalists who knew him, and the previous Commissioner who had been so heavily involved in the case.

Or was he wrong? Was there someone really high up, and close to being discovered, who thought the risk might be worth taking?

3.05 p.m.: Greve in Chianti

Officer Franchi drew up next to the other police cars and vans in the Piazza Matteotti, near the monument to Giovanni da Verrazzano, where a number of tourist coaches were parked. The little town of Greve has long benefited from its position halfway between Florence and Siena, in an area – Chianti – much valued for its agricultural produce, and especially its wine, which was already being mentioned in documents dating back to the fourteenth century. In the Middle Ages, Greve was a place where several trading routes met, and during the Renaissance – a period of great artistic, economic and cultural growth in the two main cities of Tuscany – it became a sought-after spot for the most important Florentine families to establish their country residences. Today, it is an essential destination for visitors who want to experience the genuine, rich, sweet atmosphere of a region that is unique in the world.

The shop was in one of the streets leading off the piazza, the Via Roma. The piazza had an unusual triangular shape, which some said looked like a fish. At the apex of the triangle was the church, and near the base, beneath the arcades, was the bar from which, to judge by the crowds, the phone call had been made. Among the crowds, Ferrara spotted a couple of officers from the Homicide Section asking questions.

As far as he could see, there were no journalists or TV crews – much to his relief.

A red and white tape with the words *Stop – Police* had been stretched across the entrance to the Via Roma. His men had, quite correctly, cordoned off the part of the street immediately adjacent to the crime scene.

He crossed the tape.

The shop was less than twenty yards along the street. In the two wide windows was a nicely arranged display of crucifixes, candelabras, books, postcards, and religious prints. A sign above the entrance read *Religious Articles*.

He went in.

As he did so, Rizzo came towards him. The others already there were the pathologist, Francesco Leone, with whom Ferrara continued to be on formal terms despite all the cases they had worked on together over the years, Inspector Sergi with various colleagues from Homicide, and the forensics team.

In a quiet corner, some distance from the scene of the crime, he saw a priest talking in a low voice to an elderly man. The priest, who looked nervous and upset, was unusually handsome.

There was a strange atmosphere, an unnatural absence of noise. It was almost as though the men, subdued by the surroundings, had instinctively lowered their voices and toned down the bustle normal in such situations, adapting their rhythms and movements to a sanctity the place didn't really possess.

As if to confirm that impression, Rizzo greeted Ferrara with the words, 'It's like being inside an old church.'

The room was quite large, rectangular in shape, and artificially lit. Not much light came in from outside. The walls were almost entirely covered with heavy wooden shelves, some behind glass doors, containing books, missals, votive images, and locally-made silver – or what appeared to be silver – crucifixes. The high ceiling was supported by solid beams. A half-open door on the right led to a store room. At the back was a long counter, on which candles of various sizes were displayed. Even the smell, a mixture of wood, wax, incense and damp, served to emphasise the peculiar character of the scene.

The body lay on the floor, hidden by the counter. He approached it.

The first thing he noticed was the blood, as bright as red paint, which seemed to be still gushing from under the body. The victim's slashed clothes were smeared with it, the floor was covered with a pool of it, and the shelves, the counter and the objects were spattered with it.

The dead man was lying on his left side with his head turned slightly to the right. His eyes were wide open and his mouth gaped, as if he had been caught by surprise. His face was horribly disfigured.

Francesco Leone, helped by one of the forensics team, was busy dictating his observations. He greeted Ferrara with a nod and continued without a pause.

'. . . presenting what appear to be knife wounds in the right temporal-mandibular joint, at the left corner of the lower jaw, in the right costal arch and in the mesogastric region. As well as numerous wounds all over the face . . .'

'Who's the dead man?' Ferrara asked Rizzo.

'Stefano Micali, thirty years old.'

'I checked the name in records,' Inspector Sergi said. In some ways, he had taken the place of Antonio Monaco. 'Nothing. He was clean.'

'And those two?' Ferrara asked, referring to the young priest and his companion.

'Don Sergio, from the parish church at the top of the piazza, and Alfredo Beccalossi, who owns the shop,' Rizzo replied. 'It was Don Sergio who found the body. He immediately ran to the bar to raise the alarm. Beccalossi was in the bar and they came back together. Don Sergio was scared, he didn't want to come, but Beccalossi insisted. They were here when we arrived and we asked them to stay.'

'You did the right thing. Did they resist?'

'Not at all. In fact, they seem keen to cooperate.'

While the forensics team continued with their work, Ferrara asked the two men to follow him into the store room, where they would be left in peace. He took Sergi with him, leaving Rizzo to keep an eye on the others.

Don Sergio looked a lot younger than his thirty years. He was tall, athletic-looking, and elegant: in his ecclesiastical suit he looked as if he was wearing Armani. He had fair, short hair, intense blue eyes, and gentle, almost feminine features. Raphael would surely have chosen him as a model for an angel. Alfredo Beccalossi was an elderly man, short and bent with arthritis, with unkempt white hair and nicotine-stained fingers.

Ferrara started with Beccalossi. 'Was he your employee?' he asked.

'Yes, the only one.'

'A good worker?'

'Very good. He practically ran the shop. I hardly ever set foot in here these days.'

'Married? Children?'

The old man shot a quick glance at the priest, a glance that seemed to Ferrara to be knowing and amused.

'No. No, he was a . . . lone wolf. He'd been an orphan. The priests brought him up. He started working for me when he was twenty-three. A perfect worker, never any problems, I can assure you.'

'Did he have any enemies, as far as you know?'

'Even if he'd told me he had some, I wouldn't have believed him. I can't really imagine why anyone would—'

'And yet someone did, didn't they?'

'Some petty thief, an immigrant, there are lots of them around.'

'Is that what you think, too?' Ferrara asked the priest.

'I've no idea . . . I wouldn't like to hazard a guess . . . I don't know, I really don't know!' His voice was high-pitched, and he seemed on the verge of hysterics. He was wringing his hands nervously and constantly biting his lower lip.

'But you can confirm that he was a good man?'

'Oh, yes, as good as gold.'

'Would you be so kind as to go over the facts for me, please?'

'Well, I came to get the candles for the altar—'

'What time was this?'

The priest swallowed, seeming annoyed by the interruption. 'Just after two.'

'Doesn't the shop close for lunch?' he asked, turning to Sergi.

'It's open from 9 to 1 and from 3 to 7,' Serpico replied diligently.

'Oh, but Stefanino always stays here during the lunch break,' the priest hastened to explain. 'I mean, he always stayed,' he corrected himself, lowering his voice and making the sign of the cross. 'In fact, I often came to see him during the break. He's . . . he was a good man, like I said, very dedicated.'

'Stefanino?' Ferrara asked politely, trying hard not to sound crude or tactless. Coming from the priest, the nickname sounded strange, excessively familiar.

'That was his name. I mean . . . that's what everyone here called him. He was as good as gold. Pleasant to everyone, well-liked.'

'I understand. Please go on.'

'When I arrived, it was obvious the shop was closed. I rang the bell and waited. As there was no answer I rang again, and at the same time pressed my face against the glass door, making a screen with my hands. It was quite dark inside. Except that the door wasn't locked as it usually is, and a small amount of pressure was enough to push it open. What a fright! I nearly fell flat on my face . . . my God!'

His voice had again risen in pitch. The effect was more comic than dramatic.

'And then?'

'I came in very cautiously and called, "Stefanino! Stefanino!" There was no reply, so I started walking towards the back room and then for some reason I turned my head to the left and . . . that's when I saw him! Oh my God, oh Lord, have pity on him. Have pity on us.'

'Please calm down – it's all over now.'

Don Sergio sniffled. 'I saw a heap on the floor,' he resumed. 'Behind the counter. And blood – blood everywhere. Even though it was dark, you could see it. It was almost shiny, like . . . I don't know, like liquid rubies.'

'Did you touch anything? Did you cry out, call for help?'

'I ran out. I ran to the bar and raised the alarm. The cashier called you. I wanted to go to the church and tell Father Francesco, but Signor Beccalossi begged me to come back here with him. He wanted to see for himself.'

'Did you notice anything suspicious? Did you see anyone?'

'No – nothing, nobody.'

'Did you know him well? Stefano Micali, I mean.'

'I've known him since we were children. We were at school together.'

'We'll need to talk to you again, if you don't mind. And if you think of anything, anything at all, however insignificant it may seem, please contact me. Either me or Superintendent Rizzo. There are still a few formalities to go through, so I'll hand you over to the inspector. Thank you for your time.'

Meanwhile, the cashier and the owner of the bar, as well as the customers who had seen Don Sergio come in, had been interviewed by some of the officers. Two other officers had immediately taken up guard outside the shop. Fortunately, nobody had entered before Ferrara's arrival, apart from the priest, the owner and the police.

The public have seen a lot of crime movies, Ferrara thought. *They're well trained.*

Nothing of any great interest had emerged from the interviews. They had merely confirmed that Stefano Micali was a good man – a modest, rather retiring man, hard-working and generous.

By now, the shop had been thoroughly searched. As far as could be ascertained, nothing had been stolen. The money was all in the till, and nothing valuable seemed to be missing. The owner would be able to confirm that later.

There was no sign of the murder weapon.

The forensics team and the pathologist had finished their work. The body had been wrapped in a waterproof sheet which was then zipped up and placed in a zinc casket, to be taken to the morgue at the Institute of Forensic Medicine of the University of Florence. Any objects which might turn out to be useful to the investigation – either because of the position in which they had been found or because they might be connected in some way, however remotely, with the murder – had been placed in special containers. The most interesting of these objects was some kind of missal or small Bible, bound in black and with a gold cross on the cover, which had been found lying under the body, so thoroughly drenched in blood as to be completely unreadable.

Perhaps this was the object the assistant had been showing, or intending to show, the customer, if the murderer had indeed been a customer. There were similar books displayed on the shelf behind the counter.

The shop was emptying. Soon the last men would leave and seals would be placed on the door.

Ferrara walked back to the square and got there just in time to see Gianni Fuschi of Forensics, an old friend of his, heading for one of the police cars.

He called to him.

'Can you do me a favour?' he asked when he came level with him.

'Maybe even two, Gatto,' Fuschi replied, using the

26

nickname – the Cat – that many of his men, and even some journalists, used for Ferrara. It was an affectionate term that not only showed their admiration for the shrewdness concealed beneath his often secretive exterior, but also alluded to the catlike shape of his eyes and his sharp, penetrating gaze.

'Follow me,' he said, drawing Fuschi away from the other men, who were getting into their cars and vans to return to Headquarters. Spotting Rizzo among them, he called, 'Go ahead, I'll join you!' Then, turning back to Fuschi, 'There's another thing I'd like you to take a look at. But whatever you find, I don't want anyone else to know. Just me, okay?'

From his jacket pocket he took out a plastic envelope containing the threatening letter, which he had wiped clean of fingerprints – a serious mistake, perhaps, but there was no avoiding it if he didn't want his own fingerprints or, worse still, Petra's to be identified.

He had decided that nobody, at least for the moment, should know that his life had been threatened. There were too many people who could have used it as an excuse for removing him, for his own safety, from the Monster case.

'All right, all right,' Fuschi said, amused. 'So – the upright Chief Superintendent Ferrara has taken to removing evidence from a crime scene. For his own personal use. I have a couple of friends on *La Nazione* who'd be prepared to buy me dinner at Sabatini's for a scoop like this. Maybe even two dinners. With a nice Havana cigar to finish off, not one of those disgusting pieces of charcoal you stick in your mouth!'

'This is important, Gianni,' Ferrara said.

But Fuschi had already grasped that.

On the way back Ferrara let Officer Franchi give free rein to his motor racing ambitions. There was no reason to slow down now – quite the contrary.

As they drove, they passed a white van with the letters RAI in blue on the side.

5 p.m.: the Commissioner's office

At exactly five o'clock, Ferrara reported to the Commissioner.

Riccardo Lepri, who had replaced the Mephistophelean Angelo Duranti, was almost the exact opposite of his predecessor. Where Duranti had been in a constant bad mood, Lepri was affable, sometimes even merry. A man of large build and clearly robust appetites, he very rarely lost his temper and exuded an air of calm and self-confidence. But there was something a tiny bit ambiguous in that diplomatic stance of his, something Ferrara could not quite put his finger on. It was as if, deep down, his real interests were not those his position dictated, but lay elsewhere. That was why Ferrara's relations with him, although cordial and polite, were not really as friendly as they had been with other commissioners.

'So, a difficult case,' he commented rhetorically when Ferrara had finished his report.

'Like any case where the killer isn't either caught red-handed or identified immediately. A victim with no criminal record, no witnesses, no murder weapon, no apparent motive. It may have been an attempted robbery that went wrong, but I doubt it. First, because this was an extremely violent attack, and second, because there wasn't much cash in the till, which wasn't touched anyway, and there was little or nothing of any real value in the shop.'

'The press are going to have a field day.'

'I'm surprised I haven't had them under my feet already.'

The Commissioner winked. 'A good turn from a devoted admirer of yours. As soon as I heard about the murder, I got all the journalists out of the press room and gave them an impromptu briefing on the measures we're taking to avoid or limit disorder in the stadium on Sunday. They couldn't resist.'

'Thank you, though I don't think it'll help much. The TV people have already arrived, which means the papers won't be far behind.'

'As I expected. But even a few minutes' head start can help, don't you think? If we can forestall them before they start spreading scare stories as they usually do . . .'

'It depends how long we take to get on the right track and bring the culprit to justice. My own feeling is that it's going to take a while.'

'I assume you'll be handling this personally?'

'Not exactly. I'd like to put Superintendent Rizzo in charge of the investigation. He's a good detective, he could do with the space.'

The Commissioner seemed slightly put out. Ferrara preferred not to think that he was someone else who'd have liked to see him working on something other than the Monster of Florence case for the moment.

'Of course, of course. I know Superintendent Rizzo. But his experience . . . Well, anyway, I'd be really grateful if you gave this case your special attention. You know as well as I do that when something like this happens, the police need to act quickly and efficiently, or people start to feel scared. Apart from anything else, the publicity is bad for the tourist trade, and Greve is only fifteen miles from here, practically part of Florence.'

'Don't worry, Commissioner. I stand by my men and I've

never shirked my responsibilities. The case will be pursued with due diligence and Rizzo will have my full backing. I'll keep you updated myself.'

'Thank you. I have every confidence in you.'

6 p.m.: Chief Superintendent Ferrara's office

There was a knock at the door, and Rizzo, just back from the morgue, came in.

'Sit down, Francesco.'

'Thank you, chief.'

Ferrara no longer found it strange that, although he had been calling Rizzo by his first name since early in their relationship, Rizzo, with a traditional respect for rank and seniority, continued to address him formally. Of medium height and solid, even stocky build, a down-to-earth man of few words, Francesco Rizzo was the personification of a reliable policeman and a regular guy.

'Anything interesting?'

'A few things,' he said, sitting down on one of the two small black armchairs in front of the big wooden desk and taking out a packet of cigarettes. Then, remembering that Ferrara, although not expressly forbidding it, didn't like the stench of cigarettes to clash with the smell of his cigar, put it back in his pocket.

He appeared visibly tired. His face was drawn, and his dark, prematurely greying hair slightly ruffled.

He checked in his notebook. 'The most important thing is that they were able to pinpoint the time of death very precisely: between 1.15 and 1.45. Definitely not before or after, most likely the twenty minutes between 1.20 and 1.40. From an examination of the wounds, it's clear that death was almost instantaneous, and was caused by the first or second wound to the back. They were the two deepest wounds. The weapon used was a knife with a blade about four and a half inches long.'

'How many times was he stabbed?'

'A lot. Thirty-six, and almost all of them, as I said, after he was already dead and lying on his side on the ground.'

'What do we know about the direction of the blows?'

'The first blows were struck with great force in a downward direction and from right to left, in rapid succession, which indicates that the killer is right-handed and must be as tall as, or taller than, the victim. The other blows, more cuts than blows, were inflicted from right to left, from left to right and in a downward direction.'

'Well, that's something.'

'There's more, chief.'

'Go on.'

'Leone conducted a close examination of the tissues of the rectal walls. There's no doubt about it: Micali was a practising homosexual, and had been for a long time.'

'Ah, our "Stefanino",' Ferrara said knowingly. 'What about this afternoon? Any signs of sexual assault?'

'No. Leone's ruled it out.'

'Is that all there is?'

'Yes, chief.'

'Let's see what we've got so far. The murder took place after the shop closed for lunch. According to the priest, Micali usually locked the door. And again according to Don Sergio, Micali never went out during the lunch break. On the contrary, that was when people sometimes, or maybe often, came to see him. We know the priest did. Why not some other special friends?'

'I'd say it's at least possible,' Rizzo agreed.

'Which means the killer was someone he knew. He must have opened the door to him, and trusted him enough to happily turn his back on him. He had no idea what the man's real intentions were and was genuinely surprised when he stabbed him in the back.'

'Sounds right to me.'

'The blow kills him, he doesn't even have time to cry out. He falls to the floor and the killer carries on stabbing him even though he's dead. It's as if he was so angry at him, he wanted to wipe his body from the face of the earth. But why? Why did he hate him so much? Jealousy? A quarrel over money?'

'We'll have to look into his private life. That might not be so difficult. Greve's a small place. If we're lucky, the case can be contained within the town and sooner or later we'll find the culprit.'

'I hope it's sooner rather than later. Let's try and avoid the press turning this into a soap opera. The homosexual angle will be meat and drink to them, whether it's the right line of inquiry or not. But I appreciate your optimism and I wish you good luck, because I'd like you to be in charge of the investigation. What do you think of the priest?'

'There's something strange about him,' Rizzo replied, clearly pleased with the assignment. 'Why did he run to tell the people in the bar? And why did he spend nearly half an hour with the body before he told anyone? Doing what? He gave the impression he's someone who's more likely to run away than join the fray, don't you think?'

'Yes, I do. Unless, of course, he actually ran away as soon as the crime was committed, washed off the bloodstains, got rid of the weapon and *then*, feeling repentant or whatever, ran to the bar. But frankly I don't see it. He seems too timid for that. Keep an eye on him, though, but discreetly, please, we mustn't upset anyone. This is a sensitive area, and we'd like to avoid a scandal.

'Don't worry, chief, we'll wear kid gloves with the Church. But not blinkers.'

Ferrara smiled. 'Oh, and Francesco,' he added. 'You don't need to keep me informed of everything. Just the important things, anything significant you turn up. I want you to handle as much of the case yourself as you can. I have other things on my plate at the moment. And please, as far as the press is concerned, say as little as possible. If necessary, send them to me and I'll deal with them.'

Although Rizzo was trying hard not to let it show, he was clearly surprised to be delegated such a degree of responsibility. Ferrara caught a hint of alarm in his eyes, a slight tightening of the muscles in his face.

'Let's go,' he said. 'You have things to do, and I want to watch the evening news at home for once.'

7 p.m.: Verga bookshop, Via Tornabuoni

The shiny silver Porsche Carrera parked just outside the front door of the bookshop. *Bound to get a ticket*, Rita Senesi thought, *and it's sure to be a hefty fine.* But the driver seemed quite relaxed and unconcerned with the consequences of such a glaring infraction of the rules.

The richer they are, the stupider, Rita thought.

From inside the shop, she couldn't see the occupants of the Porsche clearly but, from what she could see, the girl was certainly a looker and the driver a youngish man who, even at this hour, was still wearing sunglasses.

The girl got out – she had long, beautiful legs – and walked quickly to the front door.

Rita did not move. She had seen enough: the wisps of hair escaping from beneath her scarf, the pale freckles, the slightly upturned grey-green eyes. Customers like this girl were the exclusive reserve of her boss – who indeed, guided by his infallible antennae, had already materialised and was heading for the door, ready to hold it gallantly open for the girl.

'Please come in. It's the first time you've been here, isn't it? Are you a foreigner?'

'Yes, a foreigner from Bologna,' she replied, with a touch of sarcasm in her beautiful, silvery voice.

'You see? I've always said Florence was the wrong city. I should have opened my bookshop in Bologna!'

'Do you just flirt or do you also sell books?'

'It depends on what you're looking for. In my opinion, flirting has one advantage: it doesn't ruin the eyes.'

'I'm in a bit of a hurry,' she replied, handing him a sheet of paper with a list of titles: history and theory of Renaissance theatre, aesthetics, art history.

'We must have some of these. Fabio!' he called.

One of the assistants came running and Rita's boss gave him the list.

'It'll take five or ten minutes. While we're waiting, if you'd like to follow me upstairs I might be able to suggest something equally useful.'

The girl glanced at her watch and then looked outside, to where the car was parked. It was empty. The ticket was clearly visible, tucked under the windscreen wiper.

'Don't worry about the fine. It's too late now.'

'It's just that I have a train to catch.'

'What time does it leave?'

'8.13.'

'That gives us more than thirty minutes, plenty of time. Make the most of it, follow me. What exactly are you interested in?'

'I'm studying arts, music and drama. I'm in my last year, preparing a thesis on banquets and theatrical performances at the time of Lorenzo de' Medici.'

'And can't you find those books in Bologna?'

'I imagine I can,' she said as they climbed the stairs. 'But I'm thinking of attending a course here in Florence and that's the reading list for it.'

'So we'll be seeing you again. Florence isn't so bad after all . . .'

'I didn't say I'd made up my mind.' She smiled: the smile of a young woman keeping an older man at arm's length.

While the two hobnobbed upstairs, Rita Senesi, who had looked on in amusement as the traffic wardens had swooped on the Porsche, was now watching the young man: he had first gone into the bar-tobacconist's next door, then had come out and was pacing in front of the windows, smoking nervously.

He was really good-looking, too, and very young. Nearly six feet tall, fair-haired, slim, well dressed – though she thought the expensive buckskin jacket a trifle premature after the merest hint of autumn that had brought the city to life today. Suddenly, he seemed to tire of walking up and down. He threw away his cigarette and came in.

Rita was about to point him upstairs, but before she could he said, 'I need a pen.'

'Ball point or fountain pen?' she almost stammered.

'A fountain pen, a good one.'

The accent was not Florentine. Rita thought she detected a slight American inflection.

She led him over to the display cabinet where they kept the expensive pens, took out two trays showing different brands, and placed them on top of the glass.

'These are the latest Auroras, these are Cross, Parker and . . .'

With a determined, almost brusque gesture, the young man separated the two trays which were blocking his view of the pens inside the cabinet, and pointed. 'That one.'

It was a Montblanc Meisterstück, one of the most expensive pens they had.

'An excellent choice. Would you like it gift-wrapped?'

'It's for me. Just fill it for me, please.'

'Of course. That way you can try it.'

While Rita was inserting the cartridge, the young man took off his sunglasses. She handed him the pen and as she did so she looked him in the face. It made her shudder slightly. He had very clear grey eyes; cold eyes. As cold as ice.

The young man doodled a little on the notepad provided. 'It's fine.'

'It's better if you write something, your name, whatever . . .'

'I said it's fine. I'll take it.'

He hadn't even asked the price.

Rita made out a receipt. The young man paid the money without demur and she handed him the pen.

He left the shop.

'. . . and if you don't mind me giving you a piece of advice,' Massimo was saying, 'you shouldn't neglect the pagan aspect of those banquets and theatrical performances, the element of

36

ritual and magic. The combination of the Dionysian and the sacred in Florentine culture in the sixteenth century is a constant source of surprise. Especially in popular entertainments, but not exclusively. Think of Machiavelli and his *Mandragola*, with a plot based on the idea of gullibility: the husband deceived thanks to the supposed miraculous properties of a herb!'

'It's true, I hadn't thought of that.'

'If you're interested, I might be able to make a small contribution to your thesis. Come.' He led her to the section where the antiquarian and second-hand books were kept.

'Have a look at this,' he said, taking a volume half-bound in leather from one of the shelves. The title was printed in gold: *Common Book of the Dead and of Things Believed Lost*. 'We can't be sure, but many people think it's the only existing Italian version, translated by Giulio Delmino in Paris in 1530, of the infamous *Necronomicon*. You know what the *Necronomicon* is, don't you?'

'No.'

'It's the oldest known treatise on black magic, written by an Arab named Abdul Alhazred. Here, take it.'

'No, I couldn't do that. I could never afford it. I told you, I'm only a student.'

'Don't worry, it's not old, it's just a photostat. Not worth much, but the contents are fine. And besides, you don't have to buy it. Just promise to bring it back, that's all I ask. I insist, and when a Sicilian insists . . .'

The girl hesitated, but took the book in the end. 'You're quite something, you know? That thing about magic is a great idea – none of my teachers said anything about it.'

'Welcome to Florence, *signorina*,' he said, amused.

*

Once he got back in the car, the young man wrote a few words in block capitals on the sheet of writing paper he had bought, along with a ready-stamped envelope, from the tobacconist's:

I SAW YOU TODAY IN GREVE. I KNOW WHERE TO FIND YOU, YOU WON'T GET AWAY WITH IT. WHOEVER HAS INFLICTED TORTURE DESERVES ONLY TORTURE IN RETURN. AN EYE FOR AN EYE: THAT IS THE TRUE LAW OF THE LORD. I'LL COME AND FIND YOU. DON'T TRY AND ESCAPE. I'LL STILL FIND YOU.

And on the envelope he wrote:

FATHER SERGIO ROTONDI
PARISH CHURCH OF SANTA CROCE
GREVE IN CHIANTI (FI)

By the time the girl got back in the Porsche, he had already put everything in his pocket.

'How come it took you so long?' he asked gently.

'They couldn't find the books, they're not very organised. I only got three, in the end. But the owner's very nice, he even lent me a book.'

'Shall we go, then? It's nearly eight.'

'All right, step on it!'

He didn't need to be asked twice. He set off with a squeal of tyres. After dropping the girl he returned home, undecided whether or not to send the letter.

'Pretty girl, wasn't she?' Massimo Verga remarked.

'Don't even think about it!'

'Come on now, you're not going to tell me she's too young for me!'

'That as well, if you want me to. But what I was thinking was, she's already taken. You saw him.'

'Good-looking young man. Daddy's boy, bit of a stud. Hot blooded, like all of them, but lacking experience.'

'He's certainly good-looking. The fair hair's fake, though. There's something weird about him. And that car! If he wasn't a foreigner, I'd say he was a pimp and she was a high-class call girl.'

'That's where you'd be wrong. She's a student. A whore she may be, but I don't think she's a professional.'

She cut him short. 'I think we should stop right there, don't you?' There was no point going down that road: it was a discussion they had had a thousand times before and it invariably ended with the cynical observation – one of his favourites – 'If all women aren't bitches, how come all men are sons of bitches?'

8 p.m.: Michele Ferrara's apartment

The evening news broadcasts on the local and regional TV channels had not given much prominence to the murder. They had simply stated the facts, without jumping to any conclusions. The journalists must be desperate for leads, and for the moment were keeping things vague. Some had even managed to get through to Ferrara's home phone – for some time now, he had arranged for calls to be transferred to him from Headquarters – only to be greeted by the answer machine. He and Petra had decided today that from now on they would only answer once they knew who the caller was.

Ferrara wanted to avoid his wife being subjected to any more intimidation.

Meanwhile, Petra had responded by making one of his favourite dishes for dinner: *pappa col pomodoro*. She put it on the table with a bottle of Rosso di Montalcino from the Antinori vineyards. It was a sign that, for her, life went on. They just had to be more careful.

'Why don't you go and stay with your parents for a while?' he asked as they ate. He knew it was useless, but he had to try. He would much rather she were well away from danger.

'Because I've only just seen them and because they can cope perfectly well by themselves. You can't.'

'Come on, Petra, you know I—'

'Listen, Michele. What happened today isn't pleasant, but it's your job, right? You chose it, and I knew that when I married you. If we can't do anything about it, let's not do anything. If you can do something, let's do it. As far as I'm concerned, the only thing I can do is be there for you, and that's what I'm going to do.'

'It won't be easy, you know. And I don't want to feel as if I'm under any more pressure than I ought to be. This is a situation where my nerves need to be even steadier than usual. I have to take things very carefully, step by step. I can't afford any false moves. Above all, I need to keep a clear head. Knowing you're worried doesn't help.'

'Do you think I'd be any less worried in Baden-Baden? Don't be ridiculous, Michele. And the only pressure you're under right now is finishing your mash before it gets cold!'

Ferrara filled the two glasses almost to the brim with the excellent wine.

~~~9

> I must go.
> Cthulhu is calling my mind.
> I must go.
> Cthulhu wants my mind.
> I am going.

The words of the old book were dancing in front of Valentina's eyes, becoming blurred. She was tired: it had been a long, incredible day and it had really knocked her out.

The train sped on through the darkness, wrapped in the mists of the Apennines. She was sitting comfortably in a first-class carriage: ignoring her protests, Mike Ross had insisted on upgrading her second-class ticket.

Mike Ross. He had been a revelation. They had met by chance on an internet chat room a few weeks earlier and today she had seen him for the first time. They had arranged to meet in Greve, where he was doing research for his newspaper. She'd liked him, in an odd kind of way. Even those cold, piercing eyes of his had fascinated her.

Yes, she'd liked him, and that gave her conflicting emotions. Would he be her salvation? Would she ever find the courage to tell him everything? Could she trust him?

What a day!

It had started with that half-made decision – she was never sure of anything, that was her curse – to take an additional course at the University of Florence, some sixty-odd miles from where she lived. If she did finally make up her mind, she'd probably have to find a room there and leave Bologna, which might be a good thing.

An American stranger, Florence, black magic . . . And how would Cinzia react, Cinzia her flatmate in Bologna, to whom she was still connected in so many ways?

Confused by her own emotions, cradled by the swaying motion of the train and the warmth of the carriage, she closed her eyes.

Midnight

The pages of the black notebook with the gold cross stamped on the cover were uncut.

The hand moved rapidly and surely over the immaculately white first page. The handwriting was tiny, neat and precise.

October 1st 1999

In your name, Father, I have killed.
It was easy. Liberating.
Far more so than a Confession.
Now at last I am born!
I will go all the way, as you wish.
Do not take your support from me.
I will be the instrument of your vengeance, and mine.

PART TWO

A SERIES OF MURDERS

Florence 1999–2000

1

Michele Ferrara and his wife never got to see Placido Domingo in *Cavalleria Rusticana*, or the firework display that lit up Vienna.

They left the Austrian capital a few hours before midnight, missing the long-awaited New Year celebrations that brought the old millennium to a close and inaugurated a new one full of hope.

Two murders in a single day: there was no way Ferrara could stay out of the country. Informed of the first murder early on the morning of the 31st by Rizzo, and of the second after seven that evening by Sergeant Moschino, he had booked the first available flight, Lufthansa from Vienna to Milan. At Linate airport, a police car had been waiting for them, provided by Milan Police Headquarters, and they had reached home just before two in the morning on Saturday 1 January.

They and the driver they had been assigned had toasted the New Year in a restaurant off the autostrada near Parma, drinking poor-quality sparkling wine out of paper cups. Ferrara had felt really bad for the driver: the poor man was doing his duty, making an effort to seem as if he was in a good mood even though he was probably thinking about his girlfriend celebrating without him.

Petra, as usual, had been wonderful. With typically feminine nonchalance, she had found out the driver's tastes in
music, reading matter, drinks, even mobile phones, and had
showered him with the best gifts she could find on the shelves
of the service area shop.

They did not sleep much that night, but it was more than
sufficient for Ferrara.

The ten days they had spent in Vienna had done him a world
of good. Massimo had been on great form. He'd brought along
his new girlfriend, a very beautiful, very pleasant Venetian
woman of about forty named Lucrezia, who had even won over
Petra. Naturally, they had visited the Prater, the museum district, the Imperial Palace, and Schönbrunn Palace and park, and
Massimo had made everything even more fascinating and
enlightening with his constant anecdotes and explanations.
They had dined and danced on a boat sailing along the Danube,
laughed on the bridges, joked on the streets – in spite of the fact
that the weather was bitterly cold. Above all, they had been
struck by the remarkable contrast between the historical town
and some of the startling new architecture they came across. It
was a contrast you would never see in Florence, a museum city
par excellence, or in other Italian cities.

Ferrara had realised from the start just how much he
needed this break. Things had not been going well, and he
had been getting into an ever more sombre mood as the year
drew to its end. There was no real progress in the Monster of
Florence case, no trace of the anonymous letter writer who
had threatened his life, and Rizzo's investigation had reached
a dead end. The Micali murder seemed destined to become
one more bulging file in an already abundant archive of
unsolved cases.

And a blot on his reputation.

*

He was in his office by eight o'clock on Saturday morning.

The newspapers were waiting for him, neatly piled between his computer screen and the printer on the left-hand table. They devoted a great deal of space to the previous morning's murder, much more than to the one that had been discovered in the evening, which, according to them, was an open and shut case:

FLORENCE: MAN STABS WIFE TO DEATH was the headline in *La Nazione*. The item itself was brief.

> A startling discovery was made in Florence on the last day of the year: a mentally disturbed man who had stabbed his wife to death and kept watch over the corpse for several days. The victim was Lina Pini, 75 years old, who lived with her husband, V.R., also 75, in the Via del Confine, in the suburb of Coverciano. The murder was discovered on the evening of 31 December by *Squadra Mobile* officers responding to an emergency call from relatives who had been trying without success to contact the couple by telephone. Early investigations have established that Signora Pini had been dead for several days and that during that time her husband, who had superficial cuts on his chest, perhaps caused by a suicide attempt, had remained by her side. He was arrested for murder and is being kept under guard in hospital, where he was admitted because of his mental condition.

The tone of the various headlines about the previous morning's murder was quite different. They screamed from the front pages:

MURDER AMONG THE ANTIQUE FURNITURE
DEATH GOES SHOPPING
SLAUGHTER IN THE HEART OF SAN FREDIANO

They all said that the crime had taken place early in the morning, soon after the shop in the Via Santo Spirito had opened. The dead man was a young assistant who had worked there for some time. His name was Alfredo Lupi, and he had recently celebrated his thirty-second birthday. He had been shot twice, after which his assailant had stabbed him many times, leaving his body mutilated and his face horribly disfigured. There were no eye witnesses. As far as anyone could tell, the murder had only taken a few minutes. Nothing was yet known about the killer or the motive.

There followed interviews with friends and acquaintances of the dead man. None of them could think of any explanation as to why such a good man, a hard worker, devoted to his family – a wife and an infant son – should have been so horribly murdered.

Ferrara phoned the switchboard to find out who had dealt with the two cases. He asked to be put through to Alfredi, who had been called to the Via del Confine, and sent for Serpico, one of the two officers, along with Chief Inspector Violante, who had been handling the case in the Via Santo Spirito.

'Good morning, chief,' Alfredi said when the switchboard connected him.

'The murder last night. Is the case really closed?'

'Seems like it. The judge thinks so, too. It was the husband, poor old guy. No doubt about it.'

'Okay. Send me the file. I'd like to take a look at it before signing the final report.'

'Of course, chief.'

Ferrara hung up and lit his first cigar of the day.

*

Serpico did not have much to add to what the papers had already reported.

'When we arrived on the scene,' he said, trying to sound as official as possible, 'one of the first things we did after finding the body was to interview the neighbouring shopkeepers. We also summoned the victim's wife, Luisa Conti, twenty-six years old, to Headquarters for an initial interview.'

'Relax, Sergi. Tell it in your own words.'

The inspector went red. He ran a hand through his long curly hair, shifted his weight to his other foot, and took a deep breath.

'There's not much to tell, chief,' he resumed. 'She was devastated when she heard the news. She didn't have any explanation for her husband's murder. She kept repeating that it couldn't be true, that it was all a bad dream. She's not a strong-looking woman. She's very young, almost a girl. According to her, her husband had no enemies; all he cared about was his home and his family. In her opinion, it must have been a madman, or a case of mistaken identity. She says the reason she's so sure is because she knew her husband so well. They practically grew up together, they got engaged when they were very young . . . Neither of them had ever loved anyone else.'

'And nothing from the shopkeepers?'

'Nothing at all. Nobody saw the killer, although the street's full of people even that early in the morning. We questioned the owner of the shop, a man named Antonio Salustri, but he couldn't tell us anything either. According to him, Alfredo Lupi was extremely loyal, totally professional, and he trusted him completely. But that's it. Nobody saw anything. Or nobody wants to talk.'

'Come on, Sergi, we're not in Sicily or Calabria.'

'If you say so, chief . . .'

He knew what Sergi was getting at. The police were perfectly well aware that some of those involved in the antiques racket had strong connections with the Calabrian Mafia. But it was dangerous to jump to conclusions.

Sergi persisted. 'You know who that shop belonged to, before the current owner bought it?'

'Not if you don't tell me.'

'Ricciardi.'

Gualtiero Ricciardi had been one of the most important art and antiques dealers in Florence from the late seventies to the mid-nineties, and had amassed a considerable fortune. He and his wife had died in a fire that had almost destroyed an entire floor of their villa. They had been asleep at the time. Arson had been suspected, but the arsonist had never been found. In fact, it had been the last, and worst, of a whole series of arson attacks in Florence between 1993 and 1995. The police had investigated the possibility of underworld involvement, given that Ricciardi had long been suspected of having connections with the Calabrians, though nothing had ever been proved.

Even after his death.

'I see. Anything else? Any results yet from the autopsy, or from the search of the shop?'

'Chief Inspector Violante has everything. I left word for him to join us.'

'Where has he gone?'

'Er . . . I think he went out for a coffee.'

Ferrara smiled. The coffee break was a habit common to everyone, southerners and northerners alike: no point in getting worked up about it.

'He'll tell you about the Nucci woman. She's the only witness who claims to have seen something. He questioned her, but I'm not sure what he found out . . .'

Just then, Chief Inspector Violante knocked discreetly at the door.

'Come in!' Ferrara called.

Fabio Violante was a man of medium height, who always looked rather down at heel, and didn't exactly give the impression of efficiency Ferrara liked to see in his men. But he was close to retirement, so there was no way of getting rid of him.

He was carrying a shabby-looking brown leather briefcase.

'Talk of the devil . . .' Ferrara said.

Violante looked first at one, then at the other, uncomprehending. He was hard of hearing – another reason he and his colleagues weren't always on the same wavelength.

'Sit down, inspector. Sergi was just telling me that you interviewed a woman named . . . what was it?'

'Laura Nucci,' Serpico said.

'Laura Nucci, born in Florence, forty-one years old, secretary in a clinic on the second floor of the building directly opposite the antique shop,' Violante recited almost mechanically. 'She told me she'd just arrived at work, about eight-thirty. As she was opening the shutter of one of the windows looking out on the street she happened to see a man entering the antique shop. She described him as about six feet tall, with an athletic build and short fair hair. That was all she could say, because she had only seen him from the back, and then only briefly. She did say, though, that she'd had the impression there were no lights on yet inside the antique shop, which means the assistant hadn't yet finished opening up.'

'Anything else?'

'No, chief.'

'Have they done the autopsy?'

'They haven't finished, but I've brought you the first findings,' Violante said, opening the threadbare briefcase and taking out two files which he placed on the desk. 'And here's the forensics report.'

'Thanks. You can both go now.'

Ferrara took the first file, which contained both a report on the scene of crime investigation and the pathologist's report, and started to read the latter:

> *Following the autopsy performed by myself, in my*
> *capacity as an expert pathologist, on the corpse found at*
> *No 25 Via Santo Spirito, in the district of San Frediano,*
> *on 31 December 1999, here are the initial findings.*

The pathologist described the corpse, his garments and distinguishing marks. Then he listed the numerous wounds, two from a firearm and thirty-nine from a sharp instrument, pointing out the particular anatomical areas on which they were found. All the wounds were concentrated in the front part of the body, apart from the two bulletholes in the back, which were the only fatal ones.

The wounds from the sharp instrument had been inflicted after death and were located predominantly in the top part of the body, above all on the neck and face. Curiously, these were in unusually close proximity. Other, more isolated marks had been found on the right arm.

The time of death had been established as between 8.30 and 8.45. Death had been almost instantaneous. The cause was described as 'terminal and irreversible cardiac-respiratory failure', consequent to the traumatic lesions from the firearms.

The analysis of the stomach contents had revealed nothing of interest. The victim did not appear to be a drug-taker and his state of health prior to the murder appeared normal.

The accompanying foolscap sheets from Headquarters contained a first attempt by Violante to piece together the facts of the crime, drawing on both his observations at the crime scene and the results of the forensic tests.

According to Violante's hypothesis the killer had attacked the victim from the back, standing to the left of him. Falling to the floor, Alfredo Lupi had banged his head and rolled over onto his back, exposing his chest to further blows. The wounds on the front part of the body had bled less than those on the back, a sign that they had been struck in the final phase of the attack, by which time the victim was already dead.

Ferrara closed the file and went on to the other, which bore the stamp of the Regional Office of Forensics.

It contained dozens of photographs and two thin, typewritten pages. No useful prints had been found at the scene of the crime other than those of the victim, nor had anything significant been found in the proximity of the corpse. The only positive result was that of the ballistics test: the weapon used was a model 92 Beretta equipped with a silencer.

Not an uncommon weapon. Almost legendary, in fact. It was used by various police forces around the world, as well as the United States army, because of its stability and precision. It was a semi-automatic which normally took lethal 9mm Parabellum cartridges. The 92F model was the one used by the Italian armed forces, Carabinieri and police – as well as by a large part of the underworld.

Too common to be a useful clue, Ferrara thought.

The photographs showed the victim's mutilated face from different angles, the scene of the crime with the corpse still on the floor in the position in which it had been found, the outside of the shop and details of the objects inside, including the seventeenth-century crucifix mentioned in one of the headlines – even though it wasn't actually all that close to the body. There was also a photograph of a large eighteenth-century wardrobe which, being more or less in the middle of the large room, parallel to the front door, divided it into two almost equal parts, obstructing much of the view from outside. The body, as the newspapers had reported, had been found behind the wardrobe by two French tourists who had come in to browse even though the shop was not quite open yet.

When he had finished reading, Ferrara decided that the time had come to make a move. *Il Gatto goes into action*, he told himself with a mixture of irony and self-flattery.

The shop had only one window, a large one protected by a wire-mesh shutter that was three-quarters open. Ferrara had a warrant from the judge to have the seals taken off. He went in alone.

The interior was surprisingly large. There was a big room at the front, some sixty-five feet by twenty-five, divided more or less in half by the heavy wardrobe; a second, smaller one reached by four steps on the left just after the entrance, and a back room.

They were all cluttered with furniture, paintings, statues and a variety of objects, from crystal glasses to silver teapots and copper ladles to gilded frames. The whole place smelled of dust and damp. And death.

Ferrara switched on the light. A porcelain owl stared at him severely.

Making a mental note of the objects, he went into the back part of the main room, behind the wardrobe.

The chalk marks drawn around the body before it had been moved were still visible on the floor. Against the side wall, about five feet from the marks, stood a desk, still cluttered with notebooks, bills and papers. Ferrara went closer to have a look, but did not touch anything. Although nothing particularly attracted his attention, he stood there for a while, motionless, peering around him, even into the darkest corners. Identifying with the environment, absorbing its smells, its atmosphere, seeing what the victim must have seen a moment before dying: for Ferrara, that was worth more than any report, however detailed and conscientious.

Ten minutes later, he left the shop. He had the seals put back on and sent the officer back to Headquarters, then called Petra on his mobile to tell her he wouldn't be home for lunch. He stood there for a long time, looking along the street.

The Via Santo Spirito, which is the continuation of the Borgo San Frediano and turns into the Borgo San Jacopo after the crossroads with the Via Maggio, is a narrow street in the Oltrarno, a major destination for tourists who flood across the Ponte Vecchio to visit its many antique shops. Even that Saturday, the area was dense with people, despite the intense cold and grey skies. The bad weather, which had raged for weeks, showed no sign of abating with the New Year.

Ferrara's gaze came to rest on the buildings opposite the shop, as if they could tell him what they had seen. There was an arched door of reddish wood studded with iron nails, a small shop to its left, and then a little green door with a marble name plate beside it: *Physiotherapy Clinic – 2nd Floor*.

Looking up, he saw someone moving at the second floor window and rang the bell beside the name plate.

He heard a buzz and the lock snapped open.

On the second floor he was met by a thin, nondescript woman of about forty, wearing glasses with fake tortoiseshell frames.

'I'm looking for Signora Laura Nucci.'

'That's me.'

'Chief Superintendent Ferrara of the *Squadra Mobile*.

Pardon my intrusion, but I thought I saw someone here when I was in the street so . . .'

'I've been taking advantage of the holiday to catch up on the backlog,' the woman explained.

'May I ask you a few questions?'

'Of course. Follow me.'

She led him through the deserted reception area.

'I know you've already made a statement to Chief Inspector Violante, but I'd like to question you myself. Maybe you've thought of something else in the meantime. Do you mind if we start from the beginning?'

'Of course not. I'm quite happy to cooperate. I saw the man going into the shop, but . . .'

'Let's just start at the beginning.'

'Yes, of course, you're right, I'm sorry. Well, I'd just opened the door of the clinic. I came in, put my handbag on the desk, the desk over there, and went to open the window that looks out on the street. The window and the shutter, obviously. I do it every morning when I get in, to let the light in and air the room, obviously. When I was at the window I saw someone entering the shop. I only saw him from the back, and only for a few seconds, as I said in my statement. Unfortunately, I really can't remember anything else.'

'What time was it?'

'It might have been about half past eight.'

'Okay. And then?'

'I went back to the desk to start work, obviously. I didn't go back to the window until I heard the police cars arriving with their sirens blaring. That was when I found out the shop assistant had been murdered.'

'And between the time you opened the window and the time the police arrived you didn't hear anything unusual?'

'Obviously not. This may only be a narrow, one-way street,

but it's very noisy. Or maybe that's why it's noisy. And then the telephone was ringing, the first patients were arriving, kids were throwing firecrackers in the street as a game . . .'

'Did you know the dead man?'

'Only by sight. But he seemed a nice man – pleasant, polite. Obviously, that's only an impression.'

Obviously, Ferrara repeated to himself. Out loud, he said, 'Of course, but I'd like you to think really hard and try to describe again, as clearly as you can, the person you saw entering the shop.'

'I noticed his height and build, obviously. He was tall, I'm sure of that, about six feet tall. Good build, slim, athletic. Quite short hair – at least it looked that way from behind, I mean it was thick but didn't touch the top of his collar. He was wearing a dark suit, and I had the impression he was very young. And obviously not from round here.'

'What makes you say that?'

'Because of his clothes. The young men around here wear jeans and waterproof jackets all year long. It's like a uniform. But this man was wearing a smart, well-cut suit, dark, maybe even black. He wasn't wearing a coat.'

'A black suit? You mean like a dinner jacket and trousers? Or the kind of thing priests wear? You don't see many black suits these days.'

'No, no. I don't think so. Definitely not a dinner jacket, and not a priest's suit either, I'd say . . . though, thinking about it, I couldn't completely rule it out. I'm not even very sure it was black, like I said. It could have been dark grey, or dark blue. The street's in the shade, and at that time of day it's not easy to see things clearly.'

'But you're sure it was a man?'

'Oh, yes. If it had been a woman, she'd have had to be very tall and athletic, and very well disguised.'

'But we can't rule it out completely,' Ferrara remarked, almost to himself. 'And what about the hair? Dark, fair? Smooth, curly?'

'Wavy and fair. I already said that, it must be in my statement.'

'Of course, but you know how it is, I like to hear things for myself. Please bear with me just a little while longer. Do you remember anything else about him? Was he wearing glasses, for instance?'

'I couldn't see that. Like I said, I only saw him briefly and in passing. I don't put my nose into other people's business, obviously.' The woman sounded as if she was losing patience.

'And obviously that's the window.' He couldn't help himself.

'Yes, that one,' the woman replied curtly, responding to his involuntary provocation.

Ferrara went to the window and looked down at the shop. There was a good view from here, so good that you could tell whether or not the interior of the shop was lit. From that height, though, the angle could be deceptive, and it wasn't easy to judge how tall a person was.

If only the woman had been nosier, he thought. Or had opened the window a few minutes later, when the person was coming out . . .

'Thank you for your help,' he said. 'Please don't trouble yourself, I know the way out.'

Wrapped up warm in his overcoat and scarf, he strode along the Via Santo Spirito and stopped at the first bar-tobacconist's he found. It was already nearly one o'clock and the place was crowded with tourists and locals.

At the tables and the counter, the main topic of conversation was the murder of Alfredo Lupi.

'I always thought there was something not quite right about that one,' an elegant-looking woman was saying.

'He was a bit strange, that's for sure,' her friend replied. 'But I talked to him a few times and he seemed decent enough.'

'If you ask me, he was mixed up in something,' a man said. 'It happens all the time in that line of business.'

'A small thief shouldn't steal, because the big thief makes sure he swings for it,' the barman said, quoting an old Tuscan proverb.

'A beer and a roll,' Ferrara ordered.

'Ham and cheese okay?'

'That's fine. Did you know the young man who was murdered?'

'He had a bite to eat here a few times, like everyone.'

'What kind of man was he?'

'Fairly average. Quiet, kept himself to himself. I don't think he had any friends around here, I never saw him with anyone.'

'Did you notice anything unusual lately? Any strangers lurking around?'

'Everyone here's a stranger. Foreigners, Italians, they're all tourists. Are you a journalist?'

'No, just curious.'

He went to the cash desk, asked for two boxes of Antico Toscano cigars, paid and left.

As it was not raining, he decided to go back to Headquarters on foot, by way of the Via Tornabuoni, San Lorenzo, the Piazza del Mercato and the Via Santa Reparata. A half-hour's walk would do him good.

Halfway across the Ponte Santa Trinità he stopped to look at the Arno, swollen by the recent rains. The water swept along, as if trying to wash away every remnant of nature. But

59

it could not wash away the mysteries that continued to shroud Florence as they had always done.

A strange city, Florence, he reflected. One of the most beautiful, most beloved cities in the world, steeped in history and full of art treasures, it offers itself to visitors like a generous courtesan. But if on the one hand it flaunts itself, on the other it shuts itself up behind the heavy doors of its palatial houses, jealously guarding a privacy that has to remain inviolable, and leaving us to wonder what is concealed within those walls, what memories of past plots and betrayals.

These were the two faces of Florence. They had cast a spell on him as soon as he had arrived, and he knew they would keep him here to the end of his days – an event someone had decided to bring about sooner than anticipated.

Perhaps, he thought, if the Latin warning turned out to be accurate, his death, too, would be ascribed to the vortex of mysteries that seethe beneath the city and only occasionally bubble to the surface, almost as if to remind the world that evil, and only evil, is immortal and never fades. Not even if you cover it with the pure, virginal grace of a Botticelli Venus or try to crush it beneath the weight of Michelangelo's David.

When he got back to Headquarters he sent for Rizzo.

'Welcome back, chief,' Rizzo said, coming into the office. 'How was Vienna?'

'Like a dream. But now it's over. Nice way to start the new millennium, eh?'

'We certainly finished the old one in style,' Rizzo commented laconically. His mood seemed even grimmer than Ferrara's.

'So, nothing new on the Micali case, I gather.'

'Nothing at all. We checked everything we could. His friends, his bank account, even his relations with suppliers.

We turned his apartment upside down, examined every address book, notebook, every piece of paper. We questioned his neighbours – nobody has the faintest idea about anything.'

'What about the priest? Does his alibi still hold?'

'The parish priest confirmed that from one o'clock to just after two they went through the accounts together, then Don Sergio went off to get candles for the altar. We haven't found anything to contradict that. As for whether Don Sergio is gay, nobody's saying anything, and there's no way of proving it. If you want the truth, chief, I'm just about ready to throw in the towel. With everything else on my plate, I can't keep putting resources into this. When you get down to it, the man was a queer, pardon my language, and nobody except the priest seems at all sorry he died.'

'That's the curse of our profession, Rizzo. There's never time to concentrate on one thing, there's always something else to do. But we don't give up. Unsolved cases should never be closed. They should always stay with you, somewhere at the back of your mind. Sometimes a clue turns up out of nowhere after months or years, and you'd better be ready to grab it when it does. And anyway, the city is sorry he died, even if it doesn't know it. It's important to remember that deep down, Florence is scared. Because whatever you think of the case, there's still a killer at large. Maybe it was an 'accident', let's put it like that, and won't be repeated. But let's not forget how Micali was killed, the way the killer kept stabbing him. There was something too savage about it. It wasn't just some private settling of scores. That's my feeling, anyway.'

'Mine, too. But what should I do? Hope that the killer strikes again? And how many times?' There was bitterness in his voice.

'Keep your eyes open. That's all I'm asking. What do you know about the two murders yesterday?'

'Everything. I was with Alfonsi at the old man's place. We only just got back. Poor guy made a full confession. The case is in the hands of the judges now . . . The other murder, now that's a different story. It might turn out to be as much of a mystery as the Micali case.'

'In this case, too, the killer stabbed his victim in the face and the upper part of the body.'

'But the murder weapon was a gun. And there's no gay aspect, which I'm sure is at the root of the Micali murder. Alfredo Lupi was a married man with a little child.'

'That's true. Let's call in Violante and Serpico and have a brainstorming session. I don't know if you were told, but I've already been to the Via Santo Spirito.'

'Okay. I'll call them.'

While they were waiting, Ferrara asked Rizzo how he had spent the Christmas holidays, and he was about to reply when the telephone rang.

'There's someone called Beccalossi on the line,' the switchboard operator announced. 'He asked to speak to you or Superintendent Rizzo.'

'Beccalossi? Who's that?'

'The owner of the shop where Micali worked,' Rizzo whispered, his eyes lighting up with a sudden interest.

'Put him on,' Ferrara said, switching on the loudspeaker.

'Hello?'

'This is Superintendent Ferrara.'

'I can't hear you very well.'

'I put on the loudspeaker so that Superintendent Rizzo, who's here with me, can hear you,' Ferrara said, making sure he covered the rules for the protection of privacy.

'You sound distant.'

The advantages of technology!

'Don't worry, I can hear you perfectly well. Please go ahead.'

'I know it may not be important, but— well, you did say to let you know if . . . Anyway, I've just discovered there's something missing from the shop. I've been doing the end-of-year stocktake, and it turns out one of the black notebooks with a cross on the cover has vanished. The day before Micali died, there were twenty-two – he wrote it down in the ledger, he was very finicky. Since then I've sold four, and one ended up under poor Stefano's body, as I'm sure you remember. But there are only sixteen left.'

'I see. Anything else?'

'No, that's all. Is it any help to you?'

'Anything might be of help. Thank you very much. And don't hesitate to call if you think of anything else. You've been a great help.'

He hung up. He remembered the forensics report, how they'd had to scrape the blood off what they'd thought at first was a little Bible or prayer book, but had turned out to be only a notebook with blank pages.

The two superintendents looked at each other disconsolately. The gleam had gone from Rizzo's eyes.

'Let's begin with the motive,' Ferrara said to start the ball rolling. 'There's always a motive, however obscure. It may just be insanity, but there's always something that drives a man to commit murder. Once we pin down the motive, we're halfway there.'

They were again sitting round the rectangular meeting table, which was near the wall opposite Ferrara's desk.

'I'd rule out theft,' Chief Inspector Violante said. 'The victim's wallet was untouched, and nothing had been taken from the till.'

'And a thief wouldn't have butchered the guy like that,' Rizzo said. 'Maybe it was the work of a religious fanatic, or a psychopath, maybe someone who went inside the shop because one of the religious objects on display reminded him of some terrible thing in his past. Once he was inside, he saw the assistant and for some reason he was like the embodiment of whatever it was that had happened to him. He flew into a rage and killed him.'

'I don't like it,' Ferrara said. 'It's too literary, too much like a novel. But we can't rule it out completely. It could provide a connection between the murder in the Via Santo Spirito and the one in Greve. The latest victim also worked in a shop full of religious objects. Though the fact that the killer used a gun in this case rather contradicts the idea of a sudden fit of rage. But I wouldn't rule out the idea that there's a homicidal religious fanatic walking the streets. Maybe he carries a gun for self defence.'

'In my opinion, Alfredo Lupi was the intended victim,' Rizzo said. 'I think the murder was premeditated. Let's look into his private life, find out if it's true that he had no enemies.'

'Good idea. What about you, Sergi, what do you think?'

So far Serpico had remained silent, seeming slightly embarrassed in front of his superiors. Ferrara had noticed, and was anxious to bring him into the discussion.

'I agree with you, but . . .' he hesitated. 'Well, I wouldn't dismiss the idea that there's a connection with the antiques racket. We all know how big it is in Florence, especially in San Frediano. Don't forget, the shop used to belong to Ricciardi. There may still be some underworld involvement. Maybe Lupi knew too much. Maybe he'd somehow found out something he shouldn't and paid for it with his life.'

'Good. I think we have more than enough to be getting on with. Right, let's divide it up this way. Rizzo, you look into Lupi's private life. Violante, check the religious angle. Sergi and I will concentrate on the underworld aspect. Let's see if any of our informers know anything. We may even get a tip-off.'

Like all policemen, he knew that most cases are solved thanks to tip-offs from informers, and that whole careers have been built on such things.

Once the jobs had been assigned, Ferrara stayed in his office for a few more hours. He signed the final report on the case of the old couple in Coverciano, looked through some of the files on his desk, wrote a report on the Lupi case for the prosecutor, and got on with various bits of minor business.

By the time he got home, it was after nine. As so often in the past, the first of January had been just another working day.

Petra had his dinner ready for him: sardines in grated cheese baked in the oven, one of Ferrara's favourite dishes. Petra was in a good mood – surprisingly so, he thought, when she showed him the latest anonymous message, which she had found among the mail that had accumulated while they were away in Vienna.

Perhaps because of her down-to-earth nature, or because time had passed and nothing had happened, Petra had quickly got over the shock of the first message and now seemed to regard these things as the work of some crackpot, not be taken too seriously. Especially as this one was very different from the first, both in tone and form.

There were no red stains, and the message had been produced on a laser printer. It read:

Dear Superintendent Gatto
Did you know that in the Kingdom of the Dead the last
are already the first, but where the letters are concerned
the first will be the last? Or is smoking cigars the only
thing you know, you poor man?

That was all. No direct threat.

It was still possible that the two messages were not linked, although it did not escape Ferrara that both had arrived in conjunction with a particularly violent and mysterious crime. On the other hand, the new one could have arrived at any time while they were away, so it might not necessarily be linked to the previous day's murder. Nor was there any proof that the previous letter had been connected to the Micali murder.

He made up his mind to stick to the line of action he had decided on with his men.

He decided he wouldn't ask his friend Fuschi in Forensics to examine this second communication. He remembered only too well the strange look he'd given him when he had brought him the results of his analysis of the first message.

'I thought it was best to come in person,' he had said, the Monday after the Micali murder. 'I haven't done a written report. It's best if this thing doesn't get into the records.'

'Thanks.'

'Don't mention it. But there's not much I can tell you. The paper is ordinary A4 paper, the bloodstains are red paint, very easy to find, and the glue is the kind you can get in any stationer's. There were no prints of any kind, not on the letters, not in the glue, not on the paper. None.'

'That's fine. Thanks a lot.'

That was when Fuschi had looked at him with that strange expression on his face. 'Did you understand what I just said?'

'Yes, of course.'

'There were no prints.'

'I heard, I'm not deaf,' Ferrara had said, tensing.

'All right, you're the policeman, and I'm just a layman. But I can't help wondering how come the dead man's prints weren't on the paper. He must have touched it . . .'

'Obviously the killer must have wiped them off afterwards,' Ferrara had said, defensively.

'Instead of taking the paper away with him? He starts wasting time, when someone could come in at any moment and catch him red-handed? And for what? To let everyone know that he'd threatened him?'

Ferrara cut him short. 'Let me sort that out.' He realised that he wasn't handling this very well.

Maybe he'd have done better to show it to Massimo, who was fond of puzzles, he'd thought at the time.

Promising himself he'd talk to Massimo as soon as they got back from Vienna, Ferrara had put on a CD of arias sung by Natalie Dessay, Petra's latest discovery, determined to finish the evening with music and his wife.

2

The Ferraras had not been the only ones to interrupt their holidays.

Valentina Preti had hurried back to Bologna from San Vigilio on 29 December, two days before New Year's Eve. Exactly a week after she had arrived.

She had been close to a nervous breakdown when she left Bologna, but by the time she got back she was more confused and uncertain than ever. But one thing she knew was that she had to end the relationship that was threatening to ruin her life for ever.

Valentina went back at least twice a year to the beautiful Art Nouveau hotel her family had owned for three generations: at Christmas and either at Carnival or at Easter. Not usually in summer.

Having practically been born with skis on her feet, she loved hurling herself down the long pistes that surrounded the peak of the Plan de Corones. But in summer she preferred the beaches of southern Italy or the Greek islands, or going for weekend breaks in the Cinque Terre or on the Golfo dei Poeti.

She had been living in Bologna for four years, sharing an

apartment with her friend Cinzia Roberti. After finishing school at the age of eighteen, she had enrolled on an Arts, Music and Drama course at the University of Bologna: at last an opportunity to move away from the narrow horizons of that corner of the Dolomites.

Her friendship with Cinzia had made it easier. Two years younger than her, the daughter of a Bolognese surgeon, Cinzia Roberti was almost her exact opposite. 'A wild animal', was how her father had described her indulgently, as if that were an excuse for her behaviour. Short and thin, with black hair, she was at least as impulsive, independent, stubborn and determined as Valentina was docile and indecisive. They had known each other since they were children. The Robertis had been coming to San Vigilio di Marebbe since 1990, the year that they had discovered the Hotel Passo Selva. They had been impressed by Valentina's parents, who always welcomed their guests as if they were part of some ideal extended family, with the great Art Nouveau building as its epicentre, and had returned regularly every year for a week's skiing.

Valentina was twelve that first year and Cinzia ten.

At first, relations between the two girls had not been easy. The differences in their characters and above all in their ages, so much more obvious when they were children, had imme-diately caused friction between them. Cinzia, who was used to getting her own way, couldn't stand being in someone else's house, where she was no longer in charge, and Valentina did not understand why she had to be nice to a snotty-nosed kid who was so bossy and unpredictable. But their parents had been patient with them, and over the course of time they had developed a mutual tolerance, which eventually turned into genuine friendship.

When Valentina had chosen her university course, Cinzia had managed to convince her family that, although she was only sixteen, she absolutely had to have her own space, preferably near the university, which she herself would be attending in a couple of years' time.

The Pretis and the Robertis had put their heads together and rented an apartment for the two girls.

At first Valentina returned home every weekend, but that had soon proved tiresome, and she'd started spacing out her visits. But she always came back at Christmas.

This Christmas in particular, she really needed time to think. The end of her studies was approaching and she still had no idea what she wanted to do. And her friendship with Cinzia had deteriorated badly.

In the last few months, they had done nothing but quarrel. Cinzia had not liked the idea of Valentina taking a course in Florence, even though in nearly three months Valentina had gone there no more than four times. Nor had Cinzia approved of her friendship with that American journalist. True, he was often away for work reasons and Valentina had only seen him once since their first meeting, but they kept in regular contact over the internet and occasionally by mobile phone.

On 21 December, Valentina and Cinzia had had yet another furious row, and Valentina had decided to leave early and stay with her parents at least until Twelfth Night. She needed time to recover, and to think. What she did not know was that, instead of bringing her peace, the Christmas week would be one of torment, intensifying the passions seething inside her.

'You're more beautiful than ever!' her father said as he picked her up from the station at Brunico.

He was the same as ever. Plump, well-dressed, cheerful. And the same thing happened that always did whenever she saw him: she felt her old sense of guilt returning.

During the ride, they talked about her studies and about the latest developments at the hotel: her mother was building a gym, with sauna and massage, to replace the lofts on the top floor.

'But we haven't touched your room,' her father assured her.

Snow was falling and it was already dark, but there was the unmistakable outline of the great hotel with its pointed turret. All the lights were on, and their warmth reached out to greet her.

Her mother was waiting for her, along with Carlo, the old groom, and the doorman. As they embraced her, she felt an acute sense of nostalgia.

She walked around the ground floor and said hello to some of the guests who were playing cards or chatting in the bar as they waited for the dining room to open. Then she went down to the kitchen, where the cook was making dinner – pure Ladin cuisine – and the waiters were busy with the wines. The big room was filled with the smell of *panicia*, the local barley soup with ham and pork.

The cook, who had known Valentina since she was born, cried, 'Here's my sweetheart!' wiped her hands on the dish-cloth, flung her big arms around her and kissed her. 'Look what we've got!' she said, and lifted a napkin to reveal a large dish full of Valentina's favourite sweet: *cranfus mori*, cranberry pancakes. 'Go on, take some, there's plenty!'

'Thanks,' Valentina said, taking one. 'They're delicious, as always.' She licked her fingers as she walked away.

That evening, they had dinner in a room set aside specially for them and her father only got up a couple of times to talk to the guests at the tables, as he usually did, and make sure that everything was fine.

'If you like,' her mother said during dinner, 'you can have a room on the first floor, no 114. We've just refurbished it and it has everything. Cable TV, fax, a well-stocked minibar . . .'

'Thanks, Mummy, but I prefer mine.'

'It's up to you. It's just so small and uncomfortable. But it's ready if you want it.'

'I don't know how you can sleep up there,' her father said. 'There isn't even a toilet in the room, you have to go halfway along the corridor. And with all the work going on, it's a real mess up there.'

'My things are there – my memories . . . I like it. Don't worry.'

'If you're sure.'

Valentina wanted to be back in that room she had known as a child, she wanted to take refuge in it and forget.

Even though, as she herself had said, her memories were in that room . . .

The sloping ceiling, the Spice Girls posters, the Barbies neatly lined up on a white shelf, the lilac wallpaper, the collection of cups and medals won in skiing competitions, the television with the built-in VCR, the stereo unit and the CD rack, the books, the comics. Valentina looked around, and did not find the welcome she had expected from these objects. They were no longer childhood companions: they had suddenly become silent but accusing witnesses of her betrayal.

She had betrayed her family, her future, her hopes. She had brought it on herself, with all the unawareness of youth, and now she didn't know what to do.

Everything had started right here, in this little room that had originally been intended for the staff, and which she had been determined to have when she was ten.

She slipped into bed and turned out the light, but found it hard to get to sleep. Even the bed was accusing her.

*

It had happened on Christmas Eve 1994.

Valentina was sixteen, Cinzia fourteen.

The Robertis had arrived late in the afternoon. Valentina had been impatient to see Cinzia, eager for news of the city, and her friend had not disappointed her. After dinner they had all gone into the village, the girls to have snowball fights and the adults to drink the hot punch being distributed in the main square by skiing instructors dressed in Santa Claus costumes. There was a big Christmas tree, and multi-coloured lights were strung from house to house. Music was playing, and people greeted each other merrily and exchanged wishes. Many of them, including their parents, were waiting for midnight mass, but the two girls had managed to wriggle out of it by promising to go to bed immediately. They had run back to the hotel to try and guess from the sizes of the packages under the tree what to expect in the morning.

'Can I come to your room?' Cinzia had asked.

'Yes. But you'll have to leave before your parents get back, or they'll notice we're not asleep!'

'I have so many things to tell you,' Cinzia said. 'I'll just put my pyjamas on and I'll be right with you!'

Valentina ran to get changed and clean her teeth before her friend joined her, because the bathroom was some distance from her room.

When Cinzia came, she made Valentina's head spin with her tales of all the things she was discovering, all the exciting things that happened in a city like Bologna, the clubs she'd started going to even though she was underage, the new friends she'd made at school.

'Do you smoke?' she asked suddenly.

'No, do you?' Valentina asked.

'I smoke these,' Cinzia said, taking from her pocket some

cigarette papers, a bag of tobacco, and a small light brown cube which looked like a piece of plasticine.

There was a sly look in her eyes, and her face was lit by a crafty smile.

But she was only a child. A child playing at being adult, Valentina thought. Not that she herself wanted to stay out of the game.

Cinzia crumbled part of the little cube, mixed the shreds with the tobacco, and rolled the cigarette. Valentina admired her skill.

At that moment, she heard the noise of the lift reaching their floor. 'Shhh.'

'What is it?' Cinzia asked.

'Be quiet. It must be my parents. Turn the light out.'

They waited. They heard footsteps approaching the door, whispered words. Then silence.

'She's asleep,' her father said.

The footsteps receded.

'What about your parents?' Valentina asked, as the lift started to descend.

'I locked my door. They'll think I'm asleep, too. Don't turn the light on, it's fine like this. Maybe open the window to let the smell of smoke out.'

Cinzia lit her cigarette and inhaled deeply, filling her lungs. The moonlight lit her face, and Valentina thought she looked very beautiful.

'Here, try it,' Cinzia said, and explained what to do.

They kept on talking, passing the cigarette from one to the other.

Cinzia was becoming more and more relaxed, and laughing at the slightest thing. Valentina just felt a bit confused.

'It's cold,' Cinzia said when she had finished the cigarette. 'Let's get under the blankets.'

Valentina obeyed. She lay down flat on her back, and her friend snuggled up to her, as if in need of protection. *She's just a child*, she thought, and was moved. She almost didn't notice that Cinzia had put her hand on her breast. It may have been a natural, innocent gesture, but she felt her own nipple react to the contact.

She held her breath, embarrassed.

'Do you ever touch yourself?' Cinzia asked, in a hoarse, tremulous voice, warming her neck and ear with her breath.

Valentina realised with astonishment that her friend's hand wasn't still. With slow, gentle, circular movements, it was caressing the material of her pyjamas just over her nipple, which was becoming hard.

She turned hesitantly to her friend in search of an explanation.

Cinzia's feverish black eyes were fixed on her, her ferret-like face jutted forward, her lips curled in an inviting smile. Lips coming close, ever closer. Warm breath mingling with hers. Sickly-sweet marijuana breath fusing with her mint-fresh breath.

They exchanged a timid kiss, then another, and another.

She felt Cinzia's hand insinuating itself between the buttons of her pyjamas, exploring her soft, firm breasts.

She lost control.

That night they had become lovers, and they had remained lovers ever since. From that point on, neither of them had ever felt any curiosity about the other sex. They considered themselves uniquely happy, and their only experience of the male sexual organ – the 'hideous penis', they called it, laughing – came from magazines and pornographic videos, of which Cinzia in particular was an avid consumer.

In the years that followed, they hated to be apart and they

were constantly looking for excuses to visit one another. The Arts, Music and Drama course in Bologna was an almost obligatory choice for Valentina.

Then they'd started living together. And the quarrels had begun.

Now, for Valentina, the final reckoning had come.

She had thought that, alone in that little room, she would find the peace and quiet she needed to help her think clearly, but the first night left her confused and anxious.

It wasn't going to be easy, she realised.

'I miss you, you know.'

That was how the voice at the other end greeted her when she answered her mobile phone on the morning of 25 December. But it wasn't Cinzia's voice.

'Is that you, Mike?'

'Yes, it's me.'

'I'm glad you phoned. Happy Christmas.'

'When are you coming back to Florence?'

'I don't know yet. For the moment I'm staying here at least until Twelfth Night.' But she was already having her doubts. Perhaps she missed Cinzia, perhaps she needed to see her again in order to have the courage to say goodbye for ever. 'Why don't you come here? It's packed, but I can find you somewhere, if you like. The ski slopes are fantastic.'

'I'd like to but I can't. I have things to do.'

'All right, I'll call you when I get back to Bologna, okay?'

'I'll be waiting. Happy Christmas!'

As she ended the call, Valentina wondered if the American didn't have more to do with her quarrels with Cinzia – and the crisis she was going through – than she cared to admit. He was actually the first man she'd shown any interest in.

Until now, she had attributed this sudden attraction to the fact that he was so different from the other people she knew. Although he was not much older than her, he had already had his byline in the *New York Times*, and went around the world looking for subjects to suggest to the paper.

When she had met him again in Florence in November he had shown her a long piece he had written about San Gimignano and an exhibition of torture instruments, and had promised to take her there one day; the exhibition was fascinating, he said, and the town was beautiful.

Her English was too poor for her to understand much of the article, but she had certainly seen his name at the end.

And she couldn't ignore the fact that he was a very good-looking young man.

'Who was that?' her mother asked: she had come in and seen Valentina talking on the mobile.

'Happy Christmas, Mummy. A friend.'

'Happy Christmas, darling. Is he handsome?'

'Er . . . yes.'

'Why didn't you bring him?'

'He's working.'

'At Christmas?'

'He's a famous American journalist.'

'How old?' she asked anxiously. If he was famous, he had to be of a certain age.

'Very young, Mummy. You'd like him.'

'The important thing is that *you* like him. That's all I ask. Tell him he can come whenever he wants. Are you going skiing?'

'Of course.' She headed down to the basement, where the skiing equipment was kept.

*

But not even meeting old friends and skiing down the Plan de Corones, across the Furcia as far as the foot of the Miara, managed to settle her nerves.

'You know something?' her father said that evening. 'You seem worried.'

'It must be the exams, Daddy.'

'Really? I thought everything was fine.'

'I still have my thesis to finish. It's very demanding work . . .'

'Of course. As long as it's nothing else. You're not short of money, are you?'

'No, Daddy, don't worry. You give me more than enough.'

'What about the Panda? It must be ready for the scrapyard by now. Are you sure you don't need another car?'

'It's fine, and anyway I don't use it much in Bologna. When I go to Florence, I take the train.'

'Wise idea. Saves crossing the Apennines. This has nothing to do with that young American your mother told me about, does it?'

'No, Daddy. He's just a friend. Everything's fine.'

'What about Cinzia?' her father asked, with a hint of disappointment. 'Everything fine there, too?'

'Yes, really. Don't worry.'

Did they know? she wondered for the umpteenth time.

And her torments started over again.

Cinzia hadn't come, and she didn't know whether to be pleased or upset. She remembered the apartment they shared, which had once seemed like paradise and now increasingly seemed as suffocating as a prison. Like her attic room, where she had spent that first, agonising night. The thought of going back scared her, but at the same time she wanted once again to be clasped in the hungry arms of her childhood friend.

Perhaps that was the problem, she said to herself in a sudden moment of lucidity. That they weren't children any more. That they had become women. But who really wants to grow up in a world like this?

That night, she slept badly.

She dreamed of Cinzia at the age of thirteen in her first communion dress. She came into Valentina's room, smiling happily. Valentina was naked and ashamed. She tried to hide, but Cinzia wouldn't let her. Then she laughed and asked her if she wanted her spotless white dress. She turned her back on her and let it drop to the floor. Then she turned again and, hiding her private parts with her hands, started walking languidly towards Valentina. Valentina stared, enraptured by her friend's immature body and paralysed by her shameless exhibitionism.

Cinzia laughed, coarsely. In her hands she was now clasping a huge, hideous penis.

Valentina screamed in her sleep, but did not wake up.

The scream had smashed the image to smithereens. In her dream, she made a huge effort to put it together: she wanted to suffer again. But the fragments refused to obey. The dark hair was replaced by blonde hair, the satanic grin by a reassuring smile, the hideous penis by a male appendage as innocuous as the ones you saw on marble statues in museums.

In Valentina's sleep, it was the face and body of Mike Ross she now saw.

It snowed all day in Santo Stefano and the pistes remained closed. Still confused by that strange night, Valentina hung about the hotel, giving a hand to the waiters and cooks. She did not call Cinzia, not knowing what she would say to her, and Cinzia did not call her.

Nor did she call on the days that followed.

On the 28th, though, Mike phoned again.

'I've found the perfect Christmas present for you,' he announced.

'What is it?'

'A little apartment. As it happens, it's the apartment above mine. It's a bit of a distance from the university, but still better than going backwards and forwards from Bologna.'

'I don't understand.'

'You've only got your thesis still to finish, isn't that right? You don't need Bologna any more. You should be living in Florence. For your research. And this is a great opportunity. The way the prices are here . . .'

'But you can't just decide like that, Mike, off your own bat.'

'I don't know how you Italians do it, but I always think that if you don't make a move right away, by tomorrow it's already too late.'

'Listen, it's not as simple as that.'

'Well, do as you want. But they're only holding it for me one more day. I gave my word. Let me know.'

'I'll think about it. And thanks anyway.'

'Let me know,' he repeated.

Not even half an hour had passed – half an hour of anguish and uncertainty – when the mobile rang again.

'Valentina?'

It was Cinzia.

'Hi.'

'Why didn't you call me?'

'You didn't call me either.'

Valentina was surprised at herself. She was dissolving inside, she realised that she had wanted this phone call more than anything in the world, and yet she had found the courage to answer back.

'When are you coming back to Bologna?'

'Do you care?'

Silence.

'I can't hear you.'

'You haven't answered my question.'

'I don't know. After Twelfth Night, I think.'

'Are you having fun?'

'Are you?'

'Oh, you know, the usual.'

'Listen to me, Cinzia. I don't know if I want to go back to Bologna. I've been offered an apartment in Florence . . .'

'Your journalist friend, I suppose?' Cinzia's tone had become curt and defensive.

'He doesn't matter. What matters is what I think.'

'And what do you think?'

'I don't know. Honestly, I don't know. I have to think of my future and . . .'

'And you don't see your future with me, is that it?'

Silence.

'So that *is* it.' She sounded offended.

'I told you, I don't know. I came here to think and so many things have happened. Strange things . . .'

'Well, maybe it's just a question of making your mind up. We have to do that sometimes, in life. I made my mind up early. Maybe too early. I made my mind up that I wanted you. And I still want you. Now it's up to you.'

'I want you, too, but—'

'You see? There's a "but". In love there shouldn't be any "buts". I shouldn't have to tell you that. The truth is, you've already made your mind up. Not the way I was hoping for, but I'm not going to beg. What's the point? Unfortunately, I know you too well. Better than you know yourself.'

'Maybe that's true. You've always known too much. Right

from the start. Where to touch me, how to turn me on. You made me yours, totally yours, only yours, too much yours . . .'

'And you made me yours, don't forget that.'

'Do you really think that? If that's true, then why can't I leave Bologna? Why can't I have a man as a friend?'

'Because I don't want to lose you.'

'Maybe that's not enough. Nobody wants to lose the jewel they wear round their neck, but how do we know the jewel is only happy round that particular neck?'

'That's a bit much, comparing yourself to a jewel – and I've hardly been able to show you off. This isn't a society that accepts lesbians gladly. And that's what we are, don't forget that. If it's someone else's turn now, all I can do is wish the two of you good luck. But remember: there are jewels and there are jewels. Some are cursed, and bring bad luck to anyone who puts them on.'

That was all Valentina needed. Twenty minutes later, she called Mike.

The next day she left.

3

It was two o'clock in the morning on 9 January 2000 at the Central Park disco in the Parco delle Cascine. The music was deafening. The place was full to bursting, as it was every Saturday night. The ventilation system had been turned full on, to try and get rid of the white clouds of smoke that hung in the air. From time to time, multicoloured beams of light swept the room.

Leaning against a pillar, with a glass of whisky in his left hand and a lit cigarette in the other, Pino Ricci, a *Squadra Mobile* officer in Serpico's section, was looking around with a bored expression on his face.

Malicious rumours had been circulating for a while at Headquarters that he moonlighted as a bouncer at the Central Park on Saturdays. When Ferrara had heard the rumours, he'd shrugged his shoulders. 'He certainly has the body for it! Six and a half feet tall, built like a tank. Just looking at him is enough to scare you. Maybe they pay him just to be there.' But the rumours had never been proved.

'Hi, Pino!' came a familiar voice from behind him. 'They can't be paying you much in the Squad.'

He turned.

And smiled.

'We're used to it, Spiderman, it's part of our job.'

Fabio Nuti was an old friend. They'd known each other as children, but then their ways had parted. Pino had entered the police force and Spiderman had gone in the opposite direction. Famous from his days as a burglar for his agility at climbing the fronts of houses – hence the nickname – he was now a pusher. His speciality was selling ecstasy in discos.

The two of them hadn't seen each other for more than a year, ever since Spiderman had been arrested on his way back from Naples with a quantity of pills he had hoped to sell that weekend. It must have been a tip-off, he'd thought when he was stopped at the exit from the Florence South tollgate by an unmarked car carrying plain-clothes carabinieri from the drugs squad and asked to follow them to their barracks, where they had dismantled his brand new Rover piece by piece.

'So, Spider, how were things inside? Five-star service?'

'Fuck off, Pino. You try it some time, and tell me how many stars you'd give it.'

'Hey, just kidding. I'm pleased to see you.'

'I don't like that kind of joke, Pino, especially coming from a friend.'

Pino decided to change the subject. 'What's new on the prison grapevine? Anything hot for me? Anything that'll make me look good?'

'What?' Fabio hadn't quite heard because of the loud music.

Ricci repeated the question.

'Don't make me talk, Pino. I don't want to do that any more. People have started to cotton on. In stir, you could have cut the atmosphere with a knife.'

'What do you mean?'

'When they took me to sector A, where they keep the

remand prisoners, I swear people were looking at me suspiciously. Most of the people there were pushers, and they all knew me. Some of them had been arrested because of me. I was shit scared! When I got out of solitary, after the deputy prosecutor had interrogated me, I asked to be transferred to the other wing, where they keep convicted prisoners. Some of them I knew quite well. There was even one of the accomplices of the Monster of Florence there. He was on his own in the cell opposite mine.'

'The one Chief Superintendent Ferrara put inside.'

'Yes, that's the one. I felt sorry for him, he's quite sick. It's no joke being in prison when you're over seventy.'

'Don't forget what he did when he wasn't yet a decrepit old man, and how many families suffered because of him.'

'That's true, Pino, but when you're in prison you see things differently. Deep down we're all human beings.'

'Not all of us, Spider. People who commit certain crimes don't belong to the human race any more. But let's not talk about that, I'm fed up with all that shit about the Monster. So, nothing at all to tell me? Damn it, doesn't anyone talk any more in the slammer?'

Spiderman seemed reluctant to answer.

Pino needed to re-establish their old bond. 'Let's go to the bar, Fabio,' he said, smiling. 'I'll buy you a drink to celebrate your return to civilisation.'

Spiderman followed him.

'Two whiskies, Lucio,' Pino ordered, pretty sure he knew what Fabio would like. He was right, though his friend was quite specific: 'Make mine Glenn Grant.'

They took their two glasses and walked back to the pillar where they had met.

Pino drank a little of his whisky and asked, 'How are things with Gabriella?'

'Drop it, Pino, I don't want to talk about it. I hadn't been inside a month and the bitch had already taken up with another guy.'

'Shit! I thought you two were getting on so well . . .'

'So did I, until I got out. It's not easy for a woman to stay faithful to you when you don't come home, especially when you're locked up in prison and nobody knows when you're coming back. Anyway, let's drop it. I'll give you something, even though you don't deserve it. You didn't do anything to make things easier for me. You forgot all about me.'

'I'm just an ordinary police officer. You can't ask me for the moon.'

'I know, but if you'd talked to your boss he could have put in a good word for me.'

'Right, and then I'd have had to tell him you were my informant! My boss needs to know the information, not the source.'

Fabio nodded.

'So, what have you got for me? I hope it's clean . . .'

'You should tell the Homicide people to keep an eye on Antonio Salustri, the owner of the shop in Santo Spirito where that assistant was murdered. You know the one I mean, right?'

'Sure. You're talking to the right person, I'm working on that case. I'm not in Narcotics any more, Sergi wanted me in his squad. You remember Sergi, don't you?'

'Sure – Serpico. Is he still a hippy?'

'Oh, yes. You'd expect to see him on the barricades. Same long hair and beard, same casual clothes.'

'What a guy! I really can't see him as a policeman. He should be in the movies! How does he stand working with idiots like you?' Fabio laughed, and Pino joined him.

'And why should we keep an eye on this Salusto, or whatever you said his name was?'

'Antonio Salustri. If his name doesn't mean anything to you, you're behind the times. He's an up and comer, clean on the surface but actually a front man.'

'Carry on.'

'Lately, this Salustri's been hanging out with a guy from the Calabrian Mafia named Salvatore Dieni, who's big in the antiques racket.'

'And you're sure of this?'

'Sure I'm sure!'

'And this Salustri. Did he have anything to do with Alfredo Lupi's murder? That's the assistant.'

By now they had moved to a small table in a corner, where a few seats had become free. People had started to leave. It was getting close to closing time: four o'clock.

'There was this guy in prison – don't ask me the name because I wouldn't tell you – he told me some things in confidence.'

'What kind of things?'

'He told me the murder had something to do with the antiques racket. From what he'd heard since he'd been in prison, the guy who was killed had probably found out what his employer was up to. Maybe he'd seen something he shouldn't have seen and paid with his life.'

'Seen what?'

'He didn't tell me and I didn't ask him. When you hear something like that, you shut up and listen. Anyway, that's all I know. You keep an eye on Salustri and you won't regret it.'

'Looks like it might be worth it. But just tell me one thing.'

'What?'

'This guy from the Calabrian Mafia, Salvatore . . . what did you say he was called?'

'Salvatore Dieni.'

'Right. Who is he?'

'I met him years ago. Not a big shot, but he's got all the right contacts. The Calabrians trust him totally. They know he'd rather die than betray their code.'

In other words, as long as he stayed loyal, he and his family would live, Pino thought as he and Fabio sipped another round of whiskies. This time they'd had them brought to the table.

'What kind of guy is he?' Pino asked.

'He lives alone and whenever you see him he's alone. Officially he runs a bureau de change near the Borgo San Lorenzo. It's a front for money laundering. With all the tourists around, Florence is a great place for it.'

'Of course. People never think of organised crime in connection with Florence. We don't have Mafia killings, bombs, extortion, kidnapping . . . This is interesting. What else can you tell me?'

'Hey, I'm not going to arrest Dieni and Salustri for you! I've given you their names and told you what they're involved in – what more do you want? You're the copper, not me. I don't want anyone knowing I told you! I'd be a dead man and you'd have me on your conscience.'

'What do you think I am? You know I'd never betray you. That's why you had to do your time – because I didn't want to betray you, not even to my boss. I hope you've realised that by now.'

'Sure, I already knew it. That's why I trust you. I hope it works out for you.'

'Thanks, Spider, I'll be thinking of you.'

'Me too.'

They toasted each other, downed their whiskies and went their separate ways.

*

'Pino, tell the boss what you just told me,' Sergi began as soon as they sat down in front of Ferrara's desk. It was 8.15 on Monday 10 January.

Officer Ricci gave a faithful account of what he'd heard from his childhood friend, referred to as 'one of my most reliable sources who's proved useful on several occasions'.

'You remember two summers ago, when we caught those people who'd robbed the Central Post Office, just as they were escaping?'

'Of course I remember. It was one of your informants who tipped us off.'

'Well, chief, it's the same source. He's never been wrong. I can vouch for him.'

'Okay, Ricci, put all this in a report and give it to Inspector Sergi. Sergi, I'd like you to find out as much as you can about Salustri and Dieni. Check in the Headquarters' records, not just the Squad's.'

'Of course, chief. I'll get on to it right now and keep you informed.'

They left the room. Feeling pleased with himself, Ferrara lit a cigar. This was what he called a good start to the day.

Later that morning, the first results arrived.

'Neither of them have records, chief,' Sergi said. 'No arrests, no complaints. Absolutely nothing. There's just one thing we've corroborated so far. Dieni does indeed have a bureau de change in the Borgo San Lorenzo, just near the Piazza del Mercato. I even went past it and had a look. There was a girl cashier behind the counter, no customers.'

'I'd like that bureau de change put under surveillance, to see who uses it. When Dieni puts in an appearance, put someone on his tail. I want to see the kind of things he gets up to.'

'Yes, chief.'

'Oh, one other thing.'

'Chief?'

'Put Antonio Salustri under surveillance, too, at least for a few days.'

'Yes, chief.'

'And keep me informed.'

'Of course, chief.'

Three days later, Inspector Sergi burst into Ferrara's office.

'Sorry I didn't knock, chief,' he said, blushing, when he saw the look of surprise on Ferrara's face. 'I didn't mean to be rude.'

'Don't worry, I have nothing to hide from any of you. Sit down, take a deep breath and tell me everything.'

'We stopped Dieni. Or rather, the traffic police stopped him. They're holding him now.'

'What happened?' Ferrara asked, worried that a false move might spoil things.

'Early this morning, the boys who were tailing him saw him meet the driver of a lorry with a Reggio Calabria numberplate in a car park on the autostrada. They unloaded some things from the lorry and Dieni put them in the boot of his Mercedes. The boys got suspicious because the men were moving around furtively, as if they didn't want to be seen.'

'Okay, what happened then?'

'They asked the traffic police for help. The traffic police stopped him at the Florence North exit, as if it was just a routine check, together with the car in front and the one behind so as not to make him suspicious.'

'Good!'

'They asked him the usual questions, registration, licence,

tax . . . Then they asked him to open the boot, and he didn't want to, he said the lock was damaged. That gave the officers a good excuse to take him to the Florence North barracks, where they opened the boot. There were four paintings inside, all old. Dieni claimed he didn't know anything about them. He said someone must have put them there without his knowledge. Maybe in the car park he always uses, the one near the Santa Maria Novella station.'

'Go and get him. I want him and his car here right now. I'll call the traffic police and arrange it.'

Serpico was just about to leave the office when Ferrara called him back.

'What about the lorry?'

'It carried on along the autostrada going north. It's one of those lorries they use for transporting fruit. I gave instructions not to stop it for now, just follow it at a safe distance until further orders.'

'Good! You can go now.'

Sergi hurried out.

Ferrara prepared for the interview. He knew it wouldn't be easy. It was obvious that the provenance of the paintings was illegal, but it was also obvious that, unless Dieni cooperated, it would be difficult to trace them back to their source quickly. The traffic in stolen works of art is an area in which gathering the corroborative evidence needed to bring charges is a long, complex process. There is no up-to-date catalogue of stolen works and investigating art theft is the exclusive remit of a special unit of the Carabinieri, who guard their privileges jealously.

Less than an hour later, Dieni was in Ferrara's office. Sergi and Pino Ricci sat next to him. Ricci was looking pleased with himself: at least the tip-off he had been given was yielding results, even though there was no apparent connection between the stolen paintings and Alfredo Lupi's murder.

Salvatore Dieni was a short, thickset man with a pock-marked face, olive skin and anxious black eyes. He was clearly scared.

Ferrara took advantage of his nervousness. 'Let's cut to the chase, Dieni,' he began, in a tone of voice that left no doubt about his intentions. 'We don't have any time to waste listening to bullshit.'

'What do you mean by bullshit, Inspector?' Dieni protested, but his voice was faint and his eyes were fixed on the surface of the desk separating him from Ferrara.

'You're not talking to an inspector,' Sergi said. 'You're talking to Chief Superintendent Ferrara, head of the *Squadra Mobile*. I'm an inspector. I told you that when I introduced myself.'

'Yes, you did, Inspector, but I don't know the ranks. And anyway, you're all in plain clothes. But why have you brought me here? Maybe I should call my lawyer now. I feel as if I've been kidnapped.'

Ferrara leapt to his feet, propped the cigar he was smoking on the ashtray, looked down at the now-terrified Dieni, and in a loud but steady voice said, 'You told the traffic police a pack of lies, Dieni! I want the truth! Keep the fairy stories for your grandchildren, if you have any. This isn't the place for them. The play acting is over, is that clear? And look at the person you're talking to, not down at the floor or the desk.'

Dieni obeyed. Nobody present could tell whether the look he now gave Ferrara was one of defiance or of fear. 'I'm not a liar, Superintendent. I told the truth. It's up to you to prove those paintings are mine.'

'That means you haven't understood a thing, Dieni. Either that or you don't want to understand. I think I need to explain

myself better. That way there'll be no more misunderstand-
ings and we won't waste any more time, because time is
precious to us. So listen carefully, I'm not going to repeat
myself, is that clear?'

He paused for a moment, then sat down again, lit another
cigar and inhaled once, twice.

'For a start, one thing is certain, Dieni. You're not going to
be exchanging money any more, and you can go back to
Calabria where you came from. There's no place in this city
for someone like you. That much I can assure you.'

'What is this?' Dieni asked, stunned. 'Are you threatening
me?'

'It's not a question of threats. We found you in possession of
objects that were obtained illegally. Whatever the outcome of
any legal proceedings you may face, that's more than enough
for us to get your licence revoked. And that's not all . . .'

'But Superintendent, those paintings aren't—'

He had no time to finish his sentence. Ferrara again leapt to
his feet, and for the second time in a few minutes he raised his
voice. 'Don't you get it, Dieni? Let's stop this play acting
now!'

'What play acting?'

Ferrara's voice went up another octave, sending a shudder
through Salvatore Dieni. 'I've had enough of this, Dieni!
Maybe you'd like to see the video footage my men shot,
showing you transferring the paintings from the lorry to your
car? You're guilty of some serious offences, including aiding
and abetting. You can get up to four years in prison for that,
and that's without taking the aggravating circumstances into
account. And I can assure you you'll serve your full sentence,
even if you have had a clean record up till now.'

Dieni went limp on his chair. He had realised there was no
way out. He was completely silent, his head ever more bent

towards the ground. Ferrara took another cigar out of his leather case. His third that morning. He kept lighting them without smoking them through to the end. He needed that first taste, the strongest and best.

Sergi and Ricci were silent, too. You could have heard the proverbial pin drop.

Dieni was the first to break the almost tomb-like silence. 'It's true, I was moving those paintings. I'll tell you everything, superintendent, but I don't want the lorry driver to get into trouble. He has nothing to do with this. He's a family man, and to support his family he has to keep going up and down between Reggio Calabria and the markets in Milan, transporting fruit.'

And drugs, Ferrara thought as he sat down again. 'Carry on,' he said. 'You're doing well.'

'I'll talk, but don't send me back to Calabria. I need to keep working in Florence. You've got to believe me.'

The man was begging him. Ferrara knew what that meant. He knew all about the Calabrian Mafia, having spent more than ten years in Reggio Calabria; that was where he had leaned his trade and he often said that there was no better school. There was a real risk for Dieni that his 'godfathers' might think he wasn't reliable any more. He wasn't afraid of someone informing on him, or of going to prison, what scared him was the thought that he might have to pay, perhaps even with his life, for not being more careful while moving the paintings. If, because of him, an innocent-seeming bureau de change was closed down, he'd be depriving the clan of a valuable money-laundering operation.

It was the ideal situation, and Ferrara had to take as much advantage of it as he could.

'Where do those paintings come from and who were they intended for?'

'Could I have a coffee first?'

Without waiting for Ferrara to ask him, Ricci left the room. He returned with four coffees in paper cups and a litre bottle of mineral water.

Dieni drank his coffee quickly. 'Thank you, Superintendent, I really needed that,' he said, putting the paper cup back on the table.

'So did we,' Ferrara said. 'Now start talking. We're ready to listen.' He turned to Sergi and signalled to him to take notes.

'The paintings were stolen from a patrician villa in Sicily. I don't know who it belongs to, only that it's near Palermo. An old countess, or something like that, lives there now, on her own. I heard it was a plumber who did some work there who put the thieves on to it. That's all I know about it, but if the owner reported the theft, it should be easy enough for you to check it out.'

Let's hope so, Ferrara thought, and exchanged a knowing glance with Pino Ricci, who left the room. A few phone calls would be enough to confirm the story. If it turned out to be true, it would give at least some credence to whatever they found out in the second part of the interview, which promised to be much more interesting.

'I hope for your sake you're telling the truth, Dieni.'

'It's the truth, Superintendent, believe me. I'm sure the officer who just went out has gone to check. He'll confirm it, you'll see.'

'We'll soon know. In the meantime, carry on. Tell us where you were supposed to take the paintings. Or rather, who you were supposed to hand them over to.'

'Superintendent, you know as well as I do that Florence is a perfect market for fences to offload furniture and antiques. There are whole neighbourhoods, like Santo Spirito, where you can find craftsmen prepared to do whatever's necessary to make the objects for sale more presentable, or make it so they can't be recognised by their legitimate owners. And it all happens in broad daylight. Am I right or not?'

'We know all that, Dieni,' Ferrara said. 'We don't need you to explain it to us. What we do need is the name of the fence, or fences, you were planning to use to offload those paintings.'

'Hold your horses, I'm getting there. This isn't easy for me . . . And anyway, I can't give you names. Please, you can't make me do something like that . . .'

'So you think we should be content with your little lecture on the Florence underworld? If you want us to help you, you have to give us something in return, don't you think?'

'I realise that. I promise I'll do you a favour the first opportunity I get. Let me go and you won't regret it.'

'You haven't got it, have you? I want at least one name. Just one, as long as it's the right one.'

'I can't, I really can't . . .'

At that moment Ricci returned, and informed Ferrara that the robbery had been confirmed. Evidently the countess, or whatever she was, had reported it. That at least was a good sign.

'All right, Dieni, let's talk man to man. I think we're both men of our word.'

They looked each other straight in the eyes. The agreement they were making didn't need words on paper, didn't need signatures. It was part of an ancient code.

'We've heard you're a friend of Antonio Salustri, the antique dealer in Santo Spirito,' Ferrara resumed. 'In fact, you seem to be on very good terms indeed.'

'It's true, Superintendent, he's one of the people I use to offload merchandise, but he's not involved in this—'

'I don't care. Tell me everything you know about him. One of his assistants was murdered in his shop in Santo Spirito. You knew that, didn't you?'

The penny finally dropped. Dieni seemed relieved. 'So is that what this is about?'

'What do you know about the murder?'

'Nothing. I can only speculate . . .'

'All right, speculate, and we'll see what we think.'

'All I know, Superintendent, is that Antonio Salustri was getting ready to do a major deal, something he was sure would set him up for life.'

'What was it?'

'He'd found a buyer, a rich Swiss collector, for this painting he had by Velazquez – you know, the famous Spanish painter. A painting stolen some years ago from a church in Sicily. Salustri found it in the store room of his shop when he did an inventory of the merchandise left by the previous owner, Gualtiero Ricciardi. He knew what it was right away, but he also knew it wouldn't be an easy thing to offload. So he decided to hold on to it and wait for the right moment. Quite recently he told me about it, and asked me to help him. He needed money. I advised him to try selling it abroad. I said I could help him to carry it across the border, in return for a percentage. One of the last times we met, he told me he was in negotiation with this Swiss collector and that he might need my car. He also told me he was going to sell it for four billion lire, but the person who'd put him in touch with the Swiss guy would have to get a cut. That was the last I heard of it.'

'And what's this story of the Velazquez got to do with the murdered assistant?' Ferrara asked. He was pretty sure he knew what the answer would be, but he wanted to hear it out loud.

'I think the assistant found out what Salustri was up to. Maybe he'd even found the painting in the store room. That would be a valid motive for killing someone, don't you think?'

'How can we be sure this is just speculation on your part? Is there something else you're not telling us?'

'No, there's nothing else.'

'All right,' Ferrara said. 'Let's stop there. All this is off the record.' He looked at Sergi and Ricci in rapid succession, then back at Dieni. 'This is what we'll do. The four paintings will stay with the traffic police for the moment. You'll be charged with receiving stolen goods and released on bail. Right now you can go with the inspector and sign a statement, on the understanding that the investigation continues. Sergi, take him to your office.'

'What about my bureau de change, Superintendent?'

'I said you could go, didn't I?' Ferrara's tone left him in no doubt: he had lifted that threat, at least for the moment.

'We ought to find out where the Velazquez was stolen from,' Ferrara said as soon as Sergi had returned. 'It would be nice if we could get hold of a photo or, failing that, a good description. We need to get authorisation from the Prosecutor to remove the seals from the shop. We can always tell him we have to carry out another search to see if the painting is still there.'

'It'll be there,' Serpico said. 'Salustri comes here almost every day to ask when he can get his shop back. The last time he did, they sent him to me. I told him he'd have to apply to the Prosecutor's Department, maybe with a request from a lawyer, and that in any case he'd be able to ask for compensation for the loss of earnings. He was really upset, said he'd be reduced to stealing in order to live, things like that.'

'It couldn't be clearer, could it? We need to keep an eye on this Salustri. I want him watched twenty-four hours a day, in shifts. And I want a tap on his phones.'

'How do we present the request to the Prosecutor? We

can't tell him what we found out from Dieni or from Pino's friend. How do we justify a phone tap?'

'We won't say we suspect Salustri, just that we may get a few leads from listening in on his calls, maybe identify friends and acquaintances of the victim we don't know about yet. After all, Salustri was the victim's employer and the murder did happen in his shop.'

'So because we're asking to tap the phone of someone who's not being investigated, we don't have to mention the leads we have?'

'Precisely. I think two weeks should be long enough.'

'I'll get on to it, chief!'

At 10.28 p.m. on Sunday 16 January, in the room at the Prosecutor's Department where phone taps were monitored, the recorder connected to the phone line in Antonio Salustri's home began to show signs of life. One, two, three rings. Someone picked up the receiver.

'Salustri?' It was a man's voice, with a strong Sicilian accent.

'Yes. I know it's you.'

'What's happening, Salustri?'

'Still nothing. I can't get into the shop – we need to wait.'

'What the fuck . . .? I thought we had an understanding.'

'We do have an understanding, but I can't get in.'

'He can't wait.'

'Just be patient. It'll come.'

'He can't wait. We need that money. Let's hurry things up, shall we?'

'You'll get it all, don't worry.'

'Another week. Then we want the money.'

'I have to get it first.'

'One week.'

'But—'

The Sicilian had already hung up.

What the officer on duty had heard was more than enough for him to phone Inspector Sergi at home at that late hour and for Serpico, in his turn, to call Rizzo and Ferrara.

'We've got him, chief,' he said, concluding his account.

'Let's talk about it tomorrow,' Ferrara said. 'Let me sleep on it for now. See you tomorrow.'

'Good night, chief.'

'Good night, Sergi.'

A transcript of the telephone call was already on Ferrara's desk by eight o'clock the following morning. Ferrara had summoned his deputy and Serpico.

'Now that we have corroboration, chief,' Rizzo suggested, 'we could ask for a warrant to search the shop. It's obvious the painting's still there.'

Ferrara read the transcript again. 'The painting's there,' he said. 'There's no doubt about it. The first thing to do is stop Salustri or anyone working for him from breaking the seals and taking it away. The shop will need to be watched round the clock.'

'Right, chief, but what about the search warrant?' Rizzo insisted.

'There's no hurry. I understand your haste, but just because we've had corroboration we shouldn't lose sight of the main objective, which is to catch a killer, not a fence. Let's take this step by step. The picture's not going anywhere for the moment.'

'All right, chief. How should we proceed?'

'First of all, we check with the phone company and find out where the call came from. I want to know who he's mixed up with.'

'The phone company? That could take days, maybe even a week . . .'

'I know. We'll wait.'

'All right.'

'In the meantime we keep our eyes on Salustri. If he comes back to Headquarters, send him to me. Sergi, I want you to call the diocese in Messina and in Catania, in fact, every diocese in Sicily if you have to. Find out where this Velazquez was stolen from.'

'Superintendent Ferrara?'

'Speaking.'

'This is the officer in the guardhouse.'

'Go on.'

'A lawyer named Nicola Biffi is here with his client, a man named Salustri. They're asking to see you.'

'Bring them to my office.'

It was midday. Ferrara was overjoyed. He hadn't even needed to summon them, they'd come to him!

A few minutes later, the two men were in the room. Ferrara knew the lawyer well.

'What brings you here, Signor Biffi? It must be important if you went to the trouble of coming yourself instead of delegating the job to one of your colleagues.'

'You're quite right, Chief Superintendent. It is important.'

'Go on.'

'My client here, Signor Salustri, is the owner of the antique shop where Alfredo Lupi was murdered.'

'I know that. I haven't yet had the pleasure of meeting him personally.'

Salustri, a man in his fifties with a pale, drawn face, said nothing. He was carefully avoiding direct eye contact with Ferrara.

'After all this time, the shop is still sequestrated property,' the lawyer said. 'As I'm sure you must realise, my client is losing a great deal of money. What should he do? The shop is the only source of income for him and his family.'

'I understand, Signor Biffi, but you know I can't do anything. Signor Salustri has come here several times to ask for the sequestration order to be lifted, and he's been told that he must apply to the Prosecutor's Department. The premises are the responsibility of the legal authorities, it's not up to us.'

'Obviously I know that, but I also know that the Prosecutor's Department won't hand back sequestrated property, especially if there's a murder involved, unless they receive a favourable opinion from those conducting the investigation. We're dealing with a human tragedy here. My client hasn't committed any crime, yet he's suffering a grievous wrong.'

Salustri intervened for the first time. 'I'm ruined, superintendent,' he said, still without looking Ferrara in the eyes. That was one thing that irritated Ferrara: the other was his voice, artfully made to sound cracked in order to inspire pity. 'There are payments I'm waiting for that have been frozen. What can I do if I can't sell?'

'I understand, Signor Salustri,' Ferrara replied politely, finding it hard to hold back what he really wanted to say. 'But you really need to apply to the Prosecutor's Department, preferably through your lawyer.'

'If I've understood correctly, Chief Superintendent,' Biffi said, 'you'll give a favourable opinion.'

'No, Signor Biffi, that's not what I said. I simply explained the procedure. Your client should follow it, and I'll decide when the time comes.'

The two men left, disgruntled.

As soon as they had gone, Ferrara phoned the prosecutor and brought him up to date, making an appointment to discuss the matter in person. By the time he put the phone down, he knew for certain that Salustri would not succeed in getting the sequestration order lifted.

The following Friday, the phone company informed them of the number and location of the telephone from which Salustri had been called. It was a public phone inside an Agip service station on the autostrada a few kilometres outside Palermo, on the way to Messina.

The same day, Ferrara learned that the Velazquez painting had been stolen from the parish church of Alì Superiore, in the province of Messina, not far from Taormina.

'I spoke to the parish priest, chief,' Sergi said. 'He's very happy. He was so excited, he wanted to come to Florence straight away.'

'But what did you tell him? That we'd found it?'

'No, I didn't, but that's what he understood at first. So I explained that we still had a lot to do and that we'd keep him informed. But he was beside himself. His parishioners, which means basically the whole village, have been desperate since the painting was stolen. They consider it part of their heritage.'

'Did you ask him what the painting looks like?'

'Yes. It's from the seventeenth century, and it's attributed to the famous Spanish painter Diego Velazquez – according to him, one of the greatest portrait painters of all time.'

'What's the subject?' Ferrara asked, impatiently.

'It's the portrait of a priest or a monk, wearing a dark cloak and holding an open book in his hands. Next to him, on his right, there's a big bird that you can't see clearly, some kind of condor. The colours are very dark, he said.'

'Good. Keep your fingers crossed, this could turn out to be very useful.'

*

In the monitoring room at the Prosecutor's Department, the recorder again indicated that Salustri's phone was ringing. It rang only twice this time, and when the voices came on the line, they were the same voices as on the previous Sunday. A week had passed: it was 11.03 p.m. on Sunday 23 January. Rizzo and Sergi had been waiting with the duty officer for the call to come.

The mechanism was already in place to trace the call within a few minutes. All switchboards were being manned by an employee of the phone company and a police officer. Members of the Palermo *Squadra Mobile* had the service area where the previous call had been made under surveillance.

'What's happening, Salustri?'

'Still nothing. I can't get in.'

'What about our understanding?'

'But—'

'Get it now,' the man interrupted Salustri. 'We'll talk again tomorrow night.'

'What do you mean?'

At the other end, the line went dead.

'Too short, damn it,' Sergi said. 'I don't think there was time to trace it.'

Rizzo called the officer at the switchboard to check, then Sergi called Ferrara. 'Impossible, chief. Too short. Not even thirty seconds. All we know is that the call wasn't made from anywhere near Florence. They're trying at least to find out which area it came from.'

'We'll wait. But let them do whatever they can to identify the number.'

He was hoping it was a domestic number, but he doubted it.

They were informed by their colleagues in Palermo that nobody had used the phone in the Agip service station. They were clearly dealing with professionals, Serpico thought, professionals who wouldn't use the same phone twice.

Ferrara went to bed disappointed, but didn't have time to fall asleep. The phone rang again. It was another call from Sergi.

'Sorry to call at this hour, chief.'

'Go on.'

'Salustri has cut loose.'

'What?'

'We've just heard from the officers who've been staking out his home. They saw him leave with a suitcase in his hand. He took his car and set off in the direction of the autostrada.'

'I hope they're following him.'

'Of course. I told them not to let him out of their sight.'

'Let me know what direction he's going. Keep me updated. Doesn't matter how late it is. I don't think any of us are getting any sleep tonight.'

'Of course, chief.'

The phone calls kept coming, with Sergi keeping him up to date with every development. Salustri had taken the Autostrada del Sole heading north, had exited at Modena, and had taken a room at the Holiday Inn near the tollgate. Local officers were now keeping watch on the hotel.

He's trying to save his skin, Ferrara thought. *He can't get to the painting, his big deal has gone belly up, and he knows the Sicilians aren't joking*. At last, some time in the middle of the night, he finally managed to get to sleep. The next day was going to be busy.

'Salustri left the hotel at eight,' Ferrara said. 'Right now, he's on his way to Milan. We're following him discreetly. At this point I need a warrant to take him into custody.'

Ferrara and Rizzo were in Prosecutor Gallo's office. They had arrived first thing in the morning.

'What offence are we charging him with?' Gallo asked. 'We don't have anything against him.'

'We know there's a stolen artwork in his shop. We know he's a fence and that he has contacts with the Mafia. We've recorded two phone calls—'

'It's not sufficient, you know that – not for an arrest warrant that'll have to be endorsed within twenty-four hours by an examining magistrate from another district, perhaps Milan, who knows nothing about the case.'

'I understand the problem, chief . . .' Ferrara remembered, with a touch of regret, the days when deputy prosecutors would issue warrants with all the details left blank. But that was a long time ago, when legal procedures were different. Nowadays, maybe there was too much safeguarding of civil rights. It was always hard to find the middle way: perhaps it didn't even exist. 'But you could issue a search warrant for the shop. At least we can seize the Velazquez. In the meantime, we'll keep an eye on Salustri. If we really have to, we could get the traffic police to stop him and charge him with some traffic violation, just as an excuse to take him to their barracks. Add the painting to the phone tap evidence, and our problem is solved.'

'Good idea, Chief Superintendent. I think it's the only practical solution.'

At 10.30 a.m., Ferrara, accompanied by Rizzo, Sergi, Ascalchi and a group of officers, had the seals removed and entered the shop.

The smell of death still lingered.

The air didn't seem to have changed since the day of the murder.

The search began. In the absence of Salustri, a member of his family or a person he trusted – required for legal reasons – they had sent for Lupi's wife, on the pretext that they had to check if there were any objects there that had belonged to her husband.

They had hardly begun when they heard a mobile phone ring. It was Sergi's.

'Chief, it's the patrol that's following Salustri,' he said in Ferrara's ear, drawing him into a corner. 'They say he's coming up to Ponte Chiasso. He's obviously trying to cross the border. They're waiting for instructions.'

'He mustn't leave the country!' Ferrara cried. 'Contact customs. Have them detain him, claim they need to check his papers, search his car . . . Whatever they like, but they mustn't let him cross the border.'

'Of course, chief.'

Ferrara and Rizzo went back to supervising the search. Lupi's wife had sat down on a chair, a long way from where her husband's body had been found.

The officers began literally dismantling the shop, piece by piece. Every corner was checked, every piece of furniture shifted and inspected, every painting carefully examined.

'Chief!' Ascalchi's excited voice came from the back room. 'Come here, chief!'

Ferrara, Sergi and Rizzo ran into the back room. Ascalchi was surrounded by a group of officers, who moved aside when they saw Ferrara. In Ascalchi's hands was the painting they had been searching for.

Ferrara stared at the canvas with unexpected reverence and a touch of dismay. He felt as if the sharp, intense eyes of the clergyman in the painting, staring out of the dark background as if lit by an inner light, were staring back at him, judging him, following him when he moved.

'It was behind the bookcase, chief, propped up against the wall,' Ascalchi said, pointing to a piece of furniture next to an old desk cluttered with papers. 'We moved it and saw there was something wrapped in sheets of newspaper. We took them off and here it is.'

'Good work, boys. It should be plain sailing from now on. I'll phone the Prosecutor immediately and update him. In the meantime, carry on searching, we may find something else. Sergi, check to make sure Salustri has been detained.'

At 3 p.m., Ferrara was travelling along the autostrada on the way to Ponte Chiasso. Rizzo, Sergi and two other officers were in a car behind him.

Before leaving, Ferrara had faxed the warrant for Antonio Salustri's arrest on the charge of receiving stolen goods. In the car with him was Prosecutor Gallo, who would want to interview Salustri in person as soon as the judge in Como, who had already been informed, had endorsed the warrant.

What with the long journey and the time spent on legal procedures, it was already after nine in the evening before they finally found themselves sitting opposite the accused man at the Remand Centre in Como.

'Signor Salustri, I am the Public Prosecutor of Florence, Doctor Gallo, and this gentleman sitting beside me is the head of Florence's *Squadra Mobile*, Chief Superintendent Ferrara.'

'I know Superintendent Ferrara. My lawyer and I went to see him to ask for the sequestration order on my shop to be lifted.'

'Well, you have already been informed of the warrant I issued this morning so you know what this is about. You are under investigation for the offence of receiving stolen goods, in particular a painting by Velazquez, stolen in Sicily, which we found behind a bookcase in the back room of your shop. I have a duty to advise you that you can either choose a defence attorney for yourself or you can let me choose one for you. As you are under investigation, I need to interview you in the presence of a lawyer. That's the procedure.'

'I don't know anyone here. My lawyer's in Florence. Biffi. Do you know him?'

'Yes, but we can't wait for him to get here. The demands of the investigation require us to carry out the interview immediately.'

'So choose a lawyer for me, like you said. I have no problem answering your questions. I can explain everything. Even how I came to have that painting.'

Ferrara was following the conversation, and watching the man closely. Antonio Salustri was pale, and he had heavy rings under his eyes, but he did not seem any more submissive or humble than he'd been before.

It was obvious that he had used the time since leaving Florence to construct a line of defence, and now they would have to dismantle it without the element of surprise on their side. What Salustri didn't know was that they weren't looking to nail him for the theft of the painting, but for something else entirely.

They waited until the lawyer – the one on duty that day according to the list provided by the Como Prosecutor's Department – had arrived.

After the ritual introductions, Prosecutor Gallo continued, 'You are charged with receiving stolen goods, in that you had in your possession a priceless painting by the famous Spanish artist Velazquez, stolen some years ago from the parish church of Alì Superiore. In addition, I should like to ask you some questions about the murder of Alfredo Lupi, which took place in your shop on December 31st last year.'

Ferrara frowned.

The lawyer was listening, but did not say a word.

'What's the murder got to do with me?' Salustri protested. 'The police interviewed me the day it happened. I answered all their questions!'

'I know. I have your statement here. But I need to interview you again. Everything in its own time. Let's start with the Velazquez, since you are directly charged in connection with that. What do you have to say about that particular charge?'

'I found the painting in the shop, which I bought after the death of Gualtiero Ricciardi. I bought the shop with all the merchandise in it. After a while, as I was looking through some of the objects with a view to restoring them – I know about restoration, I've been a restorer of furniture and old paintings for years – I found the painting. I recognised it as a Velazquez. It was inside an even bigger painting with a very thick gilded frame – one of those paintings that fill an entire wall – which I was planning to restore.'

'Didn't it strike you as suspicious that the painting had been hidden like that?' Gallo asked.

'I assumed Ricciardi had been trying to protect it from thieves. The painting it was hidden inside would have been difficult to transport because of its size and weight, and wasn't particularly valuable anyway.'

'But you knew it had been stolen?'

'I didn't know and I couldn't have known. There are no catalogues of stolen art works. I thought Ricciardi had bought it legitimately. There's nothing wrong with that.'

'And who were you planning to sell the painting to?'

'Nobody. I intended to keep it for myself.'

'Are you sure?'

'Very sure.'

'I have here the transcripts of two telephone calls recorded by the police, with official authorisation. These calls were placed to your home phone at 10.28 p.m. on 16 January and 11.03 p.m. on 23 January.' He placed the two transcripts in front of Salustri. 'What do you have to say, Signor Salustri?'

The man's face clouded over. Perhaps it was the shock of

seeing the Sicilian's threats in black and white, but his self-confidence vanished in a flash and he looked desperately at this lawyer he had only just met, as if asking for help. Help was not forthcoming.

'Prosecutor Gallo, I'd like to talk to my lawyer in private, if I may.'

'That's your right. Let's adjourn for half an hour. Chief Superintendent Ferrara, if you would take them into the conference room.'

Less than fifteen minutes later, Salustri and the lawyer were again sitting opposite the Prosecutor.

'Prosecutor Gallo, I can explain everything. I think being stopped by the police today may have saved my life. I'm not a criminal, I'm a victim. I want to tell you the whole story.'

'Not before time. Trust the law. It's no accident I came here in person.'

'Then, like I said, this may be a good thing for me.'

'We'll see. In the meantime let's hear what you have to say.'

He told them about his contacts with a Sicilian, a man with a criminal record, who had acted as a go-between for a Swiss collector who wanted to buy the painting. He explained that he was supposed to have delivered the Velazquez ten days earlier in order to get the agreed price, but hadn't been able to keep the commitment because his shop had been placed under a sequestration order. He told them about the threats, how the Sicilian was pressing him to give back the advance he'd already been paid, how scared he'd been when he'd been given only twenty-four hours to come up with the money.

'Prosecutor, you know as well as I do, these people don't joke. They'd have come for me and killed me.'

'Who is this Sicilian?'

'I never found out what his name is or where he lives. I only met him once, in a bar in the centre of Florence where we'd arranged to meet. He phoned me and told me he'd found out I was looking to do a deal and that he was interested. He told me he would find a buyer. He also said that when the deal was done, he'd be there to see the money was handed over and would take twenty per cent for himself. I agreed.'

'How did this person happen to get in touch with you?'

'He wouldn't say who'd put him on to me, and I didn't insist. I'd told a few people in the antique business that I was looking to do a deal. I assumed one of them had told him about me and given him my phone number.'

'It seems to me you were a bit careless, don't you think?' Gallo observed.

'You're right, but I thought I was going to do the best deal of my life. I was naïve. I thought there were certain matters it was best not to ask too many questions about. The important thing was to make as much profit as I could and then disappear. Now I realise what a mess I got myself into.'

Gallo preferred not to insist. He considered that the moment had come to drop the subject of the Velazquez and go on to the murder of Alfredo Lupi.

'Tell us what you were doing on December 31st 1999.'

'Prosecutor, if you think I killed my assistant, you're making a big mistake. I told you. I'm not a killer and I had no motive—'

'I'm not accusing you of murder,' Gallo retorted. 'I'm simply asking you to tell me what you were doing that day.'

The lawyer intervened for the first time. 'Prosecutor, I fail to see the connection between this murder and the charge of receiving stolen goods. In any case, my client was interviewed at the time of the murder.'

'That's correct. He was questioned as a witness. But we need to ask him some more questions now because we think there may indeed be a connection between the murder and the painting. That's all.'

'But that's impossible,' Salustri protested. 'Alfredo didn't even know about the painting. He never came into the back room, where my office is, unless I was there. I checked many times. I even arranged some objects in a certain way to see if he moved them, but he never did.'

'So you say. Will you answer the question or not?'

'Of course I'll answer. It's just that I feel as if I'm being investigated for the murder.'

'No, you're not being investigated for that. If you were, I would have had to charge you with it specifically, just as I did for receiving. Your attorney can confirm that.'

The lawyer nodded.

'I was in Rome that day,' Salustri said. 'I left in the morning, on the 7.40 Eurostar. I had to take the 7.40 because there are no other trains before nine except the 8.54 which is too late. I had an appointment with a colleague of mine who has an antique shop near the Spanish Steps. He can confirm that, and so can his two assistants. As I was talking to him, about 11, 11.30, I was phoned on my mobile by a neighbour of mine who told me the police were looking for me because Alfredo had been killed. I went back to the Termini station and took the first train for Florence, where I immediately presented myself at Police Headquarters.'

'Can you tell me the name of your Roman colleague, and the name of your neighbour?'

'My colleague is Giorgio Matta, and his shop has the same name. It's right next to the Spanish Steps. My neighbour is Signor Papa, but the police know that.'

At this point, there was an exchange of looks between Gallo and Ferrara, and between Ferrara and Rizzo.

That was the end of the interview. Antonio Salustri was

taken back to his cell. There was only one charge against him: receiving stolen goods, according to article 648 of the Penal Code.

They spent the night in a hotel and left the following morning.

Ferrara was in a foul mood, and not very talkative.

He hadn't liked the way Gallo had conducted the interview. Letting Salustri know from the start that he was suspected of being involved in the murder had given him time to prepare himself psychologically and to maintain his alibi with conviction, however weak it was. Gallo should have led up to it gradually, without letting on that that was his aim. Now it would be hard to get Salustri to contradict himself.

'What do you think of his alibi?' Gallo asked at a certain point during the journey.

'I've already asked my men to check it out. But even if it's true that he was in Rome, if he didn't see his colleague until after 11, he would technically still have had time to do it even if he'd left Florence on the 8.54 train. Quite apart from the fact that he could just as easily have gone there by car. The murder took place between 8.30 and 8.45. Not much time to get to Rome, but not impossible.'

'So you're still convinced that he could be the killer?' Gallo asked, obviously puzzled.

'I have no idea,' Ferrara replied, and fell silent again.

A few days later, as if to compensate for Ferrara's frustration, he had the satisfaction of returning the Velazquez painting to its rightful owners.

When the two cars in which he, Rizzo, Sergi and Pino Ricci were travelling entered the square in front of the parish church of Alì Superiore, Ferrara and his men were astonished to see people everywhere: in the square, in the streets, on the balconies of the houses, on the steps of the church. The sound of bells filled the air.

The parish priest came out to meet them, accompanied by the mayor.

'Chief Superintendent Ferrara, the village thanks you. Look at how the people welcome you. They have been like orphans without their painting, which has been on the high altar for centuries. Thank you so much on behalf of everyone.'

Ferrara, who was not easily moved, felt strange. He was not used to this kind of public display. Apart from a single inauspicious TV broadcast he had agreed to appear on, he had always remained in the shadows, and had never exposed himself to the public.

'We were only doing our duty,' was all he managed to say. Then, to hide his embarrassment, he nodded to Sergi. The moment had come to take the painting out of the boot of the car.

Sergi and Ricci took the painting out carefully, and together they slowly climbed the steps. They entered the church, followed by the parish priest, the mayor and as many people as could crowd into the three big naves, and propped the painting on a chair in the middle of the high altar.

The ceremony that followed was something Ferrara had not been expecting.

The parish priest spoke first, emphasising the great sentimental value of the painting. Then the mayor thanked the police on behalf of all the inhabitants. The priest then asked Ferrara to join them on the altar and say a few words.

Ferrara, who thought he had got out of having to say anything more, was caught off guard and wondered what he could possibly come up with. Before he had had time to think of anything, the microphone was in his hand. He faced the crowd.

'I feel great pleasure and enormous joy in seeing the human effects of what for me and my colleagues was simply a normal police operation. We rarely get a chance to appreciate the results of our actions. Most of the time everything ends with an arrest, which is never a pleasant thing for anyone, not even for us. The benefit to society of that arrest is not something we can see or touch. So we tend to forget that the reason we chose this profession was to help people, not to persecute them. On behalf of all my colleagues, I thank you for the way you've welcomed us. Thank you with all my heart. We were only doing our duty.'

The parishioners applauded respectfully.

'Let's go to the sacristy now, Chief Superintendent,' the parish priest said. 'We've prepared some light refreshments.'

In the sacristy, they were confronted with a rectangular table more than sixty-five feet long, laden with Sicilian rustic dishes and sweets. Ferrara had a chance to savour tastes and smells he never encountered in Florence and often missed.

He and his men spent that night in Taormina. He recommended a restaurant where they could have dinner but, deaf to their protests, didn't go with them. He wasn't interested in dinner. What he wanted was to wander alone down the familiar streets, letting his memories wash over him. And the following morning, before leaving, as if he hadn't had enough nostalgia, he walked barefoot along the beach, remembering his childhood. And just as in his childhood, he was hit with a sudden craving – perhaps to make up for the disappointing breakfast at the hotel. He went into a bar and asked for a fresh brioche, half opened and filled with lemon *granita*.

4

'So you've really made up your mind.'

'Yes, Cinzia.'

It was the first of January and for two days they had done nothing but talk, moments of deep emotion alternating with recriminations and insults. The only time Valentina had been away was on the morning of the 31st. She had gone to Florence to meet the professor running the course on Renaissance theatre, who had received a request from the supervisor of her thesis for her to be admitted.

She had got up at five in the morning and for once had gone by car. By two in the afternoon she was already back. She swore over and over that she hadn't seen Mike Ross, but Cinzia did not believe her. They had started quarrelling again.

And that was how they had spent their New Year.

Now Valentina had almost finished packing her bags. Cinzia was watching her, her eyes moist with tears. For the first time since she had entered Valentina's life at San Vigilio, she seemed at a loss.

'I have to go.'

'You're not coming back.'

It was a statement, not a question: a statement she didn't expect to be contradicted.

'Listen, Cinzia. I don't want this to be goodbye. I don't think of it that way. It's only for one term. It's something I have to do. I need to concentrate on my thesis. I need to get things straight. So do you. We both need it.'

'You're wrong, as usual. I don't need it. Obviously you do. And that hurts me.'

At twenty, Cinzia had not changed much since her early teens. She was thin, not especially tall, but energetic and strong-willed. She had short, jet-black hair and intense black eyes, and a pointed chin that made her beautiful face look even more vulpine.

She was casually dressed in only a heavy beige woollen sweater that reached down to her knees, and was sitting cross-legged on the pouffe that had pride of place in the small apartment they had shared until today. Two rooms, plus kitchen and bathroom, full of evidence of their short life together. Souvenirs of journeys they had taken together, framed photographs, tasteful furniture carefully chosen in little markets over the years.

'It's a trial separation,' Valentina insisted. 'All couples do it. We just need to get away from each other for a while, that's all. It's not the end of the world!' She was speaking loudly to conceal her depression.

'Away from me, but close to that American.'

She didn't call him by his name. To her, he didn't have one.

'Please don't say that, Cinzia. I don't even know him, he's just someone nice I met by chance. I don't feel anything for him, I've never felt anything for a man.'

'I'd like to believe you. I'd really like to believe you, but I'm afraid. I'm so afraid, Vale. I beg you . . .'

Tears had run down her cheeks and gathered on the tip of

her chin, and now they glistened and vibrated as her lips quivered.

Valentina felt a strong impulse to hug her, to make love one last time. What harm could it do?

Cinzia stood up and ran to the bedroom, slammed the door and locked it.

Before going out, Mike Ross left the Philippine woman precise instructions, in English. The woman had recently arrived in Florence and did not know any Italian. That was another reason he had hired her as a part-time housekeeper.

Mike Ross lived in a three-storey villa surrounded by extensive grounds in Bellosguardo, though he only occupied the ground floor. The first floor was empty, but on the second a small apartment had been set aside, complete in every detail but never lived in. Nenita, the Filipina, had orders to open it up, to air the rooms, make sure that everything was tidy, make the beds, and arrange the flowers he'd bought the day before in vases.

It was nine o'clock. If all went well, Valentina would get to the Piazza della Stazione, where he had arranged to meet her, by about 11. He had plenty of time.

At the newsstand in the Piazza della Signoria he bought a copy of the *New York Times*, and sat calmly reading it, snug and warm in one of the many bars around the Palazzo Ducale. At 10:50, his mobile phone rang.

'It's me, Valentina.'

'I know. Your number showed up. Is everything okay?'

'It's been very foggy; I've had to drive slowly. That's why I'm late.'

'That's all right, don't worry. Where are you now?'

'About ten minutes from Barberini, I think.'

Mike made a rapid mental calculation, figuring there would not be much traffic on the first day of the year.

'You should be here by eleven-twenty, eleven-thirty at the latest. See you then. I'll be waiting.'

He called the waiter and asked for the bill.

He was astonished, as always, that breakfast in one of these bars cost almost as much as lunch, and yet they were as full as the restaurants, where at least you got decent food for your money.

He looked for his wallet in the wrong pocket and realised there was something in it. It was the letter to Father Rotondi. He had not worn this buckskin jacket since the day he had met Valentina, and had forgotten all about the letter.

He thought of throwing it away. He would find another method of establishing contact. It was too early for that anyway.

But why not keep him dangling? Smiling to himself, he walked to a post box.

'So this is the "little apartment"?'

Valentina did not know whether to be happy or worried.

It was too good to be true. Girls as young and attractive as her didn't usually get their wishes granted without having to give something in return, especially when rich men – of whatever age – were involved.

Nenita had done her work well. Light flooded in through the big windows, even on a grey overcast day like this. The drawing room with its antique furniture glowed, bright with luxuriant bouquets and warmed by a blazing fire in the eighteenth-century marble fireplace. The bedroom was large and welcoming and looked out on a veranda leading to a beautiful square terrace. The kitchen was fully fitted. The bathroom was fragrant with aromatic scents.

'It's part of the house,' Mike explained. 'When I moved in, I decided to take it as well. I didn't want to share the house with some noisy lodger. There wasn't a big difference in price.'

'How much?'

'Let's not talk about that now. The first three months are already paid. See if you like it. If you do, we'll talk again.'

'Don't even think about it. If I don't pay, I leave right now.'

'Where will you go? Florence is full, even in January. You won't find anything now.'

She could always go back to Bologna, Valentina thought. But she didn't want to.

'But you lied to me. You told me it'd be gone if I didn't say yes straight away!'

'How else could I persuade you?' the American replied, with a disarming smile. 'But let's not quarrel. Give me a month, okay? See if you like it before you commit yourself.'

Valentina looked out of one of the windows. How could she not like it? The view was breathtaking.

From this villa on a hill, there was a hundred-and-eighty-degree panorama of the whole city, dominated by Brunelleschi's dome with its miraculous harmony of line and colour. All around, like servants bowing before their master, stretched the huddle of roofs and the warren of little streets out of which rose San Lorenzo and Santa Maria Novella on the left, Santa Croce and the National Library on the right. For the first time Valentina became aware that the cathedral was by far the tallest building in the whole of Florence. It had been that way for centuries, and it would be that way for ever.

'I'll leave you now,' Mike Ross said, not giving her time to think. 'If you need anything, ask Nenita, the maid. She's only here in the mornings, but I'm sure you'll manage. Bye.'

*

It did not take Valentina long to get her bearings. In the days that followed, she managed to stop worrying about her host's possible intentions. They led totally separate lives: she was busy with her course, he with his work. He seemed to think of her as a distant acquaintance, or even just as a neighbour he was on good terms with. She did not disturb him, and he did not disturb her.

Sometimes Mike would go away for a few days, then spend whole days shut up in his apartment, listening to classical music and, Valentina supposed, writing his articles. He did not seem to have any friends. Nobody ever visited him.

At the end of the first week, he invited her out to dinner.

'It's time you started to learn the secrets of Florence,' he said.

He took her to Buca Lapi, where they had hot crostini with Colonnata lard and the best Tuscan vegetable, bread and bean soup she had ever tasted.

She was fascinated by the pages of old newspapers, some dating back to the nineteenth century, which covered the vaulted ceiling and walls.

'It's the oldest restaurant in Florence,' Mike explained. 'Originally, it was a tavern where coachmen would stop for a glass of wine and a bowl of tripe, and exchange news. They would pass around the pages of the newspaper as they finished them, crumpled and stained with sauce, oil and wine, and paste them to the wall before leaving. And there they stayed. Obviously, the host at the time wasn't too worried about cleanliness!'

Valentina noticed that at table, thanks to the wine and the conversation, Mike had become quite animated. He seemed charming, slightly affected, almost feminine in the bond he was establishing with her. His eyes, reflecting the warm lights around them in a phantasmagoria of fairy-tale colours, were no longer ice-cold, but full of life and promise.

She preferred not to think it was all due to her presence, although the thought did cross her mind.

'You know Florence well. How long have you lived in Italy? You've never told me.'

'Four years, maybe five. I like it. I think I'm here to stay. Florence has brought me luck, you know? I came here as an art student, and started to write a few articles. They were accepted and went down well.'

'And now you're a famous journalist.'

'Well, I haven't won the Pulitzer yet, but it's true, I'm quite well known. And well paid.' He sounded pleased with himself.

'Do you only write about art and exhibitions?'

'Oh, no. I cover everything. Music, theatre, celebrity interviews . . . You may not believe it, but I'm actually quite an inquisitive person. I'm interested in everything, provided I can find an angle. It could be some news item, a murder, that kind of thing . . .'

'Brrr . . .' she said, playfully.

'Actually, criminal psychology is one of the most fascinating fields nowadays. Even here in Florence there are major crimes sometimes. You remember the Monster? What a story! I'm still trying to find the best way to present it to the American public. I may even write a book about it. And in Bologna, where you come from, isn't there a serial killer around right now?'

'Let's talk about something else, please,' she said, seriously this time. He was right, a maniac was killing prostitutes in Bologna. It was an unpleasant, rather frightening subject.

'Sure, no problem,' he said. 'Let's talk about you.'

'There's not much to say. I'm just an ordinary student trying to finish her studies.'

'And after that?'

'I'm so ordinary, I don't know yet. I'd like to go into films, TV, theatre, something like that. But I could just as easily end up as an assistant in a boutique. This is Italy, not America!'

'You can find America anywhere. You just have to want it. I found it in Italy.'

'Lucky you! Anyway, it's not true. You write for the *New York Times*, not the *Corriere della Sera* or *La Repubblica*.'

He smiled. '*Touché*. But if your country hadn't given me my first ideas for articles, I'd still be paying my dues in some newsroom in New York or Chicago.'

After dinner, he took her to the Piazzale Michelangelo, from where they had a view of the city similar to the one from their villa, only closer.

She especially liked to see the Arno, shimmering with the reflected lights of the river banks and buildings. Those brown waters seemed so agitated, so pitiless, so barely contained within the rigid lines of the banks, she marvelled that they had not yet swept away the Ponte Vecchio. From here, the bridge seemed so fragile and defenceless.

Just like me, she reflected as the Porsche sped past the Pitti Palace towards the Via Senese and then home. There, she was sure he would make the pass she was dreading, and she wouldn't know how to say no, how to tell him without hurting him that she wasn't interested in men, that this wasn't the reason she'd accepted either the apartment or his dinner invitation.

But she'd accepted both, she told herself.

And now it was payback time.

She was shaking as the tyres of the Porsche squealed on the gravel of the drive leading to the villa.

She had stomach cramps, and her face was pale and tense.

'Are you all right?' he asked, concerned. 'Was I driving too fast?'

'It's probably the wine,' she said apologetically. 'I'm not used to it.'

They went inside the house.

'Can you manage?' he asked. 'If you don't mind, I won't see you upstairs. I have an article to finish and fax by tomorrow morning. Good night.'

Cheering up, Valentina climbed the first flight of stairs, looking in her handbag for the key to her apartment as she did so.

On the second floor, sure that he hadn't followed her, she breathed a sigh of relief. She felt better now. Or so she thought.

Outside her door, she hesitated, and listened carefully for the sound of footsteps on the landings.

Nothing.

She put the key in the lock with a somewhat abrupt gesture. An observant psychologist would have said she was angry.

Father Francesco divided the mail according to who it was addressed to. The bigger of the two piles was for Don Sergio, who was in charge of book-keeping and had to check the many bills and invoices they received. But today, unusually, there was also a letter addressed to him personally.

'These are for you,' he said, handing out the envelopes to Don Sergio, who was sitting opposite him on the other side of the desk. 'Aren't you going to open them?'

'Yes, of course,' Don Sergio hastened to reply, and started looking at them slowly, one by one.

It seemed to Father Francesco that Don Sergio had been behaving strangely lately. More strangely than usual. Something was bothering him, some secret that, despite all Father Francesco's discreet attempts, he was reluctant to reveal.

Don Sergio was carefully sorting the mail into categories: bills, final demands, requests for help, a few rare contributions from generous parishioners. He had not yet opened the letter addressed to him personally.

'What about that one?' Father Francesco asked. He knew he was prying, but he considered it justified. He was genuinely worried about the young priest, even though he refrained from showing it openly.

Don Sergio opened the last envelope. When he saw what it contained, a confused look came into his eyes and his face turned pale.

'Bad news?' Father Francesco asked, concerned.

'Personal,' was all Don Sergio said, his voice sounding dry and ghostly.

'Observe particularly the interplay of lines and colours. See how the straight lines of the spears form a harmonious contrast to the deliberately accentuated roundness of the crossbows and the horses. And how the bright yellows and oranges, and the unusual blue of the fallen horses at the bottom here – can you all see them? – emphasise the noise of the battle, almost relegating to second place the fighting itself, which merges with the dark colours of the landscape in the background.'

They were in Room 7 of the Uffizi Gallery. It was six days after their dinner at Buca Lapi, Valentina's first visit to the Uffizi and the second time her American friend and landlord had taken her out.

The guide was explaining Uccello's *Battle of San Romano* to a group of bored, rowdy students.

Mike gestured to her to follow him. 'Let's skip this room, we can come back another day. These kids are unbearable. We must get to the next room before they do!'

Room 8 contained seven paintings by Filippo Lippi,

including the wonderful and very modern *Madonna with Child and Two Angels*, with its angel looking out at the spectator and its landscape like a separate painting.

'Brilliant, extraordinary,' Mike Ross said. 'My favourite painter. He's a bit like me.'

'In what way?'

'Well, he was an orphan, too. Abandoned by his widowed mother in front of the Monastery of Santa Maria del Carmine.'

'Were you . . .?'

'I'll tell you one day. When we know each other better.' He gave an ambiguous smile. 'The difference between him and me is that he liked women.'

Valentina was startled. Did that mean he . . .?

'Too much in fact,' he went on. 'He couldn't stop himself. And he was a monk. Not that that means anything. Priests and monks have always got up to all sorts of things. In the fifteenth century, and now, too. Filippo Lippi was so hot-blooded that when he was working for Cosimo de' Medici, Cosimo had to lock him in until he was finished, otherwise he'd have been out chasing skirts. They say he once climbed out the window using the classic ploy of tying the bedsheets together to make a rope!'

'Do you mean . . . you're gay?' Valentina finally blurted out, more interested in Mike than in the exploits of a Renaissance painter who sounded like a character from Boccaccio. She'd had to stop herself from adding the word 'too' to her question.

Of course, if he was, that would explain a lot of things. Why he didn't flirt with her, for a start. Why he had seemed so fascinated by the statues of powerful male nudes outside the Palazzo Vecchio, why every now and again his voice sounded oddly affected.

'Hold on, kid. Don't you think you're getting a bit personal?

That's another thing I'll tell you one day. But not now, and especially not here.'

'You seem to have a lot of things to tell me. And we don't have to stay here. I've already had enough. If I see any more masterpieces my brain will turn to mush. This museum's too big.'

'You're right. Every time we come, we should concentrate on just one or two things that interest us. That's the best way to see a big collection like the Louvre or the Met.'

'Shall we go, then?'

'All right, but not to talk about me. I still have something to show you. In fact, it's the reason I invited you out. It's very near here, in San Lorenzo. And there, there's no danger your brain will turn to mush, as you put it. It's a very small collection. But your eyes will pop out of your head.' He smiled enigmatically. 'I can guarantee that.'

They left the gallery.

It was eleven o'clock on a cold, damp day in the last week of January.

They cut across the Piazza della Signoria, where an icy wind was blowing, to the Via dei Calzaiuoli – so called, Mike explained, because the hosiery merchants had their shops here from the fourteenth to the sixteenth centuries.

Valentina felt uncomfortable. She didn't know whether to be irritated or amused that an American was telling her, an Italian, all about Italian artists and Italian cities. And she didn't know if the fact that her friend might be gay reassured or disappointed her.

It would certainly pacify Cinzia when she told her. But would she tell her? Mike had implied that it was an aspect of his life about which he preferred to be discreet, that he would open up only when he was sure she was worthy of his trust. Could she betray him before he had even talked to her?

Besides, she and Cinzia hadn't been in touch very often.

Four times in all, since she had left Bologna. They had not made peace, but they had agreed to a kind of truce over the phone, promising each other that they would meet again soon, in Bologna or Florence, but 'as friends'.

There were times, though, when she missed Cinzia, when she missed her a lot. Times when she would have liked to make love to her all night. She often woke from her sleep and these thoughts would keep her awake through hours of slow agony, haunted by memories of the past. All she needed was a sign and she would have run downstairs, got in her car, and left that enchanting house in Bellosguardo for ever, without a second thought.

Perhaps at times like those, she thought, she was like Filippo Lippi. But there were no sheets long enough to let her down from her terrace and take her all the way to Cinzia's apartment in Bologna. Or she just wasn't as brave as that old painter.

Not far from the Cathedral and the Baptistry, they came to the Romanesque church of San Lorenzo, with its austere unfinished façade.

'Michelangelo designed a façade,' her 'guide' explained, 'but it was never realised. Let's go in.'

It was a relief. The church was not particularly warm, but compared with the cold outside, it was comfortable.

'This way,' he said.

He led the way to Lippi's *Annunciation*.

'Don't you think it's remarkable?'

'The painting?'

'The resemblance,' he said, almost astonished that she had not noticed it right away.

'To the Madonna in the Uffizi, you mean?' Valentina asked, uncomprehending.

'No, no, they're very different. Look closely, doesn't she remind you of anyone?'

She looked at the beautiful Madonna – eyes lowered, hand raised in an eloquent gesture, clothes softly draped in such a way as to suggest her coming pregnancy – and still she did not understand. Who was the Madonna supposed to remind her of? A famous actress? A model?

She gave him a blank look.

He looked back at her, a mixture of surprise and amusement in his eyes. 'Don't you ever look at yourself in the mirror, kid?'

Valentina almost laughed out loud. Her? A Madonna? Was he mad? If only he knew, she thought. Maybe he was gay, maybe he wasn't. But there was nothing pure or holy about her! Yes, that was something she could tell Cinzia: Valentina the Madonna!

'It's you,' he insisted, in all seriousness.

'Stop it now,' she said, starting to get a little annoyed. 'Let's go.'

The Madonna's distracted gaze now seemed like a silent rebuke.

'Look at the line of the nose, the lips. The oval shape of the face. It's you. Even those wisps of blonde hair emerging from beneath the headcloth, just like yours the day you were wearing the purple bandana, do you remember? When I first saw you I was stunned. I'd just been here for the umpteenth time, because it's my favourite place in all Florence, and I thought history was playing a trick on me. It was as if you'd stepped straight out of the picture, changed your clothes and come to meet me in Greve.'

'Let's go, please,' she said, almost imploring.

On Monday 31 January Don Sergio Rotondi walked past the church of San Salvatore al Vescovo. It was raining so hard, his umbrella barely covered him, and his shoes and the bottoms of his trousers were soaked. When he got to Number 3, Piazza San Giovanni, he went in.

Inside the Curia of the Archbishop of Florence there was a sense of discreet elegance, and a muffled murmur that testified to the constant activity of those priests assigned to the administration of the diocese.

When he had explained the purpose of his visit, Don Sergio was directed to an office on the first floor, the office of Monsignor the Archbishop.

As he climbed the stairs, he turned the letter over nervously in his hands.

He had to wait twenty minutes before being admitted to another, smaller office. Here he was greeted by a prelate of about sixty, with beautifully groomed white hair. His small hands were equally well cared for, and he moved them gracefully as he spoke. 'Please sit down. I am Monsignor Federici. His Eminence has asked me to examine your case. Yours is a very, very unusual request.'

'I realise that.'

'I assume you've given it a lot of thought.'

'I have no choice.'

Monsignor Federici was watching him closely, his chin in his right hand, his lips pursed, his brow furrowed. 'The Church is no longer as inclined as it once was to . . . turn a blind eye, if you know what I mean. If the media get hold of the story . . .'

'But the Church can make exceptions.'

'If there are very, very serious reasons why it should. The Church can do anything – with the help of God.'

'Isn't a corrupted soul serious enough?'

The prelate thought this over. 'Have you brought the letter, as I asked?'

Don Sergio held it out to him.

The prelate took it, put on a pair of half-moon glasses and studied it.

'Good,' he said. 'I think His Eminence will receive you. I hope you're just as convincing when you speak to him. The Archbishop of Florence is a holy man, but he hates being bothered unnecessarily. He has many important duties to attend to in the diocese.'

He stood up and walked to the door. 'Wait for me,' he said, and went out.

He soon returned.

'Please follow me.'

5

Busy with the Monster of Florence case as well as the Lupi murder, Ferrara had not yet had time to show the anonymous message to his friend Massimo.

He finally did it on the last Saturday of that cold, harsh January, just before leaving for Sicily. Outside the bookshop, the rain was forcing pedestrians to take shelter in shops and doorways or, if they absolutely had to get on with their business, to hug the walls in order to take advantage of the overhanging roofs.

Massimo examined the letter for a long time, puffing calmly at a black pipe with a silver ring. 'I'm not that good at riddles,' he said at last. 'Maybe you could ask one of those people who do puzzles for newspapers. They must have an e-mail address and would just love to have people contact them with problems like yours!'

'I don't think it'd be appropriate in this case,' Ferrara grunted. 'This isn't a game.' He hesitated for a moment. 'It's not the first one I've received.'

'Well, that may help us. What did the others say?'

'There was only one. To be honest, I don't even know if they're connected. It was very different, more like a threat. The Latin motto *Memento mori*, do you know it?'

Massimo thought this over. 'Was that all?'

'Does it mean anything to you?'

'Quite a bit. To begin with, it's the title of a very good novel, written by someone who's almost a fellow citizen of ours. Actually, she's Scottish but she's been living near Arezzo for ages. Her name's Muriel Spark. She used to come in here occasionally. A delightful woman! If you paid more attention to me, you'd know about her. You really must read the book. I'll give you a copy on your way out. On the house, because I'm sure you'd never buy it. Petra would, but I'll give it to her anyway. Make her read it, she'll like it.'

'Drop it, Massimo. I don't have time, you know.'

'Bullshit! The excuse of the lazy and the ignorant. If you really want to, you make the time. Winston Churchill was a big reader, even in the middle of the Second World War. With all due respect, I find it hard to believe that a police superintendent has more on his plate than Churchill.'

'Okay, you're right, as usual. But seeing as you've read this book, does it hold the solution to my problem?'

'Maybe you should ask the author,' Massimo said. 'But after you've read it, please!' Then, turning serious again, 'But there's something else, which may link the two messages. Both of them have a religious element. *The last will be the first* is a quotation from the Gospels, and *Memento mori* is the motto of a religious order, the Trappists. Maybe this man is simply trying to convert you . . .'

Obviously it was a joke, but if it was meant to cheer Ferrara up a little, it didn't succeed. *Is this something to do with Don Sergio?* he thought.

'And from a literary point of view?' he asked.

'Well, that's my speciality. And that's what bothers me: I can't find any explanation. *The first will be the last*. What does it mean? That this one's the first and you won't receive any others, which would rule out the hypothesis of a connection? But what would be the point of that? If on the other hand both are from the same person, then our man is playing with paradoxes. Because how can you have a 'first' if there isn't a 'second'? And that would mean we're dealing with an intelligent person, someone with a bit of education. If that's the case, it won't be so easy to decipher the message. It probably refers to things we're not even aware of yet. In other words: expect more messages.'

And more murders? Ferrara wondered.

The answer to his question was not long in coming.

On the afternoon of Sunday 6 February, Lapo Vanni, who lived in an apartment in the Via de' Cerchi, a side street that ran parallel to the busy Via dei Calzaiuoli, noticed a bad smell coming from his neighbour's apartment as he was returning home after a ten-day holiday. Having knocked repeatedly on the door without getting a response, he had decided to phone the police.

The *Squadra Mobile* had responded immediately, but the officers sent had had to get the fire brigade in to help them. After ascertaining that the window looking out onto the street was closed and even protected by an iron grille, the firemen had forced open the door. At that point, nobody would have been surprised if they had found a dead body inside the apartment, perhaps someone who'd suddenly been taken ill and hadn't had time to call for help. But they were not prepared for what they did in fact find.

Kneeling on the ground with his torso face down on the bed, completely naked and in an advanced state of decomposition, was the body of a man, who was identified as the owner of the apartment. It was only a studio flat, but tastefully and expensively furnished.

By the time Ferrara arrived, his men were already there, along with a team from Homicide. Soon after, the pathologist – Dr Leone as usual – arrived with the forensics team. Prosecutor Gallo had also decided to be present. After what had happened in Como, Ferrara was not too keen on the idea.

Everyone wore overshoes provided by forensics in order not to contaminate the scene.

The dead man was thirty-two, and his name was Francesco Bianchi. He was not on the police database, not even for reporting lost documents. There was nothing on him at all. The way the murder had been carried out, on the other hand, was significant, especially to Ferrara. A few differences aside, it was a carbon copy of the Micali murder.

The first difference was a broken rose stem next to the body, the second the remnants of a crumbled cigar on the bloodstained sheets, the third a length of wire around the victim's neck, knotted into a noose, which had left a deep, narrow groove in the skin. Apart from that, there were two deep wounds in the man's back, others in the left upper part of the parietal region, clearly visible when Leone turned the body over, and many others on the face, curiously concentrated as in the Micali case. There were even wounds on the arms. All caused by a sharp instrument.

'Is it possible to establish the time of death?' Ferrara asked, not expecting a positive answer.

'From the state of decomposition,' Leone said, 'I'd certainly say days, maybe several. For the moment, it's difficult to establish how many days exactly. I'll be able to make a better estimate after the autopsy.'

The air in that small space was still unbreathable. The firemen had had to open the street window wide to let in some fresh air immediately after entering, but the smell of death clung to everything.

'Never seen anything like this,' Leone said, addressing both Ferrara and the Prosecutor, who were following his examination of the wounds closely.

'It looks as if it might have been some kind of erotic game,' Ferrara said, looking around. There were several elements that suggested this: the position of the body, the red scarf over the lampshade, the traces of burned incense, the red roses in the crystal vase on the eighteenth-century overmantel, the almost empty bottle of champagne on the bedside table.

'A game he was playing with the killer,' the Prosecutor said.

'Yes,' Ferrara said, although he seemed to be thinking of something else.

'If that's right, it could make your work easier, couldn't it?' Prosecutor Gallo asked. He was ultimately responsible for the success of the investigation and he was already starting to look impatient.

'It could. But don't forget the rose stem. Red roses are frequently used in black magic rituals. There are six in the vase. Seven if we count the stem by the body. A magic number. Then there's the crumbled cigar—'

'That's a reference to you,' the Prosecutor interrupted, clearly annoyed. He did not share Ferrara's interest in black magic and Satanism, and was afraid that Ferrara might even want to include this murder in his inquiries on the Monster of Florence: if that nightmare was revived, it would throw the whole city into a panic.

'You can take the body away now,' Leone said. 'My work is done. At least for today. Tomorrow we'll see what comes out of the autopsy.'

Before leaving with the doctor, Gallo gave Ferrara his instructions. It was up to Ferrara and his men to search the apartment: a bedroom, a kitchen and bathroom. But first he had to wait for the forensics team to finish their work.

The forensics people were already moving about in their white overalls, examining every space and every object. They had found a number of prints, notably on the crystal glasses next to the champagne bottle on the bedside table, and on the rim of the toilet bowl. They had also found bloodstains on the inside of the wash basin in the bathroom, which seemed to indicate that the killer had washed the knife after the murder. The knife itself had not been found.

Once the forensics team had finished, it was the turn of Ferrara's men to carry out a thorough search.

The whole operation did not take long, because there was not a great deal in the apartment. It seemed more like a pied-à-terre than a fixed abode. They did not find anything useful.

Ferrara decided to go back to Headquarters and get on with the interviews. Lapo Vanni was asked to follow them, along with the other residents who were at home that day.

'How did you come to discover the body?' was the first question Ferrara asked Vanni when they were in his office.

'Well, I didn't exactly discover him. I smelt him. I'd been away for ten days on holiday and I was struck by the stench coming from his apartment.'

'Wasn't there anyone in your apartment while you were away?'

'No. I'm a widower and live on my own. I have a son who works in France. That's where I've been.'

'When did you leave?'

'Ten days ago, I already said.'

'Did you see or hear your neighbour as you were leaving?'

'No. I didn't even notice if the apartment was occupied, but I don't suppose it was. This Francesco Bianchi wasn't around, he usually only came at weekends.'

'How well did you know him?'

'Hardly at all. Because, like I said, he wasn't there all the time. We'd occasionally meet on the stairs or the landing and say hello.'

'What do you know about him?'

'Almost nothing. I know he lived in Siena, and taught art history in senior high school. I also know he bought the apartment about four years ago because he loved Florence and liked to come here whenever his work permitted. At least that's what he told me on one of the few occasions we spoke.'

'How long have you lived in the Via de' Cerchi?'

'I've always lived there. It was my parents' apartment.'

'So you've known Bianchi since he arrived four years ago. Four years is quite a long time. It's a small building, I find it hard to believe you never exchanged anything more than polite chit-chat.'

'But that's how it was, Superintendent. I realise it may seem strange, but you have to remember that Bianchi wasn't there all the time, like I said. It was his second home.'

'Did you ever see him with anyone? A member of his family, a friend, another neighbour?'

'He was always alone when I saw him, and I'm pretty sure none of my neighbours spent any time with him. I'd have known if they had, we all get on pretty well.'

'I'd like you to think very carefully. Are you absolutely sure you never saw him with anyone? Male or female? After all, a studio apartment is most often used as a bachelor pad, isn't it?'

'I suppose so. But I swear I never saw him with anyone. I got the impression he wasn't married. I don't think he even had a girlfriend. It seemed to me he was a real scholar.'

'Signor Vanni, I think we'll have to talk again. In the meantime, see if you can remember anything else. You do realise you haven't really told us anything, don't you?' There was a touch of irritation in Ferrara's voice. 'I think you know what we're after.'

'Yes, I think so. But frankly, I don't think I can help you. I've heard it said that he sometimes came home with other men, men who were younger than him and – well, let's say of a lower class. I didn't mention it because it was just gossip, and I don't like gossip. I don't even remember who told me.'

'Please try to remember.'

The interview was over.

In the meantime, the few other residents, interviewed by Ferrara's men, had not come up with anything useful either. It was as if the man had never lived in their building. They knew nothing about him. He might as well have been a complete stranger.

It was very late by now and Ferrara decided to go home, getting through the crowd of journalists with a laconic 'No comment for the moment.'

The next day, Headquarters was like a madhouse. It seemed to Ferrara as if history was taking an ironic revenge, because the building *had* actually been a madhouse originally: the once famous Hospital of Bonifazio, the first psychiatric hospital in the modern sense, instituted between the end of the eighteenth century and the beginning of the nineteenth. Ferrara had not been surprised to learn that such an institution should have been built in a place like Florence, with its long history of dark deeds and strange urges. He had already become familiar with the ambiguous nature of the city.

The reason for the upheaval was the newspapers, who were lumping the latest murders together, blaming the police for their inefficiency, and lambasting a city government that was giving free rein to criminals, racketeers and murderers and failing to protect honest citizens.

They were particularly angry with Ferrara. They had believed him when he had told them that the antique dealer arrested for receiving stolen goods was probably also the killer, and had considered the case of the murder in the Via Santo Spirito closed, something about which the public could rest easy.

Now Ferrara's version of that case seemed almost like a fabrication to distract public opinion from what was really happening in the city. Many journalists connected the Lupi murder with the Bianchi slaying. Some even went back as far as the murder in Greve, but most concentrated on the deaths of Bianchi and Lupi. Both killings had taken place right in the centre of the city, in areas frequented by tourists, the second occurring little more than a month after the first.

The Commissioner had lost his usual composure and was going from office to office, looking for answers that nobody could give him. The press room was packed, and the clerk, bombarded with questions, was finding it hard to fend off the journalists. The superintendents were issuing orders to their subordinates just to keep them busy and have them seen to be busy. There was a constant coming and going of patrol cars.

Ferrara immediately summoned Rizzo, Sergi, Violante, Venturi and Ascalchi to an extraordinary meeting which would take all morning, having first left strict instructions that he was not to be disturbed by anyone. Not even the Commissioner.

'Have Leone call me as soon as he's finished the autopsy,' he said to Inspector Venturi. 'I want to know the results immediately without waiting for the report. Same with forensics.'

'Right away, chief,' Venturi said, picking up the phone.

'Gentlemen,' Ferrara said without waiting for him to finish, 'we need results. And soon. As you've seen, the press are up in arms. I want every available man working on this case, round the clock. Is that clear?'

'Very clear,' everyone nodded. Except Rizzo.

'What about the Monster?' he asked.

'Continue all current operations, but give yesterday's murder priority. Now let's see what theories we can come up with. The facts are well known. Anyone not clear on them should read the papers.'

They nodded again.

'Does anyone have any ideas?'

Gianni Ascalchi cleared his throat. 'In my opinion, this was clearly a sex crime.'

'If that's the case,' Rizzo said, 'we need to know if Bianchi was involved in some kind of erotic game that went too far, or if it was something else, I don't know, a vendetta, black-mail . . .'

'Venturi, make a note to check if any large sums of money have gone in or out of Bianchi's bank account lately. In any case, the man's private life will have to be turned inside out. What else?'

'The black magic aspect,' Serpico suggested.

'Right. We need to look into that. The two things could be connected, of course.'

'The MO is very similar to that in the Micali case,' Rizzo said. 'Both men were gay.'

'Precisely. And that would open up a very disturbing pos-sibility. The newspapers are already doing everything they can to link the three murders. If they really are connected, then what we're looking at is a serial killer.'

Those two words had been in the air since the beginning of the meeting. They were already present by implication in some of the newspaper reports. Silence fell. It was as if the

Monster of Florence case, with all its complications, were hanging before them in the heavy air like a rock. There, too, they had started out with the idea of a serial killer, and years later they were still working on it!

The phenomenon of the serial killer had been practically unknown in the annals of the Italian police almost until the end of the eighties, but since then it seemed to have spread like an oil stain. Everyone was talking about it, thrillers were written about it, the media had jumped on the bandwagon, and meanwhile the police were trudging along trying desperately to keep up with the help of experts from the FBI, who were much more familiar with the subject.

What they all knew was that a serial killer was a lone wolf, which made him one of the most difficult kinds of criminal to track down.

If they really were dealing with a serial killer, the prospects were bleak.

'Lupi's murder doesn't fit,' Chief Inspector Violante protested. 'He was a married man with a son.'

'Don't forget the nature of his wounds, Inspector. Even though I myself, wrongly perhaps, thought the case was closed when we arrested Salustri, officially it isn't closed at all. I think you'd do well to look into it again, starting with Alfredo Lupi's private life. Especially as . . .'

Ferrara considered the moment had come to tell his men about the anonymous letters he had received. They might not constitute much of a lead, but with the death of Francesco Bianchi from wounds not so dissimilar from those on the other two dead men, they could no longer be disregarded.

His men reacted as he had expected, including some veiled reproaches for his having kept them in the dark about the threats, but he preferred not to tell them the real reasons he had kept silent until now.

'But there isn't a third letter,' Ascalchi said, 'even though there does seem to be a third crime.'

'Maybe the killer thought the crumbled cigar was enough. That's a message, too. To tell the truth I don't know. Maybe you're right. Maybe it's just speculation, and might lead us astray, so let's not give it any more weight than we should. Let's just keep it in mind, that's all.'

'Lupi wasn't a homosexual,' Violante insisted, annoyed perhaps at having to deal with that case again.

'The second letter in particular seems like a challenge to the police,' Rizzo said. 'That's typical of serial killers. They always think they're cleverer and more intelligent than we are.'

Again, a heavy silence fell over Ferrara's office.

Leone called just before midday. The results of the autopsy confirmed some of the theories on which they were already working, but also added some details that might subsequently prove decisive.

The death had been caused by asphyxia. The dead man had previously consumed both drugs and alcohol. The knife wounds, of which there were no less than thirty-five, had not been fatal, not even the two deep wounds in the back. The victim had been stabbed in the back first, then tortured and finally strangled to death. The crime had occurred between nine o'clock and midnight on Wednesday 2 February 2000: four days before the body was discovered.

'Finally,' Leone said, 'I found traces of sperm in the anus, as well as residues of Vaseline.'

Immediately afterwards a call came from forensics. All the fingerprints found in the apartment were the victim's, apart from those on one of the two crystal glasses and on the rim of the toilet bowl. They did not match any prints in police records. Even the blood in the wash basin had turned out to be the victim's, which confirmed that the killer had washed the knife after use.

Ferrara passed on what he had learned from these two calls, distributed tasks, and declared the meeting closed.

In the days that followed, the image of Francesco Bianchi came into clearer focus.

He was indeed gay, and a man of some social standing. He lived in Siena, but often spent weekends in Florence, as confirmed by his sister and a nephew who lived with him.

According to these two, Francesco Bianchi had left Siena on Sunday 30 January to spend a few days, perhaps even a week, in Florence, taking advantage of a short period of leave in order to make some progress with his research on an art history project. They had added that relations between them had soured recently, due to some problems connected with their inheritance, and they had both thought that he had used his research merely as a pretext to get away from home and ponder his next move.

That was why they hadn't tried to reach him by phone and hadn't been surprised that he had made no attempt to contact them. They knew nothing about his friends and acquaintances in Florence, not even if he had any.

And yet instinct told Ferrara that Florence was the place to look. Of course, it couldn't be ruled out that he may have brought a friend with him from Siena, and he had asked the police there to make all the inquiries they could. But he was just covering himself: it was more than likely that the professor had tried to keep up his image in his own city and had chosen Florence as the place where he could give free rein to his true sexual leanings, as the purchase of the apartment – and the gossip – suggested.

Ferrara had passed the case on to Serpico, authorising him to make whatever inquiries he had to make – and even mount raids if he had to – in Florence's gay circles. Homosexual encounters took place mainly in the Parco delle Cascine, the railway station of Santa Maria Novella, and – for some time now – a porno cinema in the south of the city.

For days on end, the *Squadra Mobile* offices were filled with rent boys, most of them foreigners. Foreigners were the most in demand because they didn't ask for much money.

They were unemployed young men of no fixed abode, almost all of them illegal, driven by poverty to satisfy their benefactors' desires, and sometimes their perversions, in return for a lunch, an item of clothing, the chance to call their families at home from the phone in their client's house, or even just the opportunity to take a shower.

None of them recognised, or admitted to recognising, Francesco Bianchi from the photo they were shown.

Ferrara had also asked the phone company for a printout of calls made to and from the victim's Florence apartment, and had put a tap on the home telephone of his sister in Siena.

But nothing useful had emerged.

In the end, the only clue they had found that was of any use was the traces of sperm in the victim's anus. Thanks to laboratory analysis by the forensics team, they now had the killer's DNA. But it was an abstraction. Who did it correspond to in reality? They didn't yet have a single suspect.

By the end of the week they seemed to have reached a dead end. Meanwhile, the press were becoming more strident with every day that passed. And Ferrara was starting to think they were right.

*

A similar fear was being expressed at that moment on an upper floor of Police Headquarters, where Prosecutor Gallo and Commissioner Lepri were meeting to evaluate the situation.

'I don't get the impression Ferrara knows what he's doing this time around,' Gallo was saying.

'Some investigations take time, you know that,' was Lepri's bland attempt at defence, immediately contradicted by adding, 'but time is precisely what we don't have. Two murders in a month right in the middle of the town, without a single clue, a single suspect, and nothing to give the press . . .'

'Maybe I've been too patient. Ferrara has excellent credentials, and a distinguished career behind him, but he's not himself any more. This obsession with black magic and high-level conspiracies will be the ruin of him.'

'Believe me, I've asked him to exercise a bit more caution and not let things get out of hand. It's easy to get bogged down in all this meaningless nonsense. Most of the time it turns out to be just smoke without fire. And in the meantime we're wasting time.'

'And the real murderers are still free.'

'Then there's . . .' the Commissioner fell silent, letting his gaze wander over the magnificent fresco on the ceiling of his sumptuous office: one of the privileges a State with an incomparable artistic heritage bestows on its most prestigious servants.

'Yes?' Gallo prompted him.

'Remember that TV broadcast he did? I wouldn't like him to think he can display himself to the public as some kind of hero who's better than the rest of us.'

He was referring to a popular talk show which had devoted an edition to the Monster of Florence the previous summer.

Ferrara had taken part along with a psychiatrist, a well known criminologist, a university researcher with an interest in the occult – because they were already talking at the time about the new line that Ferrara was pursuing – and to add a touch of colour, a very pretty young actress who had played a police-woman in a successful TV movie. Although Ferrara didn't usually like the limelight, he had thought it a worthwhile exercise that would make it clear to anyone who had ears to hear that the circle was closing in. But it had resulted in his becoming a popular celebrity for a while – something his superiors had not greatly appreciated.

'If he wanted to be an idol he should have become an actor,' Gallo said. 'The Prosecutor's Department has more serious things to think about. Ferrara will have to adapt. And soon.'

'What do you intend to do?'

'Nothing for the moment. But if he doesn't bring me results soon, I'll have to intervene.'

The Commissioner reflected. 'I'll talk to him,' he said.

'Go ahead, if you think it'll do any good. But I warn you that if things don't change I may have to oppose his promotion – or worse.'

'Isn't that excessive? Chief Superintendent Ferrara is still a servant of the State like us . . .'

'That's why he needs to toe the line.'

'What do you mean?'

'All he ever thinks about is the Monster of Florence, even after all these years. He almost never comes to the Prosecutor's Department, and when he does show his face, he shuts himself up in an office with a colleague of mine who's following the case. The only time I've seen him lately was over that Salustri business, and he made me go with him all the way to the border on a journey that turned out to be pointless. The deputy prosecutors come to me and complain they don't have anyone to turn to any more in Police Headquarters!'

'All right. I'll see if I can figure out a way to get him back on board.'

'Do it, but let's be clear about one thing: either Ferrara goes back to being the head of the *Squadra Mobile*, *all* the *Squadra Mobile*, or I could see myself being forced to write directly to the Head of Police asking for him to be demoted.'

On Sunday, Chief Inspector Violante came into the office.

He only had a few months to go before he retired, and he couldn't wait. He had spent his whole life in the police force and it had left him feeling bitter and unfulfilled. His sons, teenagers in the eighties, had got rich on the easy money circulating in certain circles in those days, and had never made any bones about the fact that they were ashamed their father had never risen further than being a mere cog in the machinery of State.

But he himself had never felt ashamed, and even though he was glad that he'd soon be able to rest at last, he still wanted to see his work through to the end. He knew what many of his colleagues thought of him, but he didn't care.

He had decided to take advantage of the relative calm of Sunday to go back over the file on the Lupi case, checking through all the reports and witness statements.

That was how he came across a report by the officer on duty at the switchboard on 24 January that threw new light on the case.

An anonymous phone call had come in that day. There are always a lot of them after a murder, most of them from cranks. But they always have to be checked out, especially where there are no other clues, if only to be able to say later that nothing has been neglected.

The anonymous caller had mentioned the name Antonio Gori, had described him as a 'friend' of the murdered man, and had asked the police to investigate their relationship.

The call had not been recorded, because the switchboard was not yet equipped with a tape recorder, but the officer had nevertheless prepared a detailed report in which he had emphasised how insistent the anonymous caller had been that the relationship was a homosexual one – after Violante had persisted in denying that Lupi was gay in front of everyone.

Violante felt stupid for having dismissed the report instead of passing it on to Ferrara. The call might indeed have been a crank call, but then again it might not have been.

His one excuse was that the call had come in right in the middle of the operation that had led to the arrest of Antonio Salustri. At the time, they had been sure that the murder was connected with the antiques racket, and there had been little doubt in their minds that Salustri was the killer.

But it was no excuse really: he had been a fool.

A fool, but an honest one, who would never dream of hiding his mistakes. Even when a man was close to retirement, he was still responsible for his own actions and had to account for them. Even a policeman. Especially a policeman, he told himself. How else could he presume to put handcuffs on other men's wrists?

'Congratulations, Violante,' Ferrara said on the morning of Monday 14 February. 'Excellent work!'

He was genuinely pleased. Full of admiration, too. This short-sighted, nondescript little man, who all too often seemed like a shirker, was actually one of those pillars on whom the whole apparatus of the State rests, even if nobody knew, or wanted to know about him.

'Before we summon this Gori, check him out as much as you can.'

'I've already put Inspector Venturi onto it, chief.'

Ferrara looked at him again with respect, regretting the fact that he would soon be leaving them.

Over the next two days Inspector Venturi discovered that Alfredo Lupi and Antonio Gori had indeed been seeing each other regularly for some time.

Ferrara decided it was time to question him. It had to be done immediately, before Gori had had time to think of an alibi. The judge wouldn't authorise a phone tap on the basis of an anonymous call, especially one that hadn't even been recorded. It wasn't enough to go on. So he asked Gori to come in that evening, Wednesday 16th.

'Good evening, Chief Superintendent!'

Antonio Gori was short, well shaven, neatly dressed, scented, but not effeminate.

'Good evening. Please take a seat.'

'What's this all about? Why have you asked me here at this hour? The officer who delivered the summons didn't give me any explanation. He just told me you wanted to talk to me.'

'That's right. I have to ask you some questions and take a statement from you.'

'A statement?' the man said in surprise.

'Did you know Alfredo Lupi?' Ferrara asked, abruptly. 'Before you answer, I want you to know that we haven't called you in at random. We have evidence that pointed us in your direction.'

'I knew it, I knew it!' He shook his head disconsolately. 'Yes, I knew poor Alfredo and I'm very upset about what happened to him.'

'So why didn't you come to us of your own free will?'

'Why? Should I have? I had nothing to do with . . .'

'How did you meet?' Ferrara asked, implacably.

'It happened about three years ago . . .' He broke off.

'It's all right, Signor Gori! You can talk freely here. Tell us the truth. If you have nothing to hide . . .'

'It's not that. I don't have anything to hide. It's just that it's not easy to explain.'

'It's okay. We're adults, you can talk freely. Don't be afraid – we're not charging you with anything. We have some information, and we're hoping you can confirm it, and perhaps even clarify it for us. That's all.'

'I'll tell you what you want to know, but can we keep it confidential? I wouldn't like my family to find out.'

'I'll do all I can. You have my word.'

'I met Alfredo through an ad he'd placed in a local paper. 'Thirty-year-old male seeks active partner . . .' that kind of thing. We arranged to meet in the Piazza Libertà. We both felt an immediate physical attraction to each other and decided to meet again. That first time, he told me he preferred the submissive role, which was fine with me. We arranged to meet in a week, at the Florence South tollgate.

'It wasn't easy at first because Alfredo would only have sex indoors. He was afraid we'd be spotted if we did it in the car.

'That's why we decided to get our families involved. We wanted to make our friendship look normal. My wife and his became great friends and Alfredo and I were able to meet more frequently. The four of us even went abroad on holiday together. Nobody in either family ever suspected our relationship.

'Actually, the first time we went abroad, to Romania, it was just the two of us. That's where we first made love properly. After that, there were other times when we went away together. At weekends we often went to Cortina, where I have a studio apartment. We were there for a couple of days not long before he was killed.'

'And did he tell you about any problems he had, anything he was afraid of? Please try to remember. If you know anything, now's your chance to tell us.'

'But I don't know anything. He didn't say anything about any problems, he seemed the same as usual. I can't imagine who could have killed him or why. I'd like to help you find the killer – Alfredo was a dear friend and I miss him a lot – but I don't know anything else.'

'All right, thank you. You can go now.'

Ferrara immediately asked the Prosecutor for permission to tap Gori's phone. Gallo, relieved that things had started moving again, had no hesitation in issuing the authorization. They weren't dealing just with an anonymous tip-off any more, there were concrete facts now that needed to be confirmed as soon as possible. It was even in Gori's best interests, so that they could eliminate him from their inquiries.

That was why Ferrara had preferred not to ask him what he had been doing on the morning of 31 December. They'd be in a better position to tackle that question, if they had to, once they knew a bit more.

Two officers were sent to Cortina to find out about the last time the couple had stayed there, others made discreet inquiries about Gori's other relationships, and his wife was questioned, as was Lupi's widow for the second time.

But it all led nowhere. As the days went by, the initial burst of optimism gradually gave way to a sense of frustration.

Antonio Gori turned out to have no connection with the murder, and Lupi's wife was completely unaware of her husband's double life. Ferrara took care not to reveal it to her, convinced as he was that knowing about it would only make her grief harder to bear.

On Monday 21 February – Ascalchi had just informed him that another prostitute had been found murdered in Bologna – Ferrara realised that the only thing they knew for certain after all this activity was that Lupi had been gay. With all that this discovery implied.

Just like Bologna, Florence had its very own serial killer.

Gianni Ascalchi summed up the situation with a crude comment which was to remain famous for a long time at Police Headquarters: 'What a mess! The Bolognese are butchering whores, the Florentines are slicing queers; I'd have done better staying in Rome.'

6

That night Valentina slept badly.

In her sleep she thought she heard footsteps on the floor below, someone breathing heavily, mournfully.

When she had gone to bed, about midnight, Mike Ross was still out. Being all on her own in that big, isolated villa was an unnerving experience. Especially since, following the advice of that bookseller – advice that had been greeted with enthusiasm by her supervisor in Bologna and the assistant professor in Florence – she had been immersing herself in the study of Renaissance magic, and would drop off to sleep thinking about being burned at the stake and priests officiating at human sacrifices . . .

Next morning, when she leaned out of the window, she saw Mike's Porsche parked outside, next to her Panda.

That cheered her up. She went down to the garden and walked up to the kitchen window. Inside, the Filipino woman was bustling about with the pots and pans.

'Nenita,' she called as softly as she could, in order not to wake Mike, who must still be asleep.

'Yes?' the woman replied, gesturing to her to go to the door, which she ran to open.

'I'm sorry, Nenita, but what's on the first floor?'

'Sorry, madam, no understand,' Nenita replied, smiling.

'The first floor.'

'Yes?' Nenita said again.

'What's up there?' Valentina insisted, pointing upwards. 'First floor!'

'Oh yes, first floor,' Nenita replied, smiling broadly to indicate that she had understood. 'That is first floor.'

'Yes, but . . . what's *on* the first floor?'

'Sorry, signora . . .' Nenita smiled and shrugged her shoulders.

'I see, you don't understand.'

Valentina left the house exasperated. '*If you need anything, just ask Nenita,*' she repeated to herself, mimicking Mike's accent. 'Oh, you can ask all right, but she doesn't understand a word!'

She decided she'd have it out with Mike when she got back from university . . .

The assistant professor's class focused on the first chapter of a book by the Italian historian Carlo Ginzburg, *Myths, Emblems, Clues*. The theme of the chapter was "Witchcraft and Popular Piety".

Valentina found it fascinating.

She hadn't yet read anything by Ginzburg, but promised herself she would get hold of some of his books. And maybe one day she'd go and see him. She knew Ginzburg lived in Bologna, even though he was often abroad. She had never attended any of his classes, and now she regretted it.

Thinking of Bologna reminded her of Cinzia.

When she left the university, she went to a bar to have a sandwich and took the opportunity to call her. They hadn't spoken in a long time.

From her friend's mobile the only response was the

message 'The number you have called is not available at the moment . . .'

She tried her at home.

'Hello?' The voice was female, but it wasn't Cinzia's.

'I'd like to speak to Cinzia Roberti. Is she there?'

'Who is that?'

'Valentina. Valentina Preti.'

'Just a moment.'

She could tell that the girl was covering the receiver with one hand while she conferred with Cinzia.

Cinzia's voice came on the line. 'Hi, Vale. What do you want?'

'Just wanted to say hello. How are you?'

'Fine, thanks, and you?' Her voice was neutral, neither annoyed nor affectionate.

'Me too. Who . . . who answered the phone?'

'Chiara. You don't know her. Chiara, say "hi" to my friend Valentina.'

'Hi, Valentina,' she heard in the distance. The girl was giggling, perhaps sarcastically. Or else quite innocently.

All the same, she felt offended, humiliated.

She hated this Chiara, even though she didn't know her.

'Is everything really all right?'

'Absolutely fine, don't worry. How's your course?'

'Okay.'

'And what about . . . your American friend?'

'He's . . .' She held back. 'He's harmless. Really. I'll introduce you. He's a nice man, he's never tried anything. It hasn't even occurred to him.'

'Either he's gay, Vale, or your charms are failing.'

'Not all men are the same!' she protested. Later, she would wonder why she'd felt such an immediate need to defend him.

'No, but they all want the same thing. You know that, don't you?'

'Not him, I can guarantee it. You ought to meet him, I'd like you to meet him. You'd change your mind about him.'

'If that's the only way to see you again, I'd bear even that.'

Valentina's heart skipped a beat. But if she really wanted that, why was she being so aggressive?

'It's not the only way, you know.'

'But you've never been back to Bologna. It's February 7th now. More than a month.'

She felt guilty. 'You've never come to Florence either,' she protested weakly, knowing that the fault was all hers.

Or maybe not all hers. Who was this Chiara?

'Our home is here, not there.'

'You're right. I'll come and see you soon, I promise.'

'Okay, see you. Bye.'

'Bye.'

She put down the phone, irritably. If it was 'our home', what was that bitch Chiara doing there?

'So, the *Squadra Mobile* are now looking into the possibility of – what shall we call it – there being Satanists involved?'

'Well, it's one of the areas we're investigating.'

'In other words, there are reasons for you to suspect that these crimes were initiated within some kind of occult environment. What do you think, Professor?'

'It's a fact that in Italy, indeed all over the world, there's a subculture of tiny groups who are interested in black magic and other occult practices. Within these groups, it's believed that through the most abstruse and bizarre rituals, some people can become supermen and superwomen. Some of their rituals have a strongly sexual element, and may even involve some kind of sacrifice, even human sacrifice . . .'

The voices were coming from inside the villa.

Valentina had decided not to ring at the door of his apartment, but to confront Mike directly. She had come through the garden and was now standing outside the French windows.

It was the first time she'd done this. And it would also be the first time she'd set foot in the part of the house where he lived.

He had never invited her.

She looked through the window and the white linen curtain. Mike was sitting comfortably in an armchair, his feet propped on a small, low marble table, in front of the television. The discussion she had heard was coming from the programme he was watching.

She knocked on the glass.

Surprised, Mike got up, came to the French windows and opened them.

'Hi,' he said. He seemed embarrassed.

'May I come in?' she asked.

'Sure, come in. You've never been in the lion's den before.'

'You've never asked me.'

'It didn't seem right.'

'Well, now I've summoned up the courage to do it myself. But I had to talk to you. We need to settle our accounts, it's been a month already.'

'That's true. Sit down.' He switched off the TV with the remote control.

'What was that?' Valentina asked.

'A tape I recorded last year. A programme about the Monster of Florence.'

'Are you still thinking of writing a book? Were they talking about black magic? It might be useful for my thesis.'

'If you like, I can switch it on again.'

'Maybe later. Let's talk first.'

'Okay. Can I fix you a drink?'

'No, thanks.'

'Coffee, tea?'

'No, really, I'm fine.'

Mike went to a low wooden cabinet with a beautiful inlaid surface and took out a bottle of whisky and a glass for himself.

The room was surprisingly spacious and luxurious. From the frescoed ceiling hung a huge crystal chandelier with at least two dozen drop-shaped bulbs. The walls and ceiling were decorated with elaborate stuccoes; large, valuable-looking paintings – landscapes and religious scenes – in elaborate gilded frames hung on the walls. The armchairs and sofas were beautifully upholstered, and the polished terracotta floor was strewn with large rugs. The dominant colours were red and yellow. To Valentina, it seemed like something out of a costume drama: a cardinal's drawing room, that kind of thing.

'Remarkable, isn't it?' Mike Ross said, as she looked around.

'Amazing. I thought it was just a big old house in the country originally, not a real villa.'

'Maybe it was. One of the previous owners was a famous antique dealer. He's the one who refurbished it.'

'He must have been very rich.'

'So they say.'

'How did you get it?'

'Friends at the bank.'

'It must cost a fortune.'

'If you really want to know, the newspaper pays for it! Including your apartment. That's why I can't —'

'No, Mike, it's still not right.'

He pressed a button on the remote control and sat down next to her. 'You said you were interested in the tape, right? Let's have a look.' He started the programme again.

'That's Chief Superintendent Ferrara, head of the Florence *Squadra Mobile*,' he explained, freezing the image on a close up of the policeman. 'An interesting guy. He's the one who reopened the case of the Monster of Florence after the killer had been arrested and everyone thought the case was closed. He actually tracked down two accomplices. Even the FBI had assumed the killer had acted on his own! Now he says there were other people behind him, paying him to carry out the murders. Look.'

The image jerked back into life. 'So, Chief Superintendent,' the host was saying, 'you believe that those who paid for the murders are still at large.' He turned to the criminologist. 'What do you think of that, professor?'

'It would be the first such case in history. Maniacs commit crimes, they don't commission them. Their pleasure lies in killing, cutting, disposing of the pieces . . . a serial killer obeying orders doesn't make sense to me.'

'But there is some evidence of Satanic rituals, isn't there, Chief Superintendent?'

'I'd like to stick with the facts. And it's a fact that during the trial of the Monster's accomplices, certain things emerged that . . . Here, let me read you what the judges said, and don't forget the appeal court upheld the judgement. I quote: "Clues have emerged which indicate that there may have been a third party financing the crimes we have considered in this trial." *Clues have emerged.* The implication is clear. We have to continue with our investigations. It's our duty.'

The man was about fifty, spoke with a slight Sicilian accent, and looked pleasant and well groomed. He was wearing a dark grey suit, a sky-blue shirt and a blue tie. His hair –

long black hair, combed back and streaked with white at the sides – partly covered his ears. And his sideburns were white, in contrast with the thick black eyebrows which accentuated the shape of the eyes.

A cat's eyes, Valentina thought.

He spoke calmly, quietly, measuring his words. She thought she detected a sly expression on his face as he spoke, almost as if to underline the feline effect of his eyes.

'We're going to show some file footage of Chief Superintendent Ferrara, head of the Florence *Squadra Mobile*,' the host said, 'to give our viewers some background on the man leading the hunt for the Monster's paymasters – supposing there are any.'

'Look at this,' Mike said, watching the screen with rapt attention.

The footage showed Ferrara, at least twenty years younger, in charge of a team that had surrounded a building. Beneath the image, the caption: *Reggio Calabria, August 1978.*

Michele Ferrara, wearing a bulletproof vest, had climbed onto the roof of a police car and was firing a volley, one shot after the other, at one of the windows in the building. A group of men were seen backing away from the windows to avoid the bullets.

One of the men looked as if he had been hit and fell to the floor, but it was hard to be sure. The image was blurred: the footage may have been shot by an amateur or off the cuff by one of the police officers.

'He killed that one,' Mike said.

'Maybe not,' Valentina replied, curiously involved in these images even though they were of no great interest to her.

'He did,' Mike insisted, almost irritably. 'He killed him.'

'But they were gangsters, weren't they? I don't suppose you Americans treat gangsters with kid gloves, either.'

Mike said nothing. He was following the action as if hypnotised.

The men inside the building tried to escape through the back door, but Ferrara's men were waiting for them in large numbers. The last image was of the gangsters being led in handcuffs to the police cars and vans.

Among them was a woman.

Mike pressed a button on the remote, and the screen went black.

'And the bit about magic?' Valentina asked.

'Some other time. I've had enough for today.'

He did seem tired. Valentina didn't insist. Instead, she took out her chequebook.

Mike looked at her in surprise. 'Listen, kid. Maybe I haven't made myself clear. I didn't ask you to stay here to make money on something that's already paid for by my newspaper.'

'So why *did* you ask me to stay here?'

'Because you remind me of Lippi's Madonna? I don't know. You're the only woman I've ever felt at ease with. The only one I've ever really liked.'

It sounded as if it hadn't been easy for him to say these words, and she thought it was sweet of him.

'If you want to stay, I'll be very pleased,' he said. 'If you want to pay, find a hotel.'

'I'll stay. But on one condition.'

'What's that?' he asked, smiling.

'You tell me what's on the first floor.'

Mike hesitated. 'You mean . . . up there?'

'That's right. Just below my apartment.'

'There's nothing there! Only ashes and rubble. It was almost completely destroyed in a fire when the antique dealer still lived here. The second floor was saved by a miracle. And also one bedroom on the first floor, it must have been their son's. He was a teenager at the time. The new owners never touched it. It's awful up there, dark, walls blackened by smoke, completely empty. They put new window panes in to make the front of the house look presentable, that's all.'

'And no one lives there?'

He laughed. 'How could they? There's nothing there, like I said. Apart from the one bedroom. I go in there sometimes, when I feel stressed out. For some reason, it relaxes me . . .'

'Were you in there last night?'

Mike's face seemed to harden. 'Last night?' he replied curtly. 'Absolutely not.'

'But I heard —'

'You must have imagined it.'

'It really sounded like footsteps. And someone sighing, as if they were very unhappy . . .'

Mike frowned. He seemed troubled, his thoughts in turmoil. 'I understand,' he said after a long pause. 'This house is quite isolated. It can be scary . . . I'll try to make sure you're not left alone at night any more. It's a good thing you don't have anything to fear from someone like me. You're a beautiful girl, anyone else would find the temptation too great.'

'You haven't yet explained what "someone like you" means,' she said, in a conciliatory tone.

'I don't know myself. You asked me if I'm gay. I don't know. I've had experiences with men . . . Let's go outside, I don't like talking in here.'

It was an unusually mild day, the first small sign that spring was on its way. The sun cast a soft, pale light on the garden paths. The grounds of the villa were well tended: Valentina had occasionally caught a glimpse of a gardener.

'Do I like going with men?' he said as they walked towards

the far end of the grounds, between rows of vines and olives. 'I don't think so. But it's like a curse. Every now and again, it takes me over and then it's as if I can't resist. I go looking for them. I absolutely have to find an outlet for these feelings. I think basically homosexuals disgust me. But at the same time they attract me – I don't know how to explain it, I told you, it's a curse.'

Valentina was stunned. She wondered if she too, deep down, really only wanted other women. Cinzia had cast a spell on her. Ever since they were children. But what if there was someone else besides Cinzia? What if there was a man like this, who had the same problem as hers?

'Do you have a boyfriend?'

'No. Never. It would be like admitting I'm gay, and I refuse to do that.'

She was about to say something about herself, but decided not to. Right now, Cinzia was with Chiara . . .

'So . . . what do you do?'

'To find an outlet for my feelings, you mean? I go looking for men, at night. There are plenty around. I use them, I pay them, and that's the end of it.'

'How about with a woman . . . have you ever tried?' It had come out naturally, spontaneously.

He stopped, looked her in the eyes and put a hand on her shoulder.

Valentina was moved. She felt a bond between them.

'No woman is worth the effort, Valentina. Sex is a struggle, a combat. It's like some kind of Greco-Roman wrestling contest, you know what I mean? Bodies clinging and writhing, teeth grinding, heavy breathing, the stench of sweat. It's a man's sport.'

'Only if there's no love.' She said it without thinking, and surprised even herself.

Mike's hand was touching her, and Valentina was tempted to lay her head on his strong shoulder.

The sun was setting, and they started back.

'Maybe,' he said. 'But I've never known what love is.'

What about her? Was it true love that had bound her to another woman? Suddenly she felt impoverished, as if she'd been cheated of an important part of life.

'It's a pity you're not a woman,' Mike said, 'only a vision. A Renaissance Madonna.'

'You embarrass me.'

'Why?'

'Because you don't think of me as a woman. Who knows, maybe you should try.'

It came out like sounding like a challenge. She hadn't meant to say anything like that. Perhaps it was the thought that in a few hours, in 'their' apartment in Bologna, Cinzia might be sharing 'their' bed with someone else . . .

'There'd be no point.'

They were lying completely naked on his big four-poster bed.

The room was enormous, with a fire in the hearth and heavy curtains at the windows and hanging from the canopy above the bed.

Valentina's hand was on Mike's penis, which had remained inert the whole time.

'I told you,' he said. 'It's pointless.'

She didn't mind.

She was surprised that she could touch his penis without feeling any disgust, but sympathy and tenderness instead. It didn't seem 'hideous', but soft, delicate, almost lovable. She remembered the ones she'd seen on statues, harmonious and inoffensive, so different from those obscene, erect rods in pornographic photos and films.

It was like a defenceless child, and she would have liked to continue stroking it, perhaps even kiss it.

She felt curiously free and happy. Cinzia was far from her mind. Right now, she didn't care a jot for Cinzia.

'You know something?' she said on impulse. 'I think I'm in love with you.'

The penis didn't react, and nor did Mike.

Valentina turned over.

She felt exhausted. It had been a trying day, a day of too many emotions.

Rocked by his rhythmic breathing, she fell into a deep sleep.

A languid dampness between her buttocks.

Perhaps a caress, but insistent. Insinuating.

Valentina moved slightly in her sleep, and realised that sturdy, athletic arms held her in a vice-like grip. She heard laboured breathing in her ear, and felt an unfamiliar, imposing, constricting weight on her body.

She didn't feel as if she had woken up. She didn't want to. Maybe she was only dreaming that she'd woken up . . .

She waited, frozen, terrified, yet yearning.

The unfamiliar weight was concentrated between her legs, which were wide open. It became hard and pressing. It insinuated itself with unprecedented force between the folds of her flesh and she realised all at once that it was too late to stop it now.

'No!' she cried. 'Not there!'

Now she was wide awake, feeling the pain that was ripping her open, the obscene intrusion into the wrong part of her body.

'NOOOOOOO!!!'

Mike had raised himself on his arms and was thrusting

into her, grunting 'Mother, mother' between plaintive sighs.

Valentina wept with the pain, as Mike, undaunted, unstoppable, obsessive, sodomised her.

When he came back from the bathroom, he was as white as a corpse.

He did not dare lie down next to her. He sat down on the edge of the bed, shamefaced.

Valentina was still crying. She didn't dare move, she was afraid it would hurt if she did.

'I . . . I don't know what came over me. I swear to you. It was like . . . I don't know! I'm a monster, Valentina, a monster! How *could* I?'

She turned slowly towards him. Without saying a word, she gestured to him to lie down.

She placed a hand on his chest. 'It's possible,' she murmured, 'that I still love you.'

She didn't understand what was happening. This man had just defiled her, but she was quite calm. She felt as if she were in limbo, sore but relaxed, languid, perhaps even proud of having given him an erection. Even though he'd taken her from behind, as though she were a man . . .

The thing she really didn't understand was the strange mixture of feelings that the bestial act had stirred in her. At the end she had been shaken by a violent spasm, and she wondered if it had been an orgasm.

He turned to her, his eyes moist, agonised. He looked at her for a long time, incredulously, as if his Madonna had given birth to a miracle.

Then he let his body fall on her breast, unable to contain his sobs.

Valentina stroked his hair. She felt happy and at the same

time terribly uncertain. Uncertain about her past, which may have been one big mistake, and uncertain about her future, which now seemed even more of an unknown quantity.

'What about you?' she asked.

He said nothing.

'Do you love me?'

Still he said nothing.

'It doesn't matter, you know. It doesn't matter . . .'

Mike Ross lifted his head. His cold eyes had become bright and intense, wet with tears of guilt.

For a long time, they lay staring into each other's eyes.

Then she noticed that something was moving between them, starting to press against her belly.

She smiled.

He smiled too, shyly, uncertainly.

Valentina put one arm around his shoulders and slid the other between their bodies. To guide him to the right spot.

7

Death always wins in the end.
It plays for a while with its prey
And then swallows it.
Like a cat with a mouse.
Which one of us is the cat?
You certainly don't have many lives left.
Four down, three to go!

The contents of the letter were imprinted on Ferrara's photographic memory. The letter itself was still in his office. He had a photocopy in his pocket.

It had come to Police Headquarters this time, not to his home. It had been logged along with the many anonymous letters that arrive almost every day, denouncing, threatening, claiming real crimes – or more often imaginary ones – and then, as it was addressed to him directly, it had been brought to his office.

Ferrara had immediately connected it to the two others. Instinctively, for no particular reason, even though it was quite different in both form and content. It hadn't been put together from letters cut out of a newspaper, nor had it been typed on a computer keyboard. It was handwritten: to

Ferrara, a clear sign that the killer was gaining in confidence and becoming ever more defiant.

There was no longer any doubt in his mind. The three murders had been committed by the same person, and the final target was him. The letter stated clearly that there was already a fourth victim, or would be. Then two more. And finally him.

It was still possible that this was the same person who had led the Monster and his accomplices, but he was inclined to rule it out.

The thought that the killer might be committing his latest crime at that very moment made the air inside the blue Alfa 166 even more stifling. Ferrara and the Commissioner were on their way to see the Prosecutor. They had both been summoned, separately, by Gallo in person, to an emergency meeting. It was a summons that Ferrara was duty bound to respond to, and Riccardo Lepri wouldn't have missed for anything in the world. From the Prosecutor's tone, he had gathered that Gallo had it in again for Ferrara, and he was curious to see what was going to happen. It could turn out to be a momentous occasion.

'You seem lost in thought,' he said to Ferrara as the car went along the Via Cavour. He had insisted that they take his car, saying that he only trusted his own driver. The fact was, he preferred to be seen in the most luxurious means of transport available. 'Anything wrong?'

The Commissioner's tone was as calm and cordial as ever. But his face looked drawn, his cheeks were unusually ruddy and his eyes streaked with tiny red veins. He must have eaten to excess last night, Ferrara thought.

'No more than usual,' he replied laconically.

'Do you think the Prosecutor has some bad news for us?'

'It won't be good news. He doesn't call impromptu meetings like this to praise or promote anyone.'

'You're right there,' Lepri sighed, with ostentatious resignation, as if he were the intended victim.

For the rest of the drive to the Prosecutor's Department in the Piazza della Repubblica, they were silent, each absorbed in his own thoughts.

When they had got out of the car and were standing alone together, Lepri said, 'Follow my advice, Ferrara. Drop this business about the Monster. That case will bring you nothing but trouble. If Gallo mentions it, play it down. Show him you're concentrating on these latest murders. In any case, you should be devoting more time to them, without delegating everything to your men, if you don't mind me saying so . . .'

Ferrara said nothing. These words, a clear warning of conflicts to come, merely bored him.

Instead of being taken to Gallo's office, they were led into a conference room. It was large and well lit, the bottom part of the walls covered with elegant wood panelling and the top part by frescoes that reached all the way up to the high ceiling, itself decorated with allegorical scenes. There was a screen on the wall at one end of the large table, and a projector at the other, which both jarred somewhat with the classical solemnity of the room.

Gallo was waiting for them, together with five other men and two women. Ferrara already knew the three deputy prosecutors, Luigi Vinci, Guido Fornari and Anna Giulietti, as well as Chief Superintendent Alessandro Polito, head of the Bologna *Squadra Mobile*, and Chief Superintendent Stefano Carracci, director of the Central Operational Service in Rome, which coordinated the activities of all the *Squadre Mobili* in Italy.

He had never seen the fifth man and the second woman.

They all looked slightly guilty. The men were in jackets and ties and the women, apart from a few discreet touches of colour, were wearing severe-looking tailored suits.

This was worse, much worse, than Ferrara had been expecting.

Gallo greeted them with an engaging smile. 'Come in. I think almost all of you know each other. For those of you who haven't yet had the opportunity to meet them, may I introduce Professor Stefania Prestigiacomo, lecturer in behavioural psychology at the University of Florence, and Professor Guido Marescalchi, lecturer in forensic psychopathology at La Sapienza University in Rome.' Then, for the benefit of the two professors, 'This is our Commissioner, Riccardo Lepri, and this is Michele Ferrara, head of the Florence *Squadra Mobile*.' And to everyone, 'Please, sit down.'

They all took their seats around the table as if they had all had places assigned to them, Ferrara noted. He himself sat down on one of the chairs that had remained free at the end of one side of the table. Professor Prestigiacomo sat down at the head of the table, in front of a laptop computer connected to the projector. Prosecutor Gallo remained on his feet, to her right.

'Before we begin, I'd just like to explain why Chief Superintendents Polito and Carracci are here. Chief Superintendent Polito is interested in the subject of serial killers because as head of the *Squadra Mobile* in Bologna he's been investigating a number of murders of prostitutes over the past few months, all apparently the work of a single person. Knowing that I was planning to take an in-depth look at the subject, he asked if he could take part today, to learn what there is to learn, and to make his own contribution if he can be of help in any way. Chief Superintendent Carracci, on the other hand, is here as an observer. He'll be reporting back to the Head of Police and the Minister of the Interior, who are both very concerned about the growth of this phenomenon. Naturally he is also at our disposal to provide technical support and specialised personnel if we judge it necessary.

'As I've indicated, the subject of this meeting is an examination of the type of criminal known as the serial killer. More specifically, I'd like to look more closely at the murders that have been taking place in Florence, within our jurisdiction, in the light of the theory put forward by Chief Superintendent Ferrara that these crimes are in fact the work of a serial killer.'

'*One* of the theories,' Ferrara said.

'Of course,' Gallo conceded. 'But you're an expert. You've already had to deal with similar cases, unless I'm mistaken?'

'You're not mistaken.'

'So I assume your theory has some basis in fact. Based on your experience, what, in your opinion, is the likelihood that the murders of Micali, Lupi and Bianchi are the work of one person – that is, of a serial killer?'

'One hundred per cent . . .'

His words were greeted with an astonished murmur. Given that his previous remark had suggested a note of caution, they sounded exaggerated, even provocative.

'One hundred per cent that they're the work of one person,' Ferrara continued serenely. 'Only fifty per cent that he's a so-called serial killer.'

Gallo raised his eyebrows. 'If there's only one killer, surely we have to consider him a serial killer. Unless you have any evidence, of which we're not aware, that there's a connection between the victims that has nothing to do with their being homosexuals, but involves some kind of underworld vendetta. To the best of our knowledge, their sexual preference is the one thing they have in common, which would surely support the theory of a serial killer. Isn't that right, Professor Prestigiacomo?'

The woman merely nodded. She had no desire to add to the electric tension between the two men.

'The only evidence I have points to a single perpetrator, that's all,' Ferrara said.

'Clues and conjectures, it seems to me,' Gallo said curtly. 'Not evidence. But let's look at the clues later. I suggest we take things in order and return to the subject of this meeting.'

'It's not conjecture . . .' Ferrara cut in, searching in his pocket for the photocopy of the letter he had received that morning.

'All in good time, please, Chief Superintendent. We'll get there little by little. The aim of this meeting is to sift through what we know so far and try to emerge with something that – as far as possible – we can all agree on. That's why I've asked the two professors to join us. I'd like them to start by setting the parameters within which we can then conduct the debate. Please, Professor Prestigiacomo.'

The woman stood up. She was short, plump and neat, with an aquiline nose, thick, permed black hair, and slightly too much make-up.

She cleared her throat and exchanged a knowing look with her colleague.

Il Gatto felt his hair bristle and his spine arch. He was on the defensive, ready to counterattack.

'I think it would be useful to refer to the classification drawn up in 1988 by ex-Special Agent Robert K. Ressler, who was director of the FBI's Behavioural Science Unit in Virginia. He identified two basic types of serial killers: organised and disorganised.'

She proceeded to list the characteristics of each type, starting with the *organised* type, and underlining how, with this particular type of killer, the choice of victims – completely random in the case of the *disorganised* type – is always conditioned by the presence of common factors such as age, appearance, lifestyle, race and so on.

'In the cases we're looking at,' she said, 'homosexuality could well be the common factor, as Prosecutor Gallo has pointed out.'

Pleased with himself, the Prosecutor signalled to her to continue.

'Ultimately, the characteristic profile of the organised serial killer is that of an individual who is apparently normal: middle class, and of average or above average IQ. He is often either an only child or the first-born in his families, and is deficient in the emotional sphere.'

'Possibly the hardest type to identify and catch,' Chief Superintendent Polito remarked.

'Precisely,' the professor confirmed.

Ferrara looked at his watch. While they were trading in generalisations, the killer was at large and possibly even at work.

The impatient gesture did not escape Gallo, but he said nothing.

'Before going on to the characteristics of the second type, I'd like to show you a chart highlighting the differences schematically.'

The professor started the projector, pressed some keys on the computer and a diagram appeared on the screen, comparing the salient characteristics of the two types.

'As you can see, *disorganised* serial killers act on a sudden impulse, without planning their actions. The choice of victims is random and surprise is the common characteristic of the attacks. The violence is immediate and rapidly leads to death. Sadistic sexual acts, such as mutilation, evisceration, ejaculation into open cuts in the body, are generally performed *post mortem*.' Here Professor Prestigiacomo paused.

'Any questions?' Gallo said.

'Isn't this classification out of date?' Ferrara asked. 'A lot of ink has been spilled since then about serial killers, particularly in American novels. Hasn't all that made a mockery of this distinction?'

'If you're referring to *The Silence of the Lambs*,' the professor replied, 'I've read it and enjoyed it. It's a very good thriller. But it's fiction. We have to keep to the scientific data. And to reality, like you. It's easy for a writer to identify the culprit, because he invented him! But we don't have that advantage, do we? We have to *find* him. That's why the classification we are examining was developed. The intention of those who formulated it was to make your task easier.' Her tone was acid.

'It's clear,' Professor Marescalchi intervened, trying to calm things down, 'that any effort we make to classify mental dynamics and human behaviour patterns is bound to give reductive or approximate results, which by their very nature can't convey the uniqueness of each individual. In the aim of both scientific and investigative research, however, it seems to me an overriding necessity to pinpoint different types of killer as a means of organising and refining our methods of prevention, apprehension and therapy.'

'If we really *are* dealing with a serial killer,' Luigi Vinci, one of the deputy prosecutors, remarked. 'I don't think we've established that yet.'

'Maybe a classification of the victims would be more useful,' Chief Superintendent Polito suggested, 'since that's the only thing we have to go on.'

'The dead all behave the same way, because they're dead,' Chief Superintendent Carracci joked.

'Hold on, we're coming to that,' the Prosecutor said. 'To the victims, I mean. And then we'll be able to evaluate whether or not we're dealing with a serial killer. First of all, I'd like to hear what Professor Marescalchi has to say about the things that motivate such criminals, so that we can draw our own conclusions.'

'From a behavioural point of view,' the professor began, clearly welcoming the invitation, 'serial killers can be divided into five types: the Visionary, the Missionary, the Thrill Killer, the Control Freak and the Lust Killer.'

He was a tall man of about sixty, almost bald except for a crown of white hair. His tanned, aristocratic face inspired confidence, and his bearing exuded self-assurance.

'The Visionary follows orders from voices he has heard, or visions he has seen, telling him to kill. The voice is usually that of God or Satan, who also provides instructions about how to carry out the murder.'

Ferrara could not help thinking about the priest in Greve, Don Sergio. His alibi, corroborated only by another priest, was still one of the weakest in the Micali case. Serial killer or not, it would be interesting to know where he was when the other two murders had taken place.

'The Missionary,' the professor continued, 'believes he has a mission to accomplish, usually to rid the world of those he considers the dregs of society, such as homosexuals, prostitutes – that may well be the case in Bologna, Chief Superintendent Polito – tramps, black people, drug addicts and so on. A typical example of this type of serial killer is Pedro Alonso Lopez, a thirty-one-year-old Colombian, a street peddler by trade.'

'The so-called Monster of the Andes?' the Commissioner asked.

'That's the one. Responsible for some three hundred and ten murders. A hundred little girls raped and killed in Peru, the same number in Colombia, and a hundred and ten in Ecuador. I'm sure you know all this as well as we do. What you may not all know is that in his confession, Pedro Alonso Lopez claimed that he was some kind of liberator, freeing the girls from the sufferings of their earthly lives.'

The two women shuddered in horror and even the men felt uneasy.

Guido Marescalchi let the effect of his words settle before he resumed. 'The Thrill Killer is characterised by the particular pleasure he gets from killing. The act of murder is the source of an intense feeling of pleasure, a kind of "emotional orgasm" comparable to what a gambler feels as he waits for the result.

'For the Control Freak, the act of murder comes out of a desire to exercise total control over another person. It's the idea of having the power of life and death that drives him. In such cases, acts like sodomy, rape, mutilation of the sexual organs, and so on, do not have sexual connotations, but represent the desire to exercise complete mental and physical power over the victim.

'According to some experts, the category of Control Freak is linked, although not always, with the fifth type, the Lust Killer. But the Lust Killer's principal aim isn't to gain power, but to obtain a purely sexual satisfaction.'

And with these words he concluded his presentation.

'Now,' Gallo said, 'I'd like to ask Chief Superintendent Ferrara to place the Micali, Lupi and Bianchi murders within this frame of reference, so that we can judge whether or not we are genuinely dealing with a serial killer.'

Ferrara described in detail what they had found at the three crime scenes and stated, 'The only constants in the three murders are the homosexuality of the victims, which suggests that we might be dealing with a Missionary killer, and the unusual violence with which the killer attacks the front part of the body, especially the face, which also suggests the disorganised type of serial killer. But in every other respect the murders are quite different in terms of the MO. In two cases, the first and the third, the killer used a knife, but in the second, he used a gun. The first two murders both took place in shops – shops in which religious objects were present – while the third took place in a private apartment.'

'So the third could be connected to the first as far as the MO is concerned, but not to the second,' Deputy Prosecutor Giulietti – an attractive woman of about fifty – observed thoughtfully, 'and the first could be linked to the second as regards environment, but not to the third . . .'

'And we shouldn't forget,' Gallo said, 'that there was a strong sexual element in the third murder, but not in the other two.'

'So even though there are a few coincidental similarities,' Chief Superintendent Carracci said, 'wouldn't it be better to think of these murders as three isolated occurrences? Or at least treat them as if they were?'

'Would that reassure the Head of Police and the minister?' Anna Giulietti asked.

'It would make them less worried,' Carracci chuckled.

'If this is a serial killer,' Professor Prestigiacomo said, 'the fact that the body is always left where it can easily be found would support the hypothesis of him being a disorganised killer. As does the fact that there have been a number of victims in a relatively short space of time. That should make the task of the police easier, shouldn't it?'

Which meant that the lack of results so far was a terrible stain on their reputation, Ferrara thought, admiring the nonchalance with which the woman had dealt him that low blow. He also noted that Gallo was nodding in agreement.

'On the other hand,' Alessandro Polito said, coming to his rescue, 'in all three cases the killer used his own weapons, which he took away with him, not weapons he came across by chance. And he seems to have left as soon as he had committed the murders. Both those things are characteristic of organised serial killers.'

They were all silent for a while, reflecting on this.

'Considering the MO of the last murder,' Professor Marescalchi said, 'it can't be ruled out that we are dealing with the Control Freak type of killer – just think of the wire around the neck – but there are also associations with the Lust Killer type.'

'Quite unlike the others,' Anna Giulietti intervened again, still in a thoughtful tone. 'There doesn't seem to be a single motivational pattern. It seems impossible to think they could all be the work of one person. At the same time, it's hard not to think that.'

'I agree with you, it's a real puzzle,' Professor Prestigiacomo said. 'From what we've heard so far, I don't feel I'm in a position to endorse with any certainty the theory that this is a serial killer. There are too many contrasting elements.'

'And what about the theory of Satanic rituals?' Gallo asked.

'I think we should drop that,' Ferrara said.

'But it was you who suggested it!' Gallo said in annoyance. 'And we all know it's a field of inquiry to which you've been devoting particular attention lately.'

'Yes, but on a different case,' Ferrara answered curtly.

'What about the rose stem? The leftovers of a cigar?'

'As you yourself said, they're probably intended for me. It's the killer's way of reminding me, not for the first time, that I'm the one he's after.'

'What do you mean?' Gallo asked. The others, too, seemed curious to know.

'This,' he replied, finally taking from his pocket the letter he had intended to show them earlier. 'It arrived at Police Headquarters this morning, addressed to me.'

The letter was passed around the table.

A grim silence fell over the room.

'Are you Il Gatto?' Professor Prestigiacomo asked, with a touch of sympathy in her voice that helped to relax the tension.

'Yes,' Ferrara admitted.

'Everyone in Headquarters knows that,' Lepri said, chuckling in his good-natured way.

'In Bologna too,' Polito added, amused. It was the first time that the nickname had been bandied about so openly in an official context.

'You said this wasn't the first time,' Carracci said. 'Have there been others?'

'I received anonymous letters after the first two murders as well. They were different from this one, very different, more like practical jokes. They came to my house and I didn't pay much attention to them, we all get them, the world is full of cranks. But now . . .'

'Do you still have them?' the two professors asked, almost in unison.

'Yes.'

'We need to get them examined by experts,' Gallo said. 'Handwriting and forensics. You'll get copies too, obviously,' he said to the two professors.

'Is it this letter that makes you certain we're dealing with a single killer?' Anna Giulietti asked.

'Yes,' Ferrara said.

'It sounds convincing to me,' she admitted.

'Me, too,' one of the other deputy prosecutors said.

They were all waiting for Gallo's comments.

'I don't understand,' he said, frowning. 'It says "four down". If it's referring to these murders, shouldn't it say three?'

'Ever since we've been here, I've been expecting the meeting to be interrupted,' Ferrara said. 'I don't think it'll be long before we hear about a fourth murder.'

'If we do, then I'll have to admit you're right,' Gallo said. 'But please, if and when it happens, inform us immediately. If I'm not here, I'll leave clear instructions so that whichever deputy prosecutor is on duty goes to the crime scene in person and follows the case through.' All this was, of course, for the benefit of his deputies.

Which meant that Ferrara was being placed under strict supervision. That had been the purpose of this whole *mise-en-scène* right from the start, he told himself angrily.

The blue Alfa 166 had left the courthouse ten minutes earlier. Now they were caught in a traffic jam, just a few minutes from Headquarters.

'Do you think it was useful?' the Commissioner asked.

'What?' Ferrara asked, his thoughts elsewhere.

'The meeting. Those two professors were pleasant enough. Though that Prestidiacono woman, or Prestigiacomo, or whatever the hell her name was, was a bit of a tough nut. All the same, I think you made a good impression on her in the end.'

Ferrara didn't really care. 'I don't know. Some of the things they said could turn out useful. We'll have to see how the investigation develops.'

'But at the moment it's pointing in one direction, right?'

'Mainly, but not exclusively. We can never leave any paths

unexplored. Not even the possibility that the murders are unrelated, however unlikely that seems now. I'll have different teams following up the various different leads. That's all I can do.'

The car had meanwhile extricated itself from the jam and was already driving through the gate of the former asylum.

'Congratulations, anyway,' the Commissioner said, sincerely.

'What for?'

'For holding your own against Gallo, for goodness' sake!' Lepri said with a smile, as they got out of the car. As merry, jovial and companionable as ever.

Meanwhile, a killer was at large in Florence.

And they both knew it.

Ferrara nodded goodbye, his eyes dark beneath his black eyebrows.

'Remember me to your wife!' he heard Lepri calling after him when he was already on the stairs.

'That priest, what's he called? Don Sergio . . . What happened to him?'

'He's in Greve, isn't he?'

'We need a reason to bring him in. Or maybe not, it's better if I go and see him. Best not to make him suspicious, after all this time.'

'You still think he had something to do with it?'

'No. Yes. I don't know. I can't see clearly. But something tells me I need to start over again with the first murder. And the only remaining suspect.'

They were in his office. Rizzo was sitting opposite him, the file on the Micali murder still in his hand. Ferrara was chewing his cigar, and fidgeting with his lighter without making up his mind to use it.

'Is there anything you want me to do?' Rizzo asked.

Ferrara said nothing, lost in thought. Then he gave him a knowing look. A cat's look. 'Do you mind getting me a coffee?'

Rizzo got up and placed the file on the desk in front of Ferrara.

He left the room.

He could have sent an officer, but he didn't. He wanted to be the one to get Ferrara a coffee today.

He didn't mind doing a favour for a friend.

At six, Ferrara left headquarters.

He walked.

The Via Zara, Santa Reparata, Sant'Orsola, the Piazza del Mercato, the Borgo La Noce, the magnificent San Lorenzo. Then the Via de' Conti, part of the Via de' Cerretani, the Via de' Rondinelli and finally the Via de' Tornabuoni, its pavements strewn here and there with heaps of dirty confetti.

The Verga bookshop.

He went in.

'Hello, Rita. Is Massimo here?'

'In his office. Sulking.'

'Why? Has he discovered all over again that all men are sons of bitches?'

'Worse. He's discovered that at least one woman is a bitch. The Venetian, remember?'

Ferrara smiled. It was nice to get back to normal.

He went upstairs and knocked at the door of the office.

'Come in!'

The room was filled with dense aromatic smoke. Massimo Verga was sitting reading, the stem of a long, burnished, slightly curved pipe clamped between his teeth.

'Where are the fire extinguishers?' Ferrara asked.

'I ate them to cool Lucrezia's ardour.'

'Has she beaten you down?'

'Don't play dumb. I know Rita's told you everything. She's a terrible gossip.'

'Only that you've had a disagreement.'

'I've had a disagreement. She hasn't. To her, everything's fine. Can you believe that?'

'With you around? Frankly, no. Either she's a saint or you'll end up marrying her.'

Massimo shuddered. 'Let's change the subject.'

'With pleasure. I have something to show you. Another "riddle".'

'You mean a threatening letter?'

'Judge for yourself.'

When he'd finished reading the letter, Massimo Verga let out a long whistle. 'You're in trouble, my friend.'

'I already knew that.'

'But it's worse than you think. Your secret admirer is quoting Schopenhauer! A great philosopher, but a bit gloomy.'

'What do you mean?'

'The first few lines. As far as "swallows it". Taken word for word from Schopenhauer. The rest is all his own work, and nothing special. But it means this fellow is quite well educated. A man of refined tastes, I'd say. The opposite of you, if you don't mind me saying so. You're in trouble.'

'Because he's more intelligent than me?'

'That I can't say. I don't know the man. But he's convinced he is. And he's enjoying himself playing with you like a cat with a mouse. He even says that.'

'So you agree? He's challenging me?'

'That's very clear. He feels so strong, he's even given you a handicap of two points. Two more lives before taking yours, he says.'

'And he's written it by hand. He must know we'll get our handwriting experts on to it.'

'And what will those experts tell you? That he's someone of above average IQ, well educated, meticulous, tidy, a psychopath perhaps, but clear-headed, shrewd, an excellent planner and tactician. Unless you're planning on arresting Napoleon, you're back to square one.'

'Thanks for your encouragement.'

'A pleasure.'

They both fell silent.

Massimo used the pause to relight his pipe, which he had neglected in his enthusiasm.

Ferrara would have liked to light a cigar, but his courage failed him.

'I'm thinking . . .'

'What?' Ferrara asked.

'About the riddle in the previous letter. "The last letter will be the first", you remember? I haven't solved that one yet.'

'Maybe he's more intelligent than you as well.'

'That's for sure. But I'm not the one he wants to kill.'

'You didn't add "fortunately".'

'Don't joke, Michele. This guy is serious. I'm not sure if this new message is any help in understanding the previous one. "The last will be the first" – what does that mean? Which one is this, the third?'

'Yes.'

'And he makes clear that the last one will be the seventh. But there's one missing. Does that mean it'll arrive after you're dead?'

Ferrara said nothing.

'Only if his plan works out, of course! Obviously you'll catch him first.'

'I hope so.'

'Let's think of it this way. The first letter, which wasn't sent, is the announcement of his plan, if you like. The details of what he intends to do before he gets to you. Then, after your death, as a final insult, he'll send it to the authorities to show how brilliant he's been. The first letter written, the outline, the plan, which he has seen through to the end, will be the last one sent. There you are. "The last will be the first". Clever, isn't it?'

'Yes, it is. But it's only a theory, that may not be it at all.'

'And in any case it only helps you if you're lucky enough to get your hands on a detailed plan to kill the head of the *Squadra Mobile* and also the man who wrote it.'

'Well, it's not much, but at least it's something.'

By the time he left the bookshop, it was dark.

A boy with his face painted like a cat with long black whiskers threw a handful of confetti at him and ran off to join his mother.

It was the last day of Carnival.

Carnival was over and he hadn't even noticed it had started.

8

It was the first day of Carnival, Saturday 26 February.

During the night, some wit had disguised the snow sculptures along the sloping street that leads from the first houses in the village to the main square.

Snow sculptures are a long-standing tradition in San Vigilio. There is a festival of them in the middle of January, involving the best artistic talents in the area, who spend the rest of the year expressing their genius by carving in wood whatever local tradition, the fashion of the moment or personal inspiration suggests to them.

San Vigilio di Marebbe, a village dating back to the Middle Ages, when it was subject to the abbey of Castelbadia, is in the heart of the Dolomites, to the south of the Val Pusteria: an area where Ladin culture has resisted the ravages of time and where Ladin is a spoken language even today.

It is a place that attracts skiers in winter and hikers and climbers in summer. The snow sculptures stay through the winter to greet tourists, then melt with the first warmth of spring.

'Look at that one with his trousers on his head!' Cinzia exclaimed.

They laughed heartily at an abstract composition looking something like a knight fighting a dragon. On top of the hypothetical knight the prankster had placed a pair of long johns, and the dragon on the ground, strewn with confetti and shooting stars, seemed to be splitting its sides laughing rather than lying there defeated.

They continued merrily on their way to the bar of the Hotel Posta, where they stopped to buy cigarettes for Cinzia and some punch to warm themselves.

They had arrived the day before on the same train: Valentina had got on at Florence, and Cinzia at Bologna.

They had agreed to spend this vacation together.

Only as friends, they had sworn.

Valentina hadn't told her parents anything about Florence, not only because she felt embarrassed, but also because it would have been difficult to justify the fact that she wasn't paying for the apartment where she was living. Nor did she have any desire to tell them about her relationship with Mike, which she herself did not understand.

Since that night, they hadn't had sex again.

Their life had gone back more or less to the way it had been before. He was away on business even more often. Whenever he was there, he was affectionate and considerate, even loving. But more like a shy, somewhat foolish schoolboy than a companion and a support.

More than once, she had wondered if he felt remorse for that impulsive act of sodomy and if she ought to be the one to raise the question and confront the subject, so as to have done with it once and for all. But the truth was, she wouldn't have known what to say, because she herself didn't know what she felt about what had happened. Did she feel disgust or regret, had she really suffered or had she felt a secret pleasure? How would she react if he asked her to do it again?

So things had dragged on, in a kind of limbo.

'What's new?' Cinzia asked, lighting a cigarette.

She looked beautiful, vivacious, her black eyes intense, her cheeks red with the cold.

They were sitting on wooden benches at one of the rustic tables in the bar, with their steaming glasses of punch in front of them. There were only a few regulars in the bar, some distance away, and they could talk without being either disturbed or overheard.

'You begin.'

'I miss you.'

'Cinzia, we said —'

'Okay, okay! I won't insist. I promise. I swear. We're here as friends. What do you want me to say? Bologna is a drag. The university makes me sick, my father is more fucked up than ever, my mother can't stand him but pretends nothing's wrong. She's so accepting. She doesn't even have the courage to find a lover. The only new thing in my life is CNN. I'm trying to learn English' – *seeing as how you like Americans so much*, she'd have liked to add, but she held back in order not to break the truce – 'so I've put up a satellite dish so I can get foreign channels.'

'Any new friends?'

'They're all little bitches.'

'What about what's her name?'

'Who?'

'The girl who was there once when I called you . . .'

Cinzia thought about it. Or pretended to. 'Oh, you mean Chiara? She's young, she's still at school. I give her Greek lessons, just to earn a bit of money.'

'What's she like? Is she a little bitch, too?'

'No,' Cinzia replied, feigning indifference. 'She's nice, funny. You want to know if she's sexy, don't you?' she added wickedly.

'No, I don't care.'

'I'll tell you something. She's a great shag.'

'You're such a bitch!' Valentina cried.

'Come on, I was only joking. Friends tease each other, right?'

Valentina nodded, and smiled.

But she'd felt a pang of jealousy which was hard to shake off.

'How about you? It's your turn now. How's life on the banks of the Arno?'

'I don't really know. There are tons of great things to see, but I spend almost all my time shut up at home studying.'

'You're serious, aren't you?'

'I want to graduate. Finish university and then do something – find a job, maybe travel first, change my life somehow.'

'Lucky you. I still have a long way to go.'

'Maybe we could travel together. Go abroad for a while. Would you like that?'

'Very much. We'll see. And what about that guy?'

'Mike Ross. He's working most of the time. He's nice, I told you. He took me out to dinner a couple of times. Nice restaurants, expensive.'

'Nothing else?'

'Come on, Cinzia, I told you . . .'

She didn't like talking about it. That was obvious.

By the time they left the bar, Cinzia wasn't in such a good mood any more.

*

'Ready?'

'Wait,' Cinzia said, looking around again before putting on her glasses and taking a last drag at her joint. She had never lost the habit, whereas Valentina had never caught it.

The view that sunny Monday from the peak of the Plan de Corones, at an altitude of 7,460 feet, was breathtaking. From here you could see the whole of the white valley, surrounded by a crown of perennially snowy peaks: the jagged garland of the Dolomites to the south and the mighty Aurine Alps to the north.

On Sunday, the ski slopes had been too crowded. It had been a day of renewed harmony between the friends, most of it spent with Valentina's parents, who were as kind and considerate as ever. Cinzia felt at ease with them and respected them. And they loved her as if she were their second daughter.

If they knew about the two of them, they'd never let on. But Valentina's mother had had no qualms about subjecting her daughter, in front of Cinzia, to a thorough grilling, full of innuendo, about the 'American in Florence'. Valentina had skilfully evaded her questions, suitably backed up by Cinzia in a spirit of friendship.

Now it was Monday, and they had challenged each other to a race on the most difficult of the slopes, the Sylvester, known for its downhill run of two and a half to three miles over a drop of 4,260 feet.

'Let's go!' Cinzia cried, throwing away the stub of her joint and launching herself into the run.

Typical of her, Valentina thought, still putting her gloves on, having taken them off to tuck her hair into her cap.

But she didn't mind. In fact, she smiled. The head start would add spice to the run. And, being a native of the place, she had always considered herself the stronger of the two.

She followed down the run.

Cinzia was more than fifty yards ahead of her, nimbly dodging the skiers in her way, trying to keep as straight a course as possible.

Valentina felt a vague sense of pride, seeing her friend's slender figure manoeuvring so elegantly and confidently. She shouldn't still feel pride, but she did.

She almost didn't notice the boy on the snowboard who suddenly came to a halt just ahead of her.

What the hell are snowboards doing here? she thought, swerving violently to the right to avoid him and then left again to get back on the piste.

But they were still on the red part of the piste, which deviated before the black did, and ended up at the starting post at Gripfelbaum.

The manoeuvre had cost her a few precious seconds. By now, Cinzia was nearly ninety yards ahead of her and had disappeared behind a narrow bend. Beyond it the piste divided in two, the Sylvester slope became steeper, and it was quite common to find long stretches of frozen snow.

She really had to make an effort now.

She concentrated, slowed down her breathing, and leaned forward, trying to put exactly the right amount of weight on the skis.

She took the bend.

All the skiers were advancing along the easier fork of the piste.

She immediately realised why. A sign announced that the Sylvester was closed for maintenance.

Cinzia had calmly ignored it.

Typical, she thought again, throwing herself into the gully at a speed she had never before reached. The pines on either side were a blur, the air whipped her face like a shower of sharp needles.

Although protected by her glasses, her eyes were tearing, clouding her vision, but she managed to see her friend below. She was gaining ground.

After about two miles, she had reduced the distance between them by half and was getting closer still.

She smiled, pleased with herself. She calculated that she would catch up with her after another quarter of a mile and would overtake her long before the finishing post.

She slowed down very slightly, to coordinate her movements better.

It was a mistake.

Cinzia, sensing that she was close, reduced the radius of her slalom, gaining more speed just as Valentina was losing hers.

Valentina cursed. She renewed her efforts and managed to regain ground, but more slowly.

After two and a half miles, her friend was still at least thirty yards ahead of her, and just beyond that Valentina could make out the end of the run.

She also saw that the piste rose abruptly, in a kind of makeshift ski-jump, and that to avoid it you had to make a long detour to the right or left. When Cinzia reached it, she chose to turn right.

A yellow mechanical snow shovel was working on the left. Valentina did not hesitate.

She aimed straight for the ski-jump and took it at the highest speed her skis would allow her. By the time she reached the edge, she was completely bent. She launched into the air with her body almost parallel to the skis, her arms opened wide like wings.

She was flying.

She felt an intoxicating sense of freedom. Down below, she could see Cinzia getting back on the piste and stopping to watch her.

She reached the apex of the curve and as she started descending, she began to gradually raise her body so that she would have the correct shape by the time she touched the ground.

But then cramp hit her left leg, and she was still bent double when she saw the ground coming dangerously close. She braced herself for the pain, but it was too late. One ski hit the ground before the other, throwing her off balance, the other ski came off, she saw the snow coming towards her, her right shoulder hit the ground, and her face slammed against the layer of frozen snow and her cheek scraped along it for what seemed like for ever.

She lost consciousness.

Cinzia hadn't realised what was happening at first. Once she had curved past the false ski-jump, she had looked up and seen Valentina's red and black snowsuit leaping beyond the edge of the mound, which the snow shovel had cut straight through by now, reducing it by half.

She stopped, terrified.

She saw her friend flying through the air, somehow – by the grace of God – going a long way beyond the snow shovel, and for a moment her strongest feeling was one of admiration. Then she saw Valentina's body twist in the air and fall and slam onto the piste and slide towards the woods, dragged along in an implacable movement that seemed as if it would never end.

Her eyes filled with tears.

'Vale,' she whispered, 'Vale . . .' then screamed, 'VALENTINA!!!' and rushed down the slope, thinking she would find her with her head smashed against the trunk of a tree.

She *was* near a pine, but had stopped some yards away. She

lay there, motionless, her eyes closed, her beautiful face covered in blood.

Cinzia reached her, threw off her skis and gloves, and knelt beside her.

'Vale,' she wept. 'Talk to me, I beg you. Talk to me, say something, tell me you're all right. Tell me you're fine, I beg you, I beg you. Oh my God, what have I done? It's my fault, all my fault . . . Valentina, my love, my darling . . .'

Alerted by the men on the mechanical shovel, a snow-mobile was coming towards her, dragging a stretcher behind it.

'Come on now, don't worry, everything will be all right, you'll see,' Valentina's father tried to console her, covering his own anxiety with words. 'If only you knew how many broken bones I've seen!'

Valentina's mother was silent, pale and tense. She stood and stared at the white double doors of the Emergency Department.

Cinzia was sitting stiffly on a chair, her face hidden in her hands, shaking with sobs. Signor Preti's words unwittingly made her feel worse instead of reassuring her.

The double doors opened and Doctor Werther came towards them. He seemed calm, comforting.

'Hello, Lisa, hello, Giorgio,' he greeted Valentina's parents. 'Nothing serious. She's going to be fine. All she needs is a few days in hospital and a short convalescence. A couple of weeks and she'll be good as new!'

Cinzia listened incredulously. 'But her face, all that blood . . .' She sobbed, unable to restrain herself.

Doctor Werther looked at her. 'Are you a friend of hers? Don't worry, they're just scratches. Quite a few, but superficial. She'll have a few small scabs for a while, but then she'll be more beautiful than ever. The biggest bore will be the plaster. Her right shoulder is dislocated and we'll need to immobilise it. A stiff bandage may be enough, but it's essential that for a fortnight at least she doesn't use her arm at all. And she won't be able to walk – there's been a secretion of serum, which has swollen her left knee. We've syringed it and now we're applying a light plaster cast to keep her leg firm. It can come off in two weeks. She can even cut it off herself with a pair of scissors if she's not able to come back here.'

Relieved, Valentina's parents thanked the doctor, who went back into the emergency room.

'You see?' Giorgio Preti said to Cinzia. Reassured, she sniffled and gave him a smile that lit up her tear-streaked face.

Valentina's mother, also calmer now, at last sat down.

Soon afterwards, the double doors were thrown wide open and two male nurses came out pushing a trolley. Valentina lay on it, her face swathed in bandages, her left leg in plaster and her right arm held in a stiff bandage.

Her parents and Cinzia ran to her.

Through holes in the bandages they could see her eyes, her gaze seeking each of them in turn, and her mouth: it seemed to Cinzia that she was trying to smile, but all that showed was a grimace of pain.

'Does it hurt, Vale?'

Valentina did not reply.

The nurses asked them to stand aside so that they could take her into the room she had been assigned.

'Who won?' Valentina stammered at last as they were taking her away.

Cinzia stayed by Valentina's side day and night. Lisa Preti would have liked to take over, but Cinzia had insisted, saying it was all her fault and she should be the one to attend to her.

The fact was, she was happy to be close to her. And it wasn't an unpleasant time. The hospital in Brunico was one of the few in Italy that combined the high medical standards of State hospitals with a level of comfort worthy of the best private clinics.

Valentina's parents took turns in coming to see their daughter during the day, bringing newspapers, magazines, flowers and sweets.

Valentina recovered quickly.

On the morning of 2 March the bandages were removed from the undamaged left side of her face, and the nurses explained to Cinzia how to medicate the wounded part, a network of small scabs going from the corner of the right eye and finishing in a cut across the right corner of her lips.

In the afternoon, they taught Valentina how to use crutches and that evening they dismissed her.

Giorgio Preti drove the friends back to the hotel.

'But you can't go back to Florence,' Cinzia insisted.

'I have to resume my studies. I don't want to stay here.'

'So come back to Bologna with me.'

'I can't, all my things are in Florence.'

'Don't you realise you can't look after yourself? How are you going to wash yourself? Who'll cook your food? Don't be stupid. You'll manage fine for two weeks with what you take from here. You don't need much, it's not as if you're going dancing. Bologna is still your home. I swear I won't make any attempts to steal your virtue, if that's what you're worried about.'

Valentina smiled. *And what if you did?* she thought. During this vacation she had got much closer to Cinzia, who'd been so good to her, better even than a sister would have been. She dismissed the thought.

But her friend was right. She wouldn't manage on her own in Florence, and she risked being forced into an intimacy with Mike that she didn't want to face up to at the moment. Especially in her condition.

'What about my studies . . .?' she said, weakly.

'Give me a list of books,' Cinzia said. 'I'll add exercise books, pens, ink and even an inkpot. All on the house!'

So on Sunday 5 March, Valentina set foot again in what had been her home in Bologna.

The next day, there was a text message on Valentina's mobile phone.

It was from Mike.

Having fun? When returning Florence?

She decided to call him and tell him everything. She told him she was stuck in Bologna and she would be back as soon as she was able to move. A week at the most. She was feeling fine. Her face was clear apart from a few sticking plasters and a few marks. Only the cut on her lower lip was taking time to heal and still bothered her a little, perhaps because she sometimes bit it nervously, tearing off the crust and making it bleed. But she was already moving about quite well and was thinking of cutting off the plaster on her leg as soon as she could.

Mike was sorry to hear about her accident, and offered to come and fetch her, but she said she'd prefer him not to. He made her give him Cinzia's address and phone number, however.

'Okay, if you're not here by Friday, I'll come and get you.'

'I'll let you know.'

Now she really wasn't sure she wanted Mike and Cinzia to meet.

*

Cinzia looked after her as if she were her mother.

She kept her word, too, and treated Valentina like a distinguished guest, never trying to take advantage of the thousand opportunities presented by her friend's helplessness and partial immobility. She even helped her to wash her private parts, but the touch of her hands never became too suggestive, never turned into a caress.

It was especially at such moments that Valentina would nervously bite her lower lip. At night, too, tossing and turning in a restless sleep.

They slept in the same room, but in separate beds.

The one habit Cinzia had kept from the days when they had lived together was that of walking around the apartment naked or half-naked.

She found it quite natural to flaunt her young, undeveloped body, her small, firm breasts that had never really grown, her long slim limbs and narrow buttocks which gave her a slightly boyish appearance, like one of those anorexic models so much in vogue at the time.

Valentina could not avoid the comparison between her friend's smooth, barely angular curves and the rougher, less graceful surfaces of the only male body she had ever known. Nor could she help wondering what it would be like to feel Cinzia's languid caresses again, the soft, probing kisses, the urgent, expert fingers, the delicate tongue. At times like these, she realised that what Mike had inflicted on her had been a real act of violence, the only weapon of seduction, perhaps, that a man knew.

She felt ashamed whenever she thought about it. Her mind would cloud over, and she would find it hard to reason, hard to understand. Deep down, something in her had responded to that violence.

If Cinzia ever noticed these moments of confusion, she

certainly didn't show it. She would complete whatever gesture she had begun, continue the conversation without any alteration in the tone of her voice. And, consciously or not, she would score another point in her favour.

The final move in the game came on Friday evening. In the afternoon, Cinzia had helped Valentina to cut the plaster from her leg, and finally remove the sling and plaster from her shoulder. Valentina's leg, although a little numb, had responded quickly.

'Look, I'm walking!' she cried, taking a few steps.

'*Eppur si muove*,' Cinzia remarked, solemnly.

'Let's go out!'

The days had grown longer, and the sky was clear and bright. The air smelled of spring, there were young offshoots on the horse chestnuts, everyone in the street seemed to be in a good mood, and so were the two old friends.

'Shall we go to the Bar Basso?' Valentina said.

It was a favourite meeting place for students, located in an arcade near one of the departments of the faculty of letters and philosophy, a good mile and a half from their apartment. They usually went there by public transport or in Cinzia's Scarabeo.

'Are you crazy?'

'Come on, I feel fine. I swear!'

'We'll go as far as you're able. As soon as you feel tired, tell me and we'll turn back, okay?'

'Okay.'

They managed to reach the Bar Basso.

They had coffee and cake, and bought cigarettes for Cinzia.

They went back home by taxi, in the dark.

'I'm having a shower,' Valentina announced as soon as they

got in. 'I can't wait to have a good soaping after all those sponge baths.'

'Are you sure? You've only just taken off the plaster . . .'

'You could give me a hand, one last time,' Valentina suggested, innocently.

It was only then that Cinzia realised that the slow, subtle, perhaps involuntary wearing down of her friend's defences had finally brought Valentina back to her.

She ran the water while they undressed and followed her into the big shower cabin.

'Oh, this is so nice!' Valentina exclaimed, as the wonderfully warm water gushed out. 'Soap my back, then I'll soap you.'

Cinzia took the foam-soaked sponge, and began gently sponging Valentina's shoulders, then moved down her spine. She put her left arm round her waist and placed her hand on her friend's flat, taut stomach. As she reached her buttocks with the sponge, she went up on tiptoe and lightly kissed the hollow of her neck.

Valentina did not protest.

Cinzia slid her left hand down Valentina's belly, sank her fingers into the tuft of wet pubic hair and slipped them inside the labia, searching for the clitoris.

Valentina moaned.

They ended up on her bed. Cinzia was unbridled, and Valentina let her do what she wanted, not even complaining when her friend's passionate kisses hurt her aching mouth.

Only once, when Cinzia pressed her body too firmly against her right shoulder, did she say, 'Be careful.'

They made love all night until at last, exhausted, they fell asleep, Cinzia's body clinging to Valentina's like that first time in San Vigilio.

*

The doorbell woke them the next morning. It was almost midday.

Cinzia jumped out of bed and ran to the door, still half asleep, throwing on a short dressing gown as she went. It must be a friend of hers, she thought: maybe Chiara was back from her vacation and had come to find out when their classes would be starting again. Instead, she found herself face to face with a tall, fair-haired man wearing sunglasses and carrying a huge bunch of roses.

He was smiling amiably. 'I'm looking for Valentina Preti,' he said, with a slight American accent. 'Is she here?'

You know she is, Cinzia thought, irritably.

'Yes,' she said, 'but — well . . . we're still . . .' She looked at her watch, and realised there was no point saying they were still in bed. 'We've not long woken up.'

'I see. May I come in, anyway?'

Cinzia looked desperately for a reason to say no, but couldn't find one. She couldn't very well leave him standing there in the doorway. After all, he was a friend of her friend.

'The place is a real mess . . . All right, come in. I'll tell Vale.' She pulled her dressing gown around her and let him pass.

Although she couldn't see his eyes, she felt as if she were being scrutinised, analysed, explored. She was embarrassed at being almost naked, defenceless, her hair in a tangle, her eyes bleary.

She ran into the bedroom and closed the door behind her, but not before Mike Ross had caught a glimpse of one bed that hadn't been slept in and another one, unmade, where Valentina was lying, only her outline visible under the sheet, which she had pulled up above her head.

The apartment was small. He took it all in at a glance.

Having tidied themselves up as best they could, the two

friends soon came out. Cinzia had recovered, and looked calm and almost brazen. Valentina was clearly embarrassed.

'Hi, Mike,' she said. 'What brings you here?'

'I came to pick you up, if you want me to. It's Friday, remember?'

'But I told you . . . oh, never mind. I have a headache. Would you like a coffee?'

'I'll make it,' Cinzia offered immediately, heading for the kitchenette.

'Are those . . . for me?' Valentia said, looking at the splendid bunch of roses.

'Of course.'

'Cinzia, bring a big vase, too, can you?'

'It's nice here,' he said.

'It's such a mess . . . We were up very late last night. You know, studying . . .'

Mike preferred not to delve into the nature of their studies. But what he suspected had devastated him, and his calm outward manner bore no relation to the fury he felt inside. Of course it was possible that Cinzia had woken first and had already made her bed. But ever since she had opened the door, he had been sure she had only just fallen out of bed – and not her own.

It was a side to Valentina he could never have imagined. It had caught him so completely off guard, he didn't yet know what to think of it.

Cinzia returned with a vase full of water and put the flowers in it. Then she heard the gurgling of the coffee maker and ran back to the kitchenette.

She reappeared with a tray, on which she had arranged the three cups, a sugar bowl and a small vase containing a single rose she had taken out of the bunch. She placed the tray on the coffee table between the sofa and the pouffe and handed one cup to Mike, who was sitting rather stiffly on the sofa, and another to Valentina, who was on the pouffe. As she did so she threw her a knowing glance, which did not escape Mike. Then she took her own cup and sat down on the rug.

'Have you introduced yourselves?' Valentina asked.

'There's no need,' Cinzia said.

'You must be Cinzia,' Mike said.

'Don't you ever take your glasses off?'

Mike smiled and removed them. His ice-cold eyes filled her with a sense of unease.

'I didn't want to disturb you,' he said. 'I only wanted to see how you were and, if you like, take you back to Florence.'

'I'm fine, as you see. The plaster's gone, and so has the sling. And my cheek is completely healed. But I'm still a bit weak, I don't feel up to going back today. Don't worry, though, I'll be able to do it perfectly well by myself. Cinzia has been looking after me really well – better than a nurse!'

'That's up to you. I'll be waiting for you whenever you want.' He stood up.

'Are you going already?' Cinzia said, doing nothing to hide her relief. Valentina threw her a reproving look, and this did not escape Mike either.

'I don't want to keep you any longer, and besides, I have an article to finish. I prefer to go back.'

'Come back whenever you like, we'd like that,' Cinzia lied cheerfully, putting a stress on the word 'we', as she walked him to the door.

'Bye,' he said from the door.

'Bye,' Valentina replied.

She was still sitting on the pouffe.

'He may be handsome, he may be kind, but I don't like him.' That was Cinzia's verdict.

'Why doesn't that surprise me?' Valentina said.

After what had happened last night, anyone bursting in on them would have bothered Cinzia, let alone someone who'd come to take Valentina away.

'It's not for the reason you think. There's something strange about him, something cold. Those eyes – brrr . . .'

'You're wrong, it's just an impression. At first, I also . . .' She stopped, biting her lip, so that a little drop of blood appeared. She was afraid of saying too much.

Cinzia went up to her, put her arms round her, and tried to wipe off the drop of blood with her lips.

'You're hurting me!' Valentina protested, feeling a sharp pain in her shoulder. Last night, she hadn't complained.

Cinzia moved away abruptly. 'Sorry.'

'It's nothing, I'm sorry.'

'Anyway,' Cinzia went on, 'what do you care? You're not going back to Florence, are you?'

Valentina said nothing.

Again, she didn't know. She hadn't liked seeing Mike go. Not like that, anyway. She didn't want to break off the relationship that way: it may not have got started properly, but it had left its mark on her.

How much easier everything would be if she could see everything through to the end, if she could love them both, with no ties, no obligations! But the world wasn't like that.

'You haven't answered me,' Cinzia said in alarm.

'I don't know, Cinzia . . .'

'Here we go again! We've already played this scene, Vale. It's time you grew up. It's time you made your own decisions.'

Cinzia was right. She had to make a decision. And she couldn't do that by sheltering in a corner, huddled in her friend's arms: that much suddenly became clear to her. She had to fly with her own wings. She had tried once and had fallen to earth. *Like that leap from the ski-jump,* she thought. *Exactly the same.* She'd recovered from that, maybe she should try again.

'Even if they aren't the same as yours?' she said.

Cinzia said nothing. She was chilled to the bone. All the love, the care, the affection, the two weeks of shared joys and anxieties, the passion – pointless. It had all been pointless.

In the afternoon they started quarrelling again, and the next day Valentina packed her few belongings in a bag and left.

Cinzia watched her from the window as she walked towards the bus stop.

For the first time in her life she felt really afraid. As sharply as if someone had put a scalpel through her heart, she had a premonition that this was really the end and she would never see Valentina again.

9

'Can't you sleep?' Ferrara asked his wife, not long after she had switched off the lamp on her beside table.

It was two in the morning on Ash Wednesday.

'You're the one who can't sleep,' Petra replied. 'You've been tossing and turning for an hour. Come on, get up, I'll make you a camomile tea.'

They went to the kitchen and she put the kettle on. On the table she placed two large cups, the sugar bowl and a small plate of the German biscuits – chewy biscuits that kept the jaws busy and were hell on the teeth – which her parents had sent her for Carnival.

'You're worried,' she said.

'No. But there's something about the case I'm working on that doesn't feel right.'

He didn't add anything else. He didn't like talking about his work at home, and even though it wasn't a rule, more of a habit, his wife always respected his silence.

'Isn't there always something that doesn't feel right until a case is over?' Petra said. 'It's the same with me. For example, I planted peony bulbs in the autumn and the buds should already be out by now, but they're not. What should I do? Should I worry? What's the point? I water them regularly, I give them fertiliser, and one day I'll go and check, quite calmly – because plants can sense when you're anxious – and there they'll be. We'll have beautiful flowers and I'll give you one to put in your office.'

He smiled. His wife's pragmatic philosophy had always helped him.

They continued talking about plants and flowers, finished their camomile tea, and went back to bed.

But Ferrara still couldn't get to sleep.

It wasn't Gallo's hostility that bothered him. He knew what prosecutors were like. They came and went, superintendents remained. It was the vagueness of the case, these murders that were related and at the same time unrelated, almost as if the killer wanted to display his signature and at the same time amuse himself by leaving contradictory clues, mixing up the scientifically established types like a conjuror shuffling his cards, playing with their theories like . . . yes, like the proverbial cat with the mouse.

He had to free his mind of those theories and go back to square one, start all over again with the mysterious priest, the anonymous letters, the corpses.

Right, let's start again with the corpses, he told himself. But there was one missing. Was the killer playing with the bodies, too? Leaving the first ones in full view but keeping this one hidden?

All day long he had been waiting for the call to come, announcing that another corpse had been found.

It hadn't happened.

Commissioner Lepri, Prosecutor Gallo and the deputy prosecutors must be having a great time.

'If there's another murder, I'll have to admit you're right,' Gallo had said. As if admitting one of his subordinates, the head of the *Squadra Mobile*, was right were a calamity. And in the meantime, Ferrara thought bitterly, he had again shown how little he trusted him, and had tipped the wink to his deputies to keep a close eye on him.

The grandfather clock in the living room struck three.

At two minutes past six, the telephone rang.

They had found the fourth body.

'Near the amphitheatre in the Parco delle Cascine, there's a man lying on the ground, covered in blood. He's not moving. Come quickly.'

The emergency call had come in at six in the morning.

The patrol car had got there a few minutes later, almost simultaneously with the ambulance. The man who had made the call was waiting for them. He was a pensioner, and had been walking his dog in the park, as he did every morning. A man lay face down on the ground, covered in stab wounds.

About twenty feet from the body, in full view under a tree, the police had found a bloodstained knife. The blade was about six inches long and had a mother-of-pearl handle.

Ferrara, Rizzo and Sergi soon arrived, immediately joined by Deputy Prosecutor Giulietti, who, in accordance with instructions, intended to take an active part in the scene of crime investigation and follow the operations of the forensics team in person.

The dead man was wearing a pair of old jeans and a polo-neck sweater. On his left wrist he had a watch with a metal strap: it had stopped at 3.10. On his feet were a pair of brown moccasins which showed no traces of having been dragged over the ground. Nor were there signs that there had been a struggle. The only traces of blood were where the corpse lay.

'He hasn't been moved,' Ferrara remarked. 'This is where he was killed.'

'Yes, it looks like it,' Sergi replied, crouching to have a closer look at the ground. In the meantime, Inspector Pino Fabrizi had arrived. Fabrizi was very familiar with night-time activities in the Cascine.

There were three holes in the back of the sweater, corresponding to the same number of wounds. The holes were quite close together. The sweater was soaked with blood, and blood was dripping from the sides of the body onto the ground.

Francesco Leone touched the body. The parts of it which had been exposed to the air were cold, whereas where it had been in contact with the ground, it was still slightly warm. It was also still possible to move the joints, which were not in an advanced stage of rigor mortis. Then he turned over the corpse. The blood that gushed out was still quite liquid. The front of the body showed the characteristic blue-red hypostatic marks, which are concentrated in the lower parts of a corpse. There were none on the rest of the body. As had been the case with the previous victims, the face and neck were heavily disfigured with knife wounds.

'He hasn't been dead for long,' Leone said. 'Three to four hours at the most. The hypostatic marks have only just appeared. But we'll have a more precise idea after we've done the post-mortem and determined the body temperature.'

The dead man must have been about thirty. He was of normal build and medium height.

The scene of crime officers put on their gloves and started searching the dead man's trouser pockets, under the vigilant eyes of Ferrara and Anna Giulietti. In the right pocket they found a gold key-ring with two keys, one clearly from a car, the other most likely from a house or an apartment. In the same pocket there was also a wallet containing a few banknotes, and a driving licence with the man's photo. His name was Giovanni Biagini: born in Florence, thirty-three years old. A subsequent search in the Ministry of the Interior database would show that he had no criminal record.

'Fabrizi,' Ferrara said, 'I want the whole of the surrounding area searched, including under the trees.'

Inspector Fabrizi split his men into two teams. He gave the keys found in the dead man's pocket to a couple of the men, and told them to check the cars parked in the area. There weren't many at that hour, and one of them could well be the victim's car.

In the meantime, the forensics team had started photographing the scene. They took samples of the blood present on the knife, especially on the blade, using pads soaked in a physiological solution, which they then placed in special bags. The knife itself was sealed in a separate bag.

What bothered Ferrara was the fact that the killer had abandoned the weapon at the crime scene. Why? If this killing was the work of the same person – and he was sure it was – was this another surprise move in the bizarre game he was playing with Ferrara?

As if reading his thoughts, Anna Giulietti came up to him. 'So you were right. Your killer took his time, but he struck in the end, as you predicted.'

She was wearing a grey overcoat made less forbidding by an aquamarine silk blouse the same shade as her luminous, smiling eyes. There was a sprig of mimosa in the buttonhole of her coat: Ferrara remembered that today was International Women's Day.

'A bit early to say.'

'But you'd bet on it, right?'

'I'd bet my shirt,' Ferrara said.

'Not your career?' she joked. 'That's cautious of you.'

Ferrara brushed aside her joke. He wondered what was so special about women that they should have their own day when men didn't. Petra was an exception, of course. He mustn't forget to buy her flowers.

The search of the park proved fruitless, but the two officers sent to look for the car had better luck. They found it parked near the Viale dell'Aeronautica. A white Fiat Punto, with a Florence number plate. Inside was the registration, in the name of Giovanni Biagini, a pocket diary containing a number of names and telephone numbers, and a few pornographic magazines hidden under the seat covers in the back.

'We're sequestrating the car,' Anna Giulietti said immediately, turning to Ferrara. 'Take it to the garage at Headquarters and have forensics take a look at it.'

Ferrara gave the order.

Then he called Sergi. 'Take a team to search Biagini's apartment and interview his family, if he has any. Try to find out what he was doing in the hours before he was killed and what kind of man he was.'

The house was in Galluzzo, on the edge of the city: a small house with a garden, where Giovanni Biagini had lived with his brother and sister, both unmarried.

Biagini wasn't married either.

They had to wait a few minutes before the door was opened.

When at last the Biaginis came to the door, Sergi showed his badge and said, 'Sorry to disturb you, but is Giovanni Biagini a relative of yours?'

'Our brother,' the man said. The woman looked worried.

'I'm sorry . . . May I come in? I'm afraid we have some bad news for you . . .'

When they were sitting down inside, Sergi told them the

news. Biagini's sister burst into tears. The brother looked stunned.

'But . . . are you sure it's him? Can't it be . . .?'

'I'm afraid there's no doubt about it. I'm truly sorry.'

'But how did it happen? Who was it?'

'That's what we have to find out. Prosecutor Giulietti, who's coordinating the investigation, has ordered us to carry out a search. I know this may not seem like the best time, but we can't waste a minute if we want to find the culprit.'

The brother and sister did not object. A search of their house was carried out in their presence. They found a diary and various papers, which would need to be examined carefully. What they did not find, though, were any more pornographic magazines or any other indications that the victim had been gay.

Sergi asked the Biaginis to come with him to Headquarters and left a couple of men to question the neighbours. They needed to found out as much as they could about the dead man as soon as possible.

The questioning of the brother and sister yielded no significant information.

They were interviewed together. Sergi had thought it would make things easier. Their names were Antonia and Filippo, and both were older than the dead man.

'How was Giovanni yesterday? Did you notice anything unusual about him?'

'No.' Filippo Biagini glanced at his sister, who was still very upset. 'Do you mind if I answer the questions? My sister knows exactly the same as I do. Neither more nor less.'

'No problem. So there was nothing unusual?'

'Absolutely nothing. Giovanni was exactly the same as always. I really don't understand . . .'

'Did he have a girlfriend? Did he stay with anyone?'

'No, he lived with us, he didn't have anyone. My sister and I don't have anyone. We're loners. We prefer it that way. Our parents, who are both dead now, were very much of the old school, very strict. We got used to living alone, and now . . .'

'As far as you know, did he have any problems? Could anyone have had a reason to kill him?'

'I doubt it. If there'd been anything he would have told us. We had a very close relationship. We trusted each other.'

'So you knew he had . . . "special friends" – male friends?'

The man seemed astounded. 'How dare you, Superintendent?' he protested, looking anxiously at his sister, who was still weeping quietly.

Serpico ignored the outburst. 'Thank you for the promotion,' he said, trying to play things down, 'but I'm only an inspector.'

'Sorry, I don't know the ranks. It's the first time I've ever found myself in a situation like this. I've never been in a police station in my life, not even to apply for a passport.'

'That's all right. It was just a joke, but I realise this is not the right time. And I'm sorry about the question, but we have reason to believe that —'

'No, no, no! It's not possible, I tell you. Giovanni had lots of friends, but not that kind.'

'All right. I understand.'

'It's the truth, Inspector. Don't you think I'd have noticed?'

He did think so, which made it all the more unlikely that the man had not even suspected it. But he knew that some gay men hid their leanings very carefully, and that their families often preferred not to see what they did not want to accept.

'But you knew that Giovanni often went to the Parco delle Cascine?'

'Yes, he went there from time to time. He was fond of nature.'

'What time did he leave home yesterday? When did you last see him?'

'After dinner, about ten, I'd say. He told us he was going to drive around to unwind. We didn't hear him come back, but that's normal because he slept downstairs and the two of us sleep on the first floor. And last night we went to bed straight after dinner and fell asleep almost immediately. He suffered from insomnia; we don't. In fact, we were still asleep when you rang our doorbell.'

'But when he went for a drive in his car, did he usually go on his own or did he have a friend with him?'

'I really wouldn't know. He belonged to a local sports club, and knew quite a few people there. I don't know if he went there last night and met someone. You'll have to ask at the club.'

'We will. One last question and we're finished. At least for today.'

'Go on, Inspector.'

'Do you have any explanation for your brother's murder? Someone killed him. There must have been a reason, don't you think?'

'I wouldn't know, I told you. Giovanni was a quiet man, who never got in anyone's way. It must have been a case of mistaken identity, or else someone trying to rob him. I can't think of any other reasons. Believe me.'

The sister, Antonia, who had nodded every time her brother answered a question, opened her mouth for the first time. 'That's what it was. Mistaken identity or a robber. It's more likely to have been a robber. In Florence these days, we're not safe in our houses any more. It's not like it used to be, we used to leave our front doors open. But with all the crime these days . . . Not to mention the drug addicts, who'd do anything to get money. Even kill. But I don't have to tell you. You know it as well as I do. Florence has changed. It's become as dangerous as any other city.'

True, Sergi thought. Unfortunately that was how it was. Florence wasn't just a picture postcard image. It moved at the same speed, and had the same concerns and the same vices, as every other major city in the world.

A similar picture had emerged from interviews with Giovanni Biagini's neighbours. All this was reported to Ferrara, who in the meantime had sent out teams to gather what information they could in the area where the murder had taken place.

It was an area notorious for the suspicious characters who frequented it, and this wasn't the first time it had been the subject of police attention. The Parco delle Cascine was a long strip of land, bounded like an island by the waters of the Arno, whose territory was very strictly divided according to the various sexual 'specialities' on offer.

On one side there were the transsexuals with their clients and those drawn there by curiosity. This was the most crime-ridden part of the park. Bag-snatching and other robberies were common, as were violent assaults, often with no discernable motive. Another area, closer to where the murder had taken place, was frequented by gay men and rent boys. The rent boys were often young men from the provinces, from other towns in Tuscany, or from abroad, and men from all walks of life and social classes cruised there more or less regularly. This part of the park was the most isolated.

Near to the main entrance was the traditional spot for female prostitutes.

Lastly, the far end of the Cascine, the least well lit and the hardest to keep an eye on, was the area chosen for gay sexual encounters that weren't necessarily mercenary, and was frequented by couples of all ages. This was where the murder had taken place.

For a while now, Headquarters had been compiling lists of all those who frequented the park.

The purpose was not so much to eliminate the phenomenon, which by now had reached such proportions it was impossible to suppress, as to find ways of preventing criminal acts, especially senseless acts of violence.

When the officers had left, Ferrara called for Inspector Venturi, who was the best in his squad at searching through the records, and gave him the job of carrying out a thorough check of the computer files on the Cascine. Then he sent for Ascalchi.

'I have a particularly tricky job for you.'

'Yes, chief.'

'Are you religious?'

'Well, I was baptised. But I have to say, my first communion was also my last.'

'There's a priest in Greve in Chianti . . . Do you know where that is?'

'Quite near here, isn't it?'

'Get one of the drivers to tell you how to get there. But I'd like you to go alone. Have them give you an unmarked car. When you get to the parish, ask for Don Sergio, the young priest. Don't let on that you're with the police, understand? You have a Roman accent, pretend you're a tourist, make up some story or other. I'd like you to find out where the priest was last night. If he spent the night there, if not where and why. Think you can do that?'

'Don't worry, chief, we Romans are natural actors.'

'All right, go. And don't forget, I'm trusting you.'

The idea had come to him through force of circumstance. All his best men were involved with the latest murder, which obviously had priority. And besides, the fact that Ascalchi was Roman might really trick Don Sergio into revealing something.

In another room in Headquarters, Venturi was at the computer. He had opened the *Cascine* folder and the sub-folder *Names*.

Then he'd typed in *Biagini, Giovanni* and waited while the machine carried out the search.

In a short while, lists of files containing the name began to appear. Venturi, who had not been expecting to get results, felt a rush of adrenaline.

He opened the files, selected the relevant details and printed them.

He hurried back to Ferrara's office, almost colliding with Ascalchi who was on his way out.

'Positive result, chief!' he cried as he entered. 'Very positive!'

Proudly, he placed the bundle of printed sheets on Ferrara's desk and then stood as if to attention.

'Don't just stand there,' Ferrara said. 'Sit down.'

The name had not shown up in the records at the Ministry of the Interior because Biagini did not have a record, but it did feature quite often in the *Squadra Mobile*'s own databank. The licence number of his car had been entered many times. It had been spotted in the Cascine, especially late in the evening, parked very near the scene of the crime. Biagini had also been stopped many times by the police and checked out, but he had always been on his own.

'Congratulations, Venturi,' Ferrara said. He noticed

another interesting thing: Biagini's car had often been sighted in the Cascine at the same time as a number of other cars, always with the same licence numbers.

But then Venturi saw Ferrara's face darken.

Ferrara was reading a report from a few months earlier. It had been written by two officers reporting back to their head of section some information they had received from an informer, whose name was, of course, omitted.

The information concerned the techniques used by the drivers in the parked cars. They would flash their lights at potential partners passing by, and not get out of their cars until contact had been made. But the informer had added something important. 'In the past few weeks groups of young men have been seen going up to motorists pretending to make contact with them for sexual purposes, but in fact with the intention of extorting money from them in return for being allowed to park there. Sooner or later, this is likely to lead to a serious incident.'

Could it be that Biagini had nothing to do with the supposed serial killer? That he had been killed by these young racketeers for refusing to pay, as a lesson to others?

It was pure speculation, of course, but it couldn't be ruled out, the way they could rule out a robbery because of the watch and the personal objects in the dead man's pocket.

Just then Rizzo and Sergi got back from the sports club Biagini had frequented. Biagini had not been in the previous night, not even briefly, as he usually did. No one had seen him.

Rizzo had taken a seat in the other armchair in front of Ferrara's desk, and Serpico had pulled a chair over from the nearby table.

Rizzo presented his idea of what had happened. 'Biagini must have entered the park on foot. At a certain point he was stabbed in the back. There were no signs of struggle or of the body being moved, so it's quite likely he knew the killer and was walking ahead of him along the path. It's speculation, but I think it's valid.'

'We might get information about Biagini's activities in the Cascine from the drivers of the other cars that were parked near his,' Sergi suggested. 'Fabrizi's men took down the licence numbers.'

'Venturi has just brought me a list of licence numbers of cars that have been seen a lot in the park. I want you to compare them with the ones that were there last night. Concentrate on those that recur most often. Then let's factor in the people whose telephone numbers are in Biagini's diary. Put them all together and we should be able to narrow it down to the one that interests us, even taking into account the fact that we may come up against a wall of silence.'

The men stood up to get back to work.

'Wait, Venturi,' Ferrara said. 'Seeing as you're so good with computers, could you copy for me onto a CD all the photos of the victims, starting with the Micali murder. I need them by tonight.'

Back to square one. Starting with the victims.

Night had fallen by the time Superintendent Ascalchi got back to Headquarters. He came straight to his chief's office.

'So, did Don Sergio spend last night in the parish?' Ferrara asked as soon as he saw him.

'No,' Ascalchi replied.

Ferrara felt a brief sense of triumph. 'Does he have an alibi?'

'You'd have to ask him that.'

'What do you mean? Didn't you speak to him?'

'He's not there.'

'What do you mean?'

'I mean he's gone.'

'What do you mean, gone? He can't be.'

'Gone, vanished into thin air, nowhere to be found.'

'Come on, Ascalchi, I'm not in the mood for jokes. What the hell are you trying to tell me?'

'I'm not joking, chief. He left on February 3rd, and never came back. He's already been replaced.'

February 3rd, Ferrara thought. The day after the Bianchi murder.

'Did you talk to the parish priest?'

'Of course, but he won't open up. Says he doesn't know where Don Sergio went. He left without saying a word to anyone. Not even to his relatives, apparently.'

'Impossible. A priest doesn't just vanish into thin air. The parish priest must know where he is. Why won't he say?'

'Maybe he doesn't trust Romans. He swore over and over that he was just as surprised as anyone.'

'And did you believe him?'

'You want the truth? Not in the slightest. But you didn't say I could use strong arm tactics . . . In fact, I didn't even tell him I was a policeman, like you said. But if you want me to, I can go back tomorrow and —'

'No, no, forget it. You did very well. If I want you to go back, I'll let you know. Or else I'll go myself. Anyway, you can go now.'

In the corridor, Ascalchi said as he passed an officer, 'Who rubbed him up the wrong way?' and they both laughed.

'Chief, chief!' Venturi came running after Ferrara.

It was nine o'clock, and he was on his way out. The Headquarters building was almost deserted, and the inspector's steps echoed in the corridor. He was going home. It was too late to go to Greve, and besides, it might be better to proceed with caution, and not alarm the parish priest too much. After all, he was the one who'd provided Don Sergio with his alibi for the Micali murder.

Venturi caught up with him. 'Your CD,' he said, holding out an envelope. 'The photos of Biagini are on it, too, taken in the morgue.' He smiled. 'I hurried the forensics people up a bit.'

'Thanks, I'd forgotten.'

'But you need them today, right?'

'Yes.'

He'd decided that he would have another look at the corpses that evening, try to understand what they told him, see if he could extract even the slightest shred of evidence from them.

The positions in which they were lying, the grimaces on their faces, the way their arms were bent: anything could be meaningful if you knew how to look. Not always, but often.

So, after dinner, he put the CD in his computer and, while Petra bustled about to the accompaniment of Bellini's *Sonnambula*, he started to look at the images.

First the whole bodies: comparing the positions, superimposing the images, looking for significant similarities or divergences. It was demanding work, constantly comparing each one with all the others. Then he examined the wounds to the victims' backs, leaving aside those inflicted by bullets and concentrating on the knife marks.

It seemed to him that there were some analogies in the shapes of two cuts on the bodies of Micali and Biagini, the first and last victims, but when he tried to enlarge the images even more, they became too grainy and it was impossible to compare them properly. He made a mental note to get the forensics people to take another look.

He had left the faces for last, all of them slashed to pieces, apparently indiscriminately, in a kind of blind fury, almost as if the killer had wanted to erase them, while at the same time leaving them at least slightly recognisable. This, to him, was the biggest mystery of all.

It was after midnight and Petra had already given him a goodnight kiss, knowing that it would be pointless to try and persuade him to put it off until tomorrow.

He analysed the face of the first victim. From in front, in profile, from above, from below. He isolated the part that had borne the brunt of the blows, saved everything in the computer's memory, and went on to the second, then the third and finally the fourth. He carried out the same checks on all of them, saving characteristics, peculiarities and anomalies in the memory.

To no avail. These were four different faces, as different as the faces of four individuals chosen at random could be, each with its own character, which had nothing to do with any of the others. The only thing they had in common was the large number of blows inflicted on them. Far too many, like an exercise book scrawled over by an angry child.

He found a way to put all four faces together in the same frame, two on top and two on the bottom, and spent a long time studying them.

They didn't seem to be saying anything to him, and yet he had the feeling that they wanted to speak to him, that they were screaming a message he could not catch.

Unless it was his own desire to find something, anything, that was driving him to imagine things that weren't there.

Disheartened by this thought, he thought of switching off the computer and going to bed.

Instead, he lit a cigar and decided to play with the images a little. He put up Lupi's face again, filling the screen, and subjected it to a series of special effects: changing the colour, increasing the grain, going back and increasing the contrast, and so on. He had the feeling that he was getting closer, but he didn't know to what.

He highlighted the cuts, and isolated them.

And then he saw it.

Vague, rough, and hidden as it was, now that he saw it, it appeared very clear.

While almost all the cuts seemed to be scattered randomly, there were four of them, slightly deeper and more precise than the others, that were arranged in a more regular way. One long, vertical cut and three shorter, horizontal ones, at right angles to the long cut, one at the top, one in the middle and one at the bottom.

Taken by themselves, away from the network of other cuts, they formed the letter 'E'.

Ferrara shivered.

He saved the image and went on to Micali's face.

Subjected to the same treatment, it eventually yielded a clear letter 'F'.

It was Bianchi's turn. This one was more difficult, but in the end Ferrara managed to locate a tiny 'r', and another almost identical one on Biagini's face.

Four letters. Following the order in which the murders had been committed: 'F', 'E', 'R', 'R' . . .

Ferrara felt drained, like someone who finally manages to solve a theorem after long research. There was no doubt in his mind, and he was sure the Prosecutor's Department would be convinced, too.

He felt a shudder go through him. Those four letters could mean many things, but one was the most likely: the killer was writing his, Ferrara's, name on his victims' faces.

'Ferrara' has seven letters. Seven like the roses in the

Bianchi murder. Four had been used up, and now here they were, in front of him.

Seven letters, he thought. And then, immediately: *The last will be the first.*

'Of course!' he exclaimed, so loudly he might have woken Petra if she had not been such a sound sleeper.

He and Massimo had been trying to find a solution to the puzzle the killer had set them, a solution connected with the number of messages. But there was another explanation they hadn't even thought of. The last letter of his name was, inescapably, the first letter of the alphabet!

That was it: the last letter had a very special meaning for the killer, since it was the one reserved for Ferrara.

The 'a' was the signature he would leave on his face.

Ferrara switched off the computer, put out his cigar, and turned out the lights.

He slipped into bed, careful not to wake Petra. Her calm, regular breathing would be his companion for a long time that night. He knew he wouldn't sleep. This was a night for settling accounts. With himself.

He wasn't afraid of the threat. What unsettled him was the deep hatred the man – or woman – who was carving his name in the victims' flesh must feel towards him. Why him? Did the killer have a grudge against Ferrara as a policeman, a representative of authority, or against Ferrara the man, whose life was no more devoid of faults than any other man's? What skeleton in the cupboard needed to be brought out into the light of day, what ghost from the past was demanding vengeance? If this really was a serial killer, a maniac who killed at random and challenged the forces of law and order, then the theory that the killer had a grudge against him as a policeman was the right one, and he could sleep almost soundly. But he didn't believe that.

An investigation, he knew, can force you to look inside yourself. Because, ultimately, every investigation brings you face to face with another human being, and when there's a true conflict between two human beings it's impossible not to put yourself totally on the line if you want to win.

Confronted with his own name written by his enemy, Ferrara knew that this was one of the truest and deepest conflicts he had ever known, one that concerned him more intimately than he had suspected until that moment.

His last thought before falling asleep was that he had forgotten to buy flowers for Petra. He hadn't even wished her a happy day, and he considered such neglect unforgivable. He added it to the long list of his doubts and torments. He would spend long hours drawing up that list, surrounded by the silence of the night.

10

Last Saturday's article, the English teacher wrote on the black-board.

'Today,' she announced, 'we're going to talk about the Saxon genitive.'

Cinzia was following the lesson distractedly. Every now and again she threw a glance at the brunette in the denim miniskirt sitting two desks in front of her, and fantasised. She kept wondering if she ought to forget Valentina and rebuild her life.

The girl's name was Alice and she was a secretary in a haulage firm. She was twenty-six, a bright and breezy character with none of the baggage which made Valentina's life so complicated. She wasn't married, or engaged. They had chatted amiably a couple of times.

'Before you leave,' the teacher said at the end of the lesson, 'I want each of you to take a photocopy of the *New York Times* article from the pile here on my desk. Read it for homework and we'll talk about it during the next lesson.'

They got in line and Cinzia found herself next to Alice.

'Hi,' the girl said, smiling.

'Hi,' she replied.

Alice looked at her watch. 'Did you come on your moped?' she asked as they took the copies.

'Yes,' Cinzia said, glancing at the article. 'Damn it!' She had seen Mike Ross's name at the bottom.

'What's the matter?' Alice asked in surprise, looking at the article to see what Cinzia was upset about.

'It's nothing,' Cinzia said, putting it away irritably.

'Listen,' Alice said beseechingly. 'I need to get to the Piazza Martiri and I'm late. You couldn't give me a lift, could you?'

'Sorry, I don't have an extra helmet,' Cinzia said. She was in a bad mood, and had no desire to go the long way round just for Alice. She was thinking about Valentina.

'It's all right, I have one. A friend gave me a lift here on his motorbike and he left it with me – he didn't want to take it back with him.'

Damn!

Alice got on behind Cinzia. Cinzia was aware of Alice's long legs wrapped around hers, her breasts pressed against her back, her arms squeezing her waist.

She felt nothing.

When they arrived, Alice looked at her watch again as she got off and asked Cinzia if she'd like to go to a bar for an aperitif. 'I still have a bit of time left, you went so fast. How about it?'

Was there something suggestive in her voice and her smile, or was that just in Cinzia's mind?

Cinzia felt a vague sense of guilt and a sudden dismay at the thought that someone could take Valentina's place. All at once, Alice seemed ordinary, insignificant.

'No, thanks, I really have to go,' she said, accelerating away.

'Pity. Another time, maybe?'

But Cinzia did not hear her. Her eyes were damp, but not because of the wind. She kept repeating Valentina's name under her breath.

*

Whether due to neglect by the authorities, or a deliberate policy on the part of the monks, the road which wound tortuously through the Casentine Forest for about nine and a half miles to the abbey of San Benedetto in Bosco was just a dirt road – in fact, little more than a cart track. Apart from a few farmers who sometimes used it, where it came close to the main road, to lead their flocks to pasture and helped periodically to free it from brambles and snow, few people made use of it.

The abbey was situated to the north-east of Camaldoli, in an area between Tuscany and Emilia-Romagna full of churches, hermitages and monasteries. It was built near a tributary of the Arno in 1386 on the orders of Ricci di Cambio, a Florentine banker rich enough to lend money to both the Kingdom of Naples and the Papal States.

The design complied strictly with the canons of Cistercian architecture, with a perimeter wall surrounding all the buildings, the kitchen gardens, and the grounds. To the east of the cloister the chorister monks were housed, and to the west lived the lay brothers. The two residences preserved the separation between the two groups, but they nevertheless came together to collaborate in the running of the abbey.

The church was on the north side of the cloister, protecting the rest of the complex from the north winds and allowing light to reach the other buildings. Near the porter's lodge, within the perimeter wall, were the guest quarters, consisting of a large refectory and a dormitory.

Until a few years earlier, the abbey complex had been used as a college, attended both by young men of the Florentine aristocracy destined for important posts in the public and private sectors, and by orphans from various parts of Italy being groomed for ecclesiastical careers. But then the abbey had gradually cut itself off from the world, reverting to its original vocation – helped by its unusual geographical position – and increasingly assuming the character of a hermitage.

That day in March, a van was travelling along the dirt road, driven by a monk. There had been a lot of snow that year, and patches of it still clung to vast areas of the forest.

The van jolted over the stony surface, rising and falling precipitately as the road rose and fell, but the monk didn't seem to mind too much and was whistling cheerfully.

When, after about twenty minutes of this arduous journey, the van stopped at last in front of the porter's lodge, the monk got out and went to open the rear door.

'I told you it'd be a bumpy ride, didn't I?' he laughed.

Numb with cold and almost bent double, Don Sergio emerged from the back of the van. He was no longer wearing his cassock, but instead was draped in the habit of the Benedictines, just like the monk who had driven him. 'We're born to suffer,' he said.

He picked up the bag containing his few belongings and walked towards the porter's lodge. The van drove away.

'Welcome back, brother,' the porter greeted him. 'The prior is expecting you in the chapter room.'

Don Sergio knew the way. He went along the cloister until just before the church and knocked at a door.

'Come in.'

The large, austere chapter room was exactly as he remembered it: the bare stone walls, adorned with nothing but a single large wooden crucifix, the arched windows placed close to the ceiling. Abbot Anselmo was sitting halfway along the east wall. He was alone, the stone seats to his right and left empty. He was a short, thin man, and he seemed lost in all that space, but Sergio Rotondi knew that he could dominate it with his energy.

'It really is true that the ways of the Lord are infinite,

brother,' he said when Sergi had come closer. 'Who would ever have imagined that we would see you again?'

'How are you?' Don Sergio asked.

'As you see me. Healthy, and happy that I'm still able to serve the Lord.'

'I'm pleased to hear that. Is everything ready?'

'Just as His Eminence arranged.'

'Thank you.'

'Come, I'll show you to your cell.'

Valentina had phoned Mike from the train, but couldn't get through to his mobile. She had then tried his home number, but had only managed to speak to Nenita who had answered all her questions with the words 'No home'.

At the station she had taken a taxi.

'He's gone,' Nenita had tried to explain when she finally got to the house. 'Airport, New York.'

Gone. Just like that, without saying a word.

'When's he coming back?'

'Sorry? No understand.'

'Back! When Mr Ross come back?'

The woman shrugged. 'Don't know. Didn't say.'

A week had passed, and she still had not heard from him. The days went by slowly and idly. Sometimes, in the evenings, she would get in her Panda and go down into the city to look at the shops, buy some new clothes, and check out the restaurants where she'd have liked to have dinner but wouldn't because she hated the idea of eating alone. The nights were the worst, because every now and again she would think she could hear sounds on the floor below and would cover her head with her pillow in fright, trying to blot them out.

Then morning would come and, in the clear light of day,

the fresh air and the smell of the flowers and the reassuring songs of the birds would lift her spirits, and her fears would vanish. But she was still curious to know what was beyond that padlocked door on the first floor landing.

One day, she had tried again to ask Nenita, even though she knew it would be pointless. But at least she could pretend that she'd had some kind of conversation with someone in that big, deserted house.

'Nenita, listen. Do you ever go upstairs? To the first floor.' She had pointed to the ceiling to make thing clearer.

They were in the kitchen of Mike's apartment and Nenita was making coffee.

'First floor? No, I can't. Mr Ross not want.'

On one of the walls in the kitchen Valentina had noticed a rack on which hung what she supposed were duplicate keys for the whole house, and for a second she had been tempted to grab the key to the first floor when Nenita's back was turned. But her courage had failed her.

Sunday had been the saddest day. That week spent alone had made her realise how much she missed Mike: she had hardly thought about Cinzia. She still did not know what she really felt for this man who seemed so self-assured and at the same time so shy and elusive, but she had decided there was only one way to find out: make love with him again.

So when, on Monday evening, Mike phoned from the airport to say that he was on his way back and that the next day he would finally keep his promise and take her to San Gimignano to celebrate, Valentina fell asleep happy, full of plans for seduction.

11

On the morning of Thursday 9 March, Chief Superintendent Ferrara found a document on his desk full of detailed requests from the Prosecutor's Department regarding the investigation.

Deputy Prosecutor Giulietti wasn't wasting any time. She seemed determined to make clear who was in charge from now on. The document asked for:

- an examination of the knife found at the latest crime scene, *with the purpose of obtaining fingerprints from the blade or the handle. The exact dimensions and characteristics of the knife should be established, and inquiries should be made as to whether it is on general sale or is only available in certain specialised shops;*
- a full investigation of the victim's friends and acquaintances, *obtaining information from such persons as are in a position to provide it, and from a close examination of the papers and address books found thus far in the course of the inquiries;*
- an investigation of the victim's movements on the day preceding the crime, *especially in the hours prior to his death, by interviewing such persons living with the victim*

or living in the neighbourhood of the victim as are in a
position to report circumstances that may help with a
reconstruction of the crime.

The list went on and on for another two pages in the same pedantic tone, and concluded by stating that Deputy Prosecutor Giulietti had appointed her own expert who would ascertain the nature of the substance found on the knife and, in the case of the substance being identified as human blood, as seemed likely, would also ascertain whether or not it belonged to the victim.

Ferrara called in Rizzo and made him read the document.

'But all this is exactly what we're doing! What does it mean – she doesn't trust us?'

'I'm the one she doesn't trust, not you. Read the last sentence! Anyway, that's her business. She's following Gallo's orders. Forget about it. How's our investigation going?'

'We're interviewing some of the people whose names appear in the diaries. Do you want to sit in?'

'No, I'll leave it to you. I'm going to Greve. Don Sergio has disappeared, and I want to know what's going on.'

'Disappeared? What do you mean?'

'He's not in the parish any more. Ascalchi found out about it yesterday, but that's all he was able to discover.'

'So it could be him! Shouldn't we alert the transport police, the airports, the borders —'

'Wait, let's hold our horses. It's curious, though, isn't it? By the way, Rizzo . . .'

'Yes?'

'We're definitely dealing with a single killer, and he wants me dead. I have proof.'

And he told Rizzo about the discovery he had made the previous night.

*

'Hello, father.'

'Hello, my son.'

'Could I ask you a few questions?'

'If you're not trying to sell me something, or tell me what to watch on TV, I'm all yours. The Lord gave us ears to listen.'

'Can you tell me where I can find Don Sergio Rotondi?'

Father Francesco gave a sad, doleful smile.

He finished arranging flowers in front of a little crucifix and invited Ferrara to follow him into the sacristy.

'You're not a relative of his, are you?' he asked, as they walked across the church. 'I have the feeling I've seen you somewhere before.'

'I'm not even an acquaintance of his. But we did meet once.'

'Oh, yes? When was that?'

'Last year. In October. October 1st.'

They had reached the sacristy.

'The day poor Stefanino was killed,' the old priest murmured.

'Precisely.'

'You're from the police, aren't you? I thought so.'

'I'm the head of the *Squadra Mobile*, father. My name is Michele Ferrara.'

Don Francesco sat down with considerable effort, smiling bitterly. 'My bones,' he explained. 'Now I know why your face was familiar. I've seen you in the newspapers, right? Maybe also on TV?'

'It's possible.'

'And you want to know about Don Sergio. Everyone wants to know. His relatives, the parishioners. There was even some fellow from Rome here yesterday, pretending it was a casual visit . . .'

'I have to find him. It's important, father. Other men have died since Stefano Micali. Three of them, all gay men like him.'

'And like Don Sergio, do you mean?'

'That I don't know. Is he?'

'He never confided in me, but I believe he does have those inclinations, and that they cause him great pain. But I don't see how knowing that is of any help to you. He had nothing to do with Stefanino's death. He was with me when the poor boy was killed.'

'Can you confirm that?'

'Why shouldn't I? I'm old, my memory isn't what it used to be, I sometimes fall asleep without realising it. But I'm not in my dotage yet and if I say Don Sergio was with me that day, then he was with me.'

'It was just after lunch, wasn't it?'

'Yes.'

'And you were doing the accounts.'

'Well, to tell the truth, he was doing them.'

'A boring job.'

'Extremely!'

'On a full stomach, it could make you feel drowsy . . .'

Father Francesco reflected. 'I know what you're trying to make me say. But no, it's not possible. Don Sergio liked Stefanino a lot, they grew up together, they were like brothers.'

'Careful, father, next you'll be telling me they were in love.'

'No, no, not in the way you think, God forgive you!' Father Francesco crossed himself.

'But wouldn't it be better if I found him? If he talked to me, told me what happened?'

The old man sighed. 'I suppose so.'

'So why won't you tell me where he is?'

'Because I don't know.'

'That's not possible!' Ferrara said, raising his voice despite himself. 'It isn't possible. A priest can't just vanish. A man can lose his relatives, his friends, yes, but yours is a much bigger family.' He couldn't help adding, a touch contentiously, 'And a much better organised one.'

'It is a "family", as you say, but a family that doesn't need to involve a poor provincial priest like me in its decisions.' There was genuine humility in Father Francesco's voice.

Ferrara felt as if he had been caught off guard. Suddenly, he was in a different dimension, one that went far beyond that of two flesh and blood human beings talking to each other. 'What do you mean?'

'The Church has its mysteries, my son, and its rules. Those rules aren't necessarily the same as those that ordinary mortals live by. Sometimes it's necessary to ignore normal rules for the sake of a higher good. If we're told to accept something we don't understand, we simply obey.'

The implications of these words threw a new and disturbing light on the whole case, making it, if possible, even more intangible than it had been so far. For a moment, Ferrara felt dizzy, as if he were about to be sucked into a vortex.

'I don't think I quite understand,' he said.

'Perhaps because you're following the wrong path. Or perhaps because I haven't really said anything important or shocking.'

'You've certainly told me something . . .'

'Really? I don't remember.' Father Francesco smiled wearily, and closed his eyes. 'You should know. The Lord gave us ears to listen, remember?'

Meanwhile, at Headquarters, the interviews were proceeding at a frantic pace and a true picture of the victim was starting to emerge.

Among those questioned by Rizzo and Sergi was a casual acquaintance of Biagini's, a distinctly camp individual named Pietro. He and Biagini had met by chance at a bookstall in Santa Maria Novella station while he was looking at the covers of photography magazines. It had turned out that they were both keen on photography, and Pietro had given Biagini some advice on which magazines to buy. They had subsequently met a few more times. According to Pietro, Biagini often went to the Cascine, whereas he himself only went there sometimes on Sundays.

'If you don't go to the Cascine very much, how do you know that Biagini went there often?' Sergi asked.

'He told me, didn't he? He said if I ever needed him and he wasn't at home I could find him there. One time I went there and he was there. That was when I realised!'

'That he was gay, you mean?'

'Yes.'

'Like you?' Rizzo asked.

'Look – I know that to people like you . . . But there's nothing wrong with it, okay? I'm gay and I'm not ashamed of it. On the contrary. I'm proud, right? I lead a regular life, I have a job, I've never hurt a fly.'

My God, Serpico thought. *At least one person who says it loud and clear, without beating about the bush.*

'Did you have intimate relations with Giovanni Biagini?' Rizzo asked.

'No way! He really wasn't my type. I liked talking to him, that's all, especially about photography.'

'Do you know of any particular friend of Giovanni's? Someone he saw often, someone he had a regular relationship with?'

'Oh, God, I really don't know . . . Actually, there was one time I saw him with a particular person.'

'Go on.'

'Giovanni took me to the apartment of a friend of his, near Campo di Marte, you know? There was no one there. He told me his friend lent him the apartment sometimes to bring people there.'

'For sex, I assume,' Sergi said.

'Yeah. Anyway, it was clear why he took me there, right?'

'So what happened?'

'After we'd been there a while this young guy arrives. Quite good-looking. Giovanni asked me if I minded. I told him I really didn't give a damn, but I didn't want to join in, if that's what he was planning. I don't really go for that kind of thing, you know? I stayed in the kitchenette all the time Giovanni and this young guy were in the bedroom.'

'Who was he? Did he tell you?'

'After the young guy had gone – of course I didn't ask any questions – but after he'd gone, Giovanni told me he worked in a hotel in the centre of town. He told me he'd lent this guy money recently, interest free. But the guy hadn't paid him back, even though Giovanni kept asking for his money. He seemed really angry that he hadn't been repaid, you know? I think he felt as if he'd been used.'

Meanwhile, Inspector Fabrizi had been questioning another of the dead man's friends. His name was Francesco and, apart from adding a few more details about Giovanni's homosexual activities, had provided information that would help them track down the young man Pietro had mentioned.

'One day, just a few weeks ago, Biagini told me he'd been friendly with this young guy for a while, and he'd lent him a lot of money but couldn't get it back. The young guy's name is Aldo, and he works in the Hotel Dino. Giovanni was really pissed off . . . I mean, really angry with him, because Aldo kept asking him for more money and Giovanni refused to lend him any more, obviously – he'd already lent him something like thirty million lire, Inspector! He even threatened to inform on him and lose him his job if he didn't give the money back within two weeks at the outside. He couldn't stand it any more. I was there when he said that. It was unpleasant, I tell you . . .'

Fabrizi immediately reported the results of the interview to Rizzo and Sergi. Comparing the two statements, the three of them felt reasonably satisfied. They had identified a possible culprit with a good motive for killing Biagini. It wasn't so easy for a hotel worker to find thirty million lire, and if Biagini had informed on him, not only might he have lost his job, his whole future might have been jeopardised.

'It shouldn't be difficult to track him down,' Sergi said.

'See if you can find out any more about him,' Rizzo said. 'Then we'll talk again. I'm waiting for the chief.'

Sergi was right: it wasn't difficult. The man's name was Aldo Puleo, he was thirty-two, and he came from a little village in the province of Bari which didn't even appear on road maps. He wasn't married and had been working in the hotel as a waiter for about five years. Sergi also discovered that he was a gambler, and was often seen at a gambling den in the Poggio Imperiale area.

When he reported back, he found Ferrara in a very bad mood. Rizzo was trying to cheer him up, telling him what good results they had obtained. Sergi did the same, but realised immediately that it was useless.

Having listened to Sergi, Ferrara reluctantly called the Prosecutor's Department and asked for a warrant to search Aldo Puleo's home.

'Do it as soon as the warrant arrives,' he ordered. But then

he exploded. 'There's no *point*, though! We shouldn't be looking for some hotel waiter, we should be looking for that
damned priest, Don Sergio!'

Serpico looked at him, stunned. He had never seen him in
such a state.

'But there's evidence pointing to Puleo,' Rizzo objected.
'You always say we should never leave any lead unexplored.'

'You're right. I'm sorry, boys. You've done good work,
really. This case is getting on my nerves. You carry on, I'm
going home. I've had enough for today.'

That, too, wasn't like him.

He didn't go home. At least, not immediately. He walked to
the banks of the Arno by way of the Viale Matteotti, the
Viale Gramsci and the Viale della Giovine Italia. It was the
most neglected area of Florence, an area where you heard
Tuscan spoken more often than English, German or Japanese.

He puffed at his cigar, wondering how to climb the ecclesiastical hierarchy, who to turn to, how high he would have to
go. From what the old priest had told him, it looked as if he
might have to request an audience with the Pope himself!

'*Perdone, señor.*'

It was a family of tourists who had got lost. Spaniards, the
new horde that had joined the more traditional ones.

Ferrara showed them the way, and for some reason this
banal gesture restored a little of his good mood.

He walked along the Arno as far as the Ponte alle Grazie,
and crossed to the halfway point of the bridge. There he
stopped, and looked across at the less familiar side of the
Ponte Vecchio, the upstream side along which Vasari's
Corridor ran.

Here, he thought, was the true heart of Florence. A bridge
built in the fourteenth century, at the narrowest point of the

river, on three solid arches which had defied the passage of centuries. Butchers and greengrocers had had their shops there until Grand Duke Ferdinando I had cleared them away and replaced them with goldsmiths' and silversmiths' shops. Then as now, it had been thought that the city was best represented by displays of wealth. Why shouldn't it flaunt itself like a prostitute and attract the foreigners who thronged onto the bridge to see the kiosks displaying increasingly standardised merchandise? Or the louts who swarmed everywhere and killed time while queuing to buy tickets by defacing the facades of old palaces with stupid graffiti?

'She looks like the Ponte Vecchio.' That was what the Florentines said of a woman wearing too much jewellery.

When it was no longer blood that pulsed in its veins – like the blood in the meat sold by those expelled butchers – but gold and silver, the breath of the city became laboured.

A sick city. That was how he saw it today.

A city rotting beneath the weight of appearances.

Could its Church also be rotten?

In the days that followed, the investigation started to languish again, and the newspapers redoubled their criticism of the police. With no other basis than the fact that all the victims had been gay men, they had had no hesitation in declaring that the murders were related, and had seen the latest of them as an open challenge to the head of the *Squadra Mobile*.

SERIAL KILLER HOLDS FERRARA AT BAY and THE SQUADRA MOBILE IS IMMOBILISED were the most merciful headlines. Others were bolder: FERRARA BEATEN AT HOME 4–0 and FLORENCE TREMBLES AND FERRARA DOES NOTHING.

As Ferrara had feared, the search of Aldo Puleo's apartment had yielded nothing – except an exercise book corroborating the fact that he had owed money to Giovanni

Biagini, with all the dates and amounts written down. In addition, Aldo Puleo had an alibi. He had been at work when the murder had taken place. His shift had been noted on the staff rota at the hotel, and the staff, including the manager, had all confirmed that he had been at the hotel for the whole shift and hadn't gone out once.

On Tuesday the 14th Ferrara decided to invite Deputy Prosecutor Giulietti to lunch. She had been furious about the business of the Aldo Puleo search warrant, which had achieved nothing except the harassment of an honest citizen. Nor was she happy about the lack of results in the investigation as a whole, which suggested that her clear, precise instructions had not been followed to the letter.

It wasn't Ferrara's intention, though, to attempt to justify himself, or ingratiate himself with the prosecutor in any way. He didn't really care how upset she was – he already had enough problems of his own. What he wanted from her was a favour.

Anna Giulietti belonged to an old family, which had numbered some important church dignitaries among its members, including a famous nineteenth-century cardinal.

'I don't know,' she said over the phone when he invited her. 'Do you think it's ethically correct?'

'All I'm proposing is a working lunch.'

Anna Giulietti thought it over. 'Not today perhaps, I have an appointment in Poggibonsi at three.'

'Do you know Latini's, in Certaldo? It's right near there.'

'Of course I know it.'

'I'll pick you up at midday.'

'Okay.'

'I've never married and I don't regret it. My love life is fine, but isn't really very important to me. I've always devoted

245

myself to my work. Work is my life. My father was an appeal court judge, my grandfather a notary.'

Prosecutor Giulietti was talking as they drove across the gentle hills to the south of Florence.

For the occasion, Ferrara had dusted down his old Mercedes 190, which he almost always kept in a garage and only used when he had to go outside the city. It had clocked up more than 150,000 miles, but the softly purring engine sounded as good as new.

It was a beautiful day, the air almost warm. From time to time the fragrant scents of the countryside filtered into the car – and so, occasionally, did the pungent odour of a newly fertilised field, but even that wasn't unpleasant.

Anna Giulietti had opened up during the journey. Professional and detached at first, she had allowed the conversation to become more personal as the miles sped by. It was what Ferrara had been hoping for.

'Well,' he replied, 'I am married, and I don't regret that, either. I think every choice we make in life is the right one, as long as we make it consciously.'

'I've heard about your wife. They say she's an excellent cook and an amazing gardener.'

'I consider both those statements true.'

'You're a lucky man, then.'

Ferrara thought about that for a moment. 'I suppose I am,' he concluded, as they parked in an open space in front of the petrol pump that partly hid the entrance to the restaurant.

They were greeted by Latini himself. He was one of the sons of the owner of the famous restaurant of the same name in Florence. He was a short, jovial man, who knew Ferrara well. He led them to their table, where they were joined by his wife, an American woman who was equally affable and whose great contribution to the restaurant was her superb desserts.

They ordered, but Ferrara waited until the wonderful antipasti – including the unmissable crostini with Colonnata lard – arrived before asking, 'Have you had a chance to look at my report on the victims' faces?'

'Yes, and I passed it on to the experts, along with the photographs. The "r"'s are perhaps a bit far-fetched, but the "F" and the "E" are quite clear. It's just a theory, of course, and a horrifying one. The idea of a killer playing Scrabble with the dead is pretty scary. If you're right, I have to hand it to you, you did a fantastic job. But that's nothing new.' She smiled. Latini's antipasti and wine had definitely relaxed her.

'Thanks for the compliment.'

'It wasn't a compliment. I don't do compliments. It's the truth. And besides, I'm sure you know that in the game of Scrabble, the word "Ferrara" is worth 10. The top mark . . .'

Ferrara looked at her closely.

'Are you surprised?' she asked. 'Why should you be? A lot of people think you're an outstanding detective. I know I sometimes give you the impression of being on your back. I'm sorry. I can't help it. It's my job.'

And it's what Gallo wants, Ferrara thought.

'I understand,' he said. 'A pity those people you mention don't include the press.'

'They've been down on you, that's true. But it's a sign that they identify you with the whole of the police force, and not just because you're the head of a squad. The truth is, they have confidence in you, and they're provoking you because deep down they know, or hope, that if there's anyone who can stop this killer it's you. And let's not forget they have papers to sell. Stories about serial killers, and the general public being scared, are bigger circulation boosters than football derbies. When you get down to it, they're just doing their job. I wouldn't worry too much about it.'

'I'm not the one who's worried,' he reassured her.

She knew what he meant. The Commissioner and the Prosecutor were the people directly responsible for the maintenance of public order. They were the real targets of the press campaign, and theirs were the heads that would roll if the situation got worse.

'All you have to do now is your duty. Bring us the head of the serial killer on a silver platter.' She said it in a jocular tone, as if to lighten the atmosphere.

'If my theory is correct, we're not dealing with a serial killer.'

'What do you mean?'

'This killer has a very specific plan, with a beginning and an end. He doesn't kill for any of the reasons that usually drive a serial killer. He has a very precise, clearly reasoned motive. He's practically announced seven murders, and he's carried out four of them as planned. He still has three to go. Then he'll have finished and he'll vanish for ever. He'll probably carry on with his normal life, as an office worker, a school principal, a doctor, who knows? – maybe a priest.' There was a clear insinuation in his voice as he uttered these last words.

'What do you mean?'

Ferrara hesitated, and looked into her eyes for a few moments. 'Prosecutor Giulietti, you and I are on the same side, aren't we?'

'Obviously. Always remembering that we have different roles and prerogatives, of course.' She was slightly on the defensive: she couldn't see where Ferrara was going with this.

'Obviously,' he repeated. 'So you could give me a hand, if need be.'

Anna Giulietti became even more defensive. 'In what way?'

Ferrara told her the whole story of Don Sergio, up to and including Father Francesco's veiled hints.

She followed the story with rapt attention. But she was equally attentive to the storyteller: the conviction in his eyes, the certainty in his measured gestures, the drive in the succession of sentences with their almost imperceptible Sicilian cadence, the calm vigour of the foreseen conclusion. 'Will you help me?'

She thought it over. 'Why not go to the archbishop?' she asked at last.

'Because behind Don Sergio's disappearance, there's something we don't know, something even Father Francesco doesn't know. Something the Church is trying to keep quiet. It could be that the priest is insane, but I don't think that's likely. I think there's something else, something the archbishop wouldn't hesitate to cover up, if I, a mere public official, went directly to him. You know as well as I do that the Church has the means to do that. There are secrets that a police superintendent or a deputy prosecutor will never scratch the surface of.'

They both fell silent as Signora Latini's speciality, the pear tart, arrived. Only Anna Giulietti had ordered it, not Ferrara.

'It won't be easy,' she said at last. 'I can't promise anything. But I'll try to help you . . . if you help me with the dessert!'

12

'Simple, isn't it?' Mike Ross said. 'It looks quite innocuous, like some joiner's instrument.'

They were standing in front of the Judas Cradle, a wooden pyramid supported by a tripod and surmounted by an iron ring suspended on ropes above the point of the pyramid.

The prisoner would be hung by the belt with his feet tied, above this sharp point. By means of the rope that secured him to the ceiling, he would be lowered onto the point so that it penetrated his anus – or vagina in the case of a woman.

'There's also a more subtle use,' he explained, as if the illustrations and captions accompanying the object in the exhibition at the Museum of Criminology were not enough. 'The victim was hung in such a way that he was forced to stay awake, because as soon as he relaxed his muscles he would fall onto the point of the pyramid just as if he had been dropped – and with the same results! In fact, it was also known as 'the wake'. It must have been devastating, not only physically, but psychologically as well. Of all the exhibits here, this one must have been the most humiliating, don't you think?'

Valentina did not reply. She was astonished at the extent of his fascination with the horrific depths to which man's cruelty could go. The Inquisitor's Chair, a rough wooden armchair bristling with spines even on the armrests, the Heretic's Fork, two small forks facing each other that would be brought closer together at the level of the neck and the chest, the famous Virgin of Nuremberg . . . One after another, the objects paraded before her stunned eyes. In vain, she tried not to imagine the sufferings of the men and women subjected to these obscene tortures over the centuries.

The whole thing made her nauseous.

'Let's get out of here, please.'

'Hey, kid. I didn't know you were so impressionable.'

'Let's *go*.'

Humouring her, he took her on a tour of the enchanting medieval town, in search of a gift that would make it up to her and show her the pleasanter side of life. He found what he was looking for in a little shop near the Piazza della Cisterna, not far from the museum.

It wasn't the usual tourist trap full of mass-produced trinkets, but a shop run by a young woman who made beautiful necklaces, bracelets and earrings interweaving stones with laces of waxed thread and flax. He bought Valentina two necklaces: one of green and purple crystals and one of large oval ivory-white Bohemian glass pearls. They were a perfect match for the clothes she had chosen for the occasion: an aubergine-coloured ribbed woollen sweater and a Turkish skirt that stopped just above the knees, with two zips at the front. One of the zips was half open, leaving part of her thigh bare.

It was midday, and Mike suggested they start back, and stop somewhere along the way for lunch.

Fifteen minutes' drive in the Porsche, with the hills gliding by and the olive groves shining like silver in the sun, cleared Valentina's head. She had lost her appetite after the visit to the museum, and had thought she wouldn't ever get it back, but now she was starting to feel hungry.

Mike Ross parked outside a somewhat anonymous seventies-style building half hidden by a petrol pump. A large round sign read *Ristorante Latini*.

They went in.

There were three rooms, a large one just past the entrance, and two smaller ones, one at the back and the other to the left. The larger room was fully booked, and a waiter led them to the one on the left, which had a large window looking out on a garden.

Mike let Valentina take the seat facing the window and sat down opposite her. 'Are you hungry?' he asked.

'Only a little.'

'That's a pity. They say the food here is special. It's been highly recommended to me.'

Their first course, the *pappardelle al sugo*, lived up to expectation.

'Delicious,' she said, despite herself.

'I shouldn't have taken you to see that exhibition, should I?'

'Well, it wasn't really my kind of thing . . .' She felt ill at ease. The fact was, she had been feeling uncomfortable ever since he had dampened her enthusiasm by greeting her that morning with a quick peck on the cheek. In the car, they hadn't spoken at all. He had put on Björk's latest CD, which she liked too, and they had listened to it all the way from Florence to San Gimignano.

The grim exhibition of torture instruments had not improved her mood.

'To think I devoted a whole article to it,' he said.

'How was New York?' Valentina asked, changing the subject.

'Same as usual. Work, work and more work.'

They both fell silent, at a loss what to talk about.

'Mike . . .' Valentina said at last, trying to meet his eyes through the sunglasses. She realised that he was staring at something over her shoulder. She turned, but couldn't see anything except anonymous people having animated conversations and, beyond that, the door to the kitchen, over which there was a display of calendars and the insignia of the police, the Carabinieri and the anti-Mafia brigade.

'What is this?' Mike asked the waiter bringing their second course. 'A police canteen?'

'Oh, those?' the waiter replied. 'It's just that they often come in here to eat. In fact, the famous Superintendent Ferrara is here today.'

'I see,' was all Mike said in reply, emphasising his American accent.

'This is a great opportunity for you,' Valentina said eagerly, once the waiter had gone.

'To do what?' Mike asked.

'To meet him. Maybe interview him. A journalist from a big foreign newspaper – he's bound to be flattered. It could be material for your book.'

'What book?'

'The one about the Monster of Florence. Didn't you want to write one for the American public?'

'Like hell I did! That was just something I said. Why should the American public care about some insignificant Italian provincial policeman? I don't even care about it myself. Nasty stories about uncivilised people. I'm an aesthete – if there's no art involved I'm not interested.'

It was clear he had no desire to talk any more about the subject. Again, Valentina felt ill at ease.

On the way out, she spotted the famous Ferrara sitting at a

table in the corner next to the wine cabinet with a striking blonde woman of about fifty. She thought he looked more interesting in real life than on TV.

She felt uncomfortable again when, on the way back to Florence, he said, 'That friend of yours . . . the one in Bologna . . .'

'Cinzia?'

'Yes, that's the one.'

What did Cinzia have to do with anything? She had tried not to think about her since coming back to Florence. She had wanted to concentrate only on him. She was making a desperate effort to dispel the ambiguity of the situation in which she found herself. She wanted to be free of the past, to see things clearly. She had even pulled the zip of her skirt higher than before, leaving her left thigh completely uncovered, and now here he was, dragging her back to the very thing she wanted to forget.

'What about her?' she said, a bit too abruptly.

'Are you very . . . close?'

'We've known each other since we were children.'

'That's not what I meant.'

'What *do* you mean?'

'The other day, when I came to Bologna . . . I got the impression you . . .'

'What? Why don't you just come out with it?'

But he didn't reply. He was driving fast, his eyes fixed on the road ahead.

So that was what was eating him. He'd understood, he'd seen them together, he'd caught them just after they'd got out of bed, at midday. Oh, God!

'Is there . . . anything between you?' he asked at last, hesitantly.

254

'What are you talking about? We're friends, I told you. We rented the apartment together. Actually, it was our parents who rented it for us. They know each other. We've all known each other for years.'

He said nothing, clearly unsatisfied with her answer.

'What do you want to know?' she went on in exasperation. 'If Cinzia and I sleep together? Well, what if we do? It's none of your business. Anyway it's different between girls. It happens sometimes, but it doesn't mean anything.'

'I'm sure it never happened to my mother,' Mike declared unexpectedly.

'What the hell has your mother got to do with it?'

He fell silent again, and stayed that way all the rest of the journey.

The Porsche rumbled along the drive and stopped outside the front door.

'Tell me the truth,' he said, standing beside the car. 'Are you a lesbian?'

Valentina had got out of the car, too. She looked at him angrily, on the verge of tears. 'Fuck you, Mike Ross!' She turned and ran towards the door, repeating in her mind, *Fuck you! Fuck you!*

That night, the noises on the floor below returned, insistently.

She slept restlessly, and dreamed of Mike and Cinzia changing roles constantly, but always mocking her, humiliating her, excluding her. She even saw them fucking, but couldn't figure out which of them was the woman and which the man. They each seemed to play both roles. Sometimes, they fucked like women in heat, and sometimes like effeminate men. Every scene, every shameless, obscene image was accompanied by moans and groans.

She woke up with a splitting headache.

She didn't want to go downstairs. She waited until she heard the sound of the Porsche driving away, and only then left her apartment and went down.

She knocked at the door on the ground floor and asked Nenita to make her a cup of coffee.

'Strong,' she said. 'Very strong. I have a headache.'

She didn't continue, as it was clear Nenita didn't understand a word.

They were in the kitchen again, and Valentina's eyes fell on the key rack. Maybe, she thought, that was why she'd come down here . . .

She went closer. There it was, the smallest key, with a sign next to it that said *First Floor*.

When the coffee maker emitted its triumphant gurgle, she quickly grabbed it.

Nenita was busy taking the coffee pot off the hob.

When Nenita finished her half day and left, Valentina found an excuse to phone Mike on his mobile and make sure he would not be back soon. Then she went down to the first floor and slipped the little key in the padlock, which opened immediately.

The door swung on its hinges. It was well-oiled, and didn't squeak at all.

Valentina went in.

The door closed slowly behind her and she was swallowed by the darkness.

Darkness.

When her eyes had become accustomed to it, she could just about make out half-crumbling, smoke-blackened walls in the gloom. There was a smell of old, damp ashes, like the smell of a fireplace in a house that has not been inhabited for a while.

She groped for a switch next to the door and found it. Nothing happened.

Light filtered from behind the closed windows, outlining the shutters with pale, ghostly haloes.

Driven by an irresistible impulse that overcame any residual hesitation or fear, Valentina moved forward.

She walked in short steps, careful not to trip over the heaps of rubble that lay here and there. She was moving along what seemed a long corridor. She passed the remains of two bedrooms, a room with a large, almost completely charred wooden bookcase, two bathrooms with their pipes uncovered, other rooms, other corridors.

The whole floor covered a huge space, made even larger by the ravages of the fire. Her cautious steps made a sinister echo, forcing her to stop every now and again, her heart in her throat. Then an unnatural silence would fall again over everything, and she would resume her careful walk.

At last she came to a door. The only door still intact. It was closed.

After a few seconds, which seemed to last an eternity, she pushed down the handle and went in.

A new, thicker darkness greeted her. Again she searched for a light switch, sure that this time it would work. Mike used this room.

The light came on, dazzling her with its suddenness.

Valentina looked around her.

It was a boy's bedroom, with sporting trophies, schoolbooks, and posters and pennants on the walls. There was a bed, quite intact, against the wall on the left, and on the right a large desk with a computer, neat piles of books, and bundles of files. Beside the desk, a metal shelving unit, also full of books, and on the wall above the desk, a large poster that didn't seem to belong. It showed the insignia of the

FBI and, beneath it, the words *FBI Academy, Quantico, Virginia*. Next to it was a framed photograph that showed a group of young men in T-shirts and caps with *FBI* on them. One of them was Mike, but his hair was different, longer and darker, chestnut brown perhaps. Did he dye his hair?

At the far end of the room, an armchair and a reading lamp stood beside a large French window covered with two planks of wood nailed on in the shape of an X. All the cracks were sealed with brown packing tape. To Valentina, the window seemed like an ugly blemish in a room that in every other way was pleasant and clean, and meticulously tidy.

She approached the metal shelves and looked at the books. The first two titles she saw were *Killers on the Loose: Unsolved Cases of Serial Murder* by Antonio Mendoza, and *Still at Large: A Casebook of 20th Century Serial Killers Who Eluded Justice* by Michael Newton.

The others were all in the same vein: *To Die of Horror: A Hundred Years of Serial Killers and Crimes Told as a Novel* by Enzo Catania, *I Have Lived in the Monster: Inside the Minds of the World's Most Notorious Serial Killers* by Robert K. Ressler and Tom Shachtman, *Serial Killer: Methods of Identification and Investigative Procedures* by Silvio Ciappi, *The Killers Among Us: An Examination of Serial Murder and Its Investigation* by Steven A. Egger . . .

Valentina was puzzled. Hadn't he told her he wasn't interested in the subject and that he had no intention of writing a book about the Monster of Florence? If she remembered rightly, he had dismissed her suggestion out of hand. So why . . .?

She sat down at the desk.

The books here were similar to the ones on the shelves. She turned her attention to the files. As she pulled them towards her, something slipped to the floor, but she didn't take any notice of it. She was hypnotised by the letter heading on the first document in the pile:

The other documents were also from the FBI, some stamped in blue ink with the word CLASSIFIED.

Valentina was bewildered. Who was Mike Ross? Was the journalism a cover, and was he really an FBI agent? What was he looking for in Italy?

13

On 15 March, the day after his lunch with Anna Giulietti, Ferrara received an envelope from the Prosecutor's Department. Inside was the experts' report on the weapon used to kill Giovanni Biagini, preceded by Anna Giulietti's question: *Do the experts find that the weapon found at the crime scene is the same as that used to murder and/or torture Stefano Micali on 1 October 1999, Alfredo Lupi on 31 December 1999 and Francesco Bianchi on 2 February 2000, or rather, do they find it to be compatible with the characteristics (shape, size, depth) of the wounds found on the bodies of the aforementioned Micali, Lupi and Bianchi?*

Ferrara could not help noticing that in formulating the question – linking the four murders, even Micali's, which was supposed to have been solved – Anna Giulietti seemed to have come over to his way of thinking. Pleasantly surprised, he quickly skimmed to the end of the report. The experts, having also studied the pathologist's reports which described in detail the configuration of the wounds, as well as the photos of the corpses enlarged as much as possible on their computers, came to the conclusion that *it can reasonably be stated, even though it is not possible to establish scientifically that this was the same weapon, that despite the differences between the*

various cases, the knife used to murder Giovanni Biagini is per-
fectly compatible with the wounds inflicted on the bodies of
Micali, Bianchi and Lupi.

Translated into less bureaucratic language, it was a more
than satisfactory result. Anna Giulietti must have thought the
same, since she'd taken the trouble to send it straight to him.

Almost simultaneously, a report on the fingerprints came
in from the Forensics department in Rome. The prints found
on the knife used to kill Biagini had proved to be identical to
those found on the wash basin and the glass in Francesco
Bianchi's apartment.

Ferrara sat back in his armchair and took a deep drag on
the cigar he had just lit. The pieces of the mosaic were falling
into place. True, the prints didn't match any found in the
national records, but if they got hold of a suspect there was
now an infallible way of proving that he was the culprit.

He thought about getting hold of Don Sergio's prints, and
smiled. The moment would come, sooner or later. From
Rizzo's discreet inquiries with the airline companies and the
border police, it had emerged that nobody by the name of
Sergio Rotondi had left Italy in the last two months. It was
possible, of course, that he had used a false name to get away,
or hadn't been logged because he fell into a category of trav-
ellers who weren't checked, but Ferrara didn't think so. After
all, the killer had a mission to complete.

One difficulty still remained: how to penetrate the enclosed
world of the Church. It all depended on Anna Giulietti . . .

That afternoon, when Cinzia Roberti got back from university, she switched on the TV, and went into the kitchenette to
boil water for tea.

She took the teabags and some biscotti from the sideboard,
all the while listening distractedly to the news in English on

CNN. She forced herself to do this regularly in an attempt to try and improve her English, and she was starting to get results.

As she was putting a teabag in the boiling water, she heard the name Mike Ross. Or thought she did.

It was like the man was stalking her! She went closer to the TV set in the living room. An elderly man with thin dark hair, wearing thick glasses with heavy black frames, was talking about the run-up to the Oscar nominations, which were soon to be announced.

She waited for the young journalist – she refused to utter his name – to appear on the screen.

The camera pulled back to reveal another, younger man next to the elderly man, clearly interviewing him. But he wasn't Valentina's friend either.

Cinzia didn't understand the question, but she caught the opening of it clearly enough: 'Okay, Mike, so . . .'

She must have misheard the name from the kitchen: this was obviously another Mike.

The camera zoomed in again on the older man as he started speaking.

Cinzia stood up and was about to go back to the kitchen when a caption appeared below the man's face: *Mike Ross of the* New York Times *reporting from Hollywood*.

Cinzia froze in horror.

So who was . . .?

'Fuck!' she exclaimed. 'The bastard!' She ran into the bedroom, grabbed her mobile phone and stabbed at the 1, the speed-dial for Valentina's number.

She heard it ringing.

Ferrara picked up the receiver.

'Did you get my message?' It was Anna Giulietti.

'Yes, thanks. It tallies with the forensics results from Rome – I'll send you a copy.'

'Which results are they?'

'On the fingerprints.'

'Fine, I'm curious to see them. Everything seems to be backing up your theory, doesn't it?'

'It looks that way.'

'Congratulations. And there's something else. I've made an appointment for you to see Monsignor Federici at eleven o'clock tomorrow morning at the Curia. Do you know where it is?'

'Of course.'

'Then do go. Federici is the cardinal's private secretary. From what I hear, he could be useful to you.'

The answers to all Valentina's questions about the mysterious Mike Ross lay at her feet.

After she had looked through the files, she sat back in the chair and closed her eyes. She felt dazed. When she opened them again, she caught sight of the object that had fallen from the table.

It was a small book, its cover completely black except for a gold cross. It looked like a little Bible, but opening it at random she discovered that it was a notebook, its pages filled with tiny, meticulous handwriting. On the page she was looking down at, her own name appeared three times.

Starting from that page, Valentina began reading the diary of Mike Ross, whoever he was. Goose pimples broke out on her skin.

The diary was full of the man's constant, obsessive declarations of love for her. What shook her most was the way he saw her, the way he talked about her: sometimes as a Madonna, sometimes as a bimbo, but mostly as the mother he had never known. Over and over again, the roles became con-fused, and in his imagination, as set down on the page, he addressed her as 'Mother' and told her terrible stories of childhood abuse. There were pages of violent emotion flung down on the page without punctuation, and others of strange, hallucinatory clarity.

Unable to stop, terrified and fascinated despite herself, Valentina broke off her reading, went back to the first page of the diary, and started from the beginning.

The notebook began with these words:

October 1st 1999

In your name, Father, I have killed.
It was easy. Liberating.
Far more so than a Confession.
Now at last I am born!
I will go all the way . . .

The ringing of the mobile phone echoed in the room like the thunder of the apocalypse, sending her heart into her mouth and a shudder through her body.

'Don't answer it.'

The voice was calm, ice-cold, even though his eyes were brimming with tears. Valentina turned slowly, emotionlessly, like an automaton. She was beyond fear now.

'You shouldn't have, you shouldn't have . . .' he said, weep-ing. 'I loved you, I loved you more than anyone in the world.'

He was standing in the doorway. She had no idea how long he had been watching her.

Valentina had never seen a gun, and didn't know what that metal tube was, screwed onto the barrel and pointing straight at her heart.

14

Ferrara went down to the press room, as if he had just happened to wander in that direction. The only person there was Ahmed Farah, a reporter for *La Nazione*. He was of Egyptian descent, young but very good.

'Anything new, Superintendent?'

'No, nothing,' he replied. Then, as if having second thoughts, he said, 'Actually, no, come with me.'

In the corridor he put an arm around his shoulder and whispered, conspiratorially, 'Can you keep a secret?'

'Of course. It's my job.'

'Right. This is just between you and me. We've nearly got him. We have his fingerprints, we have his DNA profile from the sperm found in Francesco Bianchi's body . . .' He paused. 'And we have a key witness.'

'Who?'

'I'm sorry, but I can't tell you that. I trust you, of course, but I have to protect him . . .'

'I understand.'

'Anyway, it won't be long now. Just wait and you'll have the scoop of your life.'

'Thanks, Superintendent. So you know his identity?'

Ferrara stopped, and pretended to think about it. 'You'll

be the first to know, but only if you can keep this secret for now.'

Ahmed replied with a broad, knowing smile.

'Remember, we haven't had this conversation,' Ferrara said, and went back to his office.

'I'll remember, boss,' Ahmed said, clicking his heels and miming a military salute.

It was a risky thing to do. If the killer thought the police were on to him, he might go to ground, making it all the harder to catch him. But if that happened, Ferrara would at least have the consolation of knowing he'd saved a couple of lives, and that was much more important than catching the man. And of course he'd continue with the investigation, because the lull wouldn't be permanent. The killer had sworn to complete his mission, and he wouldn't let go of that: that was something Ferrara was sure of.

The other possibility was that the killer might decide to complete the rest of his plan more quickly, and if he did that he would be more likely to make a mistake. It was this even-tuality that Ferrara was banking on in feeding that false information to Farah.

It was the right moment to do it.

Both public and police had become more vigilant since the latest murder. There was an atmosphere of suspicion in the city, which made it harder for the killer to operate. Fear had spread through the gay community in particular, and according to reports from the Cascine, casual encounters had become less common there. By forcing him out into the open, Ferrara was putting the killer at a clear dis-advantage.

After the third unanswered phone call in fifteen minutes, Cinzia had sent a text message.

Why no answer? Must talk to you. That man not Mike Ross. Be careful.

The man with the ice-cold eyes wrapped Valentina's lifeless body in a blanket.

The mobile had rung several times. Now a text message had come through. The man read it with a grimace of resignation.

He looked in Valentina's handbag for the keys to the Panda, and hoisted the body onto his back. He went downstairs and out to the car. The boot of the Porsche was too small, and he certainly couldn't drive around with that large bundle on the seat next to his. Nor did he want blood seeping through the blanket and leaving marks on the leather interior of the Porsche. The girl's car was much more suitable.

Once he'd put the body in the boot of the Panda, he went back inside the house. He took a long shower, changed, and burned the clothes he'd just taken off. Then he poured himself half a glass of whisky and sipped it while listening to the tragic notes of Liszt's *Dante Sonata*. Finally, he put on a pair of driving gloves and left the house.

The sun was disappearing below the horizon as he drove the Panda out through the gate of the villa and headed for the autostrada.

Signora Adele Spizzichino, who lived in the same building as Cinzia Roberti, got home late that night. As she took the front door key from her handbag, she was joined by a tall, fair-haired young man who, curiously enough, was wearing sunglasses even at such a late hour. But he had a distinguished air, a captivating smile and a small bunch of roses and tulips in one hand.

As she opened the door, she saw that the man was reading the names beside the entry phone.

'Do you want to come in?' she asked politely. The idea that he might be harbouring any evil intention was the furthest thing from her mind.

'Thank you, that's very kind of you,' he said with a slight English accent, which confirmed her good impression of him.

Nimbly, the young man started up the stairs while Adele Spizzichino, who lived on an upper floor, took the lift. *Lucky girl!* she thought, envying the woman who was expecting such a handsome young man, although she had no idea who that might be.

Halfway up the flight of stairs, the man heard the lift coming up and did an about-turn. He went back to the ground floor and continued down to the basement. The door was not locked. He moved along the damp corridor in the dark until he found a niche, where he settled to wait patiently, his long knife within easy reach in case of emergency.

Cinzia Roberti was fast asleep. By the time she went to bed, she had been exhausted, anxious, and dizzy with too much smoke and alcohol. She had spent all afternoon calling and texting Valentina, to no avail. She felt powerless. She couldn't phone Vale's parents in San Vigilio because they didn't even know their daughter had moved to Florence and she'd only alarm them. She couldn't go and look for her friend in Florence because she'd never told her where she lived, only that she had a beautiful apartment in a big villa with a view over the city. Not enough to go on.

So all she had left was her mobile phone, something she often overused, but which had turned out to be completely useless just when she needed it the most.

At dinnertime, she had opened a bottle of whisky and rolled a big joint, hoping to forget her worries at least temporarily. Later she had almost groped her way to the bedroom, had torn off her clothes and thrown herself naked on the bed, weeping.

She fell into a tortured but deep sleep. So deep was it that the click of the lock in the middle of the night did not wake her.

Nor did she notice the blade being thrust between her shoulder blades and the first vertebra on the left, abruptly stopping her heartbeat.

She passed directly from sleep to death.

The man closed the blinds carefully and turned on the light. The girl lay motionless, blood gushing from the knife wound: she was dead.

He turned her over.

He looked at her for a long time, wondering what his Valentina could possibly have seen in this thin, angular body, with its tiny, obscenely childish breasts.

The more he looked at her, the more disgusted he felt, and the more intensely he felt that total, unstoppable hatred of homosexuality which overcame him more and more these days. Men only, up until now. But this evil bitch who had stolen the love of his life from him was just the same: a filthy lesbian.

His hatred soon turned to blind rage and he began stabbing the body, as he had with the others.

This one wasn't part of the plan, but the plan had changed.

It was about three in the morning. Too early, or too late, for anyone to notice the man taking a heavy bundle out of the Panda parked outside the building where Cinzia Roberti lived, and carrying it inside. Nor did anyone see the same man come back out nearly an hour later and set off on foot towards the station.

15

Michele Ferrara entered the Curia of Florence at ten in the morning on Thursday 16 March. Monsignor Federici had been very pleasant on the phone and had intimated that he had orders from above to cooperate in every possible way.

But when at last he was in the presence of the prelate, Ferrara realised that the interview wouldn't exactly be plain sailing. The monsignor was friendly enough, but it immediately became clear that he was a consummate diplomat, capable of talking a lot without saying anything – capable, too, if need be, of concealing anything he considered it would not be in the best interests of the Holy Mother Church to reveal.

Hoping these interests would coincide with his own, Ferrara sat down in the armchair which Monsignor Federici offered him.

'I'm honoured to make your acquaintance, Chief Superintendent,' the prelate began. 'The Church owes you a great deal, and will always be grateful to you for recovering the Velazquez painting.'

'Thank you, Monsignor.'

'I've been asked by His Eminence the Cardinal to answer your questions about one of the priests in our diocese.'

'Father Sergio Rotondi, yes.'

'Precisely. I'm sure you won't mind telling me why you are searching for him?'

'Because he's vanished. And people don't just vanish into thin air.'

'If this is any comfort to you, he hasn't vanished as far as we're concerned. He's alive and, as far as we know, well.'

'Does that mean I can talk to him?'

The prelate hesitated, then let out a deep sigh. 'No,' he said at last. 'Or at the very least, it won't be easy.'

'May I ask why?'

'Of course you may. As I said, we are indebted to you and we would like to pay our debt. However . . . I'm not sure I can answer your question directly. Perhaps you'll allow me to ask you something first.'

'Please.'

'It's an obvious question, but could you tell me why it's so important to you to speak to Don Sergio?'

'Because he's a major witness to a serious crime. Perhaps you recall . . .'

'The murder of Stefano Micali, of course. Last October, wasn't it? Poor boy. And poor Don Sergio, I know he was very upset. But surely he's already been questioned by the police, hasn't he? And I also recall that Father Francesco provided him with an alibi. So why do you still need him?'

'Because whoever killed Stefano Micali has killed again, and he hasn't finished yet. I'm sure you know that. It's been in all the newspapers.'

'"Florence trembles and Ferrara does nothing".' Monsignor Federici smiled. 'I shouldn't worry about bad press if I were you. But didn't I read in the newspapers today that you have a key witness and are very close to arresting the killer? Or is that an invention? The journalist claims you already know the killer's identity. Is that why you're here? Is it Don Sergio you're after?'

'I'm sorry, Monsignor, but that's the kind of information I can't reveal in the course of an investigation,' Ferrara said: he preferred not to officially endorse a lie, but at the same time didn't deny it.

'In that case I can assure you we aren't hiding Don Sergio Rotondi here. That's what you think, isn't it?' There was something ambiguous about his smile now.

Ferrara wondered if he ought to prevaricate or tell the truth. 'I don't just think it. I know it. Or rather, I know that you know where he is, and that's all I need.'

'Of course.' The prelate thought for a moment. 'I suppose you do realise the gravity of your . . . accusation? No, let's not call it that. You haven't shown me any evidence. If you told me officially that Don Sergio Rotondi was wanted for murder, I would tell you where he is. But so far you haven't done that, and I have the impression you won't. That means we're dealing with hypotheses, suppositions, conjectures, the only result of which would be to bring the good name of the Church into disrepute. Not only because, according to your theory, one of our priests is a killer, but also, and above all, because the killer – in your theory – has been shielded by another priest, a parish priest of proven faith and exemplary honesty.'

'Father Francesco is an old man. He told me he often nods off, and he hasn't ruled out the possibility that it might have happened that day as he was going over the accounts with Father Sergio . . .'

At last something had hit home. Monsignor Federici frowned and put the fingers of both his hands together. 'I see,' he said at last, in a grave voice. 'Congratulations, Chief Superintendent. Are you a chess player?'

'No.'

'A pity, you'd be a worthy opponent. You've just checked me. But I don't think you're right. I know Father Rotondi. In fact, I know him quite well. It fell to me to interview him . . .'

'So you also suspected —'

'Oh, no, it wasn't about that. It was about something else entirely. Let's say, a spiritual matter. Please don't ask me to go into detail. But I assure you I was able to probe his soul – and his mind, too. There are many things he may be, but a killer he isn't. Don Sergio is a shy, humble man, Superintendent, a man tormented by leanings similar to those of the murder victim, leanings he has always struggled to suppress.'

'It wouldn't be the first case of a homosexual killing by those like him because he's ashamed to be that way.'

'I refuse to believe it. But even if it were true, he's no longer in a position to hurt anyone. If he is the killer, there won't be any more deaths, I can assure you, and the Church can be kept out of this unpleasant business. Divine justice will deal with him when the time comes.'

'How can you be so sure? That won't do, not as far as earthly justice is concerned.'

'What did I say? You're a good chess player. Now it's up to me to make the next move . . .' He sighed, as if surrendering. 'But I beg you, in so far as it's humanly possible, to keep to yourself what I'm about to tell you. Not that it's a secret, but the Church would prefer it not to be talked about openly, that's all.

'I'm sure you've heard of closed orders. Monks and nuns who take a vow of silence and spend their days in prayer and work, far from the eyes of the world, with just a brief pause during the day to exchange a few words and pray together.

'But perhaps you've never heard of the most extreme form of closed order. Voluntary reclusion. It's a legacy of the Middle Ages. Some people consider it a barbaric custom, which is why it's largely fallen into disuse. But it hasn't completely disappeared. Anyone who chooses this path is confined to a cell, and only leaves that cell when he is dead. It isn't unusual for him to be walled up alive, the only opening being a small window through which to pass food prepared by his brothers in the monastery. In the cell he has only the bare essentials, and he sleeps in a wooden box which will eventually be his coffin.

'There are still some individuals, inspired by a deep desire to expiate something or to be closer to the Lord, who ask for reclusion, and in very particular circumstances the Church accedes to their wishes. The last example known to the public is that of Sister Nazarena, an American woman whose real name was Julia Crotta. She lived as a recluse for forty years, and was much admired by Pope Paul VI.

'That is the path, Chief Superintendent, which Don Sergio has chosen. The situation he is in now can't be equalled even in your toughest prisons. I think it best if we leave him in peace to serve out his sentence, however long that may be.'

Ferrara was stunned. He felt an intolerable burden, a sense of inadequacy, the unpleasant sensation that he had put his eye to a keyhole and seen something he should not have seen. In comparison with this, the usual burdens of everyday life, including the burdens he carried inside him, seemed trivial. They were all forgivable, like forgetting to buy flowers for his wife on International Women's Day.

He stood up, ready to end the interview then and there, but reserving the right to come back when he had definite proof of the priest's guilt. When that happened, not even the respect he felt for the Church would stop him from doing his duty. For the moment, Monsignor Federici was right: he could not lift the veil on this secret when the only evidence he had was circumstantial.

'Believe me, Chief Superintendent,' the old prelate said, also standing up. 'What you are thinking is very, very unlikely. Father Sergio is merely a poor, frightened man.'

Ferrara stopped. 'Frightened of what?'

'His sins? The world? Who knows?'

'Or the killer? Maybe he's a split personality, and is trying to escape his other self by shutting himself up in a cell. Or maybe he knows who the killer is, but can't say anything. Doesn't it seem to you a curious coincidence that he disappeared just when someone's going around killing people like him?'

He had said all this off the top of his head, without thinking, as if from a sudden flash of inspiration. Or perhaps it was just the instinct he'd developed after so many years in the profession.

Monsignor Federici hesitated again.

There was a long silence.

'Checkmate, Chief Superintendent Ferrara,' he sighed at last. 'I'll try to obtain a dispensation for you, so that you can talk to Father Sergio. I can't promise anything, but I'll certainly try.'

16 March was Valentina's father's birthday and she always phoned to wish him many happy returns. Surprised that she hadn't heard from her during the morning, her mother had called her early in the afternoon and, not getting a reply, had tried both Cinzia's mobile phone and the apartment, without success.

She tried again half an hour later, then half an hour after that. She was starting to get worried. Finally, she made up her mind and called the hospital where Doctor Roberti worked. She apologised for disturbing him at work, and told him that she'd preferred to call him rather than passing on her worries, which were surely unfounded, to his wife. Cinzia's father reassured her and promised he'd go to the girls' apartment as soon as he was free, if he hadn't managed to get hold of them in the meantime. He gave instructions to the switchboard to keep ringing all the numbers and to put his daughter or her friend through to him as soon as they'd reached either.

A quarter of an hour later, after finishing with a patient, he called the switchboard.

'There's no answer, doctor. Either on the mobile or the home number.'

'Have you tried Valentina's mobile as well?'

'Yes, doctor.'

He frowned and looked at his watch. 5.45 p.m.

'Apologise to the other patients for me, but I'll have to reschedule my appointments,' he said, standing and taking off his white coat.

'Do you think —?'

'No, I don't think anything's happened. But it's best if I go and see.'

He got into his car and set off, cursing the traffic as he drove. He reached his daughter's building at 6.20. It took him three more interminable minutes to find a place to park, and in the end he left the car double parked with all its lights on. It wasn't right, but he had no choice. He saw Valentina's old Panda parked there, and for some reason he felt relieved.

He took the lift. By the time he reached the door of the apartment, he felt a vague sense of dizziness. The lock showed clear signs of having been forced. He opened the door and went in.

'Cinzia!' he called.

Silence.

The bedroom door was ajar and he could see that the light was on. He ran to the door and flung it open.

Doctor Roberti was a surgeon, used to seeing dead bodies. But the sight that greeted him now was more than he could bear.

Alessandro Polito, head of Bologna's *Squadra Mobile*, reached the crime scene soon after seven. There were already various police cars outside the building with their blue lights flashing, as well as two ambulances. TV crews and newspaper reporters were crowding around the main entrance. The forensics team had just arrived, too.

He ran up the stairs.

A man who must have been the father of one of the two girls sat on the sofa, looking crushed and ashen, in a state of shock, and Silvia, one of his policewomen, was holding out a glass of whisky and trying to persuade him to take a sip.

He entered the bedroom and saw a sight he could never have imagined seeing in his whole life.

The smaller of the girls lay in a pool of blood, with a gaping wound in her back. Next to her lay the other girl, who was taller and shapelier, her body strangely clean except where it was in contact with the small girl's. The expression on her face was composed, serene, almost angelic.

Above her left breast was a very noticeable bullet hole with no traces of blood around it, as if it had been carefully cleaned.

By contrast, Cinzia Roberti's body – one of his inspectors had told him her identity – was covered in blood, and it was clear that the parts still hidden because of the way she was lying must be terribly mutilated. But what made the scene uniquely horrifying was the position of the bodies, with Cinzia's hand inserted – up to, and even past, the wrist – in Valentina's vagina.

16

The TV news broadcasts that evening devoted a lot of space to the item, but Ferrara did not watch them.

He heard about the murders the following morning, from the radio. Everything about the case – the unusual circumstances, the youth and beauty of the victims, certain unpleasant details concealed by the police but partly revealed by the journalists in vague allusions that played on the morbid curiosity of the public – had aroused interest nationwide. Even in Florence, the series of murders that had shaken the city was relegated to second place.

When he got to his office, he read the newspaper reports. By mid-morning, he felt duty bound to call Polito.

'Nasty case,' he said.

'You can say that again. Never seen anything like it. Absolutely appalling. And the weirdest thing is that Valentina Preti wasn't killed in the apartment. There were no traces of her blood anywhere, but there were some in her car, which was parked outside the building. And her death took place at least eight hours earlier. It's almost as if the killer took her there just to . . .' – and he told Ferrara the details the press had merely hinted at. 'Can you imagine anything more bizarre and disgusting?'

'I don't envy you,' Ferrara said, feeling uncomfortable. 'You already have your hands full with those prostitute murders, this was all you needed. We're both going through it at the moment. What a profession we're in!'

'Well, if things go as I hope, we may be able to solve this one quickly. We've got a witness.'

'Lucky you. Did she see the murder?'

'No. But she lives in the building. Last night she let a stranger in through the front door. It was dark and she didn't see him very well, but we know that he's tall and fair-haired, has an English or American accent and wears sunglasses even at night. Young and handsome, according to the witness. He had a bunch of flowers in his hand, so she assumed he had a date and let him in without suspecting a thing. We interviewed everyone in the building last night, and no one admitted knowing him, let alone letting him in to their apartment. Of course, if he had something going with a married woman, she wouldn't have wanted to tell us straight out, especially if her husband was around. Anyway, we're working on a photofit.'

'That's good! Keep me informed, okay? If I can give you a hand, let me know.'

'Sure. Bye.'

In the middle of the afternoon, there was a phone call from Massimo Verga.

'Has something happened?' Ferrara asked. Massimo almost never phoned him at work.

'No, nothing. I just wanted to tell you something. You know that girl who was killed in Bologna?'

'Cinzia Roberti?'

'No, the other one, Valentina.'

'Right.'

'I've been thinking about it all day. I was sure I'd seen her before and then I remembered. I lent her an old book, the *Necronomicon* by Abdul Alhazred, and she never gave it back. Mind you, it wasn't valuable.'

'You knew her?' Ferrara asked, astonished.

'Not really. She came to the shop on October 1st last year. You remember, it was the day Stefano Micali was murdered. Probably just a coincidence, but that's why I decided to call you. Well, that's one reason. The other is that she told me she was studying arts, music and drama but was thinking of coming to live in Florence to do a course on popular theatre in the Renaissance. They must know something about her at the university, don't you think?'

'Good idea. I'll pass it on to Polito, who's in charge of the case. He'll be grateful to you. Was she really pretty?'

'Very.'

'And I guess you couldn't resist. Was she on her own? Did you flirt with her?'

'Yes, but it was a hopeless case, my friend. My days as a Latin lover are long over. It's a young man's world. She was alone when she came into the shop, but she'd been given a lift by a guy in a huge Porsche. A flashy dresser, this guy, and he still had sunglasses on even though it was seven o'clock in the evening. One of those tall, blond guys you see on fashion posters, you know? What can a poor old Sicilian do in a situation like that, however good-looking and —'

Ferrara had stopped listening. The description was practically identical to the one Polito had passed on to him.

'Wait, did you see him well? Can you give me a fuller description?'

'Oh God, I didn't really take much notice of him. I have to admit, I was more interested in the girl. Poor thing . . . But Rita sold him an expensive pen. She must have got a better look at him than I did.'

'Let me speak to her.'

'Is it important?'

'Let me speak to her, Massimo.'

He was shaking as he waited for Rita to come on the line.

'Hi, Superintendent, how are things?'

'Rita, do you remember the man who came into the shop on October 1st and bought a pen? He was with a pretty girl . . .'

'Valentina Preti, poor thing, I read about it. Tell me, Superintendent, I'm all ears.'

'What about him? Do you remember him?'

'Hard to forget him. Especially his eyes – hard, cold as ice.'

'What else? Can you describe him to me?'

'More than six feet tall, athletic build, short fair hair, dyed in my opinion, very light grey eyes, foreign accent, English or American, more likely American, I'd say. Smartly dressed, rich obviously, look at the car he was driving. Can you imagine? He parked it outside for nearly half an hour, didn't give a damn about the ticket.'

It wasn't possible. He couldn't believe his ears. He'd never had so much luck all in one go.

'What . . .' – he hesitated, like someone about to place a bet at the roulette table, knowing for sure he has the right number but afraid the wheel might jam at the last moment – 'what ticket?'

'The parking ticket! Right here, outside the bookshop, can you imagine? If the traffic wardens hadn't arrived, I'd have called the police! Being a piece of shit is one thing, but doing whatever you like just because you've got money, that's something else again!'

'Thanks, Rita. If you were here, I'd give you a kiss!'

'Drop in whenever you like, Superintendent. I'm not going anywhere!'

*

Ferrara called Serpico, gave him the details, and ordered him to contact the traffic police immediately. Then he summoned Rizzo and brought him up to date.

It wasn't difficult to trace the car.

Within fifteen minutes, Inspector Sergi was back.

'The ticket was issued at 7.05 on October 1st 1999. The car was a Porsche Carrera with the licence number AP 286 XS. It was registered in Florence in the name of Lorenzo Ricciardi, living at 36 Via della Campora, in Bellosguardo.'

'Ricciardi?' Ferrara repeated. 'Like the antique dealer?'

'Of course!' Rizzo exclaimed. 'Ricciardi was the previous owner of the shop where Alfredo Lupi was killed. He died in a fire in his villa. Now I come to think of it, I'm pretty sure it was in Bellosguardo.'

'Check if they're related. And send a team right now to stake out this Ricciardi's house. I'll ask the Prosecutor's Department for authorisation to tap his phone. Sergi, check if the man owns a mobile.'

When the men had gone, Ferrara dialled Anna Giulietti's number.

After talking to Anna Giulietti, he phoned Polito.

'I've found your fair-haired man,' he announced triumphantly. 'I know you're not going to believe this, but we may just possibly have killed two birds with one stone. This guy could be my man, too! His name is Lorenzo Ricciardi. He's from Florence, and I've already got his house staked out. If you come here tomorrow, we can pay him a visit together.'

'But . . . how did you . . .?' Polito said after a stunned silence.

'I'll tell you tomorrow, but trust me, I'm sure. Are you coming?'

'You bet! Why not now?'

'I need a search warrant, and I won't get it till tomorrow morning. But don't worry, everything's under control. Bring me the photos of the corpses and the ballistics report. Something tells me there might be some interesting comparisons to be made.'

The following morning, Saturday – the maid's day off – Ferrara was informed that the house was still dark. Nobody had gone in or out. The Porsche was still parked outside.

'Did you bring the photos?' he asked Polito, who had arrived punctually at nine o'clock.

'Here's the report.'

Ferrara spread the photographs on his desk and examined the faces through a powerful magnifying glass. Knowing what to look for now, he had no difficulty identifying the 'A' on Cinzia Roberti's face, half-hidden among the other wounds. He was puzzled, though. He would have expected to find that letter somewhere on the body of Valentina Preti, who had been killed first, and an 'r' on Cinzia's.

It was a troubling detail, but not enough to dent his certainty that he was on the right track. It was nearly 9.30: time for the meeting.

'Anything wrong?' Polito asked.

'No, let's go,' Ferrara said. 'No point waiting any longer.'

The *Squadra Mobile*'s conference room was not large enough to accommodate all those who had been summoned, and Ferrara had decided to hold the meeting in the reception room on the second floor which was normally used for special occasions, especially by the Commissioner. About six hundred square feet furnished in a modern style, its walls adorned with historical paintings on loan from the regional heritage board.

Ferrara sat down with Rizzo and Polito at the long conference table. Facing them, occupying the first rows of seats, were some thirty men, including inspectors. There were also a few marksmen sent all the way from Rome: that was due to Carracci, contacted by Ferrara the night before. They were from NOCS, the special forces unit usually brought in to deal with high-risk situations, who had become famous in the media for a number of major operations, including the liberation of the American general James Lee Dozier on 28 January 1982. The members of NOCS were highly trained in the use of firearms, precision shooting and assault techniques. They were distinguished from other police officers by their special black tracksuits, as well as their powerful athletic builds.

A member of the forensics team stood ready to work the projector which had been placed in the centre of the room, pointing towards a white screen to the right of the table where the three superintendents had taken their places.

The aim of the meeting was to prepare their raid on the villa in Bellosguardo down to the smallest detail. Photographs of the villa taken at dawn from a helicopter and land registry maps would be projected on the screen.

Ferrara opened the meeting.

He started by explaining the nature of the operation and the objective: to enter the villa and capture a dangerous killer.

An image of the villa appeared on the screen. It was surrounded by an extensive garden protected by high walls.

'Right, this is the place,' he said. 'The wall will have to be manned on both sides of the gate before we go in.' He went up to the screen and pointed out the positions with a wooden stick. 'Inspector Venturi has already inspected the area, and he'll put one officer on each side. They'll have to be placed so that they can keep visual contact between them.

'When they're in position, I'll ring at the gate. If it's opened, I'll go in in an armoured car, along with the NOCS commander and two of his men. Everyone agreed?'

'Of course,' the commander replied immediately, sounding very sure of himself.

'I don't agree,' Polito objected.

'Why?'

'Because I'd like to go in with you.'

He had a point. The murder had been committed within his jurisdiction, even though the area they were going into was Ferrara's responsibility.

'Okay.'

'What if there's no answer?' the NOCS commander asked.

'Then we'll open the gate ourselves. A crowbar should do it. But we'll have to move quickly – every second counts, the element of surprise is important. We have the prosecutor's authorisation to use force to remove any obstacles to our search, even if it means causing damage. Any questions?'

No one asked anything. He saw only heads nodding in agreement.

'Once inside the grounds, each man will have his own special task. We'll spread out, making sure we always keep visual contact, and advance towards the villa, under my orders. Nobody, I repeat nobody, must do anything off his own bat, understood?'

They all nodded.

Ferrara signalled to the forensics man to go on to the next image: a detail of the villa.

'This is the front door. There's another door at the back, almost at the corner, but it can't be seen in the photo. We'll try ringing again, and if there is no immediate answer we'll force this door, too. If it's metal . . .'

'We'll take over,' the NOCS commander said, as if the

scene had been rehearsed. 'We'll use explosive charges. It'll only take a few seconds.'

'Good,' Ferrara said. 'Now we come to the trickiest part. I want you all to listen very carefully because we can't afford the slightest error. Once we're inside, six officers, equipped with night sights and rifles, will immediately take up position, two on each floor, check that the corridors are basically safe, then provide cover for their colleagues to go in and search.'

Ferrara, Rizzo and Polito, each at the head of a team, would simultaneously enter and search the rooms on all three floors – Ferrara on the ground floor, Rizzo on the first floor and Polito on the second.

While Ferrara explained the operations inside the villa, the man from forensics projected images from the land registry maps showing the internal structure of the villa and the layout of the rooms.

'One very important thing,' Ferrara said. 'To communicate among ourselves, we'll use portable radios equipped with earphones. As we don't want anyone listening in, we'll be using a private frequency.'

He knew the press often listened in to police frequencies to keep up to date, and he had no desire for them to know what was happening in the villa.

'Will there still be anyone outside the villa?' Rizzo asked.

'One man on each side to make sure no one throws anything out of the windows or shoots at us or tries to escape. We already have people outside the perimeter wall, but we need to keep an eye on the villa from close up, too.'

'What about helicopters?'

'I'll tell the commander of the Airborne Squad to keep one ready. We'll use it if we need it. They can get to us in a few minutes, if necessary.'

The meeting ended. There was nothing else to say.

They went down in groups to the courtyard and took their places in various police cars and one unmarked van. They were all wearing bulletproof vests and had their weapons at the ready. Some carried sub-machine guns and M16s, others lethal-looking pump rifles.

As they were going downstairs, Polito whispered in Ferrara's ear, 'I wasn't expecting such a display of force. I thought the two of us would be going in with a few men. What if Ricciardi's not at home and sees this little army as he's coming back? Isn't that a big risk?'

'No. If he gets as far as that, he's already in our trap. There's only one access road and it'll be guarded by plain clothes men who'll keep well out of sight. Once in, he won't be able to get out. If on the other hand, he's barricaded himself inside the house, then the more precautions we take, the better. If he was inside and it was just the two of us going in, we'd be perfect targets, wouldn't we?'

Polito nodded.

The cars and the van left Headquarters, in ones and twos in order not to attract attention, especially from the journalists.

When they arrived, Ferrara went up to one of the men on guard.

'Anything new?'

'Nothing, chief. I don't think anyone's at home. No signs of life from inside.'

Ferrara rang the bell at the gate twice. There was no reply. He ordered the gate to be forced. Everything went according to plan. They swept into the grounds and reached the front door. As they had half expected, it was made of metal. The NOCS men blew it open and within a couple of minutes, they were inside the villa and proceeding as ordered.

The portable radios immediately started to crackle. Every

message said the same thing: there was no one in the house. So there was no exchange of fire, no escape, no arrest. Nothing.

They went ahead with the search of the house in a completely different frame of mind.

On the first floor, only one room seemed to have been refurbished, and it was the only room with a light switch that worked.

'Chief, come here,' Ferrara heard through his headphones.

It was Rizzo, who must be on the first floor.

Ferrara and Sergi went upstairs. With all the windows and doors flung open, daylight now illuminated the corridors and stairs.

'Careful, Sergi,' Ferrara said, stopping him from treading on a couple of stairs stained with something red that looked like congealed blood. 'I want a man to stay here and make sure no one steps on that.'

Rizzo greeted Ferrara on the first floor. 'There's something you should see, chief. Follow me.' He led him along the corridor.

'What is it?'

'You'll see. We're nearly there.'

Ferrara followed him into the one intact room on the whole floor.

'Look.'

He pointed at the bloodstains.

They had no time to say anything because at that moment Polito joined them. 'Valentina Preti lived upstairs,' he said. 'All her things are there.'

But the surprises were not over yet.

Ferrara's radio crackled.

The NOCS commander had found the entrance to the cellar.

'You should come and see this, Chief Superintendent. Immediately.'

Followed by the others, Ferrara hurried downstairs. The NOCS men showed him the way. They went down a flight of stairs into a large space surrounded by brick walls.

'What the hell is this?' Polito exclaimed.

In the centre of the room stood a rudimentary wooden tripod topped with a pyramid-shaped wedge with a sharp point. Just above it there hung an iron ring supported by ropes tethered to the walls, and another rope hung from the ceiling directly over the tip of the wedge.

'Let's leave this to forensics, boys,' Ferrara ordered. 'The villa will have to be turned over from top to bottom.'

He was clearly disappointed.

Further examination of the house might explain the purpose of that mysterious contraption and would surely give them valuable clues as to the killer's identity. He would direct the search himself, calmly and methodically. But he had lost this move, he knew that. As his friend Massimo had said after studying the messages, he was dealing with an unusually intelligent killer. And the truth, when you came down to it, was that he had let him escape. Months of searching and now that he'd had him within his grasp, he'd let him slip through his fingers!

He thought about the tip he'd fed Ahmed Farah, and felt a fool.

PART THREE

THE HUNT

1

Lorenzo Ricciardi had read Ahmed Farah's article on the train taking him back to Florence immediately after the latest murder.

He was sitting in an almost empty first-class compartment, smiling bitterly to himself. His plan had been thrown into confusion and needed to be rethought. Not because of a journalist's article, which was probably just a publicity stunt, but because of his own weakness, which had taken him by surprise. All because of a woman, as fate would have it.

Valentina . . .

He sat back in his seat and closed his eyes. He felt sad, tired, drained.

He had never known love until he had met her. He had never known a mother's affection, never had any friends, male or female. And then, on the very day he'd started carrying out his plan – the plan he'd prepared meticulously during his stay in the United States, only adding Ferrara as the final link in the chain after he'd seen him shooting wildly in that TV broadcast and had realised he was at the bottom of it all – on that very day, Valentina had burst into his life with devastating force.

Fate played strange tricks, he thought.

In the unlikely event that they tracked him down, his date

with Valentina in Greve was supposed to have been his alibi, the reason he was in that little town on the very day that Stefano had been killed. Instead it had become the start of an unsettling adventure with a bitter ending.

He had really loved her, but he would never have let her stand in the way of his plan for revenge, which was guided by the Lord and carried out in the name of the Father – both of them, the one in Heaven and the natural one.

It had been a difficult path to tread, between the cold execution of the murders and Valentina's warm embrace. Perhaps it was inevitable that it would end like this. But that didn't make it any less painful.

Now that game was over for ever and he had to think about the rest of his plan.

His mind, dulled by these sad memories and the monotonous rhythm of the train, became clear and alert again.

Knowing the press, he was sure the news about an imminent arrest was exaggerated. Knowing the police, he thought it likely they'd planted it. But even if that were the case, he decided that it wasn't worth taking any risks.

He wouldn't go home.

All he had with him was his Beretta and his knife, a little money and his diary, which was nearly finished. He was reserving the remaining blank pages for a minute description of the torture he would inflict on Ferrara.

Of course it was a problem, not being able to go home. What's more, he wouldn't be able to use his credit cards, or withdraw money from the bank, because that would help them trace him. He would have to make do with what he had, try not to be noticed, make himself as anonymous as possible. The best thing to do would be to disappear for as long as it took to figure out whether that news item was genuine and to rethink his strategy.

He knew what to do.

When he got to Santa Maria Novella station, he went straight to the toilets, where he threw his sunglasses in a litter bin and took out his contact lenses. His light chestnut-coloured eyes were no longer ice-cold. Then he set off on foot towards the eastern edge of the city, keeping his eye open for mopeds, looking for easy pickings.

He found a red Ciao, so old its owner hadn't bothered to chain it properly. Stealing it was a walkover. Its rear light was broken, but if he only used it during the day he wouldn't have any problems.

Still heading east, he stopped in a little village just before Pontassieve and entered a modest-looking barber's shop.

'How would you like it?' the hairdresser asked, once he'd sat down in the chair.

'Close shaven,' he replied in a perfect Italian accent, at last abandoning the character of the American which had served him so well. If they'd broadcast the photofit of a fair-haired foreigner, which seemed likely once he'd been seen by that woman in Bologna, nobody would pay any attention to him and he could move about with greater ease. His hair, when it had grown back, would be its natural chestnut colour.

In the next village he bought a padded anorak and a pair of mountain boots in a general store.

The prospect of a few nights in the open didn't bother him.

Ferrara turned Lorenzo Ricciardi's passport over and over in his hands. It had been found during the raid.

A week had passed.

Everything useful they had found in the villa had been brought to Headquarters, and both his own men and the forensics team had gone through it with a fine-tooth comb.

Ferrara was kept constantly up to date. Right now, the enlarged photos of the wanted man were spread out on his desk, ready to be broadcast.

He wasn't sure, though, that this was the right moment to do it.

He had managed, miraculously, to keep the press in the dark about everything, and he didn't think it would be sensible to alert Lorenzo Ricciardi again. What had seemed a good idea when he hadn't yet known the killer's identity, a way of forcing him out into the open – and the thought still nagged at him that it might have been the wrong move – might well be counterproductive now.

But he didn't want to be wrong again, and for once in his life he really didn't know what to do.

The other thing that bothered him was that Ricciardi might have gone abroad. It was common sense, after all. If he knew he'd been found out, why on earth would he stay in Italy waiting to be caught?

The day after the raid on the villa, word had gone out for a watch to be kept at airports, ports and border posts, but for someone with Lorenzo Ricciardi's intelligence and means, evading it would be child's play. That was if he hadn't already got out immediately after killing Cinzia – which was quite likely, as they'd lost all trace of him since then.

Almost everyone at Headquarters thought Ricciardi had left the country. Ferrara seemed to be the only one who still refused to accept it. This passport, which he kept turning over in his hands as if to ward off bad luck, was the only evidence he had – not very strong, admittedly – to support his stubborn belief that Ricciardi was still in the country.

In the past few days, he had taken out his frustration on Rizzo and Anna Giulietti in particular, bombarding the first with instructions on the investigation, and the second with requests for search warrants, bank checks, phone taps, even letters to police forces abroad. But both were increasingly sceptical, and his nerves were ever more on edge.

A week had gone by, seven days of constant effort, which Ferrara had directed doggedly. Officers armed with Ricciardi's photograph had checked railway stations, bus stations, taxi ranks, large stores, newsstands, pharmacies, tobacconists' shops and bars, both in Bologna and in Florence. They had discovered that no weapons permit had been issued in Lorenzo Ricciardi's name. The ownership of the villa had been traced back to a Swiss holding company, but they hadn't been able to get any information from them about their client: apparently no one in the company had ever met him personally. All the arrangements, they were told, had been made through a bank in the Bahamas, and it would be even more difficult to obtain anything useful from that source.

A trace had been put on Ricciardi's mobile phone, but he hadn't used it again. Nor had he had any dealings since 16 March with the bank which had issued the credit card he had used to pay the agency that had supplied Nenita. Nenita herself knew less about her employer than they did. Which wasn't much.

The most useful items found in the house related to the six years Lorenzo Ricciardi had spent in the United States, where he had graduated in philosophy and had then done a master's in journalism. He had apparently been an excellent student. Part of the course had involved research into the FBI's procedures and methods for identifying and capturing serial killers, a fashionable subject at the time. Through his teachers, he had been able to spend a little time at the FBI Academy in Quantico. That was obviously when the photograph above his desk had been taken. In it, his hair was chestnut brown rather than blond, a detail that didn't escape

Ferrara. He had done well on the course and his teachers had praised him as a lively and attentive pupil, who had made a notable contribution through his research.

All this, combined with his extensive library, proved beyond doubt that Lorenzo Ricciardi knew his subject well – well enough to play games with the police. He had devised each murder in such a way as to give credence to the theory that a serial killer was at work, and lead the police along lines of inquiry that had nothing to do with his real motives.

But what those motives were remained a complete mystery.

'This was in Ricciardi's VCR,' Rizzo said as he came in, waving a video cassette. Gianni Fuschi of Forensics was with him.

Ferrara shot a questioning look at Fuschi.

'I've just finished examining it,' Fuschi said. 'You should have a look at it, it's interesting.'

'Put it on,' Ferrara said to Rizzo.

To the left of the desk, on a low cabinet next to the window, there was a TV set and a VCR. Rizzo inserted the tape and started it. It was the programme about the Monster of Florence which had featured Ferrara.

'I've got the idea,' Ferrara said, irritably. 'So what?'

'Wait,' Fuschi said.

Ferrara had no great interest in watching the tape. The broadcast hadn't left him with a very pleasant memory. Fuschi stopped the tape during the file footage, freezing the image of Ferrara shooting at the building where the bosses of the Calabrian Mafia were meeting.

'Congratulations,' Fuschi said. 'I didn't know you were such a good shot. You don't even like carrying a pistol. Not a big fan of firearms, our Chief Superintendent, is he, Rizzo?'

'To be honest, he's a bit undisciplined in that area,' Rizzo said, straight-faced. 'He's supposed to have a pistol on him at all times, and he doesn't. We hardly ever see him at the rifle range. If we do it's only because he has to talk to some-one —'

'Have you come here to take the piss out of me, or do you have something important to tell me?' Ferrara exploded. It wasn't so much the jokes that bothered him as that footage. It had been the host's idea to show it, and it had come as an unwelcome surprise. Seeing it again now was intensely annoying.

'Yes, I do have something to tell you,' Fuschi replied, somewhat surprised by what seemed to him an excessive reaction on his friend's part.

'Well, what are you waiting for?'

'First the label,' Fuschi said, taking the tape out of the VCR and handing it to Ferrara. There was one word on the label: FERRARA.

'I see,' he said. '*Ferrara*, not *The Monster of Florence* or something similar, which is what you'd expect given all the other material about serial killers found in the villa . . .'

'Precisely. Secondly, the tape itself. It was originally a brand new tape, but it's been watched repeatedly, I'd even say obsessively. And the parts of the tape that are the most worn are not the discussion about the Monster, not even the bits with that actress – I must admit, I'd have spent more time watching her. No, the part he watched most is the file footage of that shootout, especially the close-ups of your face.'

'It's as if the killer wanted to memorise you,' Rizzo said. 'Especially how you are when you're in action.'

'That's possible, considering I'm one of his targets,' Ferrara said, but his mind was elsewhere. He was thinking about that night when he had lain awake wondering why the killer had chosen him. 'In your opinion,' he said, apparently going off at a tangent, 'could that shootout have been avoided?'

'How?' Rizzo said. 'It was the only way to force them out of the back of the building, where your men were waiting.'

'But we lost one of them.'

'Yes, the man who died. But come on, chief! If we had to feel guilty every time someone died . . . And what about our people? How many of them do we lose in a year?'

'I'll leave you to your philosophising,' Gianni Fuschi said, standing up. 'Especially as my contribution hasn't been much use. You don't seem to care much about this Ricciardi. Do you want to understand who you're dealing with, or not?' He walked out.

'Right, what have we learned about him?' Ferrara asked after a while, almost to himself. He and Rizzo were alone in the office.

'To begin with,' Rizzo said, 'he's done his homework, but he's obviously not a professional killer.'

'No, he's self-taught. He's clever – very clever – and he's arrogant, but he's an amateur. A professional killer wouldn't have bought a car as conspicuous as a Porsche, especially not in his own name. And he certainly wouldn't have been so stupid as to get a parking ticket! No, he's obviously not working for anyone. And he's not part of a gang. He wouldn't last five minutes.'

'He's someone who's got it in for homosexuals and for you, chief. Frankly, I don't understand the connection.'

But there had to be a connection, Ferrara thought, his nerves on edge again.

'Anyway,' Rizzo said to distract him, almost as if he had read his mind, 'I don't think there's any reason to worry. It's obvious the man's in South America or Australia or somewhere by now. Just get used to it.'

'No. I can't drop this. I'll go to Switzerland, the United States, the Bahamas if necessary, but I have to find this Ricciardi. Him or his assets: if we can get our hands on them, we can stop him moving around. Poor Anna Giulietti! She'll scream if I ask for any more letters abroad!'

'Honestly, chief, if that's the path you're planning to go down, I think you should give up now.'

'I can't *do* that. Don't forget I'm supposed to be the last victim. He could be waiting for me outside my building. He could shoot me any time he wanted.'

Not that he was worried about the possibility. In fact, he would have preferred a direct confrontation to this waiting game, this blind, meaningless activity, these endless questions without answers. But instinct told him it wouldn't happen like that. He'd only mentioned it to provoke Rizzo.

It worked. 'What do you want me to do, chief?' Rizzo asked.

'Keep going, don't let up. Concentrate on the banks. Try to find out if he has any other accounts here in Italy. I have the feeling . . .'

'Yes?'

Ferrara hesitated. 'Damn it, I still don't think he's gone abroad. I think he's hiding somewhere, not far from here. I know the most obvious thing to do would be to leave the country, but I don't believe it. And besides . . .' He hesitated again.

'Besides?' Rizzo insisted.

Ferrara said nothing for a while, chewing distractedly on a cigar he couldn't make up his mind to light.

'The two girls,' he said at last. 'I can't figure out where they fit in. They're the one false note. Everything else was done perfectly, apart from that stupid thing with the Porsche. Why kill four gay men, leaving himself enough time between the murders to carefully prepare the next one, and then suddenly kill two women, one after the other, and even let himself be seen by a woman living in the building where he was going to leave the bodies? Why did he mutilate one and not the other? Why, for that matter, did he have one of them living in his house? She wasn't his prisoner, she was his guest, the maid confirmed that. Don't you think something must have gone wrong?'

'But Cinzia Roberti had a letter carved on her face, you identified it yourself. Which proves she was part of the plan. Maybe Valentina Preti saw something connecting him to the murder and he had to get rid of her.'

'So why did he kill her first?'

'Maybe he knew that, as soon as he killed Cinzia, Valentina Preti would know it was him.'

'That may be true,' Ferrara admitted. 'But you know what? I don't buy it.'

After Rizzo had left, the switchboard put through a phonecall from the Curia.

'Hello, Chief Superintendent,' Monsignor Federici's polite voice greeted him. 'Am I disturbing you?'

'Not at all. How can I help you?'

'Actually, I was supposed to be helping you, remember? Or don't you need my help any more? Don't ask me how I heard, but I gather you've found your culprit, is that right? So poor Don Sergio had nothing to do with it, as I supposed . . .'

'You're right. It was the wrong line of inquiry, but —'

'You don't have to apologise, Superintendent. You were only doing your duty: that's what you were going to say, isn't it? And you did it well, as usual. However, I think you wanted to see Father Sergio anyway, didn't you? Are you still interested?' There was a touch of irritation in the monsignor's voice.

'I don't know,' Ferrara replied, unwilling to be distracted from matters in hand. 'Not now, perhaps later.'

'That is a pity. To help you decide, I think you should know that His Eminence was very amenable to your request and has obtained a dispensation for you to see Don Sergio, who is a recluse in the abbey of San Benedetto in Bosco. Don Sergio has been informed. At the cardinal's insistence, he has consented to break his vow of silence and speak to you.'

'Thank His Eminence. I won't forget.'

'That's all right. As I've already said, it's a great pleasure for us to be able to pay our debt to you.'

That was the end of the conversation and it left Ferrara feeling distinctly uneasy. Why had Monsignor Federici bothered to phone him, knowing there was no longer any point? In doing so, he had let him in on a secret over which the Church, by his own admission, would have preferred to draw a veil. Why? Just to let him know that the Curia had taken his request seriously? That seemed a trivial reason in comparison with the amount he had been prepared to reveal. But there was something else. He was sure the monsignor was holding something back, but he couldn't put his finger on what it was.

Grouchily, he dismissed these thoughts, and returned to the case that was causing him so much heartache.

In the years that followed, Chief Superintendent Ferrara's thoughts often went back to the second extraordinary coincidence in this complex case. It convinced him that chance, which had already come to his rescue once in the shape of Massimo Verga and Rita Senesi, was sometimes one of a policeman's best allies.

He had just put down the phone when it rang again.

'Signor Mazzorelli for you,' the officer at the switchboard announced.

'I've no idea who that is,' he replied, irritably. All he needed was another call from some pest wasting his time. 'Can't you put him through to one of the inspectors?'

'He asked for you, chief. He's the new director of the prison.'

'Okay, put him on.' He resigned himself to hearing about some request or complaint from a prisoner.

'Hello, Chief Superintendent. This is a great honour for me to speak to you. I've only recently been transferred here, but I hope we'll have many opportunities to work together.'

'Go on,' Ferrara said, in no mood for polite conversation.

If Mazzorelli was taken aback by this not very cordial welcome, he didn't let on. 'One of the prisoners has asked to see you. I thought I'd let you know personally, as it gives me an opportunity to get to know you. Naturally the interview will have to be authorised by the Prosecutor's Department, but as far as I'm concerned you can come when you like.'

'What's the prisoner's name?'

'Antonio Salustri. He says he has some information about a man called Ricciardi.'

The irritation, the boredom, even the accumulated tiredness of the last few days vanished as if by magic. Ferrara felt a rush of adrenaline which made him spring to his feet. He looked at his watch, calculating how long it would take to get authorisation from the Prosecutor's Department, which must already be in the know: the director wouldn't have phoned him without putting the request through first. He picked up his cigar case and lighter from the desk, and opened the top drawer, where he kept his pistol and holster.

'I can be there in an hour. Is that okay with you?'

He could almost see the satisfied smile on the warden's face.

2

It may have been modern once, but it wasn't any more. Built in open country near Scandicci, the new prison of Florence was a mass of grey reinforced concrete broken up by long horizontal bands of Tuscan clay. The main buildings, two semicircular blocks a short distance from each other, were longer the higher they went, like football terraces. They resembled two parentheses within which the lives of those who had shirked the responsibilities of respectable existence were enclosed. The prison had been built at the beginning of the eighties to replace the old Murature prison in the centre of the city. There was a tall iron fence on the outside, then a perimeter wall with classic sentry boxes manned by armed guards. On seeing them, anyone travelling along the Livorno-Pisa-Florence autostrada would immediately guess the purpose of the buildings.

His driver stopped the car at the main gate, and Ferrara showed his identity card. The officer at the gate authorised the car to enter the inner courtyard. Here, the driver opened the boot to allow the officer to inspect it. Then Ferrara and the driver both had to hand over their papers and their pistols, and Ferrara had to show the document from the Prosecutor's Department authorising him to enter the prison for an interview with the prisoner named Antonio Salustri.

Impatient as he was, Ferrara was not unduly bothered by this long drawn-out ritual. He knew there were strict rules about these things, and the prison staff had to keep to them, even when the visitor was the head of the *Squadra Mobile*. He hoped this was how they usually did things and they weren't just putting on a show of efficiency for his benefit.

'One moment, Superintendent,' the guard said. 'I'll just tell the boss.'

'That's fine, thanks.'

After a few minutes, another officer appeared in the guardhouse. 'Chief Superintendent Ferrara?'

'Yes.'

'If you'd like to follow me. The warden is waiting for you in his office.'

Ferrara told the driver to stay where he was until he came back, and followed the officer into the two-storey building straight ahead. The warden's office was on the first floor. The warden was a middle-aged man with a crooked nose, half hidden by a huge semi-circular desk taking up almost the whole of one wall. Ferrara wondered what effect that symbolic barrier had on the prisoners summoned to the office.

'Pleased to meet you in person, Chief Superintendent.'

'The pleasure is all mine. I don't come here often, unlike some of my colleagues. Only on occasions like this, or when the Prosecutor asks me to interrogate a prisoner.'

'Well, I'm very glad to welcome you anyway. May I offer you a coffee? In the meantime I'll have the prisoner brought to the interview room. It'll take about ten minutes.'

'Yes, I'd love a coffee.'

The warden ordered the coffee over the phone. Within a very short time, a silver tray was brought in, with the coffee in china cups: a far cry from the paper cups he was used to at Headquarters. He wondered if this luxury was a tribute to his rank or something to do with the fact that the warden was new. Whatever, the coffee was excellent and he drank it with relish.

Fortunately, he did not have to spend too long exchanging small talk with Mazzorelli, because he was soon collected by the officer who was to take him to see the prisoner.

'I hope he has something useful to tell you,' the warden said, by way of farewell.

Ferrara and the guard left the building where the offices were, went through a large iron door which had to be unlocked twice, then locked twice behind them, and crossed a courtyard about a hundred yards wide. As they walked, Ferrara sensed that he was being watched by hundreds of eyes through the barred windows of the cells.

They came to a building on the right, where another door was unlocked twice. On the first floor, he was at last admitted to the interview room, a small room not much more than ten feet by ten feet, with impersonal white walls, a table and two chairs, and a small barred window looking out onto an inner garden.

'May I send the prisoner in, Chief Superintendent?' the officer asked. 'I'll be outside – if you need me just call.'

'Thank you, send him in.'

Antonio Salustri seemed to have aged ten years. He was thinner, even paler if possible, and without a trace of his old arrogance. Ferrara almost felt sorry for him. He often felt sorry for prisoners who hadn't committed the worst crimes, like murder, rape or kidnapping. But it was a purely emotional reaction. Even the less serious crimes hurt other people, and needed to be punished.

They sat down opposite one another, with the little table in the middle.

'You asked to see me,' Ferrara began.

'Yes, Superintendent.' Salustri's tone was humble, deferential, and his tired eyes had heavy purple rings under them. 'I heard you're looking for Lorenzo Ricciardi and I decided to . . . Well, I have something to tell you.'

'How did you hear?'

'Come on, Superintendent, you know about these things. The prison grapevine is better than public radio.'

'Okay, what have you got to tell me?' Ferrara was curt and offhand. Salustri clearly wanted to get him on his side, but Ferrara preferred to keep a distance between them.

'First, I'd like your assurance that you'll help me out,' Salustri said.

'Do you think your information is that important?'

'I don't know, that's for you to say. What I do know is that I'm running a great risk by telling you. My life could be in danger when I get out of here.'

'Are you saying you were more involved with the underworld than you admitted in your original statement?'

'But you haven't yet promised —'

'Listen, Salustri, I can't promise anything, but if what you tell me is genuinely helpful to my investigation, I assure you I'll talk to the judge. There are no rules about these things, but if a prisoner cooperates it's normal for his sentence to be reduced.'

Salustri weighed up Ferrara's words. 'Thank you for that. But it's what happens afterwards that I'm afraid of.'

'If you're thinking of some kind of witness protection programme, I'm afraid we'll have to stop this interview here and now.' Ferrara was reluctant to say this: it might mean that the hopes he had placed in Salustri's testimony would come to nothing.

'I understand. I'm not asking for anything like that. All the same . . . I was wondering . . . well, if it might be possible to help me leave the country. I have relatives in Argentina, I could join them, try and start a new life . . .'

Ferrara knew that Salustri's criminal record might make such a thing unlikely, but he didn't feel compelled to go into details.

'I can't say anything for certain, but I imagine a favourable magistrate might even be able to help you with that if you really deserve it. The only thing I can promise you, if you trust me, is that I'll do what I can.'

Again, Salustri thought it over.

Ferrara counted the seconds mentally, like a poker player slowly riffling through the cards to see if the last one will give him a straight flush or a completely useless hand.

At last Salustri sighed. 'I trust you.'

'I'm not sure where to begin. It isn't true that I found the Velazquez by chance. I knew perfectly well it was in the shop, that's why I bought the damned place. I'd known Gualtiero Ricciardi for many years, I'd done lots of little jobs for him. He was heavily connected with the Calabrian Mafia, that's where all his money came from. He belonged to Nitto Santini's clan, the same Nitto Santini you arrested in '78. Gualtiero's father was a distant cousin of Pippo Calabresi's father – Pippo Calabresi who died in the shootout. The clan didn't disappear. According to Ricciardi, it gradually reformed. I can even give you the names . . .' Sweat had broken out on his forehead.

'Later,' Ferrara said. 'I'm sure the judges will be really interested. And I'm starting to think we might be able to help you after all. Go on with your story.' He was trying to encourage him, while at the same time wanting him to proceed at his own pace. In his experience it was always better to wait and see what emerged spontaneously in situations like this.

'After Ricciardi died, I managed to get my hands on the business. His son, Lorenzo, was very young and didn't know anything about antiques. His parents had already sent him to America to study, and he didn't often come back to Italy, even though . . .'

'Even though what?'

'Well, he was here when the fire happened. He was a strange guy, you know? Shy, not very talkative. He had cold eyes. In my opinion he hated his father. Actually, Gualtiero wasn't his real father. I always thought he'd started the fire himself, to kill him . . . But that's just my theory, I couldn't swear to it.'

It was quite common, Ferrara reflected, for serial killers to commit acts of arson before graduating to murder. Salustri's confession was turning out to be more and more interesting. A plausible, if complex, psychological portrait of Ricciardi was starting to emerge: a true serial killer who *pretends* to be a serial killer in order to carry out his plan. But why was Ferrara the end point of that plan? Because he was an expert on serial killers? No, that wasn't the reason, he was sure of it now.

'Anyway,' Salustri went on, 'he went back to America straight after the funeral, but not before I'd got him to promise he'd sell me the business, seeing as I was an old friend of his father. Not long after, I was contacted by a Swiss holding company. They sent me all the papers and the transaction went ahead.

'I thought I'd done the best deal of my life. I didn't plan to sell the picture straight away, I wanted to wait for the dust to settle. It was my insurance for the future. Then one morning at the end of September last year I get to the shop and see

Lorenzo Ricciardi, who's just got back from the States, chatting to Alfredo Lupi. I didn't recognise him because he'd dyed his hair and he went out without even saying hello to me. But Alfredo told me who he was, and I got scared. My first thought was that he'd found out I had the painting and wanted it back. I tried to question Alfredo, obviously without letting on what it was about, because he didn't know anything about the Velazquez, but he was vague and evasive. I was convinced that Lorenzo was on to me and that's why I decided to get rid of the painting. The rest you know.'

Salustri fell silent. Ferrara said nothing. He was thinking fast, trying to put together the pieces of the mosaic. It was starting to take shape, but was still full of holes and contradictions. Ricciardi had killed Alfredo Lupi, there was no doubt about that. But why not Salustri, who should have been the real victim, if his confession was to be believed? And where did the other victims fit in?

'But why do you think Lorenzo Ricciardi killed Alfredo Lupi, which we're absolutely certain he did, and not you?'

'I've wondered that myself. A thousand times. Maybe he tried to get him to say where the painting was hidden, and the poor boy didn't know! That's the only explanation I can think of. I can't imagine what else it could have been, especially as they were friends.'

'Friends?'

'Yes. Alfredo had been hired by Gualtiero Ricciardi just before he died, on Lorenzo's insistence.'

'What else do you know about Lorenzo?' At last, Ferrara was getting to the main object of his visit.

'A strange character, like I said. The Ricciardis couldn't have children, so they adopted him. Apparently, his real parents were the Calabresis: Pippo, who you killed, and his wife, who was arrested and later died in prison.'

Ferrara's head started to spin. Everything he had feared but hadn't dared admit, even to himself, was being confirmed. Now there was no escaping the real reason for Ricciardi's hatred, the reason he'd had that video cassette. He saw Lorenzo running it once, twice, a thousand times, obsessed with the image of his father being killed by the police, his mother being taken away in handcuffs, and above all the young police officer shooting from the car. Ferrara himself, the man responsible for making Lorenzo Ricciardi an orphan . . .

'Do you think Lorenzo knew he was adopted, or who his real parents were?' he asked, wondering for the umpteenth time if that shootout could have been avoided.

'He knew he'd been adopted. Gualtiero told me that. But he probably didn't know who his real parents were. Gualtiero would have had to tell him about his connections with the Calabrian underworld.'

'But he might have discovered it from his father's papers, after his death.'

'That's quite possible.'

Another piece had fallen into place. But where did Stefano Micali, Alfredo Lupi, Francesco Bianchi, Giovanni Biagini, Cinzia Roberti and Valentina Preti fit in?

The officer knocked discreetly at the door. Forty minutes had gone by and he wanted to make sure that everything was all right.

'Everything's fine,' Ferrara replied, although he certainly wasn't feeling fine. He looked across at Salustri, who seemed exhausted and was wiping his forehead with a handkerchief. 'Would it be possible to have two coffees, a bottle of water and some cigarettes?'

'I'll see,' the officer said, and closed the door.

'Thanks,' Salustri said.

'How long have you known Lorenzo?'

'Since '84, I think. He was just over ten. But I never saw much of him. His parents had always wanted him to go to boarding school, hoping to give him an education that would keep him out of their world. He didn't often come to Florence.'

'I see. Do you think that's why he hated them?'

'Frankly, yes. Gualtiero told me once the boy had had a bad time at boarding school, but didn't want to give up.'

The officer returned with a tray containing the coffee, the cigarettes and the water. Ferrara smiled: he was back in the world of paper cups.

'The warden would like to know if you're going to be much longer.'

'I don't think so. Ten, fifteen minutes at the most. Thank him for his patience. And thank you, too.'

The officer let the room.

Salustri lit a cigarette and took deep drags at it. Ferrara lit a cigar. The air would soon be unbreathable, but it was worth it.

'Do you have any idea how much Ricciardi's estate was worth?'

'Billions of lire, but I don't know how much.'

'And it all went to Lorenzo?'

'I don't know, but I think it's unlikely. As I said, Ricciardi senior was connected with the Calabrian Mafia and some of the money must have been used for laundering. I don't think the clan left it all to Lorenzo. It's possible he belongs to the clan, but I doubt it, as he wouldn't have stayed in America all that time and I'd probably have known about it. Most likely, they found a way to share the inheritance.'

'Do you have any idea where he might be hiding?'

'No. Abroad, I suppose. That's the likeliest. Or maybe

Reggio Calabria or Aspromonte. That's if he kept his links with the Calabrians, or contacted them again.'

That was something he hadn't thought of, and he couldn't rule it out. After all, Lorenzo Ricciardi was in unlawful possession of a firearm, which suggested he might still have underworld connections. It was unlikely he'd brought it with him from the United States.

'You said Alfredo Lupi was a friend of his. Do you know any others?'

'No. Like I said, he was a shy person. I don't think he had many friends, not even when he was at boarding school, which is when you'd expect people to make friends. I think he was a loner even there, especially as he hated the place.'

'I see. You said it wasn't in Florence, right? Was it a private school?'

'It was run by priests. Very exclusive. His father, or rather his stepfather, wanted the best for him, like I said. And to keep him away from the business, of course. I think they closed the place down later, after some scandal the Church managed to cover up.'

Ferrara's head started buzzing again. 'What was the name of this boarding school?'

'San Benedetto something . . . oh, yes, San Benedetto in Bosco, it was part of an abb —'

CLICK!

Two more pieces fell into place with military precision, echoing deafeningly in Ferrara's head. He suddenly remembered, word for word, as if he were seeing a transcript in his mind, the last part of his conversation with Monsignor Federici:

'Father Sergio is merely a poor, frightened man.'

'Frightened of what?'

'His sins? The world? Who knows?'

'Or the killer? Maybe he's a split personality, and is trying to escape his other self by shutting himself up in a cell. Or maybe he knows who the killer is, but can't say anything.'

That was the detail that had escaped him this morning! He had originally said that last sentence as part of his attempt to see Don Sergio, but it was his instinct as a detective that had suggested it to him and now it was turning out to be right.

Two separate leads pointed to the abbey of San Benedetto in Bosco.

Did Don Sergio really know the killer? Had he become a recluse to suppress a secret he could not confess? Would an interview with Don Sergio at last make it possible for Ferrara to reconstruct the entire case and understand who Lorenzo Ricciardi really was?

Rather than wait until he was back in the office, he called the switchboard from the car and obtained the number of the Curia.

He was in luck. Monsignor Federici was there, and was happy to take his call.

'I'm sorry to disturb you, Monsignor, but I'd like to ask you something.'

'Go ahead.'

'You told me you knew Don Sergio well. Could you tell me where he went to school?'

The monsignor did not seem surprised by the question. It was as if he'd been expecting it and was relieved and amused that it had finally arrived.

'Yes, San Benedetto in Bosco, the same place he's just gone back to, when it was still a boarding school. The school's closed down now. A pity, it was a good school. Quite a journey he's made, don't you think? All the way back to the place where he started.'

'That dispensation from the bishop . . . It is still valid, isn't it? I can still talk to Don Sergio?'

'Of course. After what His Eminence did to get you that interview, not to do so would be . . . well, a waste of his valuable time, I'd say. I sincerely hope it's worth it.'

'Thank you. I think it will be.'

'Call me tomorrow morning, and I'll tell you when you can see him.'

3

Once he was off the main road, Ferrara could not help regretting that he had taken his own car. A police car would at least have had the aura of officialdom.

His old Mercedes was not meant for this tortuous dirt road that wound at first through a wood full of chestnut trees and gradually emerged in a genuine forest, full of big beeches, Scots pines and the occasional silver fir. The sudden dips and ubiquitous stones really put the car's suspension to the test, and the brambles hanging over the road scratched the bodywork.

He might also have to put up the chains, because wide swathes of the forest were still under snow. He drove extremely carefully, afraid that roe bucks, wild boar, stags or fallow deer might suddenly appear and bar his way. Having travelled more than twenty-five miles – on the map he had calculated it was only about ten miles to the abbey – he noted that he was moving at a speed that varied between six and ten miles an hour! He cursed. He still had another hour of this torture.

The road was so bumpy, it made the CD jump, and Callas was hiccoughing rather than singing *Caro nome*. Ferrara finally switched off the player in exasperation. He couldn't even stand *Rigoletto* at the moment.

He was tempted to turn back, but it wouldn't make sense after coming this far. That was the way he was: once he'd started on a particular road, he couldn't turn back, not even when common sense told him that the problems still to come could well outweigh those he had left behind. The mere thought that anything he'd done thus far had been a wasted effort was more than he could bear. He was stubborn. He was Sicilian.

Twenty minutes later he caught a fleeting but distinct glimpse of the vast monastic complex. He was up on a ridge, and the monastery was down to his left. The road twisted down towards it. What struck him most from this first glimpse was the precise geometrical arrangement of the walls and buildings and the sheer size of the complex.

He checked the speedometer and realised that he had gone faster than anticipated, thanks to a few straight, clear stretches of road where he'd been able to increase speed. He had the impression that the closer he came to his target, the better the condition of the road.

He accelerated confidently, pleased with the excellence of German engineering that had allowed his old car to pass this unexpected test with flying colours.

The satisfaction, however, was short-lived. There was a huge trunk across the road, which forced him to brake sharply. The trunk had clearly been cut down recently and had been stripped bare of branches.

He had two options: either turn back, or leave the car and proceed on foot. Being Ferrara, he had no hesitation in choosing the second of these. It was two-thirty in the afternoon. It had been late morning when Monsignor Federici had phoned him and told him that Brother Anselmo would be expecting him at two o'clock.

He got out of the car and looked around. There was not a

soul in sight, and it was cold. The only sounds were the rustling of the leaves in the wind, the dull thud of snow coming loose from the foliage of the fir trees and falling to the ground, the chattering of a few distant birds and the sporadic snapping of branches as animals passed. Knowing there were wolves about, he was pleased that for once he had a pistol in the glove compartment of his car. But he felt uncomfortable having it on him, and he would never have dreamed of entering a monastery carrying a weapon.

He tried to get through to the abbey on his mobile phone, to inform them that he had been delayed, but there was no signal. He cursed again. He was just about to clamber over the trunk when he heard voices and the noise of hooves coming closer. A group of monks appeared from around the bend on the other side of the trunk, leading four oxen.

As they approached, he was struck by the monks' healthy, sturdy appearance and impressive builds.

'So sorry, it seems we've blocked your path,' the one at the front said brightly, not sounding at all sorry. 'Don't worry, it'll only take a minute.'

Ferrara thought he was joking, but the team moved with an efficiency and a precision that would have made the engineers who'd worked on his Mercedes green with envy. The trunk was secured to the oxen with thick ropes, and what with the animals pulling and the men pushing, it started to move. Ferrara would learn subsequently that one of the main activities of the monastery was the maintenance and care of the surrounding forest and that many of the monks were expert lumberjacks.

'There, it's done!' the one who had spoken before said, wiping the sweat off his forehead. 'Are you on your way to the abbey?'

It was a rhetorical question: there was nothing else in that area.

'Yes, the prior's waiting for me and I'm late,' Ferrara said, quickly getting back behind the wheel.

'Don't worry. Time has a different rhythm here. I'm sure Brother Anselmo will have found something to do while he's waiting. The road is plain sailing from here on' – there was pride in his voice – 'and with a big car like this it won't take you more than five minutes.'

Exactly five minutes later, he parked in a space in front of the main gate, between a small van and an old red Ciao moped with a broken rear light.

4

Lorenzo Ricciardi had found the perfect refuge in his former school. Not only was it isolated, but he knew that it received laymen who for whatever reason had decided to exchange – either temporarily or permanently – both the comforts and the stresses of modern society for a life of humble work and prayer. Among the guests were former bank managers, professionals, industrialists. In addition, Lorenzo knew many of the monks, and if Brother Anselmo was still there, he could hardly refuse to take him in for a short time.

At San Benedetto in Bosco, he would be able to stay safe for as long as it took to let the dust settle. Then he would strike again. Because that was his mission, and, although he'd had to change his plan slightly because of the two girls, he would still see it through to the end. One by one, those responsible for what he had become – what he hated – would fall. The first of them, and perhaps the most despicable, he had saved for last: Chief Superintendent Michele Ferrara, who had made him an orphan and condemned him to a terrible fate.

Ferrara had had to stand by powerless while the others died, had known the bitter taste of one defeat after another, and had been forced to suffer the agony of waiting, aware that a killer was after him. Finally, he, Lorenzo Ricciardi, would torture him. Torture was the most refined form of humiliation there was, as he had learned at San Gimignano. He'd read about that fascinating exhibition in an article by Mike Ross, whose name he had subsequently adopted.

If they didn't yet know his identity and were still searching for a fair-haired American, as he was sure they were, he would be able to go back to his villa, where he had prepared the Judas Cradle for the superintendent. He savoured in advance the pleasure he would feel, seeing Ferrara suspended over that sharp point, begging for mercy – a mercy that had not been shown to Lorenzo as a child. Before Ferrara died, Lorenzo wanted him to suffer as much as he himself had suffered. He wanted him to know how it felt to offer his own defenceless body to the obscene, pitiless violence of torturers.

He had arrived four days earlier, and as he had predicted, Brother Anselmo had been pleased to receive him. He had travelled the long stretch of road from Florence by moped, stopping often, sleeping in makeshift shelters along the way, buying the newspapers every day to find out how much they knew about him. By the time he arrived at the abbey, he was convinced that the newspaper article about an imminent arrest was pure invention, something planted by the police. That was just as well: he couldn't risk the monks recognising him as a wanted man.

He had to take into account the fact that the woman in Bologna must have given a description of him to the police. But the search had probably been confined to Bologna and the surrounding area, and besides, they still didn't know his true identity. Obviously they were not looking for him in Florence: those four days spent working in the fields, praying and watching the TV news with the others had left him absolutely certain about that. Now he was ready to leave the monastery.

It was then that he saw him.

5

The porter took Ferrara straight to see the prior, who was in the scriptorium, supervising the copyists who were carefully restoring the colours of the miniatures in the manuscripts from the monastery library.

Brother Anselmo, a slight old man with austere features, greeted him politely but somewhat curtly. He thanked Ferrara for having given him the opportunity to receive a rare visit from the archbishop, then handed him over to another monk who would take him to see Sergio Rotondi.

Ferrara followed his guide into the cloister and then along a narrow corridor leading to a staircase.

All the buildings, like the perimeter walls, were built out of small, irregular hewn stones, light in colour, a building material typical of the Fiorenzuola area. The architecture was simple, and Ferrara fell under the spell of its austere beauty, its clean lines, its total lack of decoration.

On the first floor they walked along more long corridors lined with large dormitories and tiny cells, all kept very tidy and equipped with just the bare necessities. At last they came to a small wooden door with a little barred window. The monk took out a huge bunch of keys. Ferrara remembered the rituals attendant on his visit to the prison where Antonio

Salustri was confined, only they seemed somewhat more human here.

Once through the door, they entered yet another corridor, this one narrower than the others, with similar doors along it, all of them with barred windows. Then they turned a corner, and Ferrara was taken aback.

They were in an empty space, some nine or ten square feet, ending in a wall that was completely blank except for a barred window through which a weak light filtered. Not far from the wall stood a rough wooden chair. Before leaving him, his guide asked him to sit down. As he sat, he glanced briefly through the barred window. He understood the true meaning of Monsignor Federici's words – *The situation he is in now can't be equalled even in your toughest prisons* – and realised the enormity of the spectacle he'd been given the somewhat dubious privilege of witnessing.

The cell was very small; just large enough to contain a wooden chest with a cross nailed to its lid, which the recluse used as a bed and which was destined – as Monsignor Federici had intimated – to become his coffin, plus an old wicker armchair, the instruments of penitence and the Bible.

Walled up alive. Sergio Rotondi had chosen the most extreme form of voluntary reclusion.

Ferrara had never before been in a situation like this and hoped he would never be in one again. He really didn't know how to react. He had a lump in his throat which made it difficult for him to speak.

He hadn't seen anyone in the cell, and assumed that Don Sergio was huddled against the wall beneath the barred window in order not to be seen.

'Are you there?' he asked at last.

'Yes,' a hoarse, tremulous, but clearly audible voice replied.

'Are you Father Sergio Rotondi?'

'I'm Sergio Rotondi.'

'Do you know who I am?'

'Yes.'

'Do you know why I'm here?'

'Yes.'

'Are you prepared to cooperate?'

'I've been asked to do so, and I will.'

'Did you know Lorenzo Ricciardi?'

'We were pupils here, when it was still a boarding school. Before the scandal . . .'

'But you were older than he was. Did you know each other?'

'Yes.'

'Do you know why we're looking for him?'

No answer.

'Do you know?'

'I can imagine.'

'Lorenzo Ricciardi is a killer.'

No answer.

'He's killed at least six people. He's a vicious killer.'

'Oh, no, no . . .' It wasn't a denial, but a lament.

'Do you think he's capable of something like that, father . . . or brother, I'm not sure what to call you.'

'Call me Sergio. That's my name.'

'Do you think he's capable of it, Sergio?'

'Yes.'

'Why?'

Sergio did not answer at once. He could be heard breathing heavily. 'I've been asked to talk . . .' he said, almost pensively. 'I should have done it before, a long time ago . . . but it was difficult . . . too difficult for me . . . I don't know why I . . . Oh, my God, why did I let all this happen?'

'What exactly?'

'Everything,' he sighed. 'I thought it was enough to take the burden of guilt on myself, but it's not enough, it could never be enough. We all had to pay.'

Ferrara clearly heard sobs from the other side of the cell and waited for Rotondi to regain his composure.

'It was 1985,' Sergio Rotondi began. 'A cursed year, the year the devil entered the monastery. We had a new Latin teacher, a Trappist monk named Brother Attanasio. He was nearly forty and incredibly handsome. He was a sodomite and lost no time in passing on his foul vice. Many of us fell victim to his charms. He was irresistible: the way he talked, the way he understood us, supported us, guided us. In other words, he had us in his power, and he took advantage of it . . .

'There were five of us, but that wasn't enough for him. He was insatiable. Towards the end of the year he set his sights on Lorenzo. He was only a child, nine, maybe ten. It was horrible. But we didn't realise it at the time.

'Lorenzo was a shy, introverted boy. He despised us, maybe even hated us. He hated everything about this place. We thought it was only fair to punish him . . . make him the same as us . . . Why, why? What came over us? I keep thinking about it, keep trying to understand how our love for Brother Attanasio and the passion and recklessness of youth could have made us stoop so low . . .'

'What happened exactly?'

'One night, we raped him. All five of us, in turn . . .'

Suddenly, the light stone walls seemed to lose the serenity Ferrara had been struck by not so long before. It wasn't the first story of this kind he'd ever heard, but hearing it told by a monk and knowing that it had taken place right here made it all the more sickening.

'And then?'

'When Brother Attanasio found out, he was furious, but he

lost no time in making Lorenzo his favourite. He had relations with the boy for many years, right up until the time Lorenzo left, I think. Soon after that, Brother Anselmo discovered what had been going on. No one knows how, but many of us thought he'd had a letter from Lorenzo, maybe an anonymous one. Anyway, he closed the school down. We'd already left by this time.'

'Stefano Micali was one of you, wasn't he?'

'Yes. And the others were Alfredo Lupi, Francesco Bianchi and Giovanni Biagini.'

Of course, Ferrara thought, bitterly. How easy it would have been to find a connection between the victims, if only they'd thought of going as far back as their childhood. But that almost never happens, unless there are particular reasons to do so. A person is generally considered within a network of adult relations – work relations, contractual ties, friendships at the time the crime is committed. These are the things detectives examine in their attempts to reconstruct a man's life.

'Did you suspect him when Stefano Micali was killed?'

'No, only later, when Alfredo died. That was when I got scared. Then I received an anonymous letter that made me almost certain it was Lorenzo taking his revenge . . . But I wasn't sure and I couldn't say anything. Think of the scandal, the repercussions for the Church . . .'

'So you let the others be executed.'

It was less an accusation than a statement of fact, and Sergio Rotondi knew it.

That withdrawal from the world, that apparently courageous gesture, had in fact been an act of the most contemptible cowardice, which had condemned his companions to death.

Ferrara abandoned him to his fate. He couldn't imagine what it must be like to have a burden like that on your conscience.

*

He was surprised that the monk who had brought him wasn't there waiting for him. He soon discovered why.

He and some of the other monks had gathered halfway down the long corridor, outside the open door of one of the cells. From the other end of the corridor, Brother Anselmo and two other monks came running.

Ferrara reached the small group almost at the same time as Brother Anselmo. The monks stood aside, silently and deferentially. It was clear from the expressions on their pale, frightened faces that something terrible had happened. Without hesitation, Ferrara followed the prior into the cell.

An elderly monk lay on his back on the bed, horribly mutilated.

Now that he knew what to look for, Ferrara immediately picked out the 'r' etched into the skin of the disfigured face.

'Who is he?' he asked, already knowing the answer.

'His name was Brother Attanasio,' the prior said in a broken voice.

'Who found him?'

'I did.' A shy young monk came forward. 'We were supposed to meet in the courtyard. When he didn't appear, I came and knocked at his door. He didn't answer, but I knew he was inside, he'd told me. I knocked again, and finally I opened the door and —'

'Stay here, all of you.' Ferrara ordered. 'Don't move! Brother Anselmo, is there a telephone I can use?'

'Come with me,' Brother Anselmo said, suddenly filled with an energy Ferrara would never have suspected.

It was risky. Lorenzo Ricciardi was armed, and they were all potential targets, but Ferrara had no choice. He absolutely had to call his men. He cursed his own lack of discipline: he'd left his damned pistol in the glove compartment of his car just when he really needed it!

They reached the prior's study without incident, and Ferrara dialled Rizzo's number.

'Lorenzo Ricciardi is at San Benedetto in Bosco,' he said, and gave him the location. 'I need a lot of men here. I need the Forest Rangers to be informed. I need helicopters to fly over the area with lights. I need the road leading here blocked at the point where it meets the main road. And I need all this NOW!'

If the killer had already escaped, it wouldn't be easy to catch him. The Casentine forest is enormous, and there was no way they could surround the whole of it. But he wouldn't find it easy to get out of it either, and they had the advantage of transport and the Forest Rangers, who knew the area.

It was also possible that he was still in the monastery, that he'd seen and recognised Ferrara, and was lying in wait somewhere. That was the possibility Ferrara had to concentrate on for now. An armed man could easily hold a whole monastery of defenceless monks at bay.

First of all he had to try and get to his own pistol.

He left Brother Anselmo and headed cautiously for the porter's lodge, running in the areas where he was most exposed to any possible fire.

By the time he got there, an eternity seemed to have passed.

The sun was setting.

'Have you seen Lorenzo Ricciardi?' he asked the porter.

'He went out about ten or fifteen minutes after you arrived, and hasn't come back.'

Ferrara was relieved. The monks were safe.

But the killer was outside, maybe waiting to kill him as soon as he set foot outside the gate. On the other hand, if Ricciardi was running and he didn't move now, he'd be giving him even more of a head start than he already had.

He had to risk it.

He ran out to his car in a zigzagging motion, and when he reached it crouched by the door.

Nothing happened.

Cautiously, he took out his keys and opened the door.

He groped for the glove compartment on the dashboard and took out his pistol.

6

After killing Brother Attanasio, Lorenzo Ricciardi had washed off the blood and gone to his cell to pick up his few belongings, including the clothes he had replaced with a habit during his stay in the abbey. Then he had calmly walked out, undisturbed.

He still couldn't believe his good luck. He had recognised his tormentor immediately he had seen him, even though the old man hadn't recognised *him*, now that he was grown up and his head was shaved. It seemed impossible – he was sure they must have dismissed Brother Attanasio from the monastery after the anonymous letter he'd sent informing on him. He'd assumed he would have a lot of trouble finding him, but as he was the last but one on the list, he hadn't been too worried about it.

When he had killed Cinzia, he had marked her with an 'A', thinking he might actually give up on Brother Attanasio and keep the 'r' for Don Sergio instead. Discovering that he was still in the abbey made it possible for him to get back to his original plan, at least to an extent. Lorenzo Ricciardi had not hesitated to attribute this unexpected turn of events to divine intervention. He was back on the right path, and the next step had been clearly signposted. All he could do was bow to the will of God.

Now he obviously couldn't go back to the villa. His escape was tantamount to a confession, but he couldn't stay here waiting for the monastery to be overrun by police. The die was cast: he was playing a game against time now, and he would see it through. Greve in Chianti first, to execute Father Sergio, then Ferrara. He wasn't sure which of them to give the last letter to. He might end up with one corpse too many, he thought with a sardonic smile.

After that, they could arrest him, kill him, it didn't matter. Once his task had been accomplished, his life would be meaningless now that he had lost Valentina.

He had tried to start the moped, but it refused to respond. After trying several times, he had thrown the vehicle to the ground and set off on foot. He knew the forest and the short cuts from his childhood, and it wouldn't be difficult for him to get back on the road long before the police got here.

With his pistol in his hand, Ferrara felt better able to protect the monks. For once he really appreciated having a weapon. He was still moving cautiously, even though the fact that Ricciardi hadn't yet shot at him led him to think that he was not in the immediate vicinity, but had vanished into the forest, where it would be harder to catch him.

He was about to turn back when the gate opened and the prior and a large group of monks came out, among whom he recognised many of the lumberjacks. They were carrying simple sticks and a few machetes.

'Go back!' he cried, irritably.

They refused to obey him.

'He escaped on foot,' Brother Anselmo said, seeing the moped lying on the ground. 'He won't get far. The brothers will find him.'

'No,' Ferrara protested. 'He's armed and dangerous. My men will be here any minute.'

But the lumberjacks had already set off.

'You can't stop them,' the prior said. 'They need to find him. The forest can be dangerous at night, and the man doesn't know the risks he's taking. There's been a lot of snow and the wolves are hungry – they've started moving around in packs again after all these years.'

Ferrara ran to catch up with them. It would have been presumptuous of him to even attempt to take command of the operation, even though he was the only one who had a firearm.

These men knew the terrain. They advanced calmly along the dirt road, spotting tracks in the dim twilight that he would never have been able to recognise.

'It'll be night soon,' one of the monks said. 'The wild boar come out at night. And so do the wolves. There are about twenty species and they're not very friendly these days.'

They continued to advance, slowly but surely.

'Here,' another monk said. He had noticed a few newly broken branches at the sides of the road, and a small space between the brambles.

At this point they moved off the road into the forest.

They walked through the thick vegetation for another half hour, occasionally returning to the road, then leaving it again. In the patches where there was snow, footprints were clearly visible, confirming that they were on the right track. It was more difficult where the snow had melted and they were walking over beds of slippery pine needles.

Ferrara kept looking at his watch, hoping at any moment to hear the rotors of helicopters followed by the roar of police cars, but all he could hear was the murmur of the forest and the howling of the wolves, subdued at first then increasingly distinct.

A gunshot rang out.

Ferrara saw the flash and immediately answered the shot, hoping he hadn't killed the fugitive.

'This way!' a monk cried.

None of them had been hurt.

Darkness had fallen suddenly.

The monks lit matches and applied them to the tips of their sticks, which burst into flame. The dense forest was immediately alive with torches.

'Look, blood!' another monk said, when they reached the spot from which the gunshot must have come.

'He must be wounded,' a third monk said, turning to Ferrara. 'The wolves will smell the blood – we have to hurry.'

'He's armed, he'll defend himself,' Ferrara said. 'Don't risk your lives. He's already shot at us once and with these torches we're a perfect target.' He was trying to persuade them to be just a little bit more careful, but they did not seem to care what happened to them.

'Look,' one of them said, pointing to bloodstains on the ground.

They were moving quickly now. Ferrara peered around him, trying to cover them as best he could.

It wasn't another gunshot that steered them in the right direction this time, but the fierce, angry snarling of wolves. The gunshot came after that, soon followed by another one, then a high-pitched whine.

They ran, found the bloodstained body of a wolf, and set off again. The snarling, more intense now, guided their steps.

A man lay on his back on the ground, being attacked relentlessly by a large pack of wolves.

'Careful!' the monk leading the group cried.

Ferrara took aim at one of the wolves. He could see the animal's eyes glowing in the dark. He fired. The wolf was hit between the eyes, and fell. The other wolves reacted by dropping their prey. He fired again and a second wolf fell.

'Get ready!' he cried, as the third shot rang out, and the remainder of the pack turned on the monks.

They easily defended themselves with the machetes, and the few wolves left soon ran off.

Ferrara and the monks approached Lorenzo Ricciardi and bent over his wounded body. He was still breathing. One hand was clutching a Beretta. There was a book sticking out of his pocket, a notebook with a black cover and a gold cross.

Only then did they hear the noise of the helicopters, and a few moments later a powerful beam of light swept over the scene.

The monks gave Lorenzo Ricciardi first aid, and then they had to walk a whole hour to reach the ambulance, which took him away.

During that hour, while Rizzo directed operations, Ferrara reflected. He wondered if he had done the right thing in not publicising the image and identity of the wanted man. As always in these cases, there was no simple answer. If he had, it was likely that Ricciardi wouldn't have sought refuge in the monastery, and so wouldn't have killed Brother Attanasio. But of course Ricciardi was cunning enough to get into the abbey anyway, if he'd wanted to. On the other hand, it was only because he hadn't known he was being hunted that he'd been bold enough to continue with his vendetta, which had finally led to his capture.

It was a meagre satisfaction. Now it was all over. Lorenzo Ricciardi had killed all his tormenters except Don Sergio – who in any case had sentenced himself to a voluntary incarceration – and Ferrara, the last link in a tragic chain that had started in Reggio Calabria and had reached its culmination within the walls of a monastery. But Ferrara wasn't thinking about himself. He was thinking about those two poor girls, who didn't fit into the vendetta.

He wouldn't learn the role they had played until that night, at home, reading the diary that began with the terrifying confession: *In your name, Father, I have killed . . .*

EPILOGUE

At Easter, Michele Ferrara and his wife visited Petra's parents in Germany, as they did every year. But instead of taking the St Gotthard tunnel, they went a longer way round, via the Brenner Pass.

Ferrara wanted to spend a few days in the mountains and had booked a long weekend for them at the Hotel Passo Selva in San Vigilio di Marebbe.

Giorgio Preti, the owner, was not there to greet them. Since the death of his daughter Valentina, he had left the running of the hotel to his nephew and now lived in seclusion with his wife in an apartment on the top floor.

They had both aged since the tragedy, and rarely went out. Ferrara only saw them twice.

The first time, they emerged from the lift in silence, both wearing dark clothes, and walked unobtrusively across the foyer, as if apologising for disturbing the life of the hotel. Their faces were sad, and there was no light in their eyes.

Petra had realised from the start that her husband hadn't chosen San Vigilio at random. Ferrara's intention had been to ask Valentina's parents to tell him more about the girl than he had learned from Lorenzo Ricciardi's diary. Her image, for some reason, had remained imprinted on his mind. Cinzia Roberti had been an innocent victim, too, but it had been

Valentina, who'd been unlucky enough to become the object of a killer's love, who had struck him the most.

When he saw the grief so clearly etched on her parents' faces, his resolution wavered. He did not have the courage to intrude on their private pain: it was the only thing they had left of their daughter.

What he did do, however, was visit the cemetery on the last day of their stay. His excuse was that cemeteries in small, historic villages were often well worth seeing.

Petra went with him: she always supported her husband's whims. At the gate, Ferrara bought a bunch of violets. They walked for a while between the graves, lingering over the ones that seemed especially curious or interesting.

And then he found her.

A simple stone, with the inscription

VALENTINA PRETI
1978–2000

and above it, an oval photograph cut into the marble.

'How beautiful she was,' Petra said, almost with surprise, while Michele placed the bunch of violets in the only free space he could find among the big vases of what were almost certainly freshly-cut flowers. 'She looks like the Madonna by Filippo Lippi. You know, the one in San Lorenzo.'

As they turned to go, they were surprised to see Valentina's parents, standing not far from them and looking at them uncertainly, almost as if trying to remember who these people were who were paying tribute to their daughter.

As they passed them, they nodded briefly by way of greeting. No one considered it necessary to ask or give explanations, and the Ferraras hurried on their way, like two children caught in a prank. But Ferrara had seen a fleeting gleam in Giorgio Preti's eyes, the age-old bond that unites human beings in the face of grief.

As they were leaving the cemetery, Petra noticed that her husband had an almost radiant expression on his face. She hadn't seen him looking like that for a long time.

'What is it, Michele?'

He smiled enigmatically. 'I don't know, maybe I just remembered that I'm going to die . . . *Memento mori*, remember that?'

His wife looked at him in surprise.

He stopped, took a cigar from his pocket, and lit it with ostentatious delight.

'Are you surprised? But what could be more beautiful than that, when you come down to it? Even death is a sign. It reminds us of what we are. Mere mortals, doomed to disappear . . .'

AUTHOR'S NOTE

In January 1978, at the age of 28, I achieved my greatest ambition by passing the examination to enter the Italian police force. I first worked in the *Squadra Mobile* of Reggio Calabria, and for more than ten years investigated kidnappings carried out by the Calabrian Mafia. Later I was appointed to the Anti-Mafia Squad, first in Naples and then in Florence, where I played a major role in the investigations into the series of Mafia killings which took place in Florence, Rome, and Milan in 1993, and helped to secure convictions which resulted in fourteen life sentences.

From October 1995 to April 2003, I was the head of the *Squadra Mobile* in Florence. I conducted several major investigations, including those into the Chinese Mafia, money laundering, and the series of double murders attributed to the so-called 'Monster of Florence'.

With regard to this latter case, my investigations led me to reject the theories of my predecessors (including American investigators who had looked at the case). I was able to demonstrate that the murders were not the work of a lone killer, but of a group of killers. The sentences passed on several of the culprits were confirmed by the court of appeal in September 2000.

Since April 2003 I have headed a special group of investigators trying to track down the person responsible for instigating the murders and to cast light on the death of Dr Francesco Narducci of Perugia, which is believed to be linked to the case. The preliminary investigations into the 'instigator' have now been concluded, and a judge's decision is currently being awaited on the possibility of a trial being held. In the meantime, I am still collaborating with the Prosecutor's Department in Perugia.

After writing two Chief Superintendent Michele Ferrara books, with another at planning stage, I completed *The Monster: Anatomy of an Investigation*, a non-fiction book about the Monster of Florence case, in order to leave a documentary record of an affair which is unique, not only in Italy, but in the world.

Although *A Florentine Death* is a work of imagination, some of it is inspired by real events. The inhabitants of Ali Superiore will recognise the episode where the Velazquez painting is handed back to them, because it really happened, although the circumstances in which the painting was found were quite different. There was an edition of the Italian TV show *Porta a Porta* which dealt with the Monster of Florence case and in which I myself participated. The police siege of a house in Reggio Calabria in which a meeting of the heads of the Calabrian Mafia was taking place is also a real event. Everything else is fictitious, and any reference to real people and events is purely coincidental. Michele Ferrara is not me. Of course he and I are alike, in that we have the same profession, but he is the Giuttari I might like to be, although I almost never succeed. I think we all have idealised versions of ourselves, to which we aspire, although most of the time we fall short of these ideals.

Michele Giuttari, November 2006

Now read the first chapter of
Chief Superintendent Ferrara's
next gripping case,
A Death in Tuscany

1

Florence, 2001

The girl, little more than a child, was found on the edge of a wood on the road above Scandicci, scantily dressed, without papers, and dying of an overdose, at dawn on Sunday 29 July, and was taken to the Ospedale Nuovo. But it wasn't until almost a week later that Chief Superintendent Michele Ferrara, head of the Florence *Squadra Mobile*, really became involved with the case.

Friday 3 August.

He was already in a bad mood when he set foot in the office. The weather was hot and muggy, even though it was only eight in the morning. Chief Inspector Violante's report on the girl's death was in his in-tray: one of the many documents that awaited his routine examination at the beginning of every day, arranged with almost maniacal care by his secretary, Sergeant Fanti, who always got in at least half an hour before he did.

It wasn't somewhere in the middle of the pile, though. It had been placed right on the top.

And Fanti wasn't the kind of person to be impressed by the death of yet another junkie.

Ferrara had picked up his pen as soon as he sat down: an automatic gesture after so many years of deskwork. Now he replaced it and took out a cigar. His morning cigar and coffee both helped to revive brain cells undermined by time and stress.

He lit his cigar without even looking at it as he read Violante's report.

He didn't like what he read.

When, the previous Sunday, he had seen the first report from the officer on duty at the hospital, he had automatically pigeonholed the case as yet another tragedy after a night at the disco, almost a commonplace event on Saturdays in the global village. The city and the surrounding hills were awash with drugs and alcohol, like the River Arno in full spate, and like the River Arno they threatened to overflow, but with even more tragic consequences than those of the flood of 1966.

Ferrara had been feeling his age for some time. The world, it seemed to him, was getting worse rather than better, and he often found himself thinking that 'things weren't the way they used to be', just like his father and presumably his grandfather before him. He had delegated the investigation – a perfectly routine one – to Chief Inspector Violante and dismissed the case from his mind. Now it came back to hit him like a slap in the face, and he didn't really know why.

Because she was dead?

That happens to junkies.

Because her age was estimated as being between thirteen and sixteen and yet, despite being so young, she had managed to shoot a lethal dose of heroin into her body?

Perhaps.

Or because, after nearly a week, they still didn't know who she was? A small detail, a mere speck, which might turn out troublesome, like a mote in the eye of justice.

But when it came down to it, if there was anything wrong with the investigation, the fault was his.

*

'Fanti!' he called.

Between his office and his secretary's, the door was always open.

Sergeant Fanti had just turned forty. He was more than six feet tall and terrifyingly thin, with hollow cheeks, blue eyes and short, wiry blond hair. He had lived in his home town of Trento until the day – almost twenty years ago – when he had joined the police. Florence had been his very first posting, and here he had stayed. He had immediately become noted for his meticulousness, his discretion, and his skill at research, whether in the records or on the internet.

Such was his passion for computers, he had even updated the office's facilities at his own expense. When Ferrara had taken up his post, he had found the new equipment already assigned by his predecessors to the secretary's office and he had okayed that, although he himself occasionally made use of it when he had some particularly sensitive information to track down.

'Yes, chief?' Fanti replied, materialising in front of Ferrara's desk almost instantaneously, as usual.

Ferrara often wondered if the man spent his time with his ear against the wall, ready to burst in as soon as he had any inkling that his chief was about to summon him. Of course if he'd been doing that, he wouldn't have had time to perform the thousand tasks around the office with the efficiency, the meticulous precision, of which he was so proud. It was by far the tidiest, best functioning office in the whole of Florence Police Headquarters. In the end, Ferrara had come to the conclusion that Fanti had a sixth sense.

'Well?' he asked without preamble.

The sergeant shrugged. It wasn't his job to draw conclusions or make judgements. But it was clear from the look on his face that he'd been expecting exactly this reaction from his boss, and that it didn't surprise him that Ferrara hadn't even opened the other files. Or that the cigar had been left in the ashtray to go out by itself.

'A young girl, maybe no more than a child,' Ferrara said, lowering his voice as if he were thinking aloud rather than addressing his subordinate – although it was also useful to have him to think aloud to – 'maybe no more than a child, right? It's hard to say these days, they grow up so quickly . . . They already have breasts when they're eleven or twelve, and go around with their navels showing. Are they trying to look like whores, or are the whores trying to look like schoolgirls? A paedophile culture, that's what we're living in, Fanti. And then everyone complains when . . . But what can you do? Children today want to look like adults, and adults want to stay children forever, no one wants to grow up, no one wants to grow old, they all think they can stay in an eternal kinder-garten without rules or restrictions, and not worry about time passing. Maybe I'm angry because I feel the weight of my years, every single one of them and maybe a few more. But in my day, damn it, this girl would have been a child! She would have been playing with her dolls, not with syringes! What kind of world is this? What kind of shitty world? And isn't there anyone looking for her? In the whole of Florence, isn't there a mother with a missing daughter, an uncle who's lost his niece, a tourist desperate to find his child?'

'Right, chief,' Fanti said, not knowing how to respond to this outburst.

'And what about us? What have we done to identify her? What has Violante done? Has he been twiddling his thumbs? Taking his children to Rimini?'

'Chief Inspector Violante's children are grown up and can look after themselves. With all due respect, I don't think they need their father to take them to the seaside any more. And

I'm sure the chief inspector hasn't been deliberately wasting time. We used to think he was a shirker, but he isn't. I think you yourself discovered that during the Ricciardi case, didn't you?'

Good old Sergeant Fanti – the voice of conscience.

Ferrara took a deep breath, then lowered his head and stared down at his desk. 'Send for him. But first bring me the complete file. Then, after Violante, I want Rizzo in here. I don't like this case at all. What are we supposed to do? Bury this girl without even finding out her name?'

'Superintendent Rizzo is on holiday, chief.'

Of course. He remembered now that at the beginning of the week Superintendent Rizzo, to all intents and purposes his deputy, had come to say goodbye before leaving for two weeks to visit his relatives in Sicily. Lucky him.

'Who's on duty?'

'Superintendent Ascalchi.'

A Roman, who knew Florence as well as Ferrara knew Asia Minor!

'Oh, great! Well, what can we do? Send for him. Then find out from the Prosecutor's Department what time the autopsy is scheduled for and who it's been assigned to. Whoever that person is, I want to speak to him as soon as possible.'

'Of course, chief,' Fanti replied, and went back to his office.

Like Rizzo, Ferrara was a Sicilian. He had been planning a journey to Sicily for months, but each time he'd had to postpone it.

While he was waiting, he phoned his wife Petra, to tell her he wouldn't be home for lunch. He didn't tell her why, there was no need. It was always like this. Even in summer. Or rather, especially in summer, when Ferrara, short-staffed because of his men's holidays, was invariably forced to give up his own.

Not that he minded: he was used to it. But he felt sorry for his wife, who insisted on staying with him all through these stifling months when the sun beat down mercilessly on Florence, the city of excess. But whenever he told her they wouldn't be going away, she would greet the announcement with a smile as predictable as the infernal heat and say that she wouldn't have been able to leave home for long anyway, because there'd be no one to water her beloved plants. He would always agree with her. They both knew this was a convenient fiction, because the terrace was equipped with a state-of-the-art irrigation system to ensure that their beautiful roof garden was always properly tended. But that was all right. It made them equal.

'All right, Michele, but whatever you do, don't go into the office tomorrow and make us miss our weekend at Massimo's, as usual. You promised him this time!'

'Don't worry, even if the sky falls, we'll be on that autostrada tomorrow morning before the tailbacks start.'

'I'll take your word for it, and I won't forgive you if—'

'So your dear Massimo takes precedence over everything, does he?'

'*Dein lieber* Massimo, you mean,' Petra replied. In spite of the many years she'd lived in Italy, she sometimes broke into a few words of her native language. It happened when she was tired, emotional or excited, but also when she wanted, however unconsciously, to underline the superiority of German precision over Italian vagueness.

'*Our* Massimo, shall we agree on that?' Ferrara said. 'See you later!' He had just seen Fanti coming in with the file on the girl.

*

Everything was in the file, starting with the record of the girl's admission to hospital, and the report by the paramedics who, alerted by an anonymous caller, had driven up the hill road leading from Scandicci to Montespertoli until they had found the girl, unconscious and barely able to breathe. They had tried to revive her, without success, and had then taken her to the nearest hospital.

The subsequent reports by Inspector Violante were detailed and irreproachable. He had examined all the missing persons reports from that period, but none of the descriptions matched. He had also checked the latest bulletin from the Ministry, but again without success. He had even gone on the internet and checked the website of a well-researched TV programme called *Has Anyone Seen Them?* which was often consulted by the police in relation to missing persons cases.

There followed copies of the telegrams, marked *Priority*, which Violante had sent to other police forces, with a summary of the case and a description of the girl, appealing for help in identifying her.

Attached to the report was a photo he had sent other forces by email. It had been taken in hospital using a digital camera, with the permission of the doctors. Given the conditions in which it was taken, the quality left something to be desired, but behind that pale, pained expression, it wasn't difficult to imagine the girl in all her radiant beauty. The features were regular, framed by soft ash-blonde hair, and the lips, even though bloodless in the photo, were full. The eyes were closed, but Ferrara – who for some reason thought they must be green – could imagine them full of life.

As was to be expected, Violante had followed the correct procedure to the letter. But the girl, who had clung on to life while they followed up various inconclusive leads, had died without either the comfort of relatives at her sickbed or the dignity of a record that at least restored her name to her.

Cardiac and circulatory failure following acute heroin poisoning was how the consultant in charge of the intensive care unit, Professor Ludovico d'Incisa, concluded his report.

RIP and amen.

'Come in!'

Nothing happened.

'COME IN!' Ferrara screamed a second time in response to the discreet knocks on his door. In the meantime, Fanti had run to open it, and Chief Inspector Violante, a grey man – grey hair, grey clothes, grey demeanour – who was deaf in one ear, came in and took up his position in front of Ferrara's desk.

Ferrara waved away the cloud of pale blue smoke from his second cigar, which he had just lit, and indicated the two armchairs for visitors.

'Choose whichever you want, but for God's sake sit down.'

Violante did as he was told, but perched on the edge of the seat, in an uncomfortable position. He was visibly nervous, as if expecting to be reprimanded.

'About this child . . . The one who died of a drug overdose . . . Where are we with that?'

'Nowhere really. Apart from the victim – did you say child, chief?'

'Why? Would you call her a woman?'

Violante's only response was to shrug his shoulders.

'I'm talking about the victim in the report I found on my desk. What has your investigation come up with?'

'Nothing in particular, chief. Time to close the file, I think . . .'

'I'll decide that, if you don't mind,' Ferrara replied. He didn't like to hear that tone of fatalistic resignation from one of his men.

Violante seemed not to understand. 'Of course, chief. But did you read the whole file?' He could see that Ferrara had it in front of him.

'Obviously. I didn't send for it just to give it an airing.'

Why was Ferrara so irritable? Violante wondered. Why was he treating him like this? He'd done his job, and he'd done it well.

'You'll have seen that we did everything we possibly could. I dealt with it personally and didn't neglect anything. But in the meantime, the girl died . . .' He shrugged his shoulders by way of conclusion.

'And yet we don't even know who she is! After nearly a week!'

Violante still did not understand.

Considering everything they had on their plates at the moment, especially with a reduced workforce, the death of a junkie wasn't exactly a priority. His many years' experience had made him cynical, and he was convinced that a girl who wasn't even missed by her family didn't really matter that much to anyone, so he was surprised by Ferrara's sudden insistence. But he also had to admit that he respected it. It was as if there was still room for a glimmer of humanity in their work: something he'd stopped believing in since he'd started counting the days until his retirement.

'A week isn't so long, chief. In fact, it's quite normal. If no one comes forward and the subject has no papers or any-thing else that makes identification possible, you know as well as I do that it can take months, and sometimes we get nowhere.'

It was true, and Ferrara wondered again why it was that he had reacted so impulsively. He was usually cautious, usually thought long and hard before blowing up. This death might have its curious aspects, but it was hardly unusual in a modern city. And Florence was no different from any other modern city in this respect.

Something about the case, though, didn't feel right. What was it? Everything, he thought, fishing out the victim's photo and taking another look at it: the pale face, the closed eyes, the tense, tormented features, heartbreaking in their still-childlike beauty.

Everything and nothing, as often happens. But he was pig-headed. If his instinct told him something was wrong, then he had to see it through to the end. Without thinking too much, at least for the moment.

'You saw her,' he said. 'How old do you think she was?'

'I'm hoping the autopsy will tell us for certain. Not very old, I'd say.'

'Old enough to be a junkie?'

'Are you asking me, chief? What do I know about kids today? I didn't understand my own children twenty years ago . . . All I know is that she died from acute heroin poisoning. That's what's written on the medical certificate. A classic overdose – all too common, unfortunately.'

'Yes,' Ferrara admitted. 'You may be right. Maybe that's the way it was. Just one more statistic for the new millennium. But I don't like it. Do you remember how we used to feel when we went to school and we hadn't done our homework? That's how I feel now. I'm not criticising your work in any way. But you've been following the case from the start. What are your impressions?'

'For what it's worth, I think the girl was almost certainly an illegal immigrant, that's why no one has come forward.'

Ferrara nodded. Although it had taken Violante to say it openly, the thought had been lurking at the back of his mind.

An illegal immigrant without a family: he refused to believe that her parents hadn't come forward simply because they were afraid of being deported. Besides, a young immigrant doesn't have the time or the inclination or the money to buy drugs. It was much more likely that she was a victim of the international traffic in human beings, which was reaching staggering proportions: the number of children who disappeared each year throughout the world and ended up in the clutches of unscrupulous traffickers was horrifying.

'From Eastern Europe . . .' he said, looking at the photo again.

'That's what I thought.'

'Anything else?'

Violante hesitated.

'Well?'

'Nothing I can put my finger on. Just an impression . . . But, all things considered, it doesn't matter, believe me.'

'What do you mean, "all things considered"?'

'You know what I mean. An illegal immigrant . . .' Violante replied with the air of resigned indifference people use to talk about subjects they'd prefer to sweep under the carpet.

Yes, he knew what Violante meant.

An unidentified illegal immigrant who'd died of a drug overdose was like a rubbish bag ready to be collected and placed in the appropriate pile: on one side those who matter and are talked about in the press and on TV, and on the other all the rest, whose records no one will ever consult. In other words, this was a case to be concluded without any fuss and without causing the Commissioner any needless worry – because, as everyone knew, he had plenty of other things on his plate.

That was the explanation for Violante's resigned attitude.

'No,' Ferrara replied, calmly, without jumping down his throat again. 'This time I don't know. Tell me your impressions and let me draw my own conclusions, okay?'

'Okay, chief, but the thing is . . . well . . . I don't really know. It's the hospital. There's something strange going on there.'

'What do you mean?'

'It's as if . . . as if once they found out no one was coming forward, they just dropped her. I mean, as if they didn't really take care of her. And now that she's dead, she's become a nuisance, and they're in a hurry to have done with her . . . like they wanted to get rid of her as quickly as possible, you know what I mean?'

'Yes, I think I'm starting to . . .'

'Since she died, they've hurried everything up. Yesterday my colleague on duty at the hospital even phoned to ask me if I could finish my report as soon as possible. As if we had nothing else to do, as if I'm bone idle.'

'Did he tell you why?'

'He says the consultant asked him. But it seems as if even the Prosecutor's Department wants to close the case as soon as possible.'

Why, for God's sake? And why was the consultant in such a hurry?

'Do you think maybe they could have saved her but made a mistake?'

'Who knows? I'm not a medical expert. But I think something strange is going on. Maybe it's just because it's August, everyone wants to get off on holiday, they're overworked, they need the beds, the case was hopeless . . .'

'Especially if she was an illegal immigrant,' Ferrara said, and realised he was getting angry again. 'If there's the slightest suspicion of malpractice we're not going to let them get away with it, okay? Do you have the medical records?'

'No – I didn't think . . .'

'What?'

'I didn't think there was any point . . . and besides, we'd need a special warrant from the deputy prosecutor who's dealing with the investigation.'

'Which deputy prosecutor is that?'

'Anna Giulietti.'

Excellent, Ferrara thought. He'd developed a good professional relationship with her during the recent Ricciardi case, and they had come out of it firm friends. He'd have to have a chat with her as soon as he could.

'Put in a request for the warrant immediately, Violante.'

'All right, chief.'

'We haven't finished with this case yet. I want you to carry on. How many men do you have on it?'

'What?'

Ferrara repeated the question, more loudly.

'Not many, chief. We're short-staffed.' Violante's tone was one of complaint, but there was a gleam of life in his eyes.

'Fanti!' Ferrara called. Before the sergeant had even come in, he asked, 'Is Sergi on holiday, too?'

'No, chief,' Fanti replied from the other room.

'I want him to work with Violante, as of now. And put as many men at their disposal as you can, okay?'

'Of course, chief,' Fanti replied as soon as he appeared, before vanishing again.

'Here,' Ferrara said, handing Violante the report. 'It needs changing.'

'How?'

'For cause of death, cross out "overdose". For the moment, assume it's homicide caused by persons unknown through the administration of narcotic substances, either of bad quality or in an excessive dose.'

'Okay, chief, I'll get on it straightaway.'

Violante left the room with a new spring in his step.

THE OXFORD MURDERS

Guillermo Martinez

On a balmy summer's day in Oxford an old lady who once helped decipher the Enigma Code is killed. After receiving a cryptic anonymous note containing only the address and the symbol of a circle, Arthur Seldom, a leading mathematician, arrives to find the body.

Then follow more murders – an elderly man on a life-support machine is found dead with needle marks in this throat; the percussionist of an orchestra at a concert at Blenheim Palace dies before the audience's very eyes – seemingly unconnected except for notes appearing in the maths department, for the attention of Seldom. Why is he being targeted as the recipient of these coded messages? All he can conjecture is that it might relate to his latest book, an unexpected bestseller about serial killers and the parallels between investigations into their crimes and certain mathematical theorems.

It is left to Seldom and a postgraduate mathematics student to work out the key to the series of symbols before the killer strikes again.

'An enthralling conflict between the heart and the mind'
Observer

978–0–349–11723–2

A DEATH IN TUSCANY

Michele Giuttari

In the picturesque Tuscan hill town of Scandicci, the body of a girl is discovered. Scantily dressed, with no purse or other possessions, she is lying by the edge of the woods. The local police investigate the case – but after a week, they still haven't even identified her, let alone got to the bottom of how she died.

Frustrated by the lack of progress, Chief Superintendent Michele Ferrara, head of Florence's elite *Squadra Mobile*, decides to step in. Although most of Florence has retreated to Rimini to escape the mercilessly hot Tuscan summer, faced with a short-staffed department, Ferrara must keep on working.

Because toxins were discovered in the girl's body, many assumed that she died of a self-inflicted drugs overdose. But Ferrara quickly realises that the truth is darker than that: he believes that the girl was murdered.

And when he delves deeper, there are many aspects to the case that convince Ferrara that the girl's death is part of a sinister conspiracy – a conspiracy that has its roots in the very foundations of Tuscan society . . .

A cleverly plotted, atmospheric mystery, *A Death in Tuscany* has been a bestseller in Italy and has been translated into nine languages. Written by former Florence police chief Michele Giuttari, it gives a unique insight into life, and police work, in Tuscany.

978-0-349-12008-9

Now you can order superb titles directly from Abacus

☐ A Death in Tuscany   Michele Giuttari   £7.99

The price shown above is correct at time of going to press. However, the publishers reserve the right to increase prices on covers from those previously advertised, without further notice.

───────────────── ⟨ABACUS⟩ ─────────────────

Please allow for postage and packing: **Free UK delivery.**
Europe; add 25% of retail price; Rest of World; 45% of retail price.

To order any of the above or any other Abacus titles, please call our credit card orderline or fill in this coupon and send/fax it to:

Abacus, P.O. Box 121, Kettering, Northants NN14 4ZQ
Fax: 01832 733076   Tel: 01832 737526
Email: aspenhouse@FSBDial.co.uk

☐ I enclose a UK bank cheque made payable to Abacus for £ . . . .
☐ Please charge £ . . . . . . to my Visa, Delta, Maestro.

Expiry Date ☐☐☐☐   Maestro Issue No.   ☐☐

NAME (BLOCK LETTERS please) . . . .

ADDRESS . . . .

. . . .

. . . .

Postcode . . . . Telephone . . . .

Signature . . . .

Please allow 28 days for delivery within the UK. Offer subject to price and availability.